George A. Henty

The Cornet of Horse

A Tale of Marlborough's Wars

George A. Henty

The Cornet of Horse
A Tale of Marlborough's Wars

ISBN/EAN: 9783337073121

Printed in Europe, USA, Canada, Australia, Japan

Cover: Foto ©Andreas Hilbeck / pixelio.de

More available books at **www.hansebooks.com**

"HE DASHED THE TORCH IN SIR RICHARD'S FACE."

THE

CORNET OF HORSE.

A Tale of Marlborough's Wars.

.

BY G. A. HENTY,

WAR CORRESPONDENT OF THE "STANDARD,"
AUTHOR OF " THE YOUNG BUGLERS," " THE YOUNG FRANC-TIREURS," ETC., ETC.

PHILADELPHIA :
PATTERSON & WHITE,
1897.

CONTENTS.

I.	WINDTHORPE CHACE	1
II.	RUPERT TO THE RESCUE	14
III.	A KISS AND ITS CONSEQUENCES	25
IV.	THE SEDAN CHAIR	39
V.	THE FENCING-SCHOOL	52
VI.	THE WAR OF SUCCESSION	68
VII.	VENLOO	77
VIII.	THE OLD MILL	91
IX.	THE DUEL	103
X.	THE BATTLE OF THE DYKES	118
XI.	A DEATH TRAP	131
XII.	THE SAD SIDE OF WAR	143
XIII.	BLENHEIM	156
XIV.	THE RIOT AT DORT	171
XV.	THE END OF A FEUD	184
XVI.	RAMILIES	197
XVII.	A PRISONER OF WAR	207
XVIII.	THE COURT OF VERSAILLES	220
XIX.	THE EVASION	234
XX.	LOCHES	248
XXI.	BACK IN HARNESS	261
XXII.	OUDENARDE	273
XXIII.	THE SIEGE OF LILLE	282
XXIV.	ADELE	292
XXV.	FLIGHT AND PURSUIT	303
XXVI.	THE SIEGE OF TOURNAI	313
XXVII.	MALPLAQUET, AND THE END OF THE WAR	326

LIST OF ILLUSTRATIONS

"He dashed the torch in Sir Richard's face" . . *Frontispiece*

"Rupert ran the highwayman right through the body" . 16

"Drawing his sword, he would have sprung upon the lad" 65

The defence of the stairs 180

"He lifted him from his seat and threw him backwards over his head" 266

"As Rupert, with the barrel poised above his head, reared himself above the bulwarks" 317

THE CORNET OF HORSE.

CHAPTER I.

WINDTHORPE CHACE.

"One, two, three, four, one, two, three, four—turn to your lady; one, two, three, four—now deep reverence. Now you take her hand; no, not her whole hand—the tips of her fingers; now you lead her to her seat; now a deep bow, so. That will do. You are improving, but you must be more light, more graceful, more courtly in your air; still you will do. Now run away, Mignon, to the garden; you have madam's permission to gather fruit. Now, M. Rupert, we will take our lesson in fencing."

The above speech was in the French language, and the speaker was a tall, slightly-built man, of about fifty years of age. The scene was a long low room, in a mansion situated some two miles from Derby. The month was January, 1702, and King William the Third sat upon the throne. In the room, in addition to the dancing-master, were the lad he was teaching, an active, healthy-looking boy between fifteen and sixteen, his partner, a bright-faced French girl of some twelve years of age, and an old man, nearer eighty than seventy, but still erect and active, who sat in a large arm-chair, looking on. By the alacrity with which the lad went to an *armoire* and took out the foils, and steel caps with visors which served as fencing masks, it was clear that he preferred the fencing-lesson to dancing. He threw off his coat, buttoned a padded guard across his chest, and handing a foil to his instructor, took his place before him.

"Now let us practise that thrust in tierce after the feint and disengage. You were not quite so close as you might have been, yesterday. Ha! ha! that is better. I think that monsieur your grandfather has been giving you a lesson, and poaching on my manor. Is it not so?"

"Yes," said the old man, "I gave him ten minutes yesterday evening; but I must give it up, my sword begins to fail me, and your pupil gets more skilful, and stronger in the wrist, every day. In the days when I was at St. Germains with the king, when the cropheads lorded it here, I could hold my own with the best of your young blades. But even allowing fully for the stiffness of age, I think I can still gauge the strength of an opponent, and I think the boy promises to be of *première* force."

"It is as you say, monsieur le colonel. My pupil is born to be a fencer; he learns it with all his heart; he has had two good teachers for three years; he has worked with all his energy at it; and he has one of those supple strong wrists that seem made for the sword. He presses me hard. Now, Monsieur Rupert, open play, and do your best."

Then began a struggle which would have done credit to any fencing-school in Europe. Rupert Holliday was as active as a cat, and was ever on the move, constantly shifting his ground, advancing and retreating with astonishing lightness and activity. At first he was too eager, and his instructor touched him twice over his guard. Then, rendered cautious, he fought more carefully, although with no less quickness than before; and for some minutes there was no advantage on either side, the master's long reach and calm steady play baffling every effort of his assailant. At last, with a quick turn of the wrist, he sent Rupert's foil flying across the room. Rupert gave an exclamation of disgust, followed by a merry laugh.

"You always have me so, M. Dessin. Do what I will, sooner or later comes that twist, which I cannot stop."

"You must learn how, sir. Your sword is so; as you lunge I guard, and run my foil along yours, so as to get power near my hilt. Now if I press, your sword must go; but you must not let me press; you must disengage quickly. Thus, you see? Now let us try again. We will practise nothing else to-day—or to-morrow—or till you are perfect. It is your one weak point. Then you must practise to disarm your opponent, till you are perfect in that also. Then, as far as I can teach you, you will be a master of fencing. You know all my *coups,* and all those of monsieur le colonel. These face guards too have worked wonders, in enabling you to play with quickness and freedom. We are both fine blades. I tell you, young sir, you need not put up with an insult in any public place in Europe. I tell you so, who ought to know."

In the year 1702 fencing was far from having attained that perfection which it reached later. Masks had not yet been invented, and in consequence play was necessarily stiff and slow, as the danger of the loss of sight. or even of death, from a chance thrust was very great. When Rupert first began his lessons, he was so rash and hasty that his grandfather greatly feared an accident, and it struck him that by having visors affixed to a couple of light steel caps, not only would all possibility of an accident be obviated upon the part of either himself or his pupil, but the latter would attain a freedom and confidence of style which could otherwise be only gained from a long practice in actual war. The result had more than equalled his expectations; and M. Dessin had, when he assumed the post of instructor, been delighted with the invention, and astonished at the freedom and boldness of the lad's play. It was, then, thanks to these masks, as well as to his teacher's skill, and his own aptitude, that Rupert had obtained a certainty, a rapidity, and a freedom of style absolutely impossible in the case of a person, whatever his age, who had been accustomed to fence with the face unguarded, and with the caution and stiffness necessary to prevent the occurrence of terrible accident.

For another half-hour the lesson went on. Then, just as the final salute was given, the door opened at the end of the room, and a lady entered, in the stiff dress with large hoops then in fashion. Colonel Holliday advanced with a courtly air, and offered her his hand; the French gentleman, with an air to the full as courtly as that of the colonel, brought forward a chair for her; and when she had seated herself, Rupert advanced to kiss her hand.

"No, Rupert, you are too hot. There, leave us; I wish to speak to Colonel Holliday and monsieur."

With a deep bow, and a manner far more respectful and distant than that which nowadays would be shown to a stranger who was worthy of all honour, Rupert Holliday left his mother's presence.

"I know what she wants," Rupert muttered to himself—"to stop my fencing lessons; just as if a gentleman could fence too well. She wants me to be a stiff, cold, finnikin fop, like that conceited young Brownlow, of the Haugh. Not if I know it, madame ma mère. You will never make a courtier of me, any more than you will a whig. The colonel fought at Naseby, and was with the king in France. Papa was a tory, and so am I." And the lad whistled a Jacobite air as he made his way with a rapid step to the stables.

The terms Whig and Tory in the reign of King William had very little in common with the meaning which now attaches to these words. The principal difference between the two was, in their views as to the succession to the throne. The Princess Anne would succeed King William, and the whigs desired to see George, Elector of Hanover, ascend the throne when it again became vacant; the tories looked to,the return of the Stuarts. ·The princess's sympathies were with the tories, for she, as a daughter of James the Second, would naturally have preferred that the throne should revert to her brother, than that it should pass to a German prince, a stranger to her, a foreigner, and ignorant even of the language of the people. Roughly it may be said that the tories were the descendants of the cavaliers, while the whigs inherited the principles of the parliamentarians. Party feeling ran very high throughout the country; and as in the civil war, the towns were for the most part whig in their predilection, the country was tory.

Rupert Holliday had grown up in a divided house. The fortunes of Colonel Holliday were greatly impaired in the civil war; his estates were forfeited; and at the restoration he received his ancestral home, Windthorpe Chace, and a small portion of the surrounding domain, but had never been able to recover the outlying properties from the men who had acquired them in his absence. He had married in France, the daughter of an exile like himself; but before the "king came to his own" his wife had died, and he returned with one son,

Herbert.   Herbert had, when he arrived at manhood, restored the fortunes of the Chace by marrying Mistress Dorothy Maynard, the daughter and heiress of a wealthy brewer of Derby, who had taken the side of parliament, and had thriven greatly at the expense of the royalist gentry of the neighbourhood.   After the restoration he, like many other roundheads who had grown rich by the acquisition of forfeited estates, felt very doubtful whether he should be allowed to retain possession, and was glad enough to secure his daughter's fortune by marrying her to the heir of a prominent royalist.   Colonel Holliday had at first objected strongly to the match, but the probable advantage to the fortune of his house at last prevailed over his political bias.   The fortune which Mistress Dorothy brought into the family was eventually much smaller than had been expected, for several of the owners of estates of which the roundhead brewer had become possessed made good their claims to them.

Still Herbert Holliday was a rich man at his father-in-law's death, which happened three years after the marriage.   With a portion of his wife's dowry most of the outlying properties which had belonged to the Chace were purchased back from their holders; but Herbert Holliday, who was a weak man, cared nothing for a country life, but resided in London with his wife. There he lived for another six years, and was then killed in a duel over a dispute at cards, having in that time managed to run through every penny that his wife had brought him, save that invested in the lands of the Chace.   Dorothy Holliday then, at the colonel's earnest invitation, returned to the Chace with her son Rupert, then five years old.   There she ruled as mistress, for her disposition was a masterful one, and she was a notable housekeeper.   The colonel gladly resigned the reins of government into her hands.   The

house and surrounding land were his; the estate whose
rental enabled the household to be maintained as be-
fitted that of a county family was hers; and both would
in time, unless indeed Dorothy Holliday should marry
again, go to Rupert. Should she marry again—and at
the time of her husband's death she wanted two or three
years of thirty—she might divide the estate between
Rupert and any other children she might have, she
having purchased the estate with her dowry, and having
right of appointment between her children as she chose.
Colonel Holliday was quite content to leave to his
daughter-in-law the management of the Chace, while
he assumed that of his grandson, on whom he doted.
The boy, young as he then was, gave every promise of
a fine and courageous disposition, and the old cavalier
promised himself that he would train him to be a soldier
and a gentleman.

When the lad was eight years old, the old vicar of the
little church at the village at the gates of the Chace died,
and the living being in the colonel's gift as master of
the Chace, he appointed a young man, freshly ordained,
from Oxford, who was forthwith installed as tutor to
Rupert.

Three years later, Colonel Holliday heard that a
French emigré had settled in Derby, and gave lessons
in his own language and in fencing. Rupert had already made some advance in these studies, for Colonel
Holliday, from his long residence in France, spoke the
language like a native; and now, after Mistress Dorothy's objection having been overcome by the assurance that French and fencing were necessary parts of a
gentleman's education if he were ever to make his way
at court, M. Dessin was installed as tutor in these
branches, coming out three times a week for the afternoon to the Chace.

A few months before our story begins, dancing had

been added to the subjects taught. This was a branch
of education which M. Dessin did not impart to the
inhabitants of Derby, where indeed he had but few
pupils, the principal portion of his scanty income being
derived from his payments from the Chace. He had,
however, acceded willingly enough to Mistress Dorothy's request, his consent perhaps being partly due to
the proposition that, as it would be necessary that the
boy should have a partner, a pony with his groom
should be sent over twice a week to Derby to fetch his
little daughter Adèle out to the Chace, where, when the
lesson was over, she could amuse herself in the grounds
until her father was free to accompany her home.

In those days dancing was an art to be acquired only
with long study. It was a necessity that a gentleman
should dance, and dance well, and the stately minuet
required accuracy, grace, and dignity. Dancing in
those days was an art; it has fallen grievously from that
high estate.

Between M. Dessin and the old cavalier a cordial
friendship reigned. The former had never spoken of
his past history, but the colonel never doubted that, like
so many refugees who sought our shore from France
from the date of the revocation of the edict of Nantes to
the close of the great revolution, he was of noble blood,
an exile from his country on account of his religion or
political opinions; and the colonel tried in every way to
repay to him the hospitality and kindness which he himself had received during his long exile in France. Very
often, when lessons were over, the two would stroll in
the garden, talking over Paris and its court; and it was
only the thought of his little daughter, alone in his dull
lodgings in Derby, that prevented M. Dessin from ac-
cepting the warm invitation to the evening meal which
the colonel often pressed upon him. During the daytime he could leave her, for Adèle went to the first

ladies' school in the town, where she received an education in return for her talking French to the younger pupils.

It was on her half-holidays that she came over to dance with Rupert Holliday.

Mistress Dorothy did not approve of her son's devotion to fencing, although she had no objection to his acquiring the courtly accomplishments of dancing and the French language; but her opposition was useless. Colonel Holliday reminded her of the terms of their agreement, that she was to be mistress of the Chace, and that he was to superintend Rupert's education. Upon the present occasion, when the lad had left the room, she again protested against what she termed a waste of time.

"It is no waste of time, madam," the old cavalier said, more firmly than he was accustomed to speak to his daughter-in-law. "Rupert will never grow up a man thrusting himself into quarrels; and believe me, the reputation of being the best swordsman at the court will keep him out of them. In M. Dessin and myself I may say that he has had two great teachers. In my young days there was no finer blade at the Court of France than I was; and M. Dessin is, in the new style, what I was in the old. The lad may be a soldier—"

"He shall never be a soldier," Madam Dorothy broke out.

"That, madam," the colonel said courteously, "will be for the lad himself and for circumstances to decide. When I was his age there was nothing less likely than that I should be a soldier; but you see it came about."

"Believe me, madam," M. Dessin said deferentially, "it is good that your son should be a master of fence. Not only may he at court be forced into quarrels, in which it will be necessary for him to defend his honour, but in all ways it benefits him. Look at his figure;

nature has given him health and strength, but fencing
has given him that light, active carriage, the arm of
steel, and a bearing which at his age is remarkable.
Fencing, too, gives a quickness, a readiness, and
promptness of action which in itself is an admirable
training. Monsieur le colonel has been good enough
to praise my fencing, and I may say that the praise is
deserved. There are few men in France who would
willingly have crossed swords with me," and now he
spoke with a hauteur characteristic of a French noble
rather than a fencing-master.

Madam Holliday was silent; but just as she was about
to speak again, a sound of horses' hoofs were heard
outside. The silence continued until a domestic entered, and said that Sir William Brownlow and his son
awaited madam's pleasure in the drawing-room.

A dark cloud passed over the old colonel's face as
Mistress Dorothy rose and, with a sweeping courtesy,
left the room.

"Let us go into the garden, monsieur," he said abruptly, "and see how your daughter is getting on."

Adèle was talking eagerly with Rupert, at a short distance from whom stood a lad some two years his senior,
dressed in an attire that showed he was of inferior rank.
Hugh Parsons was in fact the son of the tenant of the
home farm of the Chace, and had since Rupert's child-
hood been his playmate, companion, and protector.

"Monsieur mon père," Adèle said, dancing up to her
father, and pausing for a moment to courtesy deeply to
him and Colonel Holliday, "Monsieur Rupert is going
out with his hawks after a heron that Hugh has seen in
the pool a mile from here; he has offered to take me on
his pony, if you will give permission for me to go."

"Certainly, you may go, Adèle; Monsieur Rupert will
be careful of you, I am sure."

"Yes, indeed," Rupert said, "I will be very careful.

Hugh, see my pony saddled, and get the hawks. I will run in for a cloth to lay over the saddle."

In five minutes the pony was brought round, a cloth was laid over the saddle, and Rupert aided Adèle to mount, with as much deference as if he had been assisting a princess; then he took the reins and walked by the pony's head, while Hugh followed, with two hooded hawks upon his arm.

"They are a pretty pair," Colonel Holliday said, looking after them.

"Yes," M. Dessin replied, but so shortly that the colonel looked at him with surprise. He was looking after his daughter and Rupert with a grave, thoughtful face, and had evidently answered his own thought rather than the old cavalier's remark. "Yes," he repeated, rousing himself with an effort, "they are a pretty pair indeed."

At a walking pace, Rupert Holliday, very proud of his charge, led the pony in the direction of the pool in which the heron had an hour before been seen by Hugh, the boy and girl chattering in French as they went. When they neared the spot they stopped, and Adèle alighted. Then Rupert took the hawks, while Hugh went forward alone to the edge of the pool. Just as he reached it a heron soared up with a hoarse cry. Rupert slipped the hoods off the hawks, and threw them into the air. They circled for an instant, and then, as they saw their quarry rising, darting off with the velocity of arrows. The heron instantly perceived his danger, and soared straight upwards. The hawks pursued him, sailing round in circles higher and higher. So they mounted until they were mere specks in the sky. At last the hawks got above the heron, and instantly prepared to pounce upon him. Seeing his danger, the heron turned on his back, and, with feet and beak pointed upwards to protect himself, fell almost like a stone towards the earth; but more quickly still the hawks darted down upon him. One the heron with a quick movement literally impaled upon his sharp bill; but the other planted his talons in his breast, and, rending and tearing at his neck, the three birds fell together, with a crash, to the earth.

The flight had been so directly upwards that they fell but a short distance from the pool, and the lads and Adèle were quickly upon the spot. The heron was killed by the fall; and to Rupert's grief, one of his hawks was also dead, pierced through and through by the heron's beak. The other bird was with difficulty removed from the quarry, and the hood replaced. Rupert, after giving the heron's plumes to Adèle for her hat, led her back to the pony. Hugh following with the hawk on his wrist, and carrying the two dead birds.

"I am so sorry your hawk is killed," Adèle said.

"Yes," Rupert answered, "it is a pity. It was a fine, bold bird, and gave us lots of trouble to train; but he was always rash, and I told him over and over again what would happen if he was not more careful."

"Have you any more?" Adèle asked.

"No more falcons like this. I have gerfalcons, for pigeons and partridges, but none for herons. But I dare say Hugh will be able to get me two more young birds before long, and it is a pleasure to train them."

Colonel Holliday and M. Dessin met them as they returned to the house.

"What, Rupert! had bad luck?" his grandfather said.

"Yes, sir. Cavalier was too rash, and the quarry killed him."

"Hum!" said the old man; "just the old story. The falcon was well named, Rupert. It was just our rashness that lost us all our battles. What, M. Dessin, you must be off? Will you let me have a horse saddled for yourself, and the pony for mademoiselle? The groom can bring them back."

M. Dessin declined the offer; and a few minutes later started to walk back with his daughter to Derby.

CHAPTER II.

RUPERT TO THE RESCUE.

ABOUT a month after the day on which Rupert had taken Mademoiselle Adèle Dessin out hawking, the colonel and Mistress Dorothy went to dine at the house of a county family some miles away. The family coach, which was only used on grand occasions, was had out, and in this Mistress Dorothy, hooped and powdered in accordance with the fashion of the day, took her seat with Colonel Holliday. Rupert had been invited, as the eldest son was a lad of his own age. It was a memorable occasion for him, as he was for the first time to dress in the full costume of the period—with powdered hair, ruffles, a blue satin coat, and knee-breeches of the same material, with silk stockings. His greatest pleasure, however, was that he was now to wear a sword, the emblem of a gentleman, for the first time. He was to ride on horseback, for madam completely filled the coach with her hoops and brocaded dress, and there was scarcely room for Colonel Holliday, who sat beside her almost lost in her ample skirts.

The weather was cold, and Rupert wore a riding cloak over his finery, and high boots, which were upon his arrival to be exchanged for silver-buckled shoes. They started at twelve, for the dinner hour was two, and there were eight miles to drive—a distance which, over the roads of those days, could not be accomplished much under two hours. The coachman and two lackeys took their places on the box of the lumbering carriage, the two latter being armed with pistols, as it would be dark before they returned, and travelling after dark in the days of King William was a danger not to be lightly undertaken. Nothing could be more stately, or to Rupert's mind more tedious, than that entertainment. Several other guests of distinction were present, and the dinner was elaborate.

The conversation turned chiefly on county business, with an occasional allusion to the war with France. Politics were entirely eschewed, for party feeling ran too high for so dangerous a subject to be broached at a gathering at which both whigs and tories were present.

Rupert sat near one end of the table, with the eldest son of the host; as a matter of course they kept absolute silence in an assembly of their elders, only answering shortly and respectfully when spoken to. When dinner was over, however, and the ladies rose, they slipped away to a quiet room, and made up for their long silence by chatting without cessation of their dogs, and hawks, and sports, until at six o'clock the coach came round to the door, and Rupert, again donning his cloak and riding-boots, mounted his horse, and rode slowly off after the carriage.

Slow as the progress had been in the daytime, it was slower now. The heavy coach jolted over great lumps of rough stone, and bumped into deep ruts, with a violence which would shake a modern vehicle to pieces. Sometimes, where the road was particularly bad, the lackeys would get down, light torches at the lanterns that hung below the box, and show the way until the road improved.

They had ridden about six miles, when some distance ahead the sound of pistol shots, followed by loud shouts, came sharply on the ear. Rupert happened to be in front, and with the love of adventure natural to his age, he set spurs to his horse and dashed forward, not hearing, or at any rate not heeding, the shouts of his grandfather. Colonel Holliday, finding that Rupert was fairly off, bade the lackeys get down, and follow him at a run with their pistols, and urged the coachman to drive on with all possible speed.   Rupert was not long in reaching the scene of action; and hurried the more that he could hear the clinking of sword-blades, and knew that the resistance of those assailed had not ceased.

On arriving at the spot he saw, as he expected, a carriage standing by the road.   One or two figures lay stretched on the ground; the driver lay back, a huddled mass, on his seat; a man held high a torch with one hand, while with the other he was striving to re-charge a pistol.   Four other men with swords were attacking a gentleman who, with his back to the coach, was defending himself calmly and valiantly.

As he rode up Rupert unbuttoned his riding-cloak, and threw it off as he reined up his horse and dismounted.   An execration broke from the assailants at seeing this new arrival, but perceiving that he was alone, one of the four men advanced to attack him.

Just as Rupert leapt from his horse, the man holding the torch completed the loading of his pistol, and levelling it at him, fired.   The ball knocked off his hat just as he touched the ground, and the man shouted,—

"Kill him, Gervais!   Spit him like a lark; he is only a boy."

Rupert drew his sword as the highwayman advanced upon him, and was in a moment hotly engaged.   Never before had he fenced with pointed rapiers; but the swords had scarcely crossed when he felt, with the instinct of a good fencer, how different were the clumsy thrusts of his opponent to the delicate and skilful play of his grandfather and M. Dessin.   There was no time to lose in feints and flourishes; the man with the torch had drawn his sword, and was coming up; and Rupert parried a thrust of his assailant's, and with a rapid lunge in tierce ran him right through the body.   Then with a bound he dashed through the men attacking the trav-

"RUPERT RAN THE HIGHWAYMAN RIGHT THROUGH THE BODY."

eller, and took his stand beside him, while the torch-bearer, leaving his torch against a stump of a tree, also joined the combat.

Beyond a calm "I thank you, sir; your arrival is most opportune," from the traveller, not a word passed as the swords clashed and ground against each other.

"Dash in, and finish him," shouted the man who appeared the leader of the assailants, and three of them rushed together at the traveller. The leader fell back cursing, with a sword-thrust through his shoulder, just at the moment when Rupert sent the sword of the man who was attacking him flying through the air, and turning at once, engaged one of the two remaining assailants of the traveller. But these had had enough of it and as the lackeys came running up, they turned, and rushed away into the darkness. The lackeys at Rupert's order discharged their pistols after them; but a moment later the sound of four horses making off at full gallop showed that they had escaped.

"By my faith," the traveller said, turning to Rupert, and holding out his hand, "no knight-errant ever arrived more opportunely. You are a gallant gentleman, sir; permit me to ask to whom I am so indebted?"

"My name is Rupert Holliday, sir," the lad said, as the stranger shook his hand warmly, and who, as the lackey approached with the torch, exclaimed,—

"Why, by the king's head, you are but a stripling, and you have run one of these fellows through the body, and disarmed the other, as neatly as I ever saw it done in the schools. Why, young sir, if you go on like this you will be a very Palladin."

"I have had good masters, sir," Rupert said, modestly; "and having been taught to use my sword, there is little merit in trouncing such rascals as these."

"By my faith, but there is though," the stranger said. "It is one thing to fence in a school with buttoned foils,

another to bear oneself as calmly and as well as you did.
But here are your friends, or I mistake not."

The coach came lumbering up, at a speed which for
coaches in those days was wonderful, and as it stopped
Colonel Holliday leapt out, sword in hand.

"Is it all over?" he exclaimed. "Is Rupert hurt?"

"It is all over, sir; and I have not so much as a
scratch," Rupert said.

"Sir," the stranger said, uncovering, and making a
courtly bow to the old cavalier, and to Mistress Dorothy, who was looking from the open door, "your
son—"

"My grandson," the colonel, who had also uncovered,
corrected.

"Your grandson arrived in time to save me from
grievous peril. My coachman and lackey were shot at
the first fire, and I fancy one of the horses. I disposed
of one of the rascals, but four others pressed me hard,
while a fifth held a light to them. Your grandson ran
one through in fair fight, and disarmed another; I dis-
abled a third, and they ran. I have to thank him for
my life; and, if you will permit me to say so—and I have
been in many frays—no man ever bore himself more
coolly, or used his sword more skilfully, than did this
young gentleman."

"I am very proud indeed to hear that the lad bore himself so well; although I own that he caused some anxiety
to his mother and myself, by rushing forward alone to
join in a fray of whose extent he knew nothing. However, all is well that ends well. And now, sir, as your
servants are killed, and but one horse remains to your
carriage, will you permit me to offer you for the night
the hospitality of Windthorpe Chace? I am Colonel
Holliday, sir, an old servant of King Charles the First."

"I accept your offer, sir, as frankly as it is made. I
have often heard your name. I, sir, am John Churchill."

"The Earl of Marlborough!" exclaimed Colonel Holliday.

"The same," the Earl said, with a smile. "I am not greatly loved, sir; but my name will, I am sure, do me no ill service with one of the men of Naseby."

"No, indeed!" Colonel Holliday said, warmly; "it is at once a pleasure and an honour to me to entertain so great a general at the Chace."

"And now," the earl said, "a truce to compliments. Pray resume your seat in the coach, sir. I will cut loose the horse from the coach, and will follow you in company with your grandson."

Colonel Holliday in vain tried to persuade the earl to take his place in the carriage.

The latter, however, firmly declined, and the colonel took his place in the coach, and drove off at once, to make preparation for the reception of his guest.

The earl had even declined the offer to leave one or both of the lackeys behind. And when the carriage had driven off, he said to Rupert, who had stood looking with respectful admiration at the greatest general of the age, "Now, young sir, let us have a look at this carrion; maybe their faces will throw some light upon this affair."

So saying, he took the torch which had been left burning, and turned over the body of the man he had slain before Rupert arrived on the scene.

"I do not know him," he said, looking steadily at the dead man's face.

"I know him," Rupert exclaimed in surprise. "He is a saddler of Derby—a fierce nonconformist and whig, and a preacher at conventicles. And to think of his being a highwayman!"

"An assassin is a better term," the earl said, contemptuously. "I guessed from their number it was my life, and not my money, that they sought. Now let us look at the fellow you sent to his account."

Rupert hung back as they approached the man he
had killed.   In those days of rebellions, executions, and
duels, human life was regarded but lightly.   Still, to a
lad of little over fifteen the thought that he had killed a
man, even if in fair fight, was very painful.

"Ah, I thought so," the earl said.   "This is a creature
of a political enemy.   I have seen him in his ante-chamber.   So the order came from London, and the tools
were found here.   That will do.   Now let us get this
horse out of the traces.   It is some years since I have
ridden bare-backed.   No, I thank you," in answer to
Rupert's offer of his own horse; "a saddle matters not
one way or the other.   There, now for the Chace; and
I shall not be sorry to fall to on the supper which, I
doubt not, the good gentleman your grandfather will
have prepared."

So saying, he vaulted on his horse, and with Rupert
rode quietly along the road to the Chace.   The great
door opened as they approached, and four lackeys with
torches came out.   Colonel Holliday himself came
down the steps and assisted the earl to alight, and led
the way into the house.

They now entered the drawing-room, where Mistress
Dorothy was seated.   She arose and made a deep
courtesy, in answer to the even deeper bow with which
the earl greeted her.

"My lord," she said, "welcome to Windthrope
Chace."

"Madam," the earl said, bowing over the hand she
extended, until his lips almost touched her fingers, "I
am indeed indebted to the fellows who thought to do me
harm, in that they have been the means of my making
the acquaintance of a lady whose charms turned all
heads in London, and who left the court in gloom when
she retired to the country."

Nowadays, such a speech as this would be thought to

savour of mockery, but gentlemen two hundred years since ordinarily addressed women in the language of high-flown compliment.

Mistress Holliday, despite her thirty-seven years, was still very comely, and she smiled as she replied,—

"My lord, ten years' absence from court has rendered me unused to compliments, and I will not venture to engage in a war, even of words, with so great a general."

Supper was now announced, and the earl offered his hand to lead Mistress Dorothy to the dining hall.

The meal passed off quietly, the conversation turning entirely upon country matters. The earl did full justice to the fare, which consisted of a stuffed carp, fresh from the well-stocked ponds of the Chace, a boar's head, and larded capon, the two latter dishes being cold. With these were served tankards of Burgundy and of sherries. Rupert, as was the custom of the younger members of families, waited upon the honoured guest.

The meal over, Mistress Holliday rose. The earl offered her his hand and led her to the door, where, with an exchange of ceremonious salutes, she bade him good-night.

Then the earl accompanied Colonel Holliday to the latter's room, hung with rapiers, swords, and other arms. There ceremony was laid aside, and the old cavalier and the brilliant general entered into familiar talk, the former lighting a long pipe, of the kind known at present as a "churchwarden." The earl told Colonel Holliday of the discovery that had been made, that the attack was no mere affair with highwaymen, but an attempt at assassination by a political rival.

"I had been down," he said, "at Lord Hadleigh's, where there was a gathering of many gentlemen of our way of thinking. I left London quietly, and thought that none knew of my absence; but it is clear that through some spy in my household my enemies learned both my journey and destination. I came down on horseback, having sent forward relays. When I arrived last night at Hadleigh my horse was dead lame. I misdoubt now 'twas lamed in the stable by one of the men who dogged me. Lord Hadleigh offered me his coach, to take me back the first stage—to the inn where I had left my servants and had intended to sleep. I accepted—for in truth I sat up and talked all last night, and thought to doze the journey away. Your Derbyshire roads are, however, too rough, and I was wide awake when the first shot was fired!"

"Do you think of taking steps to punish the authors of this outrage?" Colonel Holliday asked.

"By no means," the earl answered. "I would ask you to send over a man, with the horse I rode on and another, at daybreak. Let him put them into the coach and drive back to Hadleigh, taking with him the bodies of the lackey and coachman. With him I will send a note to my lord, asking that no stir be made in the matter. We need not set the world talking as to my visit to this house; but lest any magistrate stir in the matter, I will leave a letter for him saying that the coach in which I travelled was attacked by highwaymen, and that two of them, as well as the two servants, were killed, and that no further inquisition need be made into the matter. You may be sure that the other side will say naught, and they will likely enough go back and carry off their dead to-night, and bury them quietly."

"Very well, sir," Colonel Holliday said. "My grandson will ride over with you in the morning to Ashby-de-la-Zouche. Two well-armed lackeys shall accompany you."

"Oh, there is no fear of another attempt," the earl said, smiling. "Besides, your grandson and I could fight a whole troop of cut-throats by daylight. What a swordsman that boy is! and as cool as a veteran! He is your pupil with the sword, I presume?"

"Only partly; he owes most of his skill to a French emigré, who calls himself M. Dessin, but who had, I suspect, a far higher title across the water. He is a magnificent swordsman; and as I was able to teach the lad a few thrusts which in their time did me good service, and the boy has a clear eye, a cool head, and a firm wrist, he can, young as he is, hold his own, go where he will."

"What do you mean to do with him? You ought to make a soldier of him. It is the career of a gentleman, and we shall have a stirring campaign on the Rhine next spring. He will have plenty of opportunities to distinguish himself, and I need not say he will have my best favour and protection!"

"I thank you heartily," the colonel said, "and doubt not that one day the lad may claim the fulfilment of your promise. At present his mother dreams of his being a Parliament-man, and shining at court. But you might as well expect to teach a falcon to dance. Besides, the lad is a soldier heart and soul, and has, saving your presence, little of the whig in him; and his mother will find ere long, that if he goes to Parliament it will not be to vote as she wishes. Besides," he said, moodily, "I foresee changes here which he, young as he is, will not brook. If then at present I decline your kind offer in his name, I think that the time is not far off when he may remind you of it."

"Let him do so," the earl said, "and a commission in horse, foot, or artillery is at his service. And now, with your permission, I will to bed, for my eyelids are consumedly heavy."

Colonel Holliday rang a hand bell, and a lackey appeared with lighted candles. Preceded by him the old cavalier accompanied his guest to the door of his apartment, and seeing that a posset cup of spiced cordial was steaming on the table, and that everything else was properly prepared, left him to repose.

CHAPTER III.

A KISS AND ITS CONSEQUENCES.

THREE months have passed since the Earl of Marlborough's visit to the Chace. Changes have taken place in England, for on the 8th of March King William died from the effects of a fall from his horse, and the Princess Anne ascended the throne. After her accession, one of her first steps had been to shower honour upon the Earl of Marlborough. A whig cabinet was formed, of which he and Lord Godolphin were the leading spirits, two tories, however—Harley and St. John—having seats in the ministry. The Earl of Marlborough was her most trusted adviser. He had during the reign of the late monarch been always a firm friend of the Princess Anne, and was at one time regarded almost as a tory. He had indeed plotted for the restoration of the Stuarts, and had entered into negotiation with the French king for that purpose. The plot having been discovered, he had with other noblemen been sent to the Tower, and had continued in disgrace until a year before the death of William.

Anne appointed him one of her ministers, and made the duchess her most intimate friend. In fact, in politics the Duke of Marlborough took no very strong part. He was attached to the Stuarts, for under them he had at first risen to rank and honour; but he was a strong Protestant, and therefore in favour of the maintenance of the Act of Succession, fixing the reversion of the throne on the Elector of Hanover, who, although not the nearest in the line of succession, had been selected because the nearest heirs to the throne were Catholics.

At the Chace things have gone on as before. Rupert

has worked hard at his lessons and his fencing, and M. Dessin allows that, save for his extra length of reach, he should have no advantage now over his pupil. In the afternoon the lad spent his time with his hawks, or practised firing with pistol or carbine, or roamed over the country with Hugh. Nevertheless, things had somehow changed. Colonel Holliday had become gloomy and silent; and although he and his daughter-in-law were studiously ceremonious and polite to each other, it was clear that a cloud had risen between them. Rupert saw but little of this, however, and was surprised one day when, as he was going out for a ride, his grandfather said to him gravely,—

"Take a turn in the garden with me, Rupert; I want to have a talk with you. I think it well, Rupert," he said, after walking for some time in silence, "to prepare you for what, if you have not guessed already, you will be told ere long. Madam will no doubt herself inform you of it; and it is as well, my lad, that you should be prepared, for you might in your surprise say something hasty, and so cause a breach which it would take long to heal."

Rupert looked in astonishment at his grandfather. He had not the most remote idea of what was coming.

"You have doubtless noticed," Colonel Holliday went on, "the frequency of Sir William Brownlow's visits here?"

"Yes, sir, I have noticed that, but do not often see him. I keep out of his way, for in truth I like him not, nor that son of his, who, on the strength of his three years' seniority, looks down upon me, and gives himself as many airs as madam my mother's peacock."

"And you have never even thought why he comes here so frequently?"

"No, sir," Rupert said, surprised; "it was no business of mine, and I gave no single thought to it."

"He is a suitor for your lady mother's hand," Colonel Holliday said, gravely.

"What!" almost shouted Rupert; "what, sir! he, with his sneering face, dares to think—"

"My dear boy, he not only dares to think, but madam approves of the thought, and has promised him her hand."

Rupert stood motionless.

"It shall not be," he burst out. "We must stop it, sir. Why do not you?"

"I have no shadow of authority over Mistress Holliday," the old colonel said. "As far as I could go, for your sake I have gone—farther, perhaps, than was wise. It has been a great blow for me, Rupert. I had hoped that in the time to come you would be master of the Chace, and of all the broad acres I owned when young; now it will never be. This house and the home farm are mine, and will be yours, lad; but the outlying land will never come back to the Chace again, but will go to swell the Haugh estate on the other side. My lady can leave it as she likes. I have begged her to have it settled upon you, but she has declined. She may have another family, and, infatuated as she is with her suitor, she is more likely to leave it to them than to you, especially as I fear that you will not take kindly to the new arrangement."

"I will not submit to it, sir; I will not have it. I will insult him, and force him to fight me," the lad gasped, his face white with passion.

"No, Rupert, it won't do, lad. Were you four or five years older you might interfere; now he would laugh at you for a headstrong boy. You would gain his hate, and forfeit your mother's favour utterly. It was because I feared an outbreak like this that I told you to-day what you will in a few hours learn from her."

"What is to be done?" Rupert said, despairingly.

"Nothing, my boy. At her marriage, your mother will of course live at the Haugh with Sir William. This house is mine, and if you cannot get on at the Haugh, it will be always open to you."

"I will never set my foot inside the Haugh," Rupert said, firmly. "My lady mother may leave her lands where she will; but if I am to have them only at the price of being the humble servant of this new father-in-law, I care not for them. He has an evil face, grandfather, and I hated him before I knew what he came for."

"My boy," Colonel Holliday said, "we have all many things to go through in life that we like not. This is your trial, and I trust that you will come out of it worthily. Your respect and duty are due to your mother. If you will not feign gladness that you do not feel, I do not blame you; but when she tells you the news, answer her with that respect which you owe her. She has a clear right to choose for herself. She is still a comely dame, and no one will blame her for taking another husband. To me and to you the thing may seem hard, even unnatural, but it is not so. I like Sir William no more than you do. Report says that he has deeply dipped into his estates over the dice-box; and your lady mother's estates, and the sum that many years of quiet living has enabled her to save, are doubtless items which he has not overlooked."

Rupert remained for some time silent.

"I will be perfectly respectful to my mother," he said, "but I will not disguise my feelings. If I did so at first, it would in the end be useless, for Sir William I could never treat with respect. Sooner or later a quarrel would come, and I may therefore as well have it understood first as last. The estates I care for only because they were part of the Chace, and I know that they will never be mine if this match is made. You feel that yourself, do you not, sir?"

"Yes," the colonel said, reluctantly, "I have felt that all along."

"Very well, sir," Rupert said; "in that case I have nothing to gain by affecting a satisfaction at this match. I shall respectfully but firmly warn my mother against it, and tell her that if she persists in it I will never put my foot under the roof of Sir William Brownlow."

The next morning the servant brought word to Rupert, that Mistress Holliday wished to speak to him in her room. Knowing what was coming, Rupert went with slow steps and a heavy heart to the little drawing-room which was known as madam's room.

"Rupert," she said, as he stood respectfully before her, "I have sent for you to tell you that I have accepted the offer of marriage of Sir William Brownlow. Sir William has much court influence, and will be able to do you much service, and he has promised me to look upon you as a son of his own."

"Madam," Rupert said, calmly and respectfully, "that you should marry Sir William Brownlow is a matter as to which, alas! I have no right to say aught. I trust that the marriage will bring you happiness, although my mind sorely misgives me as to whether it will be so. As to myself, I decline Sir William's offer of protection. It is enough for me that my fathers have for generations owned Windthorpe Chace. Come what may, madam, I neither acknowledge Sir William as my father, nor do I put a foot under his roof."

"Malapert boy!" Mistress Holliday said, angrily, "this is the teaching of Colonel Holliday."

"Pardon me," Rupert said, quietly, "Colonel Holliday begged me to submit to what could not be helped; but I declined. This man is not worthy of you, madam. Were you about to marry a good man, I would gladly receive him as my father. I should be glad to know when out in the world that you were cared for and happy; but this is not a good man."

"Hush, sir," Mistress Holliday said. "I will not suffer you to speak thus. And know, Rupert, if you do not know it already, that I have absolute power over the estates of the Chace, and that if you defy me I can leave them where I will."

"I know it, madam," Rupert said, sadly; "but this will in no way alter my determination. If when you marry you give me your permission to remain here with my grandfather, I will do so; if not, I will go forth into the world, to seek my fortune."

"Insolent boy!" Mistress Holliday said; furiously, "I have a mind to call the lackeys in and bid them beat you."

"Madam," Rupert said, drawing himself up and touching his sword lightly, "if you value your lackeys you will give no such order; for the first man, lackey or lord, who lays his hand on me, I would kill like a dog. With your permission, madam, I will retire, since this morning I take my dancing lesson."

So saying, with a ceremonious bow Rupert left his mother's presence. M. Dessin and his daughter were already with Colonel Holliday when Rupert joined them, and he went through his dancing lesson as usual. Then Adèle went as usual out into the garden, and the fencing lesson began. When it was half over, Rupert's brow clouded angrily for he heard horsemen ride up to the door, and felt sure who they were.

"Steady, my dear pupil, steady," M. Dessin cried, as with knitted brow Rupert pressed him hotly, fancying at the moment that Sir William Brownlow stood in front of him.

"*Peste!*" he exclaimed, as the lad lunged and touched him in the chest, "you are terrible. Monsieur le colonel," he went on, dropping his sword, "I resign my post. I have seen it coming for some time, and now it has arrived. Your grandson is more than a match for me. He has all my skill, some of yours, and has besides an activity and suppleness greater, I think, than I ever had. You young islanders are trained to use hand and eye; and although French lads may have as much activity, they have far less strength, far less aptitude for such exercises. Besides, there are other reasons. Go, Monsieur Rupert, and take care of my daughter; I would talk with monsieur your grandfather."

Slowly, and brooding over the change which the late twenty-four hours had made in his fortune, Rupert sought the garden. As he sauntered along the walks he heard a cry, and looking up saw Adèle struggling in the arms of James Brownlow, who was trying to kiss her, while a young fellow his own age stood by laughing. Rupert's pent-up fury found a vent at last, and rushing forward, he struck the aggressor so violent a blow between the eyes that, loosing his hold of Adèle, he fell to the ground.

"Thunder and lightning," the other young man exclaimed, drawing his sword, "what means this, young cockerell?"

Rupert's sword flew from its sheath, but before he could cross it, James Brownlow sprang to his feet and crying to his friend,—

"Stand back! I will spit the saucy knave!" rushed upon Rupert.

The swords clashed, and almost simultaneously Brownlow's weapon flew far through the air.

With a cry of fury he ran to fetch it, while his companion burst into a coarse laugh.

Rupert did not move from his position, but stood passive, until his antagonist again rushed at him.

"Mind this time," Rupert said, between his teeth, "for I will kill you like a dog."

Warned by the lesson, James Brownlow fought more carefully; but he was too enraged to continue these tactics long, and after a short bout he lunged furiously. Rupert turned aside the point and straightened his arm, and his antagonist fell to the ground, run completely through the body.

"You are a witness that I killed him in fair fight," Rupert said, turning to the young man, who gazed stupefied at the body of his comrade, and then sheathing his sword bounded away to the stables. Hugh was there.

"Quick, Hugh; saddle Ronald. I have just killed young Brownlow, and must ride for it."

Hugh stood for a moment astonished, and then calling a helper ran into the stables. In a minute he came out with two horses saddled. Without a word Rupert leapt on one, while he vaulted on the other, and the two dashed off at full speed.

"Where are you going, Master Rupert?"

"To London," Rupert said. "This is no place for me now. I killed him in fair fight, and after warning; still, what with Sir William and my lady mother, there will be no stopping here. You had better ride back, Hugh, and tell my grandfather, privately, that I am going to the Earl of Marlborough, to ask him to give me the cornetcy he promised me."

"With your leave, Master Rupert, I shall do nothing of the sort. Where you go, I go. My grandfather rode out with yours to Naseby, and died there. My people have been the tenants of the Chace as long as the Hollidays have been its lords, and have always followed their master to the field. My old father would beat me out of the house with a broom-handle, if I went back and said I had let you go to the wars alone. No, Master Rupert, wherever you go, Hugh Parsons goes too."

Rupert held out his hand, which his companion

grasped, and the two galloped rapidly along the road towards London.

In the meantime all was consternation at the Chace.

Colonel Holliday and M. Dessin were deeply engaged in conversation when Adèle burst in upon them.

"Quick, quick!" she exclaimed, "M. Rupert is fighting with a wicked young man!"

"Then," said M. Dessin, grimly, "it will be very bad for the wicked young man, whoever he is."

"Where are they?" exclaimed Colonel Holliday.

"In the garden," the girl said, bursting into tears. "The wicked young man was rude to me, and wanted to kiss me, and M. Rupert knocked him down, and then they began to fight, and I ran away."

M. Dessin swore a very deep oath in French, and was about to hurry out with Colonel Holliday. Then he stopped, and putting his hand on the colonel's shoulder, said, coldly, "Do not let us hurry, sir. M. Rupert has taken the matter in his hands. It is as well that he should kill this fellow as that I should have to do so."

Just at this moment they reached the door, and a young man came running up to the house shouting,—

"Young Brownlow is killed. Help! help!"

"I think, M. Dessin," Colonel Holliday said, stopping, "it would be as well if you and mademoiselle were for the present to leave us. There will be trouble enough, and the fewer in it the better. Sir William is a hot man, and you are not a cool one. Enough mischief has been done."

"You are right," M. Dessin said. "Will you tell M. Rupert that so long as my arm can lift a sword it is at his service, and that I am his debtor for life. Come, Adèle, let us leave by the front of the house."

Colonel Holliday now hurried out into the garden, just as Sir William Brownlow, accompanied by his son's friend, rushed out of the house, followed by some lackeys with scared faces.

Not a word was spoken as they ran to the spot where young Brownlow was lying.

Sir William and Colonel Holliday both knelt beside him, and the latter put his finger to his pulse.

"He is not dead," he said, after a moment. "Ralph, saddle a horse, and ride with all speed to Derby for a doctor."

"Ay," Sir William said, "and tell the chief magistrate that he is wanted here, with one of his constables, for that murder has been done."

"You will do nothing of the sort," Colonel Holliday said. "Sir William Brownlow, I make every excuse for you in your grief, but even from you I will permit no such word to be used. Your son has been wounded in fair fight, and whether he dies or not, alters the circumstances no whit. My grandson found him engaged in offering a gross insult to a young lady in the garden of my house. He did what I should have done had I so found him—he knocked him down. They fought, and your son was worsted. I think, sir, that for the credit of your house you had best be quiet over the matter. Hush, sir," he went on sternly, seeing that the baronet was about to answer furiously, "I am an old man, but I will put up with bluster from no man." Colonel Holliday's repute as a swordsman was well known, and Sir William Brownlow swallowed his passion in silence. A door was taken off its hinges, and the insensible young man was carried into the house. There he was received by Mistress Holliday, who was vehement in her reproaches against Rupert, and even against Colonel Holliday, who had, as she said, encouraged him in brawling. The colonel bent quietly before the storm; and leaving the wounded man in the care of his daughter-in-law and the attendants, made his way to the stables, to

inquire what had become of Rupert. There he found
that a few minutes before, Rupert, accompanied by
Hugh Parsons, had ridden off at full speed, having
placed valises and a brace of pistols in the holsters on
their saddles. The colonel was glad to hear that Rupert had his humble friend with him, and doubted not
that he had made for London. With a somewhat light-
ened heart he went back to the house.

After galloping fast for the first two miles, Rupert
drew rein, for he had now time to think, and was assured that even should Sir William at once send into
Derby for a warrant for his apprehension, he would be
across the borders of the county long before he could be
overtaken.

"Have you any money with you, Hugh?" he asked,
suddenly; "for I have not a penny with me."

"I have only two shillings, Master Rupert. I got
that yesterday in Derby for a nest of young owlets I
found in the copse."

Rupert reined up his horse in dismay.

"Two shillings between us, Hugh! and it is 126 miles
to London. What are we to do?"

Hugh thought a moment. "We can't go on with
that, sir. Do you take these two shillings and ride on
to the Red Dragon, you will be outside the county there.
I will ride back to father's. It's under two miles, and I
shall be back here in half-an-hour again. He will give
me any money he may have in the house. I may as
well fill my valise too, while I am about it; and he's got
a pair of pistols too, that he will give me."

It was clearly the best course to take, and Rupert
trotted forward on his way, while Hugh galloped back
at full speed. In a quarter of an hour the latter drew
rein at his father's door.

"Hullo, Hugh, lad," the farmer, a hearty man of some
fifty years of age, said, as he came to the door, "be'est

thou? What **art** doing on the squire's horse? He looks as if thou had ridden him unmercifully, surely?"

In a few words Hugh related what had taken place, and told him of his own offer to go to the wars with Rupert.

"That's right, lad; that's right and proper. It's according to the nature of things that when a Holliday rides to the war a Parsons should ride behind him. It's always been so, and will always be so, I hope. Mother will grieve, no doubt; but she won't want to fly in the face of nature. Here, mother, come out; Master Rupert's killed Sir William Brownlow's son, and is off to the wars, and so our Hugh's, natural-like, going with him."

Mrs. Parsons, after her first ejaculation of surprise, burst into tears, but, as her husband had predicted, offered no objection whatever to what seemed to her, as to him, a matter of plain duty on the part of her son. Hugh now explained the reason of his return.

"Ay, ay, lad; thou shalt have the money. I've got fifty pounds for next quarter's rent. Colonel Holliday will be glad enough for some of it to go to his grandson. I'll gin ye half o't, Hugh, and take my chance of the colonel agreeing to it. I'll give'e as much more out of my old stocking upstairs. Put it carefully by, lad. Money is as useful in war as at other times, and pay ain't always regular; may be the time may come when the young master may be short of money, and it may come in useful. Now put on thy riding coat; and mother will put thy best clothes in a valise. Bustle up, mother, there bain't no time to lose.",

Thus addressed, Mrs. Parsons dried her tears and hurried away. Hugh, hitching the bridle over a hook, made his way to his room to change his clothes. When he came down, all was ready.

"Thy clothes are in the valise, Hugh. I have put on

the holsters, and the pistols are in them.   They are loaded, boy.   In the bottom of one are the master's twenty-five pounds.   Thy own money is in the valise. Here, boy, is my father's sword; it hasn't been used since Naseby, but it's a good blade.   Thou are a deft hand at quarterstaff and single-stick though, and I doubt not that thy hands can guard thy head.   I need not say, Hugh Parsons, you will, if need be, die for thy master, for I know thou will do it, lad.   Now kiss thy mother, boy; and God speed you."

A long embrace with his father and mother, and then Hugh, blinded by his tears, mounted his horse, and rode off in the track of Rupert.

After an hour's sharp riding he overtook him, at a wayside inn, just across the boundary between Derby and Leicestershire.

"Is it all right, Hugh?" he asked, as Hugh drew up at the door.

"All right, Master Rupert.   Father has sent thee twenty-five pounds out of the rent that will be due at Lady day; and he doubts not that the colonel will approve of what he has done.   How long have you been here?"

"Only some five minutes, Hugh.   We had best let the horses feed, and then ride quietly into Leicester, it's only fifteen miles away.   I see you've got a sword."

"A sword and pistols, Master Rupert; and as you have the same, methinks any highwayman chaps we might meet would think twice ere they venture to cry 'Stand and deliver!' "

"You heard no word of whether James Brownlow was alive or dead, Hugh?   I should be very glad to hear that he is not killed."

"No word of the matter had come to the farm when I came away," Hugh said; "but I should not worry about it one way or the other, Master Rupert.   You'll kill lots more when you get to the wars; and the country won't grieve over James Brownlow. Young as he was, he was a bad one; I've heard more than one dark story whispered of him. Folks say he took after his father, who was as wild and as bad as any man in Derbyshire when he was young."

CHAPTER IV.

THE SEDAN CHAIR.

"This is our last stage, Hugh, and to-night we shall be in London," Rupert said, as they rode out of Watford. "Methinks we shall find it very strange in that great city. I am glad I thought of asking our host the name of an inn at which to put up; the Bell in Bishopsgate Street, he said. It will seem less strange asking the way there than it would be to be wandering about gazing for a place at which to alight."

"Ay, truly, Master Rupert; and I've heard say those London folk are main fond of making game of strangers."

"So I have heard, Hugh; any reasonable jest we had best put up with with good temper; if they push it too far, we shall be able, I doubt not, to hold our own. The first thing to do will be to get clothes of the cut in vogue, for I have come away just as I stood; and I fear that even your clothes will have a marvellously country air about them in the eyes of the city folk. There is London," he said, as they passed over the crest of Hempstead Hill. "That great round dome that stands up so high must be St. Paul's; and look how many other church towers and spires there are. And there, away to the right, those must be the towers of Westminster."

"It is a big place, surely, Master Rupert. How many people do you think live there?"

"I believe there are near 300,000 souls there, Hugh. It seems wonderful, does it not?"

"It's too big to think of, Master Rupert," Hugh said, and they continued their journey southward.

They entered the city at Aldersgate, but they had

ridden some distance through houses before they arrived at the boundary, for the city was already spreading beyond its ancient limits.

Once inside the walls, the lads were astonished at the bustle and noise.

Hugh inquired the way to Bishopsgate Street of a respectable citizen, who directed them to follow the road until they came to a broad turning to their left, this would be Chepeside, and they were to follow this until they came to the Exchange, a large building straight in front of them. Passing this, they would find themselves in Bishopsgate Street.

If Aldersgate Street had surprised them, much more were they astonished at the din and turmoil of Chepeside, and Hugh, having twice narrowly escaped riding over a citizen, and being soundly rated for a country gawk, Rupert turned to him.

"Look at your horse's head, Hugh, and pay no attention to aught else. When we have reached our destination, we shall have plenty of time to look at all these wonders."

The advice was good, and without mischance they reached the Bell in Bishopsgate Street, and rode into the yard. The host at once came out, and after a momentary look of surprise at the youth of the new arrivals, he asked Rupert courteously if he needed a room.

"Two rooms if it please you," Rupert said, "and together."

The host called a hostler, who at once took charge of the horses, and led them to the stable, the lads first removing the valises and holsters, which a servant carried up to their rooms.

"We would have supper," Rupert said; "and while that is preparing we would, if it is not too late, order some clothes more in the mode than these. Can you direct us to a tailor?"

"You cannot do better," the landlord said, "than visit my neighbour, Master John Haliford. His shop is just opposite, and he makes for many of our best city folk, and for more than one of the gentry of the Court."

Rupert thanked him, and they crossed the street to the shop indicated.

The landlord looked after them with a puzzled air.

"It is not often that Joe Miles cannot guess the quality and errand of his guests, but this time he is floored. Has that young spark run away from home? I hardly think so, for he speaks gravely, and without haste; lads who have run away may generally be known by their speaking in a hurry, and as if anxious. They are both well mounted; the younger is clearly of the higher estate, although but meanly dressed; nor does the other seem like his lackey. What are they talking about outside neighbour Haliford's shop, I wonder? I would give a silver penny to know. I will walk over presently, and smoke a pipe with him, and hear what he thinks of them."

The conversation which the host of the Bell had wished he could overhear was as follows:—

Hugh began it.

"Look, Master Rupert, before we go into the shop, let us talk over what you are going to order."

"I am going to order a walking suit, Hugh, and a court suit for myself, and a suit for you."

"Yes, but what sort of a suit, Master Rupert?"

"I should say a walking suit, Hugh, such as would become a modest citizen."

"That's just it, Master Rupert. So far you have treated me as a friend; but now, sir, it must be different, for to do so any longer would not be seemly. You are going to be an officer; I am going to follow you as a trooper; but till we go to the war I must be dressed as your retainer. Not a lackey, perhaps, but a sort of con-

fidential retainer. That will be best, Master Rupert, in
every way."

Rupert was silent for a moment.

"Well, Hugh, perhaps that would be best; but you
must remember that whatever we are before others, we
are always friends when we are alone."

"Very well," Hugh said, "that is understood; but you
know that alone or before others, I shall always be your
faithful servant."

"What can I make you, sir?" the tailor asked, as the
lads entered his shop.

Master Haliford was a small man; neat in his dress; a
little fussy in manner. He was very upright, and
seemed to look under rather than through the pair of
horn spectacles which he wore. His look changed from
affability to doubt as he took a nearer look at his intending customers.

"I need a suit such as a gentleman might wear at
court," Rupert said, quietly, "and a walking or ordinary
suit for myself; and a suit such as would be worn by a
trusted retainer for my friend here."

The tailor put his head on one side, and rubbed his
chin thoughtfully.

"Have I had the honour of being recommended to
you by the honourable gentleman your father?" he
asked.

"No, indeed," Rupert said, "it was mine host at the
Bell, who advised me that I could not do better than
come to your shop."

"Ah, you are known to him, beyond doubt," John
Haliford said, brightening.

"No, indeed," Rupert answered, "he was a stranger to
me to within five minutes back."

"You must excuse my caution, young sir," John Haliford said, after another minute's reflection, "but it is the
custom of us London tradesmen with those gentlemen

who may honour us with their custom, and whom we have not the honour of knowing, to require payment, or at least a portion of payment, at the time of giving the order, and the rest at the time of delivery of the goods. In your case, sir, I am sure, an unnecessary piece of caution, but a rule from which I never venture to go."

"That is only fair and right," Rupert said. "I will pay half now, and the other half when the garments are completed, or if it please you, will pay the whole in advance."

"By no means, by no means," the tailor said with alacrity; "one-third in advance is my rule, sir. And now, sir, what colour and material do you affect?"

"As sober both in hue and in material as may be," Rupert said, "and yet sufficiently in the fashion for me to wear in calling upon a nobleman of the court."

"Pardon me," the tailor said, "but perhaps you would condescend to take me into your confidence. There are noblemen, and noblemen. A tory lord, for instance, is generally a little richer in his colour than a whig nobleman, for these affect a certain sobriety of air. With some again, a certain military cut is permitted, while with others this would be altogether out of place."

"I am going to the Earl of Marlborough," Rupert said, briefly.

"Dear me, dear me! indeed now!" the little tailor said with an instant and great accession of deference, for the Earl of Marlborough was the greatest man in the realm. "Had your honour mentioned that at first, I should not have ventured to hint at the need for previous payment."

"What!" Rupert said, with a smile, "you would have broken your fixed rule! Surely not, Master Haliford."

The tailor looked sharply at his young customer. Whoever he might be, he was clearly no fool; and without more ado he brought forward his patterns and bent himself to the work in hand.

Having chosen the colours and stuffs for the suits of clothes, the lads returned to the Bell, where a supper of cold chicken and the remains of a fine sirloin awaited them, with two tankards of home-brewed ale. The next morning, before sallying out to see the town, Rupert wrote to his grandfather, asking his pardon for running away, expressing his intention of applying to the Earl of Marlborough for a cornetcy of horse, and giving his address at the Bell; asking him also to make his humble excuse to his lady mother, and to assure her of his devotion and respect, although circumstances had caused his apparent disobedience to her wishes.

Although there was a much greater amount of filial respect and obedience expressed in those days than now, human nature has differed but slightly in different ages of the world; and it is probable that sons went their own way quite as much as they do now, when there is very little talk either of obedience or respect. Indeed, the implicit obedience, and almost servile respect, which our forefathers expected from their sons, could not but in a great number of cases drive the sons to be hypocrites as well as undutiful; and our modern system of making our boys companions and friends, of taking an interest in all they do, and in teaching them to regard us as their natural advisers, has produced a generation of boys less outwardly respectful, no doubt, but as dutiful, and far more frank and truthful than those of the bygone times.

Rupert, finding that few of the citizens wore swords, and feeling that in his present attire he would attract attention by so doing, left his sword at the inn, and bought for Hugh and himself a couple of stout sticks— Hugh's a cudgel which would be useful in a hand well accustomed to single-stick, his own a cane of a wood such as he had never before seen—light, strong, and stiff. He chose it because it was well balanced in the hand. Then they sallied out into Cornhill, past the Exchange, erected by the worshipful citizen Sir Thomas Gresham, and then into Chepeside, where they were astonished at the wealth and variety of the wares displayed in the shops. Gazing into the windows, they frequently got into the way, and were saluted many times with the query, "Where are you going, stupids?" a question which Hugh was largely inclined to resent, and would have done so had not Rupert told him that evidently they did get into the way of the hurrying citizens, and that it was more wise to put up with rudeness than to embark in a series of quarrels, in which, moreover, as strangers, they were likely to get the worst of the dispute. St. Paul's Cathedral, then but newly finished, astonished them vastly with its size and magnificence, and they returned to the mid-day dinner at the Bell delighted with all that they had seen.

Asking the landlord how he would recommend them to pass the afternoon, he said that they could do no better than take a boat at London Bridge, and be rowed up to the village of Chelsea, where many of the nobility did dwell, and then coming back to Westminster might get out there, see the Abbey and the great Hall, and then walk back along the Strand.

The lads followed the advice, and were soon delighted and surprised with the great river, then pure and limpid, and covered with boats proceeding rapidly in all directions, for it was at that time the great highway of London. Tide was flowing and the river nearly full, and having given their waterman the intimation that time did not press, he rowed them very gently along in the centre of the stream, pointing out to them, when they had passed above the limits of the city, the various noblemen's houses scattered along the banks of the river. Off Westminster the waterman ceased rowing, to allow them to view the grand old Abbey; and then

as they went on again, they marvelled at the contrast of
the low, deserted marshes of Lambeth and Bankside,
which contrasted so strongly with the magnificence and
the life they had left behind.   At Chelsea they admired
the grand palace for the reception of old soldiers, and
then—for the tide was turning now—floated back to
Westminster.   So long were they in going round the
Abbey, and examining the tombs of the kings, that it
was getting dark when they started eastward again, up
past the Palace of Whitehall, and then along the Strand.
Already the distance between the city and Westminster
was connected with houses, and the junction of the two
cities had fairly taken place.

Dim oil lamps were lighted here and there as they
went along, foot passengers bore lanterns to enable
them to pick their way across rough places, and link-
men carried torches in front of sedan-chairs, in which
ladies were being taken to fashionable entertainments,
which then commenced at six o'clock.

All this was new and amusing to the boys; and having
gone into a tavern near the Abbey, and partaken of
some refreshment, they were not pressed for time; and it
was near eight before they seriously thought of proceeding towards the city.

When a few hundred yards from Temple Bar, they
heard a shouting and a scream down one of the streets
leading to the river.

The street was deserted, but down at the farther end
they could see the flash of sword blades, in the light of
an oil lamp.

"Come along, Hugh; that is a woman's scream."

"Better not interfere, Master Rupert," Hugh said.

But Rupert had already darted off, and Hugh without
a moment's hesitation followed in his steps.

At the end of the street they came upon a sedan-chair.
The two porters stood surily against the wall, menaced

by the drawn swords of two men, standing over them, while two other men—evidently of higher rank, but enveloped in cloaks—were forcibly dragging a lady from the chair. They had thrown a cloak over her head to drown her cries.

As the lads came up, one of the men uttered a furious oath.

"Rolf, Simon! leave those fellows and keep these springalls back. They are but boys. I will whistle when I am in the boat. Now, mistress!" and he began to carry the lady away.

As the lads arrived, the servitors—for such they were by their appearance—leaving the chairmen, turned upon them. One of the chairmen at once ran off as fast as his legs could carry him; but the other, a sturdy fellow, leaped on the back of the man who had been guarding him, as the latter turned upon Rupert. Hugh was attacked by the other.

"Be careful, Hugh! keep out of reach of his point," Rupert cried; and darting past, he struck the man who had hold of the lady a sharp blow across the ankle, which brought him instantly to the ground with his burden.

The other gentleman drew his sword, and rushed upon Rupert. It was fortunate for the latter that he had chosen his stick for lightness and balance, for it moved as quickly and easily as a foil. Without a thought of guarding, his assailant rushed at him to run him through; but Rupert parried the thrust, and in turn drove the end of his stick, with all his force, into his opponent's stomach. The man instantaneously doubled up with a low cry, and fell on the ground.

Then the other man, who had by this time risen to his feet, in turn rushed furiously at Rupert. A few times the sword and stick scraped and rasped against each other, and then Rupert lunged full at the other's face!

There was a loud cry, an oath, and then, as the sound of the watch running down the street, led by the chairman who had run away, was heard, the man took to his feet and fled. The lackey who had engaged Hugh, and who had in vain endeavoured to get to close quarters with the lad, imitated his example; but the prostrate man on the ground, and the fellow held by the chairman, were seized by the watch.

Rupert turned to the young lady, who, having now disencumbered herself of the folds of the cloak over her head, was leaning, half fainting, against the chair.

Taking off his hat and bowing deeply, he expressed his hope that she had suffered no harm through the unmannerly assault upon her.

"I thank you greatly, sir," she said, speaking with a slightly foreign accent. "I am unhurt, although somewhat breathless. I owe you my deep gratitude for rescue from these evil-minded men."

"What may be your name, mistress?' one of the watch asked. "You will be needed to-morrow to testify against these men."

"My name is Maria Von Duyk, and I reside at present with the worthy alderman, Peter Hawkins, to whom I was returning in the chair, as the chairmen will tell you, after a visit to Mistress Vanloct, whose house we had just left when molested."

"And yours, young sir?" the watchman asked.

"My name is Rupert Holliday. I am staying at the Bell, in Bishopsgate Street."

"You will both have to be present to-morrow morning before the worshipful magistrate Master Forman, at Westminster."

The watch now secured the man on the ground, who was recovering from the effect of the violent thrust in the stomach, and putting handcuffs on him and the other, led them away.

"You will permit me, I trust, to escort you to your door," Rupert said, as he ceremoniously handed the young lady into her chair.

"Yes, indeed, sir; and I trust that you will enter, and allow Dame Hawkins to add her thanks to mine."

Rupert bowed, and the chair being closed the chairmen lifted it, and with Rupert and Hugh following, proceeded eastward.

When they arrived at the house of Alderman Hawkins, in Lawrence Pulteney, the young lady on alighting begged Rupert to enter; but the latter excused himself on account of the hour, but said that he would call next morning, and would, if allowed, accompany her and the alderman to give evidence as to the assault.

On arriving next morning, Rupert was overwhelmed with thanks by the alderman, his wife, and Mistress Maria Von Duyk, all of whom were much surprised at his youth, for in the dim light of the preceding evening the young lady had not perceived that her rescuer was a mere lad.

Rupert found that there was no occasion to go before the magistrate, for the alderman having sent down early to the watchhouse to inquire at what hour their presence would be required, found that the prisoners had been rescued on their way to the watchhouse, by a party of armed men.

"We are," the alderman said, "well aware who was the leader of the assailants, the man who escaped. Sir Richard Fulke is a ruined gamester, and is a distant relation of Dame Vanloct, whom my young friend was yesterday visiting. Knowing the wealth of Mistress Von Duyk's good father, he has sought to mend his ruined fortune by a match with her. At the urgent request of Mistress Von Duyk I wrote to him, saying that his attentions were unpleasing to her, and that they must be discontinued, or that she could no longer visit

4

at Dame Vanloct's where she usually had met him. This was a week since. He replied courteously, regretting that the deep devotion he felt was unrequited but withdrawing from the undertaking of trying to win her, and promising that henceforth she should be no longer troubled with his presence when she visited Dame Vanloct. This was of course done to lull our suspicion. When the chair was stopped yesterday, Maria at once recognized his voice. As they dragged her from the chair, he said,—

" 'Quick! hurry her down to the boat.'

"There is no doubt upon my mind that he intended to carry her off, and compel her to marry him. I bethought me at first of applying to the secretary of state for a warrant for his arrest to answer for this outrage, but Mistress Maria leaves us to-morrow for Holland, and the process would delay her departure, and would cause a scandal and talk very unpleasant to herself, and which would greatly offend my good friend her father. Had the men in custody been brought up this morning, there would have been no choice but to have carried the matter through. It was then a relief to us to find that they had escaped. I have told you this, young sir, as your due after having rescued Mistress Von Duyk from so great a peril. Now, as to yourself, believe me if my friendship and assistance can in any way advantage you, they are at your service. Even of your name I am yet in ignorance."

Rupert thanked the worthy alderman, and then stated that he was the grandson of Colonel Holliday, of Windthorpe Chace, in Derbyshire, and had come up to London to wait upon the Earl of Marlborough, who had promised him his protection and a cornetcy in a regiment of horse for service in Holland.

"In that case, sir," Mistress Von Duyk said, "it is like you may come to Dort. If so, believe me that my father, whom I shall tell how much we are indebted to you, will not be backward in manifesting his gratitude for the great service that you have rendered to his daughter."

"How were you thinking of passing the day?" the alderman asked.

"I had no plan," Rupert said. "In truth, I am waiting to call upon the Earl of Marlborough until Master Haliford has fashioned me a suit of clothes fitted for such an occasion; he has promised them for this evening."

"Would it please you to go down the river? I have a boat, and if you would like to see the shipping of this great port, and the palace at Greenwich for our seamen, my boatmen will take you down; and you will, I trust, return and take your mid-day meal with us."

And so it was arranged; and as Rupert and Hugh were rowed down the river, lost in wonder at the numerous craft that lay there, Hugh admitted that Rupert's interference in a business which was no concern of his had turned out a fortunate occurrence.

CHAPTER V.

THE FENCING-SCHOOL.

It was with no small trepidation that Rupert Holliday ascended the steps of the Earl of Marlborough's residence in Pall Mall. Hugh accompanied him thus far and stopped at the door, outside which, in the courtyard, and in the hall were standing many lackeys who had attended their masters. Rupert felt very young, and the somewhat surprised looks of the servants in the hall at his appearance, added to his feeling of youth. He was shown into an ante-chamber, where a number of officers of all ranks, of courtiers, and politicians, were assembled, talking in groups. Rupert felt alone and uncomfortable among this crowd of distinguished men, none of whom did he know, and no one paid the smallest attention to him. He had on entering written his name down in a book in the hall, whence it would be taken in with others to the great man.

Presently an officer in general's uniform came out from an inner room, and an instant afterwards the earl himself appeared. Not only was John Churchill one of the most handsome men in Europe, but he was the most courtly and winning in manner; and Rupert, shrinking back from observation, watched with admiration as he moved round the room, stopping to say a few words here, shaking hands there, listening to a short urgent person, giving an answer to a petition, before presented, by another, giving pleasure and satisfaction wherever he moved. Rupert saw, however, that even while speaking his eye was wandering round the room, and directly he perceived him he walked straight towards him, those standing between falling back as he advanced.

"Ah, my young friend," he said, warmly, holding out his hand to Rupert, "I was expecting you. Sir John Loveday, Lord Fairholm," he said, turning to two young gentlemen near, "let me present to you Master Rupert Holliday, grandson of Colonel Holliday, one of the bravest of our cavaliers, and who I can guarantee has inherited the skill and courage of his grandfather. He will make the campaign in Holland with you, gentlemen, for his commission has been made out to-day in her Majesty's fifth regiment of dragoons. I will speak to you more, presently, Rupert."

So saying, the earl moved away among his visitors, leaving Rupert flushed with pleasure and confusion. The young gentlemen to whom the earl had introduced him, much surprised at the flattering manner in which the great general had spoken of the lad before them, at once entered into conversation with him, and hearing that he was but newly come to London, offered to show him the various places where men of fashion resorted, and begged him to consider them at his disposal. Rupert, who had been carefully instructed by his grandfather in courtly expression and manner, returned many thanks to the gentlemen for their obliging offers, of which, after he had again spoken to the earl, and knew what commands he would lay upon him, he would thankfully avail himself.

It was nearly an hour before the Earl of Marlborough had made the round of the ante-chamber, but the time passed quickly to Rupert. The room was full of men whose names were prominent in the history of the time, and these Sir John Loveday, and Lord Fairholm, who were lively young men, twenty-two or twenty-three years old, pointed out to him, often telling him a merry story or some droll jest regarding them. There was St. John, handsome, but delicate-looking, with a half sneer on his face, and dressed in the extremity of fashion,

with a coat of peach-coloured velvet with immense
cuffs, crimson leather shoes with diamond buckles; his
sword was also diamond hilted, his hands were almost
hidden in lace ruffles, and he wore his hair in ringlets of
some twenty inches in length, tied behind with a red
ribbon.   The tall man, with a haughty but irritable face,
in the scarlet uniform of a general officer, was the Earl
of Peterborough.   There too were Godolphin and Or-
ford, both leading members of the cabinet, the Earl of
Sutherland, the Dukes of Devonshire and Newcastle,
Lord Nottingham, and many others.

At last the audience was over, and the minister, bowing to all, withdrew, and the visitors began to leave.   A
lackey came up to Rupert and requested him to follow
him; and bidding adieu to his new friends, who both
gave him their addresses and begged him to call upon
them, he followed the servant into the hall and upstairs
into a cosey room, such as would now be called a bou-
doir.   There stood the Earl of Marlborough, by the
chair in which a lady of great beauty and commanding
air was sitting.

"Sarah," he said, "this is my young friend, Rupert
Holliday, who as you know did me good service in the
midlands."

The countess held out her hand kindly to Rupert, and
he bent over it and touched it with his lips.

"You must remember you are my friend as well as
my husband's," she said.   "He tells me you saved his
life; and although I can scarce credit the tale, seeing
how young you are, yet courage and skill dwell not
necessarily in great bodies.   Truly, Master Holliday, I
am deeply indebted to you; and Sarah Churchill is true
in her friendships."

"As in her hates, eh?" laughed the earl.

Between the Earl of Marlborough and his wife there
existed no common affection.   They were passionately

attached to each other; and the earl's letters show that at all times, even when in the field surounded by difficulties, harassed by opposition, menaced with destruction by superior forces, his thoughts were turned affectionately towards her, and he was ever wishing that the war would end that he might return to her side. She on her part was equally attached to him, but much as she strove to add to his power and to forward his plans, her haughty and violent temper was the main cause of the unmerited disgrace into which he fell with his royal mistress, who owed so much to him personally, and whose reign he did so much to render a brilliant and successful one. At the present time, however, she stood upon the footing of the closest intimacy and affection with Queen Anne. The earl then introduced Rupert to those other ladies who were present; the eldest, his daughter Lady Harriet, recently married to Mr. Godolphin; the second, Anne, married to Lord Spencer; and the two daughters still unmarried, aged sixteen and seventeen respectively.

Rupert was so confused with the earl's kindness, that he had difficulty in finding words, but he made a great effort, and expressed in proper set terms his thankfulness to the countess for her great kindness to him, and of his own want of deserts.

"There," the countess said, "that will do very nicely and prettily; and now put it aside until we are in public, and talk in your own natural way. So you have been fighting again, have you, and well-nigh killing young Master Brownlow?"

Rupert was completely astounded at this address; and the earl said, laughing,—

"I told you that I expected you. The worthy colonel your grandfather wrote me a letter, which I received this morning, telling me the incident which had taken place, and your sudden disappearance, stating that he doubted not you had made for London, and begging—which indeed was in no way necessary—my protection on your behalf."

"Did my grandfather say, sir," Rupert asked, anxiously, "aught of the state of Master Brownlow?"

"Yes; he said that the leech had strong hopes that he would recover."

"I am indeed glad of that," Rupert said; "for I had no ill will to him."

"We must be careful of you, Master Holliday," the countess said; "for if you go on like this you will much diminish the number of the queen's subjects."

"I can assure your grace," Rupert said, earnestly, "that I am no brawler, and am not quarrelsome by nature, and that the thought of shedding blood, except of the foes of my country in battle, pains me much."

"I'll warrant me you are the mildest-tempered boy alive," the earl said. "Now tell me frankly: you have been in London some forty-eight hours; have you passed that time without getting into a fray or quarrel of any kind?"

Rupert turned scarlet with confusion.

"His looks betray him," the earl laughed. "Look, girls, at the mild-tempered young gentleman. Now, out with it. How was it?"

Thus exhorted, Rupert stammeringly gave an account of the fray in which he had been engaged.

"Von Duyk!" the earl said. "She must be a daughter of the great merchant of Dort—a useful friend to have made, maybe, Master Holliday; and it may be that your adventure may yet be of service to the state. Never speak now, Master Rupert, of your peaceful intentions. You take after your namesake, the Prince, and are a veritable knight-errant of adventure. The sooner I have you over in Holland fighting the queen's enemies, and not the queen's subjects, the better. Now tell me, where have you taken up your abode?"

"At the Bell, at Bishopsgate Street," Rupert answered.

"And your follower, for I know one accompanied you; where is he?"

"He waits without, sir."

The earl touched a hand bell.

"Fetch in Master Holliday's retainer; you will find him without. Make him at home in the servant's hall. Send a messenger down to the Bell at Bishopsgate, fetch hither the mails of Master Holliday; he will remain as my guest at present."

Rupert now entered upon a life very different to that which he had led hitherto. He received a letter from Colonel Holliday, enclosing an order on a London banker for fifty pounds, and he was soon provided with suits of clothes fit for balls and other occasions. Wherever the earl went, Rupert accompanied him as one of his personal followers; and the frank, straightforward manners of the lad pleased the ladies of the court, and thus "Little Holliday," as he was called, soon became a great favourite.

It was about a fortnight after his arrival in town that, for the first time, he accompanied his friends Sir John Loveday and Lord Fairholm to the fencing-school of Maitre Dalboy, the great fencing-master of the day. Rupert had been looking forward much to this visit, as he was anxious to see what was the degree of proficiency of the young court gallants in the art which he so much loved.

Maitre Dalboy's school was a fashionable lounge of the young men of the court and army. It was a large and lofty room, and some six assistants were in the act of giving instructions to beginners, or of fencing with more advanced students, when the trio entered. Maitre

Dalboy himself came up to greet them, for both Rupert's friends had been his pupils.

"You are strangers," he said, reproachfully. "How are your muscles to keep in good order, and your eye true, if you do not practise? It is heartrending! I take every pains to turn out accomplished swordsmen; and no sooner have my pupils learned something of the business, than they begin to forget it."

"We shall begin to put your teaching into effect before long, Maitre Dalboy," Sir John Loveday said, with a smile, "for we are going over to join the army in Holland in a few weeks, and we shall then have an opportunity of trying the utility of the parries you have taught us."

"It is too bad," the Frenchman said, shrugging his shoulders, "that my pupils should use the science I have taught them, against my countrymen; but what would you have? It is the fortune of war. Is this young gentleman a new pupil that you have brought me?"

"No, indeed," Lord Fairholm said; "this is Master Rupert Holliday, a cornet in the 5th regiment of dragoons, who is also about to start for Holland."

"I have had the advantage of learning from a countryman of yours, M. Dalboy," Rupert said, "a M. Dessin, who is good enough to teach the noble art in the town of Derby."

"Dessin! Dessin!" Maitre Dalboy said, thoughtfully. "I do not remember the name among our maitres d'escrime."

"The Earl of Marlborough himself vouches for the skill of Master Holliday with the sword. His grandfather, Colonel Holliday, was, I believe, noted as one of the finest blades at the court of St. Germains."

"I have heard of him," M. Dalboy said, with interest. "Let me think; he wounded the Marquis de Beauchamp, who was considered one of the best swordsmen in

France. Yes, yes, his fame as a swordsman is still re-membered. And he is alive yet?"

"Alive and active," Rupert said; "and although, as he says himself, he has lost some of his quickness of reposte there are, M. Dessin says, few fencers who could even now treat him lightly."

"And you have had the benefit of his instruction as well as that of my countryman?" M. Dalboy asked.

"Yes," Rupert said, "my grandfather, although he cares not at his age for prolonged exercise, has yet made a point of giving me for a few minutes each day the benefit of his skill."

"I should like to have a bout with you, Master Hol-liday," M. Dalboy said; "will you take a foil? I am curious to see what the united teaching of my country-man and that noted swordsman Colonel Holliday may have done. To me, as a master, it is interesting to dis-cover what is possible with good teachers, when the science is begun young. What may your age be, Mas-ter Holliday?"

"I am four months short of sixteen," Rupert said, "and I shall be very proud of the honour of crossing swords with so famed a master as yourself, if you think me worthy of so great a privilege."

There was quite a sensation in the fencing-school, round which were gathered some forty or fifty of the young men of the day, when Maitre Dalboy called for his plastron and foil, for it was seldom indeed, and then only with swordsmen of altogether exceptional strength, that M. Dalboy condescended to fence, contenting him-self ordinarily with walking about the school and giving a hint now and then to those fencing with his assistants, not, perhaps, more than once a week taking a foil in his hand to illustrate some thrust or guard which he was inculcating. At this call, therefore, there was a general silence; and every one turned to see who was the fencer whom the great master thus signally designed to honour.

Great was the astonishment when, as M. Dalboy divested himself of his coat and vest, the lad who had entered with Lord Fairholm and Sir John Loveday was seen similarly to prepare for the contest.

"Who is he? What singular freak is this of the maitre to take up a foil with a boy?" was the question which ran round the room.

Several of those present had met Rupert Holliday, and could give his name; but none could account for the freak on the part of the master.

Fortunately Rupert was unacquainted with the fact that what seemed to him a natural occurrence was an extraordinary event in the eyes of all assembled, and he therefore experienced no feeling of nervousness whatever. He knew that Colonel Holliday was a master of the sword, and his grandfather had told him that M. Dessin was an altogether exceptional swordsman; as he knew himself to be fully a match for the latter, he felt sure that, however perfect a master M. Dalboy might be, he need not fear discrediting his master, even if his present opponent should prove more than his match.

There was a dead silence of curiosity at the singularity of the affair, as Rupert Holliday took his post face to face with the master; but a murmur of surprise and admiration ran round the room at the grace and perfection of accuracy with which Rupert went through the various parades which were then customary before the combatants crossed swords.

Rupert felt as calm and as steady as when fencing at home,and determined to use all his caution as well as all his skill; for not only did he feel that his own strength was upon trial, but that the honour of the teachers who had taken such pains with him was concerned in the result. The swords had scarcely crossed when an expres-

sion of surprise passed across Maitre Dalboy's face.
The first few passes showed him that in this lad he had
found an opponent of no ordinary character, and that
all his skill would be needed to obtain a victory over
him. For the first few minutes each fought cautiously,
feeling each other's strength rather than attempting to
attack seriously. Then the master dropped his point.

"Ma foi! young sir, you have done monsieur le colonel and my compatriot justice. I offer you my congratulations."

"They are premature, sir," Rupert said, smiling; "you
have not as yet begun."

The silence in the school was even more profound
when the swords again crossed than it had been when
the bout began, for wonder had now taken the place of
amused curiosity. The struggle now commenced in
earnest. Several times at first Rupert narrowly escaped
being touched, for the master's play was new to him.
The thrusts and feints, the various attacks, were all familiar; but whereas Colonel Holliday had fought simply
with his head, standing immovably in one place, and M.
Dessin had, although quick to advance and fall back,
fought comparatively on the defensive, while he himself
had been the assailant from his superior activity, M.
Dalboy was as quick and as active as himself, and the
rapidity of the attacks, the quick bounds, the swift
rushes, at first almost bewildered him; but gradually,
as he grew accustomed to the play, he steadied himself,
and eluded the master's attacks with an activity as great
as his own.

In vain M. Dalboy employed every feint, every combination in his repertoire. Rupert was always prepared,
for from one or other of his teachers he had learnt the
defence to be employed against each; and at last, as the
master, exhausted with his exertions, flagged a little,
Rupert in turn took the offensive. Now M. Dalboy's

skill stood him in equal stead to defend himself against
Rupert's rapid attacks and lightning-like passes and
thrusts; and although the combat had lasted without a
second's interruption for nearly a quarter of an hour,
neither combatant had touched the other.

At last Rupert saw by his opponent's eye that a new
and special combination was about to be put into action
against him, and he instantly steadied himself to resist
it. It came with the rapidity of thought, but Rupert
recognized it by the first pass as the very last combination which M. Dessin had taught him, assuring him at
the time that he would find it irresistible, for that there
were not three men in Europe acquainted with it. He
met the attack then with the defence which M. Dessin
had showed him to be the sure escape, ending with a
wrench which nearly tore the sword from the hand of
his opponent. M. Dalboy sprang back on guard, with
a look of profound astonishment; and then throwing
down his foil, he threw himself, in the impetuous manner of his countrymen, on Rupert's neck, and embraced
him.

"Mon dieu! mon dieu!" he exclaimed, "you are in-
croyable, you are a miracle. Gentlemen," he said, turning to those present, when the burst of enthusiastic ap-
plause which greeted the conclusion of this extraordinary contest subsided, "you see in this young gentleman
one of the finest swordsmen in Europe. I do not say
the finest, for he has not touched me, and having no
idea of his force I extended myself rashly at first; but I
may say he is my equal. Never but once have I crossed
swords with such a fencer, and I doubt if even he was
as strong. His parry to my last attack was miraculous.
It was a *coup* invented by myself, and brought to perfection with that one I speak of. I believed no one else
knew it, and have ever reserved it for a last extremity;
but his defence even to the last wrench, which would

have disarmed any other man but myself, and even me had I not known that it should have come then, was perfect; it was astounding. This maître of yours—this M. Dessin," he went on, turning to Rupert, "must be a wonder. Ah!" he said suddenly, and as if to himself; "c'est bien possible! What was he like, this M. Dessin?"

"He is tall, and slight except as to his shoulders, where he is very broad."

"And he has a little scar here, has he not?" the fencing master said, pointing to his temple.

"Yes," Rupert said, surprised; "I have often noticed it."

"Then it is he," M. Dalboy said, "the swordsman of whom I spoke. No wonder you parried my *coup*. I had wondered what had become of him. And you know him as M. Dessin? and he teaches fencing?"

"Yes," Rupert said; "but my grandfather always said that M. Dessin was only an assumed name, and that he was undoubtedly of noble blood."

"Your grandfather was right," the master said. "Yes, you have had wonderful masters; but unless I had seen it, I should not have believed that even the best masters in the world could have turned out such a swordsman as you at your age."

By this time the various couples had begun fencing again, and the room resounded with the talk of the numerous lookers-on, who were all discoursing on what appeared to them, as to M. Dalboy, the almost miraculous occurrence of a lad under sixteen holding his own against a man who had the reputation of being the finest maître in Europe. Lord Fairholm, Sir John Loveday, and other gentlemen, now came round.

"I was rather thinking," Sir John said, with a laugh, "of taking you under my protection, Master Holliday, and fighting your battles for you, as an old boy does for a young one at school; but it must even be the other way. And by my faith, if any German Ritter or French swordsman should challenge the British dragoons to a trial of the sword, we shall put you forth as our David."

"I trust that that may not be," Rupert said; "for though in battle I hope that I shall not be found wanting, yet I trust that I shall have nought to do in private quarrels, but be looked upon as one of a peaceful disposition."

"Very peaceful, doubtless!" laughed Lord Fairholm. "Tell me, Master Rupert, honestly now, didst ever use in earnest that sword that you have just shown that you know so well how to wield?"

Rupert flushed up crimson. "Yes," he said, with a shame-faced look, "I have twice used my sword in self-defence."

"Ha, ha! our peaceful friend!" laughed Lord Fairholm. "And tell me, didst put an end to both unfortunates?"

Rupert coloured still more deeply. "I had the misfortune to slay one, my lord; but there are good hopes that the other will recover."

A general shout of laughter greeted the announcement, which together with Rupert's evident shamefaced look, was altogether too much for their gravity.

Just at this moment a diversion was caused by a young man dressed in the extreme of fashion who entered the school. He had a dissipated and jaded air.

"Fulke, where hast been?" one of the group standing round Rupert asked. "We have missed you these two weeks. Some one said you had been roughly mauled, and had even lost some teeth. Is it so?"

"It is," the new-comer said, with an angry scowl. "Any beauty I once may have had is gone for ever. I have lost three of my upper teeth, and two of my lower, and I am learning now to speak with my lips shut, so as to hide the gap."

"But how came it about?"

"DRAWING HIS SWORD, HE WOULD HAVE SPRUNG UPON THE LAD."

"I was walking down a side street off the Strand, when four men sprang out and held my hands to my side, another snatched my watch and purse, and as I gave a cry for the watch, he smote me with the pommel of his rapier in my mouth, then throwing me on the ground the villains took to their heels together."

The exclamations of commiseration and indignation which arose around, were abruptly checked by a loud laugh from Rupert.

There was a dead silence and Sir Richard Fulke, turning his eyes with fury towards the lad who had dared to jeer at his misfortune, demanded why he laughed.

"I could not help but laugh," Rupert said, "although doubtless it was unmannerly; but your worship's story reminded me so marvellously of the tale of the stout knight, Sir John Falstaff's adventure with the men of buckram."

"What mean you?" thundered Sir Richard.

"I mean, sir," Rupert said, quietly, "that your story has not one word of truth in it. I came upon you in that side street off the Strand, as you were trying to carry off by force, aided by a rascal named Captain Copper, a lady, whose name shall not be mentioned here. I had not my sword with me, but with a walking-stick I trounced your friend the captain, and then, with my stick against your rapier, I knocked out those teeth you regret, with a fair thrust. If my word is doubted, gentlemen, Alderman Hawkins, who heard the details of the matter from the young lady and her chairmen, can vouch for it."

A cry of fury burst from Sir Richard Fulke; and drawing his sword he would have sprung upon the lad, who had not only disfigured him for life, but now made him the laughing-stock of society, for the tale would, he knew, spread far and wide. Several of the gentlemen threw themselves between him and Rupert.

5

"I will have his life's blood!" he exclaimed, struggling in the arms of those who would hold him back. "I will kill the dog as he stands."

"Sir Richard Fulke," Lord Fairholm said, "Master Holliday is a friend of mine, and will give you an honourable meeting when you will; but I should advise you to smother your choler. It seems he proved himself with a stick your superior, although armed with a sword and Master Dalboy will tell you that it is better to leave him alone."

Master Dalboy was standing by, and going up to Sir Richard, said,—

"Sir, if you will take my poor advice you will go your way, and leave Master Holliday to himself. He has, as those here will tell you, proved himself fully my equal as a swordsman, and could kill you if only armed with a six-inch dagger against your sword. It would be safer for you to challenge the whole of those in this present company than to cross swords with him."

A few words from those standing round corroborated a statement which at first appeared fabulous; and then finding that an open encounter with Rupert would be the worst possible method of obtaining satisfaction for the injuries he had received, Sir Richard Fulke flung himself out of the school, muttering deep vows of future vengeance.

"You have made a dangerous enemy," Lord Fairholm said, as the three friends walked homeward. "He bears a bad character, and is a reckless and ruined man. After what he has heard of your skill as a swordsman he will, we may be sure, take no open steps against you; but it is certain that he will scheme night and day for vengeance. When the report gets abroad of his cock-and-bull story, and the true history of the loss of his teeth, he will not be able to show his face in public for some time; but he will be none the less dangerous.

Through that notorious ruffian, Captain Copper, he can dispose of half the cut-throats about the town, and I should advise you not to go out after dark until you have put the seas between you and him, and even then you had better be cautious for a time."

Rupert agreed with his friend's advice, and the next day begged his patron to let him embark at once for Holland, in a ship that was to sail with troops from London Bridge. He urged as his reason for desiring to go at once, his wish to learn something at least of his duties before the campaign began.

As the earl had already heard a rumour of the scene in the fencing-school, he made no opposition to the plan, and the next day Rupert, accompanied by Hugh, sailed down the Thames, bound for Rotterdam.

CHAPTER VI.

THE WAR OF SUCCESSION.

THE war which was about to commence, and which
Rupert Holliday sailed for the Hague to take part in,
was one of the grandest and most extensive struggles
that ever devastated Europe, embracing as it did the
whole of the central and western nations of the continent.   In fact, with the exception of Russia, still in the
depths of barbarism, and Italy, which was then a battle-
field rather than a nation, all the states of Europe were
ranged on one side or the other.

As Charles the Second of Spain approached his end,
the liveliest interest was felt as to his succession.   He
had no children, and the hopes and fears of all the continental nations were excited by the question of the disposal of the then vast dominions of Spain.   The principal powers of Europe, dreading the consequences of
this great empire being added to the power of any one
monarch, entered into a secret treaty, which was signed
at the Hague in 1698, by which it was agreed that Spain
itself should be ceded to the Electoral Prince of Bavaria, with Flanders and the Low countries; Naples,
Sicily, Tuscany, and Guipuscoa, were to fall to France;
and the Duchy of Milan to the archduke, son of the
Emperor of Germany.   Holland was to gain a considerable accession of territory.   England, one of the signa-
tories to the treaty, was to gain nothing by the division.

The contents of this treaty leaked out, and the king of
Spain, after a consultation with Austria, who was also
indignant at the secret treaty, made a will bequeathing
all his dominions to the Elector of Bavaria.   Had that
prince lived, all the complications which ensued would
probably have been avoided, but he died, the 9th

February, 1699, and the whole question was thereby again opened. Another secret treaty was made, between England, France, and Holland, and signed on the 13th March, 1700, at the Hague. By this treaty it was agreed that France was to receive Naples, Sicily, Guipuscoa, and Lorraine; the Archduke Charles— Spain, the Low Countries, and the Indies, and the Spanish colonies were to be divided between Holland and England. As both England and Holland were at the time in alliance with Spain, it must be admitted that their secret arrangement for the partition of her territories was of a very infamous character.

Louis of France, while apparently acting with the other powers, secretly communicated the contents of the treaty to Charles II. The Spanish king was naturally dismayed at the great conspiracy to divide his kingdom at his death, and he convened his council of state and submitted the matter to them. It was apparent that France, by far the most powerful of the other continental states, could alone avert the division, and the states-general therefore determined to unite the interests of France and Spain by appointing the Duc d'Anjou, grandson of the King of France, sole heir to the vast empire of Spain.

The news that Spain and France were henceforth to be united caused the greatest consternation to the rest of the States, and all Europe began to arm. Very shortly after signing the bequest, the old King of Spain died, and the Duc d'Anjou ascended the throne. The Spanish Netherlands, governed by the young Elector of Bavaria, as Lieutenant-General of Spain, at once gave in their adhesion to the new monarch. The distant colonies all accepted his rule, as did the great Spanish possessions in Italy; while the principal European nations acknowledged him as successor of Charles II.

The new empire seemed indeed of preponderating

strength. Bavaria united herself in a firm alliance with France and Spain; and these three countries, with Italy and Flanders, appeared capable of giving the law to the world. England, less affected than the continental powers by the dominance of this powerful coalition, might have remained quiet, had not the French King thrown down the gauntlet of defiance. On the 16th September, 1701, James II., the exiled King of England, died, and Louis at once acknowledged his son as King of Great Britain and Ireland. This act was nothing short of a public declaration of war, not only against the reigning monarch of England, but against the established religion of our country. The exiled prince was a Roman Catholic, Louis was the author of the most terrible persecution of the Protestants that ever occurred in Europe. Thus the action of the French king rallied round William III. all the Protestant feeling of the nation, both Houses of Parliament voted loyal addresses, and the nation prepared for the great struggle before it. The king laboured to establish alliances and a plan for common action, and all was in readiness, when his sudden death left the guidance of affairs in other hands. These hands were, happily for England, those of the Earl of Marlborough, the finest diplomatist, as well as the greatest soldier, of his time.

The struggle which was approaching was a gigantic one. On one side were France and Spain, open to attack on one side only, and holding moreover Flanders, and almost the whole of Italy, with the rich treasures of the Indies upon which to draw for supplies. The alliance of Bavaria, with a valiant population, extended the offensive power of the coalition into the heart of Austria.

Upon the other hand were the troops of Austria, England, Holland, Hanover, Hesse Cassel, and the lesser states of Germany, with a contingent of troops, from Prussia and Denmark. In point of numbers the nations ranged on either side were about equal; but while France, Spain, and Bavaria formed a compact body under the guidance of Louis, the allies were divided by separate, and often opposing interests and necessities, while Austria was almost neutralized by a dangerous Hungarian insurrection that was going on, and by the danger of a Turkish invasion which the activity of French diplomacy kept continually hanging over it. The coalition was weakened in the field by the jealousies of the commanders of the various nationalities, and still more by the ignorance and timidity of the Dutch deputies, which Holland insisted on keeping at headquarters, with the right of veto on all proceedings.

On the side of the allies the following were the arrangements for the opening of the campaign. A German army under Louis, Margrave of Baden, was to be collected on the upper Rhine to threaten France on the side of Alsace; a second corps, 25,000 strong, composed of Prussian troops and Dutch, under the Prince of Saarbruck, were to undertake the siege of Kaiserwerth, a small, but very important fortress, on the right bank of the Rhine, two leagues below Dusseldorf. The main army, 35,000 strong, under the Earl of Athlone, was destined to cover the frontier of Holland, from the Rhine to the Vecun, and also to cover the siege of Kaiserwerth; while a fourth body, of 10,000 men, under General Cohorn, were collected near the mouth of the Scheldt, and threatened the district of Bruges.

Upon the other side the French had been equally active. On the Lower Rhine a force was stationed to keep that of Cohorn in check. Marshal Tallard, with 15,000 men, came down from the Upper Rhine to interrupt the siege of Kaiserwerth, while the main army, 45,000 strong, under the Duke of Burgundy and Marshal Boufflers, was posted in the Bishopric of Liege, resting on the tremendous chain of fortresses of Flan-

ders, all of which were in French possession, and
strongly garrisoned by French and Spanish soldiers.

At the time, however, when the vessel containing Rupert Holliday and Hugh Parsons sailed up the Scheldt,
early in the month of May, these arrangements were not
completed, but both armies were waiting for the conflict.

The lads had little time for the examination of the
Hague, now the dullest and most quiet of European
capitals, but then a bustling city, full of life and energy;
for, with the troops who had arrived with them, they
received orders to march at once to join the camp
formed at Breda. Accustomed to a quiet English country life, the activity and bustle of camp life were at once
astonishing and delightful. The journey from the
Hague had been a pleasant one. Rupert rode one of
the two horses with which the Earl of Marlborough had
presented him, Hugh the other; and as a portion of the
soldiers with them were infantry, the marches were
short and easy; while the stoppages at quaint Dutch villages, the solemn ways of whose inhabitants, their huge
breeches, and disgust at the disturbance of their usual
habits when the troops were quartered upon them, were
a source of great amusement to them.

Upon reaching the camp they soon found their way to
their regiment. Here Rupert presented to Colonel
Forbes the letter of recommendation with which the
Earl of Marlborough had provided him, and was at once
introduced by him to his brother officers, most of them
young men, but all some years older than himself. His
frank, pleasant, boyish manner at once won for him a
cordial acceptance, and the little cornet, as he was called
in the regiment, soon became a general favourite.

Hugh, who had formally enlisted in the regiment before leaving England, was on arrival handed over to a
sergeant; and the two lads were, with other recruits,

incessantly drilled from morning till night, to render them efficient soldiers before the day of trial arrived.

Rupert shared a tent with the other two officers of his troop, Captain Lauriston, a quiet Scotchman, and Lieutenant Dillon, a young Irishman, full of fun and life.

There were in camp three regiments of British Cavalry and six of infantry, and as they were far from the seat of war, there was for the present nothing to do but to drill, and prepare for the coming campaign. Rupert was delighted with the life, for although the work for the recruits was hard, the weather was splendid, supplies abundant—for the Dutch farm-wives and their daughters brought ducks, and geese, and eggs into the camp —and all were in high spirits at the thought of the approaching campaign. Every night there were gatherings round the fire, when songs were sung and stories told. Most of the officers had before campaigned in Holland, under King William, and many had fought in Ireland, and had stirring tales of the Boyne, of the siege of Athlone, and of fierce encounters with the brave but undisciplined Irish. At the end of a month's hard work, Rupert began to understand his duties, for in those days the amount of drill deemed necessary for a trooper was small indeed in proportion to that which he has now to master. Rupert was already a good rider, and soon learnt where was his proper place as cornet in each evolution, and the orders that it behoved him to give. The foot drill was longer and more difficult, for in those days dragoons fought far more on foot than is now the case, although at this epoch they had already ceased to be considered as mounted infantry, and had taken their true place as cavalry. Rupert's broadsword drill lasted but a very short time; upon the drill sergeant asking him if he knew anything of that weapon, he said that he could play at singlestick, but had never practised with the broadsword. His instructor, however, found that a very few lessons were sufficient to enable him to perform the required cuts and guard with sufficient proficiency, and very speedily claimed the crown which Rupert promised him on his dismissal from the class.

Week after week passed in inactivity, and the troops chafed mightily thereat, the more so that stirring events were proceeding elsewhere. The siege of Kaiserwerth, by a body of 15,000 German troops, had begun on the 18th of April, and the attack and defence were alike obstinate and bloody. The Earl of Athlone, with his covering forces lay at Cleves, and a sharp cavalry fight between 1000 of the allied cavalry and 700 French horse took place on the 27th of April. The French were defeated, with the loss of 400 men; but as the victors lost 300, it is clear that both sides fought with extreme determination and bravery, such a loss—700 men out of 1700 combatants—being extraordinarily large. The spirit shown by both sides in this the first fight of the war, was a portent of the obstinate manner in which all the battles of this great war were contested. For two months Kaiserwerth nobly defended itself. Seventy-eight guns and mortars thundered against it night and day. On the 9th of June the besiegers made a desperate assault and gained possession of a covered way, but at a cost of 2000 killed and wounded. A week later the place capitulated after a siege which had cost the allies 5000 men.

General Boufflers with his army of 37,000 men, finding himself unable to raise the siege, determined to make a dash against Nimeguen, an important frontier fortress of Holland, but which the supineness of the Dutch Government had allowed to fall into disrepair. Not only was there no garrison there, but not a gun was mounted on its walls. The expedition seemed certain of success, and on the evening of the 9th of June Boufflers moved out from Xanten, and marched all night.

Next day Athlone obtained news of the movement and started in the evening, his march being parallel with the French, the hostile armies moving abreast, and at no great distance from each other. The cavalry covered the British march, and these were in the morning attacked by the French horse under the Duke of Burgundy. The British were outnumbered, but fought with great obstinacy, and before they fell back, with a loss of 700 men and a convoy of 300 waggons, the infantry had pushed forward, and when the French army reached Nimeguen, its ramparts bristled with British bayonets. Boufflers disappointed in his aim, fell back upon the rich district of Cleves, now open to him, and plundered and ravaged that fertile country. Although Kaiserwerth had been taken and Nimeguen saved, the danger which they had run, and the backward movement of the allied army, filled the Dutch with consternation.

The time, however, had come when Marlborough himself was to assume the command, and by his genius, dash, and strategy to alter the whole complexion of things, and to roll back the tide of war from the borders of Holland. He had crossed from England early in May, a few days only after Rupert had sailed; but hitherto he had been engaged in smoothing obstacles, appeasing jealousies, healing differences, and getting the whole arrangement of the campaign into something like working order. At last, everything being fairly in trim, he set out on the 2nd of July from the Hague, with full power as commander-in-chief of the allied armies, for Nimeguen. There he ordered the British troops from Breda, 8000 Germans from Kaiserwerth, and the contingents of Hesse and Luneburg, 6000 strong, under the Prince of Zell, to join him.

As these reinforcements brought his army up to a strength superior to that of the French, although Marshal Boufflers had hastily drawn to him some of the garrisons of the fortresses, the Earl of Marlborough prepared to strike a great blow.   The Dutch deputies who accompanied the army—and whose timidity and obstinacy a score of times during the course of the war thwarted all Marlborough's best-laid plans, and saved the enemy from destruction—interfered to forbid an attack upon two occasions, when an engagement would, as admitted by French historians, have been fatal to their whole army.   Marlborough therefore was obliged to content himself by outflanking the French, compelling them to abandon Cleves, to cross the Meuse, and to fall back into Flanders, with some loss, and great haste and disorder.

In vain the French marshal endeavoured to take post so as to save the Meuse fortresses, which stood at the gates of Flanders, and by their command of the river prevented the allies from using the chain of water communications to bring up supplies. Marlborough crossed the line by which his siege train was coming up, and then pounced upon Venloo, a very strong fortress standing across the Meuse—that is to say, the town was on one side, the fort of St. Michael on the other.

After this chapter, devoted to the necessary task of explaining the cause and commencement of the great War of Succession, we can return to the individual fortunes of our hero

CHAPTER VII.

VENLOO.

UPON the 5th dragoons being, with the others lying with it in camp at Breda, ordered up to join the main army at Nimeguen, Rupert was, to his great delight, declared to be sufficiently advanced in his knowledge of drill to take his place regularly in the ranks; and Hugh and the other recruits also fell into their places in the various troops among which they were divided. Hugh being, at Rupert's request, told off to Captain Lauriston's troop. With drums beating and colours flying, the column from Breda marched into the allied camp at Duckenberg in front of Nimeguen, where the troops crowded out to greet this valuable addition of eight infantry regiments and three of cavalry.

Scarcely were the tents pitched than Rupert heard himself heartily saluted, and looking round, saw his friends Lord Fairholm and Sir John Loveday, who being already in camp had at once sought him out.

"By my faith, Master Holliday, the three months have done wonders for you; you look every inch a soldier," Lord Fairholm said.

"His very moustache is beginning to show," Sir John Loveday said, laughing.

Rupert joined in the laugh, for in truth he had that very morning looked anxiously in a glass, and had tried in vain to persuade himself that the down on his upper lip showed any signs of thickening or growing.

"Well, and how many unfortunate English, Dutch, and Germans have you despatched since we saw you?"

"Oh, please hush," Rupert said, anxiously. "No one knows that I have any idea of fencing, or that I have

ever drawn a sword before I went through my course of
the broadsword here. I would not on any account that
any one thought I was a quarrelsome swordster. You
know I really am not, and it has been purely my misfortune that I have been thrust into these things."

"And you have never told any of your comrades that
you have killed your man? or that Dalboy proclaimed
you in his *salle* to be one of the finest blades in Europe?"

"No, indeed," Rupert said. "Why should I, Sir
John?"

"Well, all I can say is, Rupert, I admire your modesty
as much as your skill. There are few fellows of your
age, or of mine either, but would hector a little on the
strength of such a reputation. I think that I myself
should cock my hat, and point my moustache a little
more fiercely, if I knew that I was the cock of the whole
walk."

Rupert smiled. "I don't think you would, Sir John,
especially if you were as young as I am. I know I
have heard my tutor say that the fellow who is really
cock of a school, is generally one of the quietest and
best-tempered fellows going. Not that I mean," he
added hastily, as his companions both laughed, "that I
am cock, or that I am a quiet or very good-tempered
fellow. I only meant that I was not quarrelsome, and
have indeed put up more than once with practical jok-
ings which I might have resented had I not known how
skilful with the sword I am, and that in this campaign I
shall have plenty of opportunities of showing that I am
no coward."

"Well spoken, Rupert," Sir John said. "Now we have
kept you talking in the sun an unconscionable time;
come over to our tent, and have something to wash the
dust away. We have some fairly good Burgundy, of
which we bought a barrel the other day from a vintner
in Nimeguen, and it must be drunk before we march.
Are these the officers of your troop? pray present me."

Rupert introduced his friends to Captain Lauriston and Lieutenant Dillon, and the invitation was extended to them. For the time, however, it was necessary to see to the wants of the men, but later on the three officers went across to the tents of the king's dragoons, to which regiment Lord Fairholm and Sir John Loveday both belonged, and spent a merry evening.

Upon the following day the Earl of Marlborough sent for Rupert, and inquired of him how he liked the life, and how he was getting on; and begged of him to come to him at any time should he have need of money, or be in any way so placed as to need his aid. Rupert thanked him warmly, but replied that he lacked nothing.

The following day the march began, and Rupert shared in the general indignation felt by the British officers and men at seeing the splendid opportunities of crushing the enemy—opportunities gained by the skill and science of their general, and by their own rapid and fatiguing marches—thrown away by the feebleness and timidity of the Dutch deputies. When the siege of Venloo began the main body of the army was again condemned to inactivity, and the cavalry had of course nothing to do with the siege. The place was exceedingly strong, but the garrison was weak, consisting only of six battalions of infantry and 300 horse. Cohorn, the celebrated engineer, directed the siege operations, for which thirty-two battalions of infantry and thirty-six squadrons of horse were told off, the Prince of Nassau Saarbruch being in command.

Two squadrons of the 5th dragoons, including the troop to which Rupert belonged, formed part of the force. The work was by no means popular with the cavalry, as they had little to do, and lost their chance of taking part in any great action that Boufflers might fight with Marlborough to relieve the town.

The investment began on the 5th of September, the

efforts of the besiegers being directed against Fort St. Michael at the opposite side of the river, but connected by a bridge of boats to the town.

On the 17th the breaches were increasing rapidly in size, and it was whispered that the assault would be made on the evening of the 18th, soon after dusk.

"It will be a difficult and bloody business," Captain Lauriston said, as they sat in their tent that evening. "The garrison of Fort St. Michael is only 800, but reinforcements will of course pour in from the town directly the attack begins, and it may be more than our men can do to win the place. You remember how heavily the Germans suffered in their attack on the covered way of Kaiserwerth."

"I should think the best thing to do would be to break down the bridge of boats before beginning the attack," Lieutenant Dillon remarked.

"Yes, that would be an excellent plan if it could be carried out, but none of our guns command it."

"We might launch a boat with straw or combustibles from above," Rupert said, "and burn it."

"You may be very sure that they have got chains across the river above the bridge, to prevent any attempt of that kind," Captain Lauriston said.

Presently the captain, who was on duty, went out for his rounds, and Rupert, who had been sitting thoughtfully, said, "Look here, Dillon, I am a good swimmer, and it seems to me that it would be easy enough to put two or three petards on a plank—I noticed some wood on the bank above the town yesterday—and to float down to the bridge, to fasten them to two or three of the boats, and so to break the bridge; your cousin in the engineers could manage to get us the petards. What do you say?"

The young Irishman looked at the lad in astonishment.

"Are you talking seriously?" he asked.

"Certainly; why not?"

"They'd laugh in your face if you were to volunteer," Dillon said.

"But I shouldn't volunteer; I should just go and do it."

"Yes, but after it was done, instead of getting praise —that is, if you weren't killed—you'd be simply told you had no right to undertake such an affair."

"But I should never say anything about it," Rupert said. "I should just do it because it would be a good thing to do, and would save the lives of some of our grenadiers, who will, likely enough, lead the assault; besides, it would be an adventure, like any other."

Dillon looked at him for some time.

"You are a curious fellow, Holliday; I would agree to join you in the matter, but I cannot swim a stroke. Pat Dillon cares as little for his life as any man; and after all, there's no more danger in it than in going out in a duel; and I could do that without thinking twice."

"Well, I shall try it," Rupert said, quietly. "Hugh can swim as well as I can, and I'll take him. But can you get me the petards?"

"I dare say I could manage that," Dillon said, entering into the scheme with all an Irishman's love of excitement. "But don't you think I could go too, though I can't swim? I could stick tight to the planks, you know."

"No," Rupert said, seriously, "that would not do. We may be detected, and may have to dive, and all sorts of things. No, Dillon, it would not do. But if you can get the petards, you will have the satisfaction of knowing that you have done your share of the work; and then you might, if you could, ride round in the evening with my uniform and Hugh's in your valise. If you go on to the bank half a mile or so below the town, every one will be watching the assault, and we can get ashore, put on our clothes, and get back home without a soul being the wiser."

"And suppose you are killed?"

"Pooh, I shall not be killed!" Rupert said. "But I shall leave a letter, which you can find in the morning if I do not come back, saying I have undertaken this adventure in hope of benefiting her Majesty's arms; that I do it without asking permission; but that I hope that my going beyond my duty will be forgiven, in consideration that I have died in her Majesty's service."

The next day at two o'clock, Lieutenant Dillon, who had been away for an hour, beckoned to Rupert that he wanted to speak to him apart."

"I have seen my cousin Gerald, but he will not let me have the petards unless he knows for what purpose they are to be used. I said as much as I could without betraying your intentions, but I think he guessed them; for he said, 'Look here, Pat, if there is any fun and adventure on hand, I will make free with her gracious Majesty's petards, on condition that I am in it.' He's up to fun of every kind, Gerald is; and can, I know, swim like a fish. What do you say, shall I tell him?"

"Do, by all means," Rupert said. "I have warned Hugh of what I am going to do, and he would never forgive me if I did not take him but if your cousin will go, all the better, for he will know far better than I how to fix the petards. You can tell him I shall be glad to act under his orders; and if it succeeds, and he likes to let it be known the part which he has played in the matter—which indeed would seem to be within the scope of his proper duties, he being an engineer—I shall be glad for him to do so, it always being undestood that he does not mention my name in any way."

Half-an-hour later Dillon entered, to say that his cousin agreed heartily to take a part in the adventure, and that he would shortly come up to arrange the details with Rupert. Rupert had met Gerald Dillon before, and knew him to be as wild, adventurous, and harum-scarum a young officer as his cousin Pat; and in half-an-hour's talk the whole matter was settled.

Gerald would take two petards, which weighed some twenty pounds each, to his tent, one by one. Hugh should fetch them in a basket, one by one, to the river bank, at the spot where a balk of wood had been washed ashore by some recent floods. At seven in the evening Gerald should call upon his cousin, and on leaving, accompany Rupert to the river bank, where Hugh would be already in waiting. When they had left, Pat Dillon should start on horseback with the three uniforms in his valise, the party hiding the clothes in which they left the camp, under the bank at their place of starting.

The plan was carried out as arranged, and soon after seven o'clock Rupert Holliday and Gerald Dillon, leaving the camp, strolled down to the river, on whose bank Hugh was already sitting. The day had been extremely hot, and numbers of soldiers were bathing in the river. It was known that the assault was to take place that night, but as the cavalry would take no part in it, the soldiers, with their accustomed carelessness, paid little heed to the matter. As it grew dusk, the bathers one by one dressed and left, until only the three watchers remained. Then Rupert called Hugh, who had been sitting at a short distance, to his side; they then stripped, and carefully concealed their clothes. The petards were taken out from beneath a heap of stones, where Hugh had hid them, and were fixed on the piece of timber, one end of which was just afloat in the stream. By their side was placed some lengths of fuse, a brace of pistols, a long gimlet, some hooks, and cord. Then just as it was fairly dark the log was silently pushed into the water, and swimming beside it, with one hand upon it, the little party started upon their adventurous expedition.

The log was not very large, although of considerable length, and with the petards upon it, it showed but little above water. The point where they had embarked was fully two miles above the town, and it was more than an hour before the stream took them abreast of it. Although it was very dark, they now floated on their backs by the piece of timber, so as to show as little as possible to any who might be on the look out, for of all objects the round outline of a human head is one of the most easily recognized.

Presently they came, as they had expected, to a floating boom, composed of logs of timber chained together. Here the piece of timber came to standstill. No talk was necessary, as the course under these circumstances had been already agreed to. The petards and other objects were placed on the boom, upon which Rupert, as the lightest of the party, crept, holding in his hand a cord fastened round the log. Hugh and Gerald Dillon now climbed upon one end of the log, which at once sank into the water below the level of the botom of the boom, and the current taking it, swept it beneath the obstacle. Rupert's rope directed its downward course, and it was soon alongside the boom, but on the lower side.

The petards were replaced, and the party again proceeded; but now Hugh swam on his back, holding a short rope attached to one end, so as to keep the log straight, and prevent its getting across the mooring chains of the boats forming the bridge; while Rupert and Gerald, each with a rope, also attached to the log, floated down some ten or twelve yards on either side of the log, but a little behind it. The plan answered admirably; the stream carried the log end foremost between two of the boats, which were moored twelve feet apart, while Gerald and Rupert each floated on the other side of the mooring chains of the boats; round these chains they twisted the ropes, and by them the log lay anchored as it were under the bridge, and between two of the boats forming it. If there were any sentries on the bridge, these neither saw nor heard them, their attention being absorbed by the expectation of an attack upon the breaches of Fort St. Michael.

The party now set to work. With the gimlet holes were made a couple of feet above the water. In them the hooks were inserted, and from these the petards were suspended by ropes, so as to lie against the sides of the boats, an inch only above the water's level. The fuses were inserted; and all being now in readiness for blowing a hole in the side of the two boats, they regained the log, and awaited the signal.

The time passed slowly; but as the church clocks of the town struck eleven, a sudden outburst of musketry broke out round St. Michael's. In an instant the cannon of the fort roared out, the bells clanged the alarm, blue fires were lighted, and the dead silence was succeeded by a perfect chaos of sounds. The party under the bridge waited quietly, until the noise as of a large body of men coming upon the bridge from the town end was heard. At the first outbreak Gerald Dillon had, with some difficulty, lit first some tinder, and then a slow-match, from a flint and steel—all of these articles having been most carefully kept dry during the trip, with the two pistols, which were intended to fire the fuses, should the flint and steel fail to produce a light.

As the sound of the reinforcements coming on to the bridge was heard, Gerald Dillon on one side, Rupert Holliday on the other, left the log, and swam with a slow match in hand to the boats. In another instant the fuses were lighted, and the three companions swam steadily down stream.

In twenty seconds a loud explosion was heard, followed almost instantaneously by another, and the swimmers knew that their object had been successful, that two of the boats forming the bridge would sink immediately, and that, the connection being thus broken, no reinforcements from the town could reach the garrison of the Fort St. Michael. Loud shouts were heard upon the bridge as the swimmers struck steadily down stream, while the roar of the musketry from Fort St. Michael was unremitting.

Half an hour later the three adventurers landed, at a point where a lantern had, according to arrangement, been placed at the water's edge by Pat Dillon, who was in waiting with their clothes, and who received them with an enthusisatic welcome. Five minutes later they were on their way back to their camp.

In the meantime the battle had raged fiercely round Fort St. Michael. The attack had been made upon two breaches. The British column, headed by the grenadiers, and under the command of Lord Cutts, attacked the principal breach. The French opposed a desperate defence. With Lord Cutts as volunteers were Lord Huntingdon, Lord Lorn, Sir Richard Temple, and Mr. Dalrymple, and these set a gallant example to their men.

On arriving at a high breastwork, Lord Huntingdon, who was weakened by recent attack of fever, was unable to climb over it.

"Five guineas," he shouted, "to the man who will help me over!"

Even among the storm of balls there was a shout of laughter as the nobleman held out his purse, and a dozen willing hands soon lifted him over the obstacle.

Then on the troops swept, stormed the covered way, carried the ravelin, and forced their way up the breach. The French fought staunchly; and well it was for the

British that no reinforcements could reach them from Venloo, and that the original 800 garrisoning the fort were alone in their defence. As it was, the place was stormed, 200 of the French made prisoners, and the rest either killed or drowned in endeavouring to cross the river.

The French in Venloo, upon finding that the fort had fallen, broke up the rest of the bridge; and although there was some surprise in the British camp that no reinforcements had been sent over to aid the garrison, none knew that the bridge had been broken at the commencement of the attack, consequently there were neither talk nor inquiries, and those concerned congratulated themselves that their adventure had been successful, and that, as no one knew anything of it, they could, should occasion offer, again undertake an expedition on their own account.

The day after the capture of St. Michael's, strong fatigue parties were set to work, erecting batteries to play across the river on the town.

These were soon opened, and after a few days' further resistance, the place surrendered, on the condition of the garrison being free to march to Antwerp, then in French possession.

The towns of Ruremond and Stevenswort were now invested, and surrendered after a short resistance; and thus the Maas was opened as a waterway for the supplies for the army.

The Dutch Government, satisfied with the successes so far, would have now had the army go into winter quarters; but Marlborough, with great difficulty, persuaded them to consent to his undertaking the siege of Liege, a most important town and fortress, whose possession would give to the allies the command of the Meuse—or Maas—into the very heart of Flanders.

Marshal Boufflers, ever watching the movements of

Marlborough, suspected that Liege would be his next object of attack, and accordingly reconnoitered the ground round that city, and fixed on a position which would, he thought, serve admirably for the establishment of a permanent camp.

The news was, however, brought to Marlborough, who broke up his camp the same night; and when the French army approached Liege, they found the allies established on the very ground which the Marshal had selected for their camp. All unsuspecting the presence of the English, the French came on in order of march until within cannot-shot of the allies, and another splendid opportunity was thus given to Marlborough to attack the main body of the enemy under most advantageous circumstances.

The Dutch deputies again interposed their veto, and the English had the mortification of seeing the enemy again escape from their hands.

However, there was now nothing to prevent their undertaking the siege of Liege, and on the 20th of October the regular investment of the place was formed.

The strength of Liege consisted in its citadel and the Fort of Chatreuse, both strongly fortified. The town itself, a wealthy city, and so abounding in churches that it was called "Little Rome," was defended only by a single wall. It could clearly offer no defence against the besiegers, and therefore surrendered at the first summons, the garrison, 5000 strong, retiring to the citadel and Fort St. Chatreuse, which mounted fifty guns. Siege was at once laid to the citadel, and with such extraordinary vigour was the attack pushed forward, under the direction of General Cohorn, that upon the 23rd of October, three days only after the investment commenced, the breaches in the counter-scarp were pronounced practicable, and an assault was immediately ordered. The allies attacked with extreme bravery, and the citadel was carried by storm—here as at Venloo, the British troops being the first who scaled the breach. Thus 1000 prisoners were taken; and the garrison of Fort Chatreuse were so disheartened at the speedy fall of the citadel, that they capitulated a few days later.

This brought the first campaign of the war to an end. It had been very short, but its effect had been great. Kaiserwerth had been taken, and the Lower Rhine opened; four fortified places on the Meuse had been captured; the enemy had been driven back from the borders of Holland; and the allied army had, in the possession of Liege, an advanced post in the heart of Flanders for the recommencement of the campaign in the spring. And all this had been done in the face of a large French army, which had never ventured to give battle even to save the beleaguered fortresses.

The army now went into winter quarters, and Marlborough returned at once to England.

Upon the voyage down the Meuse, in company with the Dutch commissioners, he had a very narrow escape. The boat was captured by a French partisan leader, who had made an incursion to the river. The earl had with him an old servant named Gill, who, with great presence of mind, slipped into his master's hand an old passport made out in the name of General Churchill. The French, intent only upon plunder, and not recognizing under the name of Churchill their great opponent Marlborough, seized all the plate and valuables in the boat, made prisoners of the small detachment of soldiers on board, but suffered the rest of the passengers, including the earl and the Dutch commissioners, to pass unmolested.

Thus, had it not been for the presence of mind of an old servant, the Earl of Marlborough would have been taken a prisoner to France; and since it was his genius and diplomatic power alone which kept the alliance together, and secured victory for their arms, the whole issue of the war, the whole future of Europe, would have been changed.

CHAPTER VIII.

THE OLD MILL.

A CONSIDERABLE portion of the allied army were quartered in the barracks and forts of Liege, in large convents requisitioned for the purpose, and in outlying villages. The 5th dragoons had assigned to them a convent some two miles from the town. The monks had moved out, and gone to an establishment of the same order in the town, and the soldiers were therefore left to make the best they could of their quarters. There was plenty of room for the men, but for the horses there was some difficulty. The cloisters were very large, and these were transformed into stables, and boards were fastened up on the open faces to keep out the cold; others were stalled in sheds and outbuildings; and the great refectory, or dining hall, was also strewn thick with straw, and filled with four rows of horses.

In the afternoon the officers generally rode or walked down into the town. One day, Rupert Holliday with Pat Dillon had met their friends Lord Fairholm and Sir John Loveday, whose regiment was quartered in the town, at the principal wine-shop, a large establishment, which was the great gathering place of the officers of the garrison. There an immense variety of bright uniforms were to be seen, English, German, and Dutch, horse, foot, and artillery, while the serving men hurried about through the throng with trays piled with beer mugs, or with wine and glasses.

"Who is that officer," Dillon asked, "in the Hessian cavalry uniform? Methinks he eyes you with no friendly look."

Rupert and his friends glanced at the officer pointed out.

"It is that fellow Fulke," Sir John said. "I heard he had managed to obtain a commission in the army of the Landgrave of Hesse. You must keep a smart look out, Master Rupert, for his presence bodes you no good. He is in fitting company; that big German officer next to him is the Graff Muller, a turbulent swashbuckler, but a famous swordsman—a fellow who would as soon run you through as look at you, and who is a disgrace to the Margrave's army, in which I wonder much that he is allowed to stay."

"Who is the fellow you are speaking of?" Dillon asked.

"A gentleman with whom our friend Rupert had a difference of opinion," Sir John Loveday laughed. "There is a blood feud between them. Seriously, the fellow has a grudge against our friend, and as he is the sort of man to gratify himself without caring much as to the means he uses, I should advise Master Holliday not to trust himself out alone after dark. There are plenty of ruined men in these German regiments who would willingly cut a throat for a guinea, especially if offered them by one of their own officers."

"The scoundrel is trying to get Muller to take up his quarrel, or I am mistaken," Lord Fairholm, who had been watching the pair closely, said: "They are glancing this way, and Fulke has been talking earnestly. But ruffian as he is, Muller is of opinion that for a notorious swordsman like him to pick a quarrel with a lad like our friend would be too rank, and would, if he killed him, look so much like murder that even he dare not face it; he has shaken his head very positively."

"But why should not this Fulke take the quarrel in his own hands?" Dillon asked, surprised. "Unless he is the rankest of cowards he might surely consider himself a match for our little cornet?"

"Our little cornet has a neat hand with the foils,"

Lord Fairholm said, drily, "and Master Fulke is not un-acquainted with the fact."

"Why, Rupert," Dillon said, turning to him, "you have never said that you ever had a foil in your hand!"

"You never asked me," Rupert said, smiling. "But I have practised somewhat with the colonel my grand-father. And now it is time to be off, Dillon; we have to walk back."

Four days later, as Rupert Holliday was standing in the barrack-yard, his troop having just been dismissed drill, a trooper of the 1st dragoons rode into the yard, and after asking a question of one of the men, rode up to him and handed him a note.

Somewhat surprised he opened it, and read as fol-lows:—"My dear Master Holliday,—Sir John Loveday and myself are engaged in an adventure which promises some entertainment, albeit it is not without a spice of danger. We need a good comrade who can on occa-sion use his sword, and we know that we can rely on you. On receipt of this, please mount your horse and ride to the old mill which lies back from the road in the valley beyond Dettinheim. There you will find your sincere friend, FAIRHOLM. P. S.—It would be as well not to mention whither you are going to ride."

It was the first note that Rupert had received from Lord Fairholm, and delighted at the thought of an ad-venture, he called Hugh, and bade him saddle his horse.

"Shall I go with you, Master Rupert?" Hugh asked, for he generally rode behind Rupert as his orderly.

Rupert did not answer for a moment. Lord Fair-holm had asked him to tell no one; but he meant, no doubt, that he should tell none of his brother officers. On Hugh's silence, whatever happened, he could rely, and he would be useful to hold the horses. At any rate, if not wanted, he could return.

"Ay, Hugh, you can come; and look you, slip a brace of pistols quietly into each of our holsters."

With a momentary look of surprise, Hugh withdrew to carry out his instructions; and ten minutes later, Rupert, followed by his orderly, rode out of the convent.

The mill in question lay some three miles distant, and about half a mile beyond the little hamlet of Dettinheim. It stood some distance from the road, up a quiet valley, and was half hidden in trees. It had been worked by a stream that ran down the valley. It was a dark, gloomy-looking structure; and the long green weeds that hung from the great wheel, where the water from the overshot trough splashed and tumbled over it, showed that it had been for some time abandoned. These things had been noticed by Rupert when riding past it some time before, for, struck with the appearance of the mill, he had ridden up the valley to inspect it. On his ride to Lord Fairholm's rendezvous, he wondered much what could be the nature of the adventure in which they were about to embark. He knew that both his friends were full of life and high spirits, and his thoughts wandered between some wild attempt to carry off a French officer of importance, or an expedition to rescue a lovely damsel in distress. Hugh, equally wondering, but still more ignorant of the nature of the expedition, rode quietly on behind.

The road was an unfrequented one, and during the last two miles' ride they did not meet a single person upon it. The hamlet of Dettinheim contained four or five houses only, and no one seemed about. Another five minutes' ride took them to the entrance to the little valley in which the mill stood. They rode up to it, and then dismounted.

"It's a lonesome dismal-looking place, Master Rupert. It doesn't seem to bode good. Of course you know what you're come for, sir; but I don't like the look of the place, nohow."

"It does not look cheerful, Hugh; but I am to meet Lord Fairholm and Sir John Loveday here."

"I don't see any sign of them, Master Rupert. I'd be careful if I were you, for it's just the sort of place for a foul deed to be done in. It does not look safe."

"It looks old and haunted," Rupert said; "but as that is its natural look, I don't see it can help it. The door is open, so my friends are here."

"Look out, Master Rupert; you may be running into a snare."

Rupert paused a moment, and the thought flashed across his mind that it might, as Hugh said, be a snare; but with Lord Fairholm's letter in his pocket, he dismissed the idea.

"You make me nervous, Hugh, with your suggestions; nevertheless I will be on my guard;" and he drew his sword as he entered the mill.

As he did so, Hugh, who was holding the horses' bridles over his arm, snatched a brace of pistols from the holsters, cocked them, and stood eagerly listening. He heard Rupert walk a few paces forward, and then pause, and shout "Where are you, Fairholm?" Then he heard a rush of heavy feet, a shout from Rupert, a clash of swords, and a scream of agony.

All this was the work of a second; and as Hugh dropped the reins and rushed forward to his master's assistance, he heard a noise behind him, and saw a dozen men issue from behind the trees, and run towards him.

Coming from the light, Hugh could with difficulty see what was taking place in the darkened chamber before him. In an instant, however, he saw Rupert standing with his back to a wall, with a dead man at his feet, and four others hacking and thrusting at him. Rushing up, Hugh fired his two pistols. One of the men dropped to the ground, the other with an oath reeled backwards.

"Quick, sir! there are a dozen men just upon us."

Rupert ran one of his opponents through the shoulder, and as the other drew back shouted to Hugh,—

"Up the stairs, Hugh! Quick!"

The two lads sprang up the wide steps leading to the floor above, just as the doorway was darkened by a mass of men. The door at the top of the steps yielded to their rush, the rotten woodwork giving, and the door falling to the ground. Two or three pistol bullets whizzed by their ears, just as they leapt through the opening.

"Up another floor, Hugh; and easy with the door."

The door at the top of the next ladder creaked heavily as they pushed it back on its hinges.

"Look about, Hugh, for something to pile against it."

The shutters of the window were closed, but enough light streamed through the chinks and crevices for them to see dimly. There was odd rubbish strewn all about, and in one corner a heap of decaying sacks. To these both rushed, and threw some on the floor by the door, placing their feet on them to keep them firm, just as with a rush the men came against it. This door was far stronger than the one below, but it gave before the weight.

The hinges will give, Hugh exclaimed; but at the moment Rupert passed his thin rapier through one of the chinks of the rough boards which formed it, and a yell was heard on the outside. The pressure against the door ceased instantly; and Rupert bade Hugh run for some more sacks, while he threw himself prone on them on the ground. It was well he did so, for, as he expected, a half dozen pistol-shots were heard, and the bullets crashed through the woodwork.

"Keep out of the line of fire, Hugh."

Hugh did so, and threw down the sacks close to the door. Several times he ran backwards and forwards across the room the assailants still firing through the door. Then Rupert leapt up, and the pile of sacks were rapidly heaped against the door, just as the men outside, in hopes that they had killed the defenders, made another rush against it.

This time, however, the pile of sacks had given it strength and solidity, and it hardly shook under the assault. Then came volleys of curses and imprecations, in German, from outside; and then the lads could hear the steps descend the stairs, and a loud and angry consultation take place below.

"Open the shutters, Hugh, and let us see where we are."

It was a chamber of some forty feet square, and, like those below it, of considerable height. It was like the rest of the mill, built of rough pine, black with age. It had evidently been used as a granary.

"This is a nice trap we have fallen into, Hugh, and I doubt me if Lord Fairholm ever saw the letter with his name upon it which lured me here. However, that is not the question now; the thing is how we are to get out of the trap. How many were there outside, do you think?"

"There seemed to me about a dozen, Master Rupert, but I got merely a blink at them."

"If it were not for their pistols we might do something Hugh; but as it is, it is hopeless."

Looking out from the window they saw that it was over the great water-wheel, whose top was some fifteen feet below them, with the water running to waste from the leet, which led from the reservoir higher up the valley.

Presently they heard a horse gallop up to the front of the mill, and shortly after the sound of a man's voice raised in anger. By this time it was getting dark.

"What'll be the end of this, Master Rupert? We

7

could stand a siege for a week, but they'd hardly try that."

"What's that?" Rupert said. "There's some one at the door again."

They came back, but all was quiet. Listening attentively, however, they heard a creaking, as of some one silently descending the stairs. For some time all was quiet, except that they could hear movements in the lower story of the mill.

Presently Rupert grasped Hugh's arm.

"Do you smell anything, Hugh?"

"Yes, sir; I smell a smoke."

"The scoundrels have set the mill on fire, Hugh."

In another minute or two the smell became stronger, and then wreaths of smoke could be seen curling up through the crevices in the floor.

"Run through the other rooms, Hugh; let us see if there is any means of getting down."

There were three other rooms, but on opening the shutters they found in each case a sheer descent of full forty feet to the ground, there being no outhouses whose roofs would afford them a means of descent.

"We must rush down stairs, Hugh. It is better to be shot as we go out, than be roasted here."

Rapidly they tore away the barrier of sacks, and Rupert put his thumb on the latch. He withdrew it with a sharp exclamation,—

"They have jammed the latch, Hugh. That was what that fellow we heard was doing."

The smoke was now getting very dense, and they could with difficulty breathe. Rupert put his head out of the window.

"There is a little window just over the wheel," he said; "if we could get down to the next floor we might slip out of that and get in the wheel without being noticed. Look about, Hugh," he exclaimed, suddenly;

"there must be a trap-door somewhere for lowering the sacks. There is a wheel hanging to the ceiling; the trap must be under that."

In a minute the trap was found, and raised. The smoke rushed up in a volume, and the boys looked with dismay at the dense mirk below.

"It's got to be done, Hugh. Tie that bit of sacking, quick, over your nose and mouth, while I do the same. Now lower yourselves by your arms, and drop; it won't be above fifteen feet. Hold your breath, and rush straight to the window. I heard them open it. Now, both together; now."

The lads fell on their feet, and were in another minute at the window. The broad top of the great wheel stretched out level with them, hiding the window from those who might have been standing below. The wheel itself was some thirty feet in diameter, and was sunk nearly half its depth in the ground, the water running off by a deep tail-race.

"We might lie flat on the top of the wheel," Hugh said.

"We should be roasted to death when the mill is fairly in flames. No, Hugh; we must squeeze through this space between the wall and the wheel, slip down by the framework, and keep inside the wheel. There is no fear of that burning, and we shall get plenty of fresh air down below the level of the mill. I will go first, Hugh. Mind how you go, for these beams are all slimy; get your arm well around, and slip down as far as the axle."

It was not an easy thing to do, and Rupert lost his hold and slipped down the last ten feet, hurting himself a good deal in his fall. He was soon on his feet again, and helped to break the fall of Hugh, who lost his hold and footing at the axle, and would have hurt himself greatly, had not Rupert caught him, both boys falling with a crash in the bottom of the wheel.

They were some little time before regaining their feet, for both were much hurt. Their movements were, however, accelerated by the water, which fell in a heavy shower from above, through the leaks in the buckets of the wheel.

"Are you hurt much, Master Rupert?"

"I don't think I am broken at all, Hugh, but I am hurt all over. How are you?"

"I am all right, I think. It's lucky the inside of this wheel is pretty smooth, like a big drum."

The position was not a pleasant one. A heavy shower of water from above filled the air with spray, and with their heads bent down it was difficult to breathe; the inside planks of the wheel were so slimy that standing was almost impossible, and at the slightest attempt at movement they fell. Above, the flames were already darting out through the windows and sides of the mill.

"Do you not think we might crawl out between the wheel and the wall, and make our way down the tail-race, Master Rupert? This water is chilling me to the bones."

"I think it safer to stop where we are, Hugh. Those fellows are sure to be on the watch. They will expect to see us jump out of the upper window the last thing, and will wait to throw our bodies—for of course we should be killed—into the flames, to hide all trace of us. We have only to wait quietly here. It is not pleasant; but after all the trouble we have had to save our lives, it would be a pity to risk them again. And I have a very particular desire to be even with that fellow who is, I doubt not, at the bottom of all this."

Soon the flames were rushing out in great sheets from the mill, and even in the wheel the heat of the atmosphere was considerable. Presently a great crash was heard inside.

"There is a floor fallen," Rupert said. "I think we

may move now; those fellows will have made off, secure that—Hullo! what's that?"

The exclamation was caused by a sudden creaking noise, and the great wheel began slowly to revolve. The fall of the floor had broken its connection with the machinery in the mill, and left free, it at once yielded to the weight of the water in its buckets. The supply of water coming down was small, and the wheel stiff from long disuse, therefore it moved but slowly. The motion, however, threw both lads from their feet, and once down, the rotatory motion rendered it impossible for them to regain their feet. After the first cry of surprise, neither spoke; across both their minds rushed the certainty of death.

How long the terrible time that followed lasted, neither of them ever knew. The sensation was that of being pounded to death. At one moment they were together, then separated; now rolling over and over in a sort of ball, then lifted up and cast down into the bottom of the wheel with a crash; now with their heads highest, now with their feet. It was like a terrible nightmare; but gradually the sharp pain of the blows and falls were less vivid—a dull sensation came over them—and both lost consciousness.

Rupert was the first to open his eyes, and for a time lay but in dreamy wonder as to where he was, and what had happened. He seemed to be lying under a great penthouse, with a red glow pervading everything. Gradually his thoughts took shape, and he remembered what had passed, and struggling painfully into a sitting position, looked round. The wheel no longer revolved; there was no longer the constant splash of water. Indeed the wheel existed as a wheel no longer.

As he looked round the truth lighted upon him. The burning mill had fallen across the wheel, crushing, at the top, the sides together. The massive timber had given no further, and the wheel formed a sort of roof, sloping from the outer wall, built solidly up against it, to the opposite foot. Above, the timber of this wall glared and flickered, but the soddened timber of the wheel could have resisted a far greater amount of heat. The leet had of course been carried away with the fall, and the water would be flowing down the valley. The heat was very great, but the rush of air up the deep cut of the mill-race rendered it bearable. Having once grasped the facts—and as he doubted not the fall must have occurred soon after he lost consciousness, and so saved him from being bruised to death—Rupert turned to Hugh.

He was quite insensible, but his heart still beat. Rupert crawled out of the wheel, and found pools of water in the mill-race, from which he brought double hand-fuls, and sprinkled Hugh's face. Then as he himself grew stronger from fresh air and a copious dousing of his face and head with water, he dragged Hugh out, and laying him beside a pool dashed water on his face and chest. A deep sigh was the first symptom of re-turning consciousness. He soon, to Rupert's delight, opened his eyes.

After a time he sat up, but was too much hurt to rise. After some consultation, Rupert left him, and went alone down to the hamlet of Dettinheim, where, after much knocking, he roused some of the inhabitants, who had only a short time before returned from the burning mill. Sodden and discoloured as it was, Ru-pert's uniform was still recognizable, and by the author-ity this conveyed, and a promise of ample reward, four men were induced to return with him to the mill, and carry Hugh down to the village. This they reached just as the distant clock of Liege cathedral struck two. A bed was given up to them, and in half an hour both lads were sound asleep.

CHAPTER IX.

THE DUEL.

GREAT was the excitement in the 5th Dragoons when, upon the arrival of Rupert and Hugh—the former of whom was able to ride, but the latter was carried by on a stretcher—they learned the attack which had been made upon one of their officers. The "Little Cornet" was a general favourite, short as was the time since he had joined; while Hugh was greatly liked by the men of his own troop. Rupert's colonel at once sent for him, to learn the particulars of the outrage. Rupert was unable to give farther particulars as to his assailants than that they were German soldiers; that much the dim light had permitted him to see, but more than that he could not say. He stated his reasons for believing Sir Richard Fulke was the originator of the attack, since he had had a quarrel with him in England, but owned that, beyond suspicions, he had no proof. The colonel at once rode down to head-quarters, and laid a complaint before the Earl of Athlone, who promised that he would cause every inquiry to be made. Then the General commanding the Hesse contingent was communicated with, and the colonel of the cavalry regiment to which Sir Richard Fulke belonged was sent for. He stated that Captain Fulke had been away on leave of absence for three days, and that he had gone to England. The regiment was, however, paraded, and it was found that five troopers were missing. No inquiry, however, could elicit from any of the others a confession that they had been engaged in any fray, and as all were reported as having been in by ten o'clock, except the five missing men, there was no clue as to the parties engaged. The five men might have deserted, but the grounds for suspicion were very strong. Still, as no proof could be obtained, the matter was suffered to drop.

The affair caused, however, much bad feeling between the two regiments, and the men engaged in affrays when they met, until the order was issued that they should only be allowed leave into the town on alternate days. This ill-feeling spread, however, beyond the regiments concerned. There had already been a good deal of jealousy upon the part of the Continental troops of the honour gained by the British in being first in at the breaches of Venloo and Liege, and this feeling was now much embittered. Duels between the officers became matters of frequent occurrence, in spite of the strict orders issued against that practice.

As Rupert had anticipated, the letter by which he had been entrapped turned out a forgery. Lord Fairholm was extremely indignant when he heard the use that had been made of his name, and at once made inquiries as to the trooper who had carried the note to Rupert. This man he found without difficulty; upon being questioned, he stated that he had just returned from carrying a message when he was accosted by a German officer who offered him a couple of marks to carry a letter up to an officer of the 5th Dragoons. Thinking that there was no harm in so doing, he had at once accepted the offer. Upon being asked if he could recognize the officer if he saw him, he replied that he had scarcely noticed his face, and did not think that he could pick him out from others.

The first three or four duels which took place had not been attended with fatal result; but about three weeks after the occurrence of the attack on Rupert, Captain Muller, who had been away on leave, returned, and publicly announced his attention of avenging the insult to his regiment by insulting and killing one of the officers of the 5th Dragoons.

The report of the threat caused some uneasiness among the officers, for the fellow's reputation as a swordsman and notorious duellist was so well known, that it was felt that any one whom he might select as his antagonist would be as good as a dead man. A proposition was started to report the matter to the general, but this was decisively negatived, as it would have looked like a request for protection, and would so affect the honour of the regiment.

There was the satisfaction that but one victim could be slain, for the aggressor in a fatal duel was sure to be punished by removal into some corps stationed at a distance.

Rupert was silent during these discussions, but he silently determined that he would, if the opportunity offered, take up the gauntlet, for he argued that he was the primary cause of the feud; and, remembering the words of M. Dessin and Maître Dalboy, he thought that, skilful as a swordsman as Muller might be, he would yet have at least a fair chance of victory, while he knew that so much could not be said for any of the other officers of his regiment.

The opportunity occurred two days later. Rupert, with his friend Dillon, went down to the large saloon, which was the usual rendezvous with his friends Fairholm and Loveday. The place was crowded with officers, but Rupert soon perceived his friends, sitting at a small table. He and Dillon placed two chairs there also, and were engaged in conversation when a sudden lull in the buzz of talk caused them to look up. Captain Muller had just entered the saloon with a friend, and the lull was caused by curiosity, as his boast had been the matter of public talk; and as all noticed that two officers of the 5th were present, it was anticipated that a scene would ensue.

A glance at Dillon's face showed that the blood had

left his cheek; for, brave as the Irishman was, the prospect of being killed like a dog by this native swordsman could not but be terrible to him, and he did not doubt for a moment that he would be selected. Captain Muller walked leisurely up to the bar, drank off a bumper of raw Geneva, and then turned and looked round the room. As his eyes fell on the uniform of the 5th, a look of satisfaction came over his face, and fixing his eyes on Dillon, he walked leisurely across the room. Rupert happened to be sitting on the outside of the table, and he at once rose and as calmly advanced towards the German.

There was now a dead silence in the room, and all listened intently to hear what the lad had to say to the duellist. Rupert spoke first; and although he did not raise his voice in the slightest, not a sound was lost from one end of the room to the other.

"Captain Muller," he said, "I hear that you have made a boast that you will kill the first officer of my regiment whom you met. I am, I think, the first, and you now have the opportunity of proving whether you are a mere cut-throat or a liar."

A perfect gasp of astonishment was heard in the room.

Dillon leapt to his feet, exclaiming,—

"No, Rupert, I will not allow it! I am your senior officer." And the gallant fellow would have pushed forward, had not Lord Fairholm put his hand on his shoulder and forced him back, saying,—

"Leave him alone; he knows what he is doing."

The German took a step back, with a hoarse exclamation of rage and surprise at Rupert's address, and put his hand to his sword. Then, making a great effort to master his fury, he said,—

"You are safe in crowing loud, little cockerel; but Captain Muller does not fight with boys."

A murmur of approval ran round the room; for the prospect of this lad standing up to be killed by so noted a swordsman was painful alike to the German and English officers present.

"The same spirit seems to animate you and your friend Sir Richard Fulke," Rupert said, quietly. "He did not care about fighting a boy, and so employed a dozen of his soldiers to murder him."

"It is a lie!" the captain thundered. "Beware, young sir, how you tempt me too far."

"You know it is not a lie," Rupert said, calmly. "I know he told you he was afraid to fight me, for that I was more than his match; and it seems to me, sir, that this seeming pity for my youth is a mere cover of the fact that you would rather choose as your victim some one less skilled in fence than I happen to be. Are you a coward, too, sir, as well as a ruffian?"

"Enough!" the German gasped. "Swartzberg," he said, turning to his friend, "make the arrangements; for I vow I will kill this insolent puppy in the morning."

Lord Fairholm at once stepped forward to the Hessian captain.

"I shall have the honour to act as Mr. Holliday's second. Here is my card. I shall be at home all the evening."

Rupert now resumed his seat, while Captain Muller and his friend moved to the other end of the saloon. Here he was surrounded by a number of German officers, who endeavoured to dissuade him from fighting a duel in which the killing of his adversary would be condemned by the whole army as child murder.

"Child or not," he said, ferociously, "he dies to-morrow. You think he was mad to insult me; it was conceit, not madness. His head is turned; a fencing-master once praised his skill at fence, and he thinks himself a match for me—me! the best swordsman, though I say it, in the German army. No, I would not have forced a quarrel on him, for he is beneath my notice; but I am right glad that he has taken up the glove I meant to throw down to his fellow. In killing him I shall not only have punished the only person who has for many years ventured to insult Otto Muller, but I shall have done a service to a friend."

No sooner had Rupert regained his seat than Dillon exclaimed,—

"Rupert, I shall never forgive myself. Others think you are mad, but I know that you sacrifice yourself to save me. You did me an ill-service, my lord," he said, turning to Lord Fairholm, "by holding me back when I would have taken my proper place. I shall never hold up my head again. But it will not be for long, for when he has killed Rupert I will seek him wherever he may go, and force him to kill me too."

"My dear Dillon, I knew what I was doing," Lord Fairholm said. "It was clear that either he or you had to meet this German cut-throat."

"But," Dillon asked, in astonishment, "why would you rather that your friend Rupert should be killed than I?"

"You are not putting the case fairly," Lord Fairholm said. "Did it stand so, I would certainly prefer that you should run this risk than that Rupert should do so. But the case stands thus. In the first place, it is really his quarrel; and in the second, while it is certain that this German could kill you without fail, it is by no means certain that he will kill Rupert."

Dillon's eyes opened with astonishment.

"Not kill him! Do you think that he will spare him after the way he has been insulted before all of us?"

"No, there is little chance of that. It is his power, not his will, that I doubt. I do not feel certain; far from it, I regard the issue as doubtful; and yet I feel a strong confidence in the result; for you must know, Master Dillon, that Rupert Holliday, boy as he is, is probably the best swordsman in the British army."

"Rupert Holliday!" ejaculated Dillon, incredulously. Lord Fairholm nodded.

"It is as I say, Dillon; and although they say this German is also the best in his, his people are in no way famous that way. Had it been with the best swordsman in the French army that Rupert had to fight, my mind would be less at ease. But come now, we have finished our liquor, and may as well be off. We are the center of all eyes here, and it is not pleasant to be a general object of pity, even when that pity is ill-bestowed. Besides, I have promised to be at home, to wait for Muller's second. I will come round to your quarters, Rupert, when I have arranged time and place."

The calm and assured manner of Rupert's two friends did more to convince Dillon that they were speaking in earnest, and that they really had confidence in Rupert's skill than any asseveration on their part could have done, but he was still astounded at the news that this boy friend of his, who had never even mentioned that he could fence, could by any possibility be not only a first-rate swordsman, but actually a fair match for this noted duellist. Upon the way up to the barracks, Rupert persuaded his friend to say nothing as to his skill, but it was found impossible to remain silent, for when the officers heard of the approaching duel there was a universal cry of indignation, and the colonel at once avowed his intention of riding off to Lord Athlone to request him to put a stop to a duel which would be nothing short of murder.

"The honour of the regiment shall not suffer," he said, sternly, "for I myself will meet this German cutthroat."

Seeing that his colonel was resolute, Rupert made a sign to Dillon that he might speak, and he accordingly related to his astonished comrades the substance of what Lord Fairholm had told him. Rupert's brother officers could not believe the news; but Rupert suggested that the matter could be easily settled if some foils were brought, adding that half-an-hour's fencing would be useful to him, and get his hand into work again. The proposal was agreed to, and first one and then another of those recognized as the best swordsmen of the regiment took their places against him, but without exerting himself in the slightest, he proved himself so infinitely their superior that their doubts speedily changed into admiration, and the meeting of the morrow was soon regarded with a feeling of not only hope, but confidence. It was late before Lord Fairholm rode up to the cornet's.

"Did you think I was never coming?" he asked, as he entered Rupert's quarters. "The affair has created quite an excitement, and just as I was starting, two hours back, a message came to me to go to head-quarters. I found his lordship in a great passion, and he rated me soundly, I can tell you, for undertaking to be second in such a disgracefully uneven contest as this. When he had had his say, of course I explained matters, pointed out that this German bully was a nuisance to the whole army, and that you being, as I myself could vouch, a sort of phenomenon with the sword, had taken the matter up to save your brother officer from being killed. I assured him that I had the highest authority for your being one of the best swordsmen in Europe, and that therefore I doubted not that you were a match for this German. I also pointed out respectfully to him that if he were to interfere to stop it, as he had intended, the matter would be certain to lead to many more meetings between the officers of the two nationalities. Upon this the general after some talk decided to allow the matter to go on, but said that whichever way it went he would write to the generals commanding all the divisions of the allied army, and would publish a general order to the effect that henceforth no duels shall be permitted except after the dispute being referred to a court of honour of five senior officers, by whom the necessity or otherwise of the duel shall be determined; and that in the case of any duel fought without any such preliminary, both combatants shall be dismissed from the service, whether the wounds given be serious or not. I think the proposal is an excellent one, and likely to do much good; for in a mixed army like ours, causes for dispute and jealousy are sure to arise, and without some stringent regulation we should be always fighting among ourselves."

At an early hour on the following morning a stranger would have supposed that some great military spectacle was about to take place, so large was the number of officers riding from Liege and the military stations around it towards the place fixed upon for the duel. The event had created a very unusual amount of excitement, because, in the first place, the attempt to murder Rupert at the mill of Dettinheim had created much talk; the intention of Captain Muller to force a quarrel on the officers of the 5th had also been a matter of public comment, while the manner in which the young cornet of that regiment had taken up the gage, added to the extraordinary inequality between the combatants, gave a special character to the duel. It was eight in the morning when Rupert Holliday rode up to the place fixed upon, a quiet valley some three miles from the town. On the slopes of hills on either side were gathered some two or three hundred officers, English, Dutch, and German, the bottom of the valley, which was some forty yards across, being left clear. There was, however, none of the life and animation which generally characterize a military gathering. The British officers looked sombre and stern at what they deemed nothing short of the approaching murder of their gallant young countryman; and the Germans were grave and downcast, for they felt ashamed of the inequality of the contest. Among both parties there was earnest though quiet talk of arresting the duel, but such a step would have been absolutely unprecedented. The arrival of the officers of the 5th, who rode up in a body a few minutes before Rupert arrived with Lord Fairholm and his friend Dillon, somewhat changed the aspect of affairs, for their cheerful faces showed that from some cause, at which the rest were unable to guess, they by no means regarded the death of their comrade as a foregone event. As they alighted and gave their horses to the orderlies who had followed them, their acquaintances gathered round them full of expressions of indignation and regret at the approaching duel.

"Is there any chance of this horrible business being stopped?" an old colonel asked Colonel Forbes, as he alighted. "There is a report that the general has got wind of it, and will at the last moment put an end to it by arresting both of them."

"No, I fancy that the matter will go on," Colonel Forbes said.

"But it is murder," Colonel Chambers said, indignantly.

"Not so much murder as you think, Chambers; for I tell you this lad is simply a marvel with his sword."

"Ah," the colonel said, "I had not heard that; but in no case could a lad like this have a chance with this Muller, a man who has not only the reputation of being the best swordsman in Germany, who now has been in something like thirty duels, and has more than twenty times killed his man."

"I know the ruffian's skill and address," Colonel Forbes said; "and yet I tell you that I regard my young friend's chance as by no means desperate."

Similar assurances had some effect in raising the spirits of the English officers; still they refused to believe that a lad like a recently-joined cornet could have any real chance with the noted duellist, and their hopes faded away altogether when Rupert rode up. He was, of course, a stranger to most of those present, and his smooth boyish face and slight figure struck them with pity and dismay. Rupert, however, although a little pale, seemed more cheerful than any one on the ground, and smiled and talked to Lord Fairholm and Dillon as if awaiting the commencement of an ordinary military parade.

"That is a gallant young fellow," was the universal exclamation of most of those present, whatever their nationality. "He faces death as calmly as if he were ignorant of his danger."

Five minutes later Captain Muller rode up, with his second; and the preparations for the conflict at once began.

All except the combatants and their seconds retired to the slopes. Lord Fairholm and Captain Swartzberg stood in the middle of the bottom; Rupert stood back at a short distance, talking quietly with Dillon and his colonel; while Captain Muller walked about near the foot of the slope, loudly saluting those present with whom he was acquainted.

There was but little loss of time in choosing the ground, for the bottom of the valley was flat and smooth, and the sun was concealed beneath a grey bank of clouds, which covered the greater part of the sky, so that there was no advantage of light.

When all was arranged the length of the swords was measured. Both had come provided with a pair of duelling rapiers, and as all four weapons were of excellent temper and of exactly even length, no difficulty was met with here. Then a deep hush fell upon the gathering as the seconds returned to their principals.

It had been arranged by the seconds that they should not fight in uniform, as the heavy boots impeded their action. Both were accordingly attired in evening dress. Rupert wore dark puce satin breeches, white stockings, and very light buckled shoes. His opponent was in bright orange-coloured breeches, with stockings to match. Coats and waistcoats were soon removed, and the shirt sleeves rolled up above the elbow.

As they took stand face to face, something like a groan went through the spectators. Rupert stood about five feet nine, slight, active, with smooth face, and head covered with short curls. The German stood six feet high, with massive shoulders, and arms covered with muscle. His huge moustache was twisted upwards towards his ears; his hair was cropped short, and stood erect all over his head. It was only among a few of the shrewder onlookers that the full value of the tough, whipcordy-look of Rupert's frame, and the extreme activity promised by his easy pose, were appreciated. The general opinion went back to the former verdict, that the disparity was so great that, even putting aside the German's well-known skill, the duel was little short of murder.

Just before they stood on guard, Captain Muller said, in a loud voice,—

"Now, sir, if you have any prayer to say, say it; for I warn you, I will kill you like a dog."

A cry of "Shame!" arose from the entire body of spectators; when it abated Rupert said, quietly but clearly,—

"My prayers are said, Captain Muller. If yours are not, say them now, for assuredly I will kill you—not as a dog, for a dog is a true and faithful animal, but as I would kill a tiger, or any other beast whose existence was a scourge to mankind."

A cheer of approbation arose from the circle; and with a grin of rage Captain Muller took his stand. Rupert faced him in an instant, and their swords crossed. For a short time the play was exceedingly cautious on both sides, each trying to find out his opponent's strength. Hitherto the German had thought but little of what Fulke had told him that he had heard, of Rupert's skill; but the calm and confident manner of the young Englishman now impressed him with the idea that he really, boy as he was, must be something out of the common way. The thought in no way abated his own assurance, it merely taught him that it would be wiser to play cautiously at first, instead of, as he had intended, making a fierce and rapid attack at once, and finishing the struggle almost as soon as it began.

The lightning speed with which his first thrusts were parried and returned soon showed him the wisdom of the course he had adopted; and the expression of arrogant disdain with which he had commenced the fight speedily changed to one of care and determination. This insolent boy was to be killed, but the operation must not be carelessly carried out.

For a time he attempted by skilful play to get through Rupert's guard, but the lad's sword always met him; and its point flashed so quickly and vengefully forward, that several times it was only by quick backward springs that he escaped from it.

The intense, but silent excitement among the spectators increased with every thrust and parry; and every nerve seemed to tingle in unison with the sharp clink of the swords. The German now endeavoured to take advantage of his superior height, length of arm, and strength, to force down Rupert's guard; but the latter slipped away from him, bounding as lightly as a cat out of range, and returning with such rapid and elastic springs, that the German was in turn obliged to use his utmost activity to get back out of reach.

So far several slight scratches had been given on both sides, but nothing in any way to affect the combatants. As the struggle continued, gaining every moment in earnestness and effort, a look of anxiety gradually stole over the German's face, and the perspiration stood thick on his forehead. He knew now that he had met his match; and an internal feeling told him that although he had exerted himself to the utmost, his opponent had not yet put out his full strength and skill. Rupert's face was unchanged since the swords had crossed. His mouth was set, but in a half smile; his eye was bright; and his demeanor rather that of a lad fencing with buttoned foils than that of one contending for his life against a formidable foe.

Now thoroughly aware of his opponent's strength and tactics, Rupert began to press the attack, and foot by foot drove his opponent back to the spot at which the combat had commenced. Then, after a fierce rally, he gave an opening; the German lunged, Rupert threw back his body with the rapidity of lightning, lunging also as he did so. His opponent's sword grazed his cheek as it passed, while his own ran through the German's body until the hilt struck it. Muller fell without a word, an inert mass; and the surgeon running up, pronounced that life was already extinct.

The crowd of spectators now flocked down, the English with difficulty repressing their exclamations of delight, and congratulated Rupert on the result, which to them appeared almost miraculous; while the senior German officer present came up to him, and said,—

"Although Captain Muller was a countryman of mine, sir, I rejoice in the unexpected result of this duel; it has rid our army of a man who was a scourge to it."

Plaisters and bandages were now applied to Rupert's wounds; and in a few minutes the whole party had left the valley, one German orderly alone remaining to watch the body of the dead duellist until a party could be sent out to convey it to the town for burial.

CHAPTER X.

THE BATTLE OF THE DYKES.

FOR some time after his duel with Captain Muller, it is probable that the little cornet was, after Marlborough himself, the most popular man in the British army in Flanders. He however bore his honours quietly, shrinking from notice, and seldom going down into the town. Any mention of the duel was painful to him; for although he considered that he was perfectly justified in taking up the quarrel forced upon his regiment, yet he sincerely regretted that he should have been obliged to kill a man, however dangerous and obnoxious, in cold blood.

Two days after the duel he received a letter from his grandfather. It was only the second he had received. In the previous letter Colonel Holliday alluded to something which he had said in a prior communication, and Rupert had written back to say that no such letter had come to hand. The answer ran as follows,—

"My dear Grandson,—Your letter has duly come to hand. I regret to find that my first to you miscarried, and by comparing dates I think that it must have been lost in the wreck of the brig 'Flora,' which was lost in a tempest on her way to Holland a few days after I wrote. This being so, you are ignorant of the changes which have taken place here, and which affect yourself in no slight degree. The match between your lady mother and Sir William Brownlow is broken off. This took place just after you sailed for the wars. It was brought about by our friend, M. Dessin. This gentleman—who is, although I know not his name, a French nobleman of title and distinction—received, about the time you left, the news that he might shortly expect to hear that the decree which had sent him into exile was reversed. Some little time later a compatriot of his came down to stay with him. M. Dessin, who I know cherished ill-feeling against Sir William for the insult which his son had passed upon his daughter, and for various belittling words respecting that young lady which Sir William had in his anger permitted himself to use in public, took occasion when he was riding through the streets of Derby, accompanied by his friends, Lord Pomeroy and Sir John Hawkes, gentlemen of fashion and repute, to accost him. Sir William swore at him as a French dancing-master; whereupon M. Dessin at once challenged him to a duel. Sir William refused with many scornful words to meet a man of such kind, whereupon M. Dessin, drawing Lord Pomeroy to him, in confidence disclosed his name and quality, to which his compatriot—also a French nobleman—testified, and of which he offered to produce documents and proofs. They did then adjourn to a tavern, where they called for a private room, to talk the matter over out of earshot of the crowd; and after examining the proofs, Lord Pomeroy and Sir John Hawkes declared that Sir William Brownlow could not refuse the satisfaction which M. Dessin demanded. It has always been suspected that Sir William was a man of small courage, though of overbearing manner, and he was mightily put to when he heard that he must fight with a man whom he justly regarded as being far more than his match. So craven did he become, indeed, that the gentlemen with him did not scruple to express their disgust loudly. M. Dessin said that, unless Sir William did afford him satisfaction, he would trounce him publicly as a coward, but that he had one other alternative to offer. All were mightily surprised when he stated that this alternative was that he should write a letter to Mistress Holliday renouncing all claim to her hand. This Sir William for a time

refused to do, blustering much; but finally, having no
stomach for a fight, and fearing the indignity of a public
whipping, he did consent so to do; and M. Dessin
having called for paper and pens, the letter was then
written, and the four gentlemen signed as witnesses.
The party then separated, Lord Pomeroy and Sir John
Hawkes riding off without exchanging another word
with Sir William Brownlow. Your lady mother was
in a great taking when she received the letter, and
learned the manner in which it had come to be written.
M. Dessin left the town, with his daughter, two days
later. He came over to take farewell of me, and expressed himself with great feeling and heartiness as to
the kindness which he was good enough to say that I
had shown him. I assured him, as you may believe,
that the action he had forced Mistress Holliday's suitor
to take left me infinitely his debtor. He promised to
write to me from France, whither he was about to
return. He said that he regretted much that a vow he
had sworn to keep his name unknown in England, save
and except his honour should compel him to disclose it,
prevented him from telling it; but that he would in the
future let me know it. After it was known that he had
left, Sir William Brownlow again attempted to make
advances to your lady mother; but she, who lacks not
spirit, repulsed him so scornfully that all fear of any
future entanglement in that quarter is at an end; at the
which I have rejoiced mightily, although the Chace,
now that you have gone, is greatly changed to me.
Farmer Parsons sends his duty to you, and his love to
Hugh. I think that it would not be ill-taken if, in a
short time, you were to write to Mistress Holliday.
Make no mention of her broken espousal, which is a
subject upon which she cares not to touch. The Earl
of Marlborough has been good enough to write me a
letter speaking in high terms of you. This I handed to

her to read, and although she said no word when she handed it back, I could see that she was much moved. My pen runs not so fast as it did. I will therefore now conclude.

"Your loving Grandfather."

This letter gave great pleasure to Rupert, not because it restored to him the succession of the estates of the Chace, for of that he thought but little, but because his mother was saved from a match which would, he felt sure, have been an unhappy one for her.

The winter passed off quietly, and with the spring the two armies again took the field. The campaign of 1803 was, like its predecessor, marred by the pusillanimity and indecision of the Dutch deputies, who thwarted all Marlborough's schemes for bringing the French to a general engagement, and so ruined the English general's most skilful plans, that the earl, worn out by disappointment and disgust, wrote to the Queen, praying to be relieved of his command and allowed to retire into private life, and finally only remained at his post at his mistress's earnest entreaty. The campaign opened with the siege of Bonn, a strongly fortified town held by the French, and of great importance to them, as being the point by which they kept open communication between France and their strong army in Germany. Marlborough himself commanded the siege operations, having under him forty battalions, sixty squadrons, and a hundred guns. General Overkirk, who, owing to the death of the Earl of Athlone, was now second in command, commanded the covering army, which extended from Liege to Bonn.

The siege commenced on the 3d of May, and with such vigor was it carried on that on the 9th the fort on the opposite side of the Rhine was carried by storm; and as from this point the works defending the town could all be taken in reverse, the place surrendered on

the 15th, the garrison, 3600 strong, being permitted by
the terms of capitulation to retire to Luxemburg.
Marshal Villeroi, who commanded the French army on
the frontier, finding that he could give no aid to Bonn,
advanced against Maestrich, which he hoped to surprise, before Overkirk could arrive to its aid. On the
way, however, he had to take the town of Tangres,
which was held by two battalions of infantry only.
These, however, defended themselves with astonishing
bravery against the efforts of a whole army, and for
twenty-eight hours of continuous fighting arrested the
course of the enemy. At the end of that time they were
forced to surrender, but the time gained by their heroic
defence afforded time for Overkirk to bring up his
army, and when Villeroi arrived near Maestrich, he
found the allies already there, and so strongly posted
that although his force was fully twice as strong as
theirs, he did not venture to attack.

Marlborough upon the fall of Bonn marched with
the greatest expedition to the assistance of his col-
league. His cavalry reached Maestrich on the 21st, his
infantry three days later. On the 26th of May he broke
up the camp and advanced to undertake the grand operation of the siege of Antwerp. The operation was to
be undertaken by a simultaneous advance of several
columns. Marlborough himself with the main wing
was to confront Marshal Villeroi, General Spaar was to
attack that part of the French lines which lay beyond
the Scheldt, Cohorn was to force the passage of that
river in the territory of Hulst, and unite Spaar's attack
with that of Obdam, who with twenty-one battalions
and sixteen squadrons was to advance from Bergen-op-
Zoom. The commencement of this operation was well-
conducted. On the night of the 26th Cohorn passed
the Scheldt, and the next morning he and Spaar made
a combined attack on that part of the French lines

against which they had been ordered to act, and carried them after severe fighting and the loss of 1200 men. Upon the following day the Earl of Marlborough riding through the camp saw Rupert Holliday, standing at the door of his tent. Beckoning him to him, he said,—

"Would you like a ride round Antwerp, Master Holliday? I have a letter which I desire carried to General Obdam, whose force is at Eckeron on the north of the city."

Upon Rupert saying that he should like it greatly, the earl bade him be at his quarters in an hour's time.

"There is the despatch," he said, when Rupert called upon him. "You will give this to the general himself. I consider his position as dangerous, for Marshal Villeroi may throw troops into the town, and in that case the Marquis Bedmar may fall in great force upon any of our columns now lying around him. I have warned Obdam of his danger, and have begged him to send back his heavy baggage, to take up a strong position, and if the enemy advance in force to fall back to Bergen-op-Zoom. Should the general question you, you can say that you are aware of the terms of the despatch, and that I had begged you to assure the general that my uneasiness on his account was considerable."

The general then pointed out to Rupert on a map the route that he should take so as to make a sweep round Antwerp, and warned him to use every precaution, and to destroy the despatch if there should be danger of his being captured.

"Am I to return at once, sir?"

"No," the earl said. "If all goes well we shall in three days invest the place, advancing on all sides, and you can rejoin your corps when the armies unite."

Rupert's horse was already saddled on his return, and Hugh was in readiness to accompany him as his orderly.

It was a thirty miles' ride, and it was evening before he reached Eckeron, having seen no enemy on his line of route.

He was at once conducted to the quarters of the Dutch general, who received him politely, and read the despatch which he had brought. It did not strike Rupert that he was much impressed with its contents, but he made no remark, and simply requested one of his staff to see to Rupert's wants, and to have a tent pitched for him.

He spent a pleasant evening with the Dutch general's staff, most of whom could talk French, while Hugh was hospitably entertained by the sergeants of the staff.

The next morning the tents were struck, and the heavy baggage was, in accordance with Lord Marlborough's orders, sent to the fortress of Bergen-op-Zoom, but, to Rupert's surprise and uneasiness, no attempt was made to carry out the second part of the instruction contained in the despatch.

The day passed quietly, and at night the party were very merry round a camp fire.

At eight o'clock next morning a horseman rode into camp with the news that the French were attacking the rear, and that the army was cut off from the Scheldt!

The Earl of Marlborough's prevision had proved correct. The French marshals had determined to take advantage of their central position, and to crush one of their enemy's columns.

On the evening of the 29th, Marshal Villeroi detached Marshal Boufflers with thirty companies of grenadiers and thirty squadrons of horse. These marching all night reached Antwerp at daybreak without interruption, and uniting with the force under the Marquis Bedmar, issued out 30,000 strong to attack Obdam. Sending off detached columns, who moved round, and—unseen by the Dutch, who acted with as

great carelessness as if their foes had been 500 miles
away—he took possession of the roads on the dykes
leading not only to Fort Lille on the Scheldt, but to
Bergen-op-Zoom, and fell suddenly upon the Dutch
army on all sides.

Scarcely had the messenger ridden into Eckeron,
when a tremendous roar of musketry broke out in all
quarters, and the desperate position into which the
supineness of their general had suffered them to fall,
was apparent to all.

In a few minutes the confusion was terrible.

Rupert and Hugh hastily saddled their horses, and
had just mounted when General Obdam with twenty
troopers rode past at full gallop.

"Where can he be going?" Rupert said. "He is not
riding towards either of the points attacked."

"It seems to me that he is bolting, Master Rupert,
just flying by some road the French have not yet occupied."

"Impossible!" Rupert said; but it was so, and the next
day the runaway general himself brought the news of
his defeat to The Hague, announcing that he had escaped with thirty horse, and that the rest of his army
was destroyed.

It is needless to say that General Obdam never afterwards commanded a Dutch army in the field. The second part of the news which he brought The Hague was
not correct. General Schlangenberg, the second in
command, at once assumed the command; the Dutch
rallied speedily from their surprise, and the advancing
columns of the enemy were soon met with a desperate
resistance. In front General Boufflers attacked with
twenty battalions of French troops, headed by the grenadiers he had brought with him, while a strong Spanish
force barred the retreat. Under such circumstances
many troops would at once have laid down their arms;

but such a thought never occurred to the Dutchmen of
Schlangenberg's army.

While a portion of this force opposed Bouffler's
troops pressing on their front, the rest threw themselves
against those who barred their retreat to Fort Lille.
Never was there more desperate fighting; nowhere
could ground have been selected more unsuited for a
battle-field.

It was by the roads alone running upon the dykes
above the general level of the country the troops could
advance or retreat, and it was upon these that the heads
of the heavy columns struggled for victory.

There was little firing.

The men in front had no time to reload, those behind
could not fire because their friends were before them;
it was a fierce hand-to-hand struggle, such as might
have taken place on the same ground in the middle
ages, before gunpowder was in use. Bayonets and
clubbed muskets, these were the weapons on both sides,
while dismounted troopers—for horses were worse than
useless here, mixed up with the infantry—fought with
swords. On the roads, on the sides of the slopes, waist
deep in the water of the ditches, men fought hand-to-
hand. Schlangenberg commanded at the spot where
the Dutchmen obstinately and stubbornly resisted the
fury of the French onslaught, and even the chosen
grenadiers of France failed to break down that desperate defence. All day the battle raged.

Rupert having no fixed duty rode backwards and
forwards along the roads, now watching how went the
defence against the French attack, now how the Dutch
in vain tried to press back the Spaniards and open a
way of retreat. Late in the afternoon he saw a party
of the staff officers pressing towards the rear on foot.

"We are going to try to get to the head of the column," one said to Rupert; "we must force back the
Spaniards, or we are all lost."

"I will join you," Rupert said, leaping from his horse. "Hugh, give me my pistols and take your own; leave the horses, and come with me."

It took upwards of an hour to make their way along the dyke, sometimes pushing forward between the soldiers, sometimes wading in the ditch, but at last they reached the spot where, over ground high heaped with dead, the battle raged as fiercely as ever. With a shout of encouragement to the men, the party of officers threw themselves in front and joined in the fray. Desperate as the fighting had been before, it increased in intensity now.

The Dutch, cheered by the leading of their officers, pressed forward with renewed energy; the Spaniards fought desperately, nor indeed could they have retreated, from the crowd of their comrades behind. The struggle was desperate; bayonet clashed against bayonet, heavy muskets descended with a showering thud on head and shoulders, swords flashed, men locked together struggled for life, those who fell were trampled to death, and often those in front were so jammed by the pressure, that their arms were useless, and they could do nought but grasp at each other's throats, until a blow or a bayonet thrust from behind robbed one or other of his adversary. Slowly, very slowly, the Dutch were forcing their way forward, but it was by the destruction of the head of their enemy's column, and not by any movement of retreat on their part.

After a few minutes of desperate struggles, in which twice Hugh saved his life by shooting a man on the point of running him through with a bayonet, Rupert found himself on the edge of the road. He drew out of the fight for an instant, and then making his way back until he came to a Dutch colonel, he pointed out to him that the sole hope was for a strong body of men to descend into the ditch, to push forward there, and to open fire on the flank of the enemy's column, so as to shake its solidity.

The officer saw the advice was good; and a column, four abreast, entered the ditches on each side, and pressed forward. The water was some inches above their waists, but they shifted their pouches to be above its level, and soon passing the spot where the struggle raged as fiercely as ever on the dyke above, they opened fire on the flanks of the Spaniards. These in turn fired down, and the carnage on both sides was great. Fresh Dutchmen, however, pressed forward to take the place of those that fell; and the solidity of the Spaniards' column being shaken, the head of the Dutch body began to press them back.

The impetus once given was never checked; slowly, very slowly, the Dutch pushed forward, until at last the Spaniards were driven off the road, and the line of retreat was open to the Dutch army. Then the rear guard began to fall back before the French; and fighting every step of the way, the last of the Dutch army reached Fort Lille long after night had fallen.

Their loss in this desperate hand-to-hand fighting had been 4000 killed and wounded, besides 600 prisoners and six guns. The French and Spaniards lost 3000 killed and wounded.

It was well for Rupert that Hugh kept so close to him, for nearly the last shot fired by the enemy struck him, and he fell beneath the water, when his career would have been ended had not Hugh seized him and lifted him ashore. So much had the gallantry of the little cornet attracted the attention and admiration of the Dutch, that plenty of volunteers were glad to assist Hugh to carry him to Fort Lille. There during the night a surgeon examined his wound, and pronounced that the ball had broken two ribs, and had then glanced out behind, and that if all went well, in a month he would be about again.

The numbers of wounded were far beyond the resources of Fort Lille to accommodate, and all were upon the following day put into boats, and distributed through the various Dutch riverine towns, in order that they might be well tended and cared for. This was a far better plan than their accumulation in large military hospitals, where, even with the greatest care, the air is always impure, and the deaths far more numerous than when the men are scattered, and can have good nursing and fresh air.

Rupert, with several other officers, was sent to Dort, at that time one of the great commercial cities of Holland. Rupert, although tightly bandaged, and forbidden to make any movement, was able to take an interest in all that was going on.

"There is quite a crowd on the quay, Hugh."

"Yes, sir; I expect most of these Dutch officers have friends and acquaintances here; besides, as yet the people here cannot tell who have fallen, and must be anxious indeed for news."

The crowd increased greatly by the time the boat touched the quay; and as the officers stepped or were carried ashore, each was surrounded by a group of anxious inquirers.

Hugh, standing by his master's stretcher, felt quite alone in the crowd—as, seeing his British uniform, and the shake of his head at the first question asked, none tried to question him—and looked round vaguely at the crowd, until some soldiers should come to lift the stretcher. Suddenly he gave a cry of surprise, and to Rupert's astonishment left his side, and sprang through the crowd. With some difficulty he made his way to a young lady, who was standing with an elderly gentleman on some steps a short distance back from the crowd. She looked surprised at the approach of this British soldier, whose eyes were eagerly fixed on her;

but not till Hugh stepped in front of her and spoke did she remember him.

"Mistress Von Duyk," he said, "my master is here wounded; and as he has not a friend in the place, and I saw you, I made bold to speak to you."

"Oh! I am sorry," the girl said, holding out her hand to Hugh. "Papa, this is one of the gentlemen who rescued me, as I told you, when Sir Richard Fulke tried to carry me off."

The gentleman, who had looked on in profound astonishment, seized Hugh's hand,—

"I am indeed glad to have an opportunity of thanking you. Hasten home, Maria, and prepare a room; I will go and have this good friend brought to our house."

CHAPTER XI.

A DEATH TRAP.

NEVER did a patient receive more unremitting care than that which was lavished upon Rupert Holliday in the stately old house at Dort. The old housekeeper, in the stiffest of dresses and starched caps, and with the rosiest although most wrinkled of faces, waited upon him; while Maria von Duyk herself was in and out of his room, brought him flowers, read to him, and told him the news, and her father frequently came in to see that he lacked nothing. As for Hugh, he grumbled, and said that there was nothing for him to do for his master; but he nevertheless got through the days pleasantly enough, having struck up a flirtation with Maria's plump and pretty waiting-maid, who essayed to improve his Dutch, of which he had by this time picked up a slight smattering. Then, too, he made himself useful, and became a great favourite in the servants' hall, went out marketing, told them stories of the war in broken Dutch, and made himself generally at home. Greatly astonished was he at the stories that he heard as to the land around him; how not unfrequently great subsidences, extending over very many square miles, took place; and where towns and villages stood when the sun went down, there spread in the morning a sea very many fathoms deep. Hugh could hardly believe these tales, which he repeated to Rupert, who in turn questioned Maria von Duyk, who answered him that the stories were strictly true, and that many such great and sudden catastrophes had happened.

"I can't understand it," Rupert said. "Of course one could imagine a sea or river breaking through a dyke and covering low lands, but that the whole country should sink, and there be deep water over the spot, appears unaccountable."

"The learned believe," Maria said, "that deep down below the surface of the land lies a sort of soil like a quicksand, and that when the river deepens its bed so that its waters do enter this soil it melts away, leaving a great void, into which the land above does sink and is altogether swallowed up."

"It is a marvellously uncomfortable feeling," Rupert said, "to think that one may any night be awoke with a sudden crash, only to be swallowed up."

"Such things do not happen often," Maria said; "and the districts that suffer are after all but small in comparison to Holland. So I read that in Italy the people do build their towns on the slopes of Vesuvius, although history says that now and again the mountain bubbles out in irruption, and the lava destroys many villages, and even towns. In other countries there are earthquakes, but the people forget all about them until the shock comes, and the houses begin to topple over their heads."

"You are right, no doubt," Rupert said. "But to a stranger the feeling, at first, of living over a great quicksand, is not altogether pleasant. To-morrow the doctor says I may leave my room. My own idea is that I need never have been kept there at all."

"If there had been any great occasion for you to have moved about, no doubt you might have done so," Maria said; "but you might have thrown back your cure, and instead of your bones knitting well and soundly, as the leech says they are in a fair way to do, you might have made but a poor recovery. Dear me, what impatient creatures boys are!"

"No, indeed I am not impatient," Rupert said. "You have all made me so comfortable and happy, that I should indeed be ungrateful were I to be impatient. I only want to be about again that I may spare you some of the trouble which you bestow upon me."

"Yes, that is all very well and very pretty," Maria said, laughing; "but I know that you are at heart longing to be off to join your regiment, and take part in all their marching and fighting. Do you know, an officer who came here with you after that terrible fight near Antwerp, told me that you covered yourself with glory there?"

"I covered myself with mud," Rupert laughed. "Next day, when I had dried a little, I felt as if I had been dipped in dough and then baked. I am sure I looked like a pie in human shape when you first saw me, did I not?"

"It would have been difficult to tell the colour of your uniform, certainly," Maria smiled. "Fortunately, neither cloth nor tailors are scarce in our good town of Dort, and you will find a fresh suit in readiness for you to attire yourself in to-morrow."

"Oh, that is good of you," Rupert said, delighted; for he had been thinking ruefully of the spectacle he should present the next day. As to Hugh, he had been fitted out in bourgeois clothes since he came, and had said no word as to uniform.

In another fortnight Rupert was thoroughly restored to health, his wound had healed, his bones had perfectly set, and he was as fit for work as ever. Even his host could not but allow that there was no cause for his further detention. During this time Rupert had talked much with the Burgomaster, who spoke French fluently, and had told him frequently and earnestly of the grievous harm that was done to the prospects of the war by the mischievous interference with the general's plans by the Dutch deputies, who, knowing nothing whatever of war, yet took upon themselves continually to thwart the plans of the greatest general of the age. Van Duyk listened with great attention, and promised that when he went shortly to Haarlem he would use all his influence to abbreviate the powers which the deputies so unwisely used.

Two or three days before the date fixed for Rupert's departure, he was walking in the town with Mynheer Von Duyk and his daughter, when he observed a person gazing intently at him from the entrance to a small bye-lane. He started, and exclaimed,—

"There is that rascal, Sir Richard Fulke!"

"Where?" exclaimed both his companions.

"He has gone now," Rupert said. "But he stood there in shadow, at the entrance to that lane."

So saying, he hurried forward, but no sign of his enemy was visible.

"Are you sure it was he?" Mynheer Von Duyk asked. "What can he be doing in Holland?"

Rupert then in a few words recounted their meeting in Liege, the subsequent attempt to murder him at the mill, and the disappearance of Sir Richard Fulke, and his exchange into some other regiment.

Von Duyk was much disturbed.

"This touches me nearly," he said. "It is from your interference on behalf of my daughter that you have incurred this fellow's enmity, and it is clear that he will shrink from nothing to gratify it. Moreover, I cannot consider my daughter to be in safety, so long as so reckless a man is in the town. I will go at once to the magistrates, and urge that my daughter goes in danger of him, and so obtain an order to search for and arrest him. In a few hours we will have him by the heels, and then, after a while in prison, we will send him packing across the frontier, with a warning that if he comes back he will not escape so lightly."

The search, however, was not successful; and Mynheer Von Duyk was beginning to think that Rupert must have been mistaken, when the officer of the magistracy discovered that a man answering to the description given had been staying for three days at a small tavern by the water, but that he had hastily taken a boat and sailed, within a half-hour of being seen by Rupert.

"It is a low resort where he was staying," Von Duyk said, "a tavern to which all the bad characters of the town—for even Dort has some bad characters—do resort. If he came here to do you harm, or with any fresh design upon my daughter, he would find instruments there. I had intended to have left Maria behind, when I travelled to the Hague next week; but I will now take her with me, with two or three stout fellows as an escort. As for you, friend Rupert, you have but two more evenings here in Dort, but I pray you move not out after dusk, for these long wars have made many men homeless and desperate, and it is not good for one who has an enemy to trust himself abroad at night, alone."

The next morning Hugh went down to the quay with one of the clerks of Von Duyk, and struck a bargain with some boatmen to carry Rupert and himself to Bergen-op-Zoom.

It was a craft of some four or five tons burden, with a good-sized cabin. The next day Hugh went down early to the boat with the bags containing Rupert's luggage and his own, and a servant of Von Duyk accompanied him, bearing some provisions and a few choice bottles of wine for their use on the way.

"Do you know, Master Rupert," he said, on his return, "I don't much like the look of that boatman chap. When we got down to the quay this morning, he was talking with two men whose faces I did not see, for they walked suddenly and hastily away, but who seemed to me to flavour much of the two men we disturbed that evening when they were carrying off Miss Von Duyk. I could not swear to them, for I did not get a fair sight of them before, but they were about the same size and height, and it was clear that they did not wish to be recognized."

Rupert made no reply for a while, but thought the matter over.

"Well, Hugh, I wish it had not been so, for I hate quarrels and brawls, but I do not think that we need be uneasy, especially now that we are warned. The boat carries but three men, and as we shall have our pistols and swords, I imagine that we are a match for these Dutch boatmen. See that the pistols are loaded, and say naught to our kind friends here as to your suspicions; I would not make them uncomfortable."

Before taking leave of their friends, Rupert was drawn aside by Mynheer Von Duyk, who begged to know if he had any necessity for money, and assured him that then or at any other time he should be glad to honour any drafts that Rupert might draw upon him.

"I am not a man of many words," he said, "but in saving my daughter from that ruffian you have laid me under an obligation which I should be glad to discharge with half my fortune. I am, as you know, a rich man— I may say a very rich man. Had you been a few years older, I would gladly have given my daughter to you did your inclination and hers jump that way; as it is, I can only regard you as a younger brother of hers, and view you as a sort of son by adoption. Young men in cavalry regiments require horses and have many expenses, and you will really pain me much if you refuse to allow me to act as your banker. I have, believing that you would not take it wrongly, paid in to your account with the paymaster of your regiment the sum of two hundred pounds, and have told him that the same sum would be paid to your account annually so long as the regiment might be in Flanders, and that he may further cash any order drawn by you upon my house.

There now, my daughter is waiting, and the hour for sailing is at hand. Do not let us say any more about it."

So saying he hurried Rupert out into the hall where Maria Von Duyk was waiting, before he could have raised any objection had he wished to do so. But in truth Rupert felt that he could not refuse the kind offer without giving pain, and he knew moreover that this allowance, which to the rich merchant was a mere trifle, would add greatly to his comfort, and enable him to enter more freely than he had yet done in the plans and pursuits of his brother officers, who were for the most part young men of fortune. With a word or two of sincere thanks therefor, he accompanied the worthy Dutchman, and twelve minutes later the party were on their way down to the quay.

"A surly looking knave is your captain," Mynheer Von Duyk said, as they stood by the boat while the men prepared for a start. "I see he belongs not to this town, but to Bergen. However, the voyage is not a long one, and as you know but little of our language, it will matter but slightly whether his temper be good or bad. There, I see he is ready. Good-bye, Master Holliday; good-bye, my good Hugh. All fortune attend you, and God keep you both from harm."

Maria added her affectionate adieux to those of her father, and in a few minutes the boat was moving down the river under full sail.

"Hugh, you may as well overhaul the cabin at once," Rupert said; "we have paid for its sole use during the voyage. Cast your eye carefully round, and see if there is anything that strikes you as being suspicious. I see no arms on deck; see that none are hidden below."

Hugh returned on deck in a few minutes.

"It seems all right, Master Rupert. There are some provisions in a locker, and in another are a cutlass, a couple of old pistols, and a keg half full of powder; I should say by its weight there are ten pounds in it. The arms are rusted, and have been there some time, I should say. There is also a bag of heavy shot, and there is a long duck gun fastened to the beam; but all these things are natural enough in a boat like this. No doubt they fire a charge or two of shot into a passing flight of wild-fowl when they get a chance."

"That's all right then, Hugh, especially as they evidently could not go down into the cabin without our seeing them; and as with our pistols and swords we could make short work of them even if they did mean mischief, we need not trouble ourselves any further in the matter. It's going to be a wet night, I am afraid; not that it makes much difference, but one would rather have stayed on deck as long as one could keep awake, for the smells of the cabin of a Dutch fishing-boat are not of the sweetest."

Rupert was not mistaken. As the darkness came on a thick heavy mist began to fall steadily; and he and Hugh descended through the half door from the cockpit into the cabin.

"Now let us have supper, Hugh; there are plenty of good things; and I have a famous appetite."

The thoughtfulness of Mynheer Von Duyk's housekeeper had placed two candles in the basket together with two drinking glasses; and the former were soon lighted, and by the aid of a drop or two of their own grease, fixed upright on the rough table. Then a splen-did pie was produced; the neck was knocked off a bottle; the lads drew out their clasp-knives, and set to work.

"Here is a bottle of schnaps," Hugh said, examining the basket when they had finished a hearty meal.

"You may as well give that to the boatman, Hugh. I expect the good frau had him in her thoughts when she put it in, for she would hardly give us credit for such bad taste as to drink that stuff when we could get good wine."

Hugh handed out the bottle to the boatman, who took it with a surly grunt of satisfaction. It was raining steadily, and the wind had almost dropped. An hour later the lads agreed that they were ready for sleep. Hitherto the door had been slightly open to admit air.

"Shall I shut the door, Master Rupert?"

"Well, perhaps you had better, Hugh. We have got into the way of sleeping heavily at Dort, without any night guard or disturbance. I doubt not that these Dutchmen mean us no harm; still it is well to be on the safe side."

"There is no fastening to it, Master Rupert."

"Well, take your sword out of its scabbard, Hugh, and put the scabbard against the door, so that it will fall with a crash if the door is opened. Then, if we have a pistol close at hand, we can sleep in security."

Hugh obeyed his instructions; and in a few minutes, wrapped in their military cloaks, they were fast asleep on the lockers, which served as benches and beds.

How long they slept they knew not; but both started up into a sitting attitude, with their hands on their pistols.

"Who's there?" both shouted; but there was no answer. The darkness was intense; and it was clear that whoever had tried to open the door had shut it again.

"Have you your tinder-box handy, Hugh? if so, let us have a light. Those fellows are moving about overhead, Hugh; but we had better stay where we are. The scabbard may have shaken down, for the wind has got up, and the boat is feeling it; and if they mean foul play they could knock us on the head as we go out from under the low door. Hallo! what's that?"

The "that" was the falling of some heavy substance against the door.

"Those are the coils of cable, Hugh; they have blocked us in. Go on striking that light; we can't push the door open now."

Some more weight was thrown against the door, and then all was still.

Presently Hugh succeeded in striking a light—no easy task in the days of flint and steel—and the candles being lighted, they sat down to consider the position.

"We are prisoners, Master Rupert; no doubt about that."

"None at all, Hugh. The question is what do they mean to do with us. We've got food enough here to last us with ease for a week; and with our pistols and swords, to say nothing of the duck-gun, we could hold this cabin against any number."

Presently they heard the men on deck hailing another boat.

"I suppose that is that rascal Fulke," Rupert said. "I hope that I am not quarrelsome by disposition, Hugh; but the next time I meet that fellow I will, if time and place be suitable, come to a reckoning with him."

There was a movement above, and then a bump came against the side. The other boat had come up.

"Now we shall see what they are up to."

Nothing, however, came of it; there was some low talking above, and some coarse laughter.

"Master Rupert," Hugh exclaimed, suddenly, "I am standing in water!"

Rupert had half lain down again, but he leapt up now.

"They have scuttled the boat, Hugh, and mean to drown us like rats; the cowards."

"What's to be done now, Master Rupert?" Hugh asked.

"Let us try the door, Hugh."

A single effort showed that they were powerless here. The door was strong, it was fastened outside, and it was heavily weighted with coils of rope and other substances.

"The water rises fast, it's over our ankles," Hugh said, quietly.

The bumping of the boat was again heard outside, then a trampling of feet, and all was still again.

"They have taken to the boats."

Not all, however, for through the door there came a shout,—

"Good-bye, Master Holliday," and a loud, jeering laugh.

"Au revoir, Sir Richard Fulke," Rupert shouted back; and when we meet next, beware!"

"Ha, ha! it won't be in this world;" and they heard their enemy get into the boat.

"Now, Hugh, we must set to work; we have got the boat to ourselves."

"But what are we to do, Master Rupert?"

Rupert was silent for a minute.

"There is but one way, Hugh; we must blow up the boat."

"Blow up the boat!" Hugh repeated, in astonishment.

"Yes, Hugh; at least, blow the deck up. Give me that keg of powder."

Hugh opened the locker; it was, fortunately, still above water.

"Now, Hugh, put it in that high locker there, just under the deck. Knock its head out. Now tie a pistol to those hooks just above, so that its muzzle points at the powder; now for a piece of cord."

"But it will blow us into smash, Master Rupert."

"I hope not, Hugh; but we must take our chance. I would rather that than be drowned gradually. But look, the water is up nearly to our waists now; and the boat must be pretty nearly sinking. I will take hold of the cord, then both of us throw ourselves down to the floor, and I will pull the string. Three feet of water over us ought to save us; but mind, the instant you feel the shock, jump up and rush for the opening; for it is pretty safe to sink her. Now!"

The lads dived under water, and the instant afterwards there was a tremendous explosion; the deck of the boat was blown into the air in a hundred fragments, and at the same moment the boat sunk under the water.

A few seconds later Rupert and Hugh were swimming side by side. For a while neither spoke—they were shaken and half stunned by the shock.

"It is a thick fog, Hugh; all the better; for if those scoundrels come back, as is likely enough, there is no chance of their finding us, for I can hardly see you, though I am touching you. Now we must paddle about, and try to get hold of a spar or a bit of plank."

CHAPTER XII.

THE SAD SIDE OF WAR.

BEFORE firing the keg of powder, Rupert and Hugh had rid themselves of their jack-boots, coats, and vests, and they therefore swam easily and confidently.

"Listen, Hugh! Here is the boat coming back again," Rupert exclaimed. "This thick mist is fortunate, for they can't see twenty yards. We can always dive when they come near. Mind you go down without making a splash. We are all right at present; the boat is going to our right, let us swim quietly in the other direction."

Presently they heard a voice in English say,—

"It is no use our troubling ourselves. It's a mere waste of time; the young rascals are dead; drowned or blown up, what matters it? they will never trouble you again."

"You don't know the villains as well as I do. They have as many lives as cats. I could have sworn that they were burned at that mill, for I watched till it fell, and not a soul came out; and to this moment I don't know how they escaped, unless they flew away in the smoke; then I thought at any rate the chief rogue was done for, when Muller wrote to tell me he was going to finish him for me the next day; then they both got through that day's fighting by the Scheldt, though I hear they were in the front of it; and now, when I leave them fastened up like puppies in a basket, in a sinking boat, comes this explosion, and all is uncertain again."

"Not a bit of it," the other voice said; "they simply preferred a sudden death to a slow one; the matter is simple enough."

"I wish I could think so," the other said. "But I tell you, after this night's work I shall never feel my life's

safe for one hour, till I hear certain news of their death.
Stop rowing," he said, in Dutch; "there is a bit of a
plank; we must be just on the place where she blew up!
Listen, does any one hear anything?"

There was a long silence, and then he said,—

"Row about for half an hour; it's as dark as a wolf's
mouth, but we may come upon them."

In the meantime, the two lads were swimming steadily and quietly away.

Presently Hugh said,—

"I must get rid of my sword, Master Rupert, it seems
pulling me down. I don't like to lose it, for it was my
grandfather's."

"You had better lose the grandfather's sword, Hugh,
than the grandson's life. Loose your belt, Hugh, and
let it go. Mine is no weight in comparison. I'll stick
to it as long as I can, for it may be useful; but if needs
be, it must follow yours."

"Which way do you think the shore lies?" Hugh
asked, after having, with a sigh of regret, loosed his
sword-belt and let it go.

"I have no idea, Hugh. It's no use swimming now,
for with nothing to fix our eyes on, we may be going
round in a circle. All we need do is to keep ourselves
afloat till the mist clears up, or daylight comes."

For an hour they drifted quietly. Hugh exclaimed,—

"I hear a voice."

"So do I, Hugh; it may be on shore, it may be in a
boat. Let us make for it in either case."

In five minutes they saw close ahead of them a large
boat, which, with its sail hanging idly by the mast, was
drifting down stream. Two boatmen were sitting by
the tiller, smoking their pipes.

"Heave us a rope," Hugh said, in Dutch. "We have
had an upset, and shall be glad to be out of this."

The boatmen gave a cry of surprise, but at once leapt

to their feet, and would have thrown a rope, but by this time the lads were alongside, and leaning over they helped them into the boat. Then they looked with astonishment at their suddenly arrived guests.

"We are English soldiers," Hugh said, "on our way to Bergen-op-Zoom, when by some carelessness a keg of powder blew up, our boat went to the bottom, and we have been swimming for it for the last couple of hours."

"Are you the English officer and soldier who left Dort this afternoon?" one of the men said. "We saw you come down to the quay with Mynheer Von Duyk and his daughter; our boat lay next to the boat you went by."

"That is so," Hugh said. "Are you going to Bergen? We have enough dollars left to pay our passage."

"You would be welcome in any case," the boatman said. "Hans Petersen is not a man to bargain with shipwrecked men. But go below, there is a fire there; I will lend you some dry clothes, and a glass of hot schnaps will warm your blood again."

Arrived at Bergen, one of the boatmen, at Rupert's request, went up into the town, and returned with a merchant of ready-made clothes, followed by his servant bearing a selection of garments such as Rupert had said that they would require, and in another half hour, after a handsome present to the boatmen, Rupert and Hugh landed, dressed in the costume of a Dutch gentleman and burgher respectively. Their first visit was to an armourer's shop, where Hugh was provided with a sword, in point of temper and make fully equal to that with which he had so reluctantly parted; then, hiring horses, they journeyed by easy stages to Huy, a town on the Meuse, six leagues above Liege, which Marlborough, again forbidden by the Dutch deputies to give battle when he had every prospect of a great victory, was besieging.

The capture of the fortress, and subsequently of Limberg, was all the campaign of 1703 effected; whereas, had the English commander been allowed to have his way, the great results which were not obtained until after three years' further fighting might at once have been gained.

Rupert was greeted with enthusiasm by his comrades on his return. After the battle before Antwerp the duke had caused inquiries to be made as to the fate of his young friend, and had written to Dort, and had received an answer from Rupert announcing his convalescence and speedy return to duty.

Upon hearing his tale of the fresh attempt upon his life by Sir Richard Fulke, the commander-in-chief wrote to the states-general, as the government of Holland was called, and requested that orders should be issued for the arrest of Sir Richard Fulke, wherever he might be found, upon a charge of attempt at murder. Nothing was, however, heard of him, and it was supposed that he had either returned to England or passed into Germany.

After the capture of Limberg the army went into winter quarters, and the 5th dragoons were allotted their old quarters near Liege.

During the campaign of 1703, although slight advantages had been gained by the allies in Flanders, it was otherwise in Germany and Italy, where the greatest efforts of the French had been made. Beyond the Rhine the French and Bavarians had carried all before them, and Villars, who commanded their armies here, had almost effected a junction across the Alps with Vendome, who commanded the French troops in Italy. Had success crowned their efforts, the armies could have been passed at will to either one side or the other of the Alps, and could have thrown themselves with overwhelming force either upon Austria, or upon Prince Eugene, who commanded the imperial troops in Italy. The mountaineers of the Tyrol, however, flew to arms, and held their passes with such extreme bravery that neither the Bavarians on the north, nor the French on the south, could make any progress, and the design had for a time been abandoned. Austria was paralyzed by the formidable insurrection of Hungary, and it appeared certain that Vienna would in the ensuing campaign fall into the hands of the French.

During the winter Marlborough laboured earnestly to prepare for the important campaign which must take place in the spring, and after the usual amount of difficulties, arising from private and political enemies, at home and in Holland, he succeeded in carrying out his plan, and in arranging that the Dutch should hold their frontier line alone, and that he should carry the rest of his army into Germany. The position there seemed well-nigh desperate. Marshal Tallard, with 45,000 men, was posted on the Upper Rhine, in readiness to advance through the Black Forest and join the advanced force and the Bavarians, who also numbered 45,000 men, and the united army was to advance upon Vienna, which, so weakened was the empire, was defended only by an army of 20,000 men, placed on the frontier.

On the 8th of May, Marlborough set out with his army, crossed the Meuse at Maestricht, and arrived at Bonn on the 28th of that month. Marching up the Rhine, he crossed it at Coblentz on the 26th, and pushed on to Mundlesheim, where he met Prince Eugene, who now commanded the allied force there. Next only to Marlborough himself, Eugene was the greatest general of the age—skilful, dashing yet prudent, brave to a fault —for a general can be too brave—frank, sincere, and incapable of petty jealousy.

Between him and Marlborough, from the date of their
first meeting, the most cordial friendship, and the most
loyal co-operation, prevailed. Each was always anxious to give the other credit, and thought more of each
other's glory than their own. So rapidly had Marlborough marched, that only his cavalry had come up; and
Prince Eugene, reviewing them, remarked that they
were the finest body of men he had ever seen.

A few days later the Prince of Baden came down from
the Austrian army of the Danube to meet him. Eugene and Marlborough wished the prince to take command of the army of the Rhine, leaving the army of the
Danube to their joint command. The prince, however,
stood upon his rank; and it was finally arranged that
Eugene should command the army of the Rhine, and
that Marlborough and the Prince of Baden should command the army of the Danube on alternate days—an arrangement so objectionable that it is surprising it did
not terminate in disaster.

Marlborough at once marched with his force, and
making his way with great difficulty through the long
and narrow defile of Geislingen, effected a junction with
the Prince of Baden's army; and found himself on the
2nd of July at the head of an army of 96 battalions, 202
squadrons of horse, and 48 guns, confronting the
French and Bavarian army, consisting of 88 battalions,
160 squadrons, 90 guns, and 40 mortars, in a strong
position on the Danube.

The bulk of the army was on the right bank. On the
left bank was the height of Schellenberg, covering the
passage of the river at Donauwörth, and held by 12,000
men, including 2500 horse. Along the front of this hill
was an old rampart, which the French were engaged in
strengthening when the allied army arrived. The latter
were not when they came up, according to the ordinary
military idea, in a condition to attack. Their camp had

been broken up at three in the morning, and it was two in the afternoon before they arrived, after a long and fatiguing march, in front of the enemy's position.

Thinking that it was probable that he would be forced to fight immediately upon arriving, Marlborough had selected 130 picked men from each battalion, amounting to 6000 men, together with thirty squadrons of horse, as an advance guard, and close behind them followed three regiments of Imperial grenadiers, under Prince Louis. The total strength of this force was 10,-500 men.

The French and Bavarian generals did not expect an attack, knowing the distance that the troops had marched, and therefore quietly continued their work of strengthening the entrenchments. The Duke of Marlborough, seeing the work upon which they were engaged, determined to attack at once, for, as he said to the Prince of Baden, who wished to allow the men a night's rest, "Every hour we delay will cost us a thousand men." Orders were therefore given for an instant assault upon the hill of Schellenberg. Not only was the position very strong in itself, but in front of it was a wood, so thick that no attack could be made through it. It was necessary, therefore, to attack by the flanks of the position, and one of these flanks was covered by the fire of the fortress of Donauwörth.

"This is as bad as a siege," Rupert said, discontentedly, to his friend Dillon, for their squadron formed part of the advance, "we are always out of it."

"You are in a great hurry to get that bright cuirass of yours dinted, Rupert; but I agree with you, the cavalry are always out of it. There go the infantry."

In splendid order the 6000 picked men moved forward against the face of the enemy's position, extending from the wood to the covered way of the fortress; but when they arrived within range of grape, they were swept by so fearful a storm of shot that the line wavered. General Goor and his bravest officers were struck down, and the line fell into confusion.

The Bavarians seeing this, leapt from their entrenchments, and pursued their broken assailants with the bayonet; but when disordered by their rush, a battalion of English guards, which had kept its ground, poured so tremendous a fire into their flank that they fell back to their entrenchments.

"This looks serious," Dillon said, as the allies fell back. "The enemy are two to our one, and they have got all the advantage of position."

"There is the duke," Rupert exclaimed, "reforming them. There they go again, and he is leading them himself. What a terrible fire! look how the officers of the staff are dropping! Oh, if the duke should himself be hit! See, the infantry are slackening their advance in spite of the shouts of their officers; they are wavering! Oh, how dreadful; here they come back again."

"The duke is going to try again, Rupert; see how he is waving his hand and exhorting the men to a fresh attack. That's right, lads, that's right; they have formed again: there they go."

Again the troops wavered and broke under the terrible rain of bullets; and this time the Bavarians in great force leapt from their entrenchments, and pounced down upon the broken line.

"Prepare to charge!" shouted General Lumley, who commanded the cavalry. "Forward, trot, gallop, charge!"

With a cheer the cavalry, chafed at their long inaction while their comrades were suffering so terribly, dashed forward, and threw themselves furiously upon the Bavarians, driving them headlong back to their lines, and then falling back under a tremendous fire, which rolled over men and horses in numbers.

At this moment a cheer broke from the dispirited infantry, as the heads of the three regiments of Imperial grenadiers, led by the Prince of Baden, arrived on the ground. These, without halting, moved forward towards the extreme left of the enemy's position—which had been left to some extent unguarded, many of the troops having been called off to repulse Marlborough's attack—pushed back two battalions of French infantry, and entered the works.

General D'Arco, the French commanding officer, withdrew some of his men from the centre to hold the Prince of Baden in check; and Marlborough profited by the confusion so caused to endeavour, for the fourth time, to carry the hill. His force was, however, now fearfully weakened; and General Lumley, after conferring with him for a moment, rode back to the cavalry.

"The 5th dragoons will dismount and join the infantry," he said.

In a moment every soldier was on his feet; and five minutes later the regiment, marching side by side with the infantry, advanced up the hill.

This time the assault was successful. The enemy, confused by the fact that the allies had already forced their line on the left, wavered; their fire was wild and ineffectual; and with a tremendous cheer the allies scaled the height and burst into the works. Close behind them General Lumley led his cavalry, who made their way through the gaps in the entrenchments, and fell upon the fugitives with dreadful slaughter. The French and Bavarians fled to a bridge across the Danube below Donauwörth, which, choked by their weight, gave way, and great numbers were drowned. The rest retreated through Donauwörth, their rear being gallantly covered by General D'Arco, with a small body of troops who held together. Sixteen guns and thirteen standards fell into the victors' hands.

The loss of the allies, considering the force that they
brought into the field—for the main army had not arrived when the victory was decided—was extraordinary, for out of a total of 10,500 men, including cavalry, they lost 1500 killed, and 4000 wounded, or more
than half their force; and the greater part of these were
English, for upon them fell the whole brunt of the fighting.

The enemy suffered comparatively little in the battle,
but great numbers were killed in the pursuit or drowned
in the Danube; still greater numbers of Bavarians scattered to their homes; and out of 12,000 men, only 3000
joined the army on the other side of the Danube.

The Elector of Bavaria fell back with his army to
Augsburg, under the cannon of which fortress he encamped, in a position too strong to be attacked. His
strong places all fell into the hands of the allies; and
every effort was made to induce him to break off from
his alliance with France. The elector, however, relying
upon the aid of Marshal Tallard, who was advancing
with 45,000 men to his assistance, refused to listen to
any terms; and the allied powers ordered Marlborough
to harry his country, and so force him into submission
by the misery of his subjects. Such an order was most
repugnant to the duke, who was one of the most hu-
mane of men, and who by the uniform kind treatment of
his prisoners, not only did much to mitigate the horrors
of the war in which he was engaged, but set an example
which has since his time been followed by all civilized
armies. He had, however, no resource but to obey orders; and the cavalry of the allies were sent to carry fire
through Bavaria. No less than 300 towns and villages
were destroyed in this barbarous warfare.

This duty was abhorrent to Rupert, who waited on
the duke, and begged him as the greatest of favours to
attach him for a short time to the staff, in order that he

might not be obliged to accompany his regiment. The
duke—who had already offered Rupert an appointment
on his staff, an offer he had gratefully declined, as he
preferred to do duty with his regiment—at once acceded
to his request, and he was thus spared the horror of seeing the agony of the unhappy peasantry and townspeo-
ple, at the destruction of their houses. Rupert, in his
rides with messages across the country saw enough to
make him heartsick at the distress into which the people
of the country were plunged.

One day when riding, followed by Hugh, he came
upon a sad group. By a hut which had recently been
burned, after some resistance, as was shown by the dead
body of a Hessian trooper, a peasant knelt by the body
of his wife, a dead child of some five years old lay by,
and a baby kicked and cried by the side of its mother.
The peasant looked up with an air of bewildered grief,
and on seeing the British uniform sprang to his feet,
and with a fierce but despairing gesture placed himself
as if to defend his children to the last.

Rupert drew his rein.

"I would not hurt you, my poor fellow," he said, in
Dutch.

The man did not understand, but the gentleness of the
tone showed him that no harm was meant, and he again
flung himself down by his wife.

"I do not think that she is dead, Hugh," Rupert said.
"Hold my horse, I will soon see."

So saying, he dismounted and knelt by the woman.
There was a wound on her forehead, and her face was
covered with blood. Rupert ran to a stream that
trickled by the side of the road, dipped his handkerchief
in water, and returning, wiped the blood from the face
and wound.

"It is a pistol bullet, I imagine," he said to him; "but
I do not think the ball has entered her head; it has, I

think, glanced off. Fasten the horses up to that rail, Hugh; get some water in your hands, and dash it in her face."

The peasant paid no attention to what was being done, but sat absorbed in grief, mechanically patting the child beside him.

"That's it, Hugh; now another. I do believe she is only stunned. Give me that flask of spirits out of my holster."

Hugh again dashed water in the woman's face, and Rupert distinctly saw a quiver in her eyelid as he did so. Then forcing open her teeth, he poured a little spirit into her mouth, and was in a minute rewarded by a gasping sigh.

"She lives," he exclaimed, shaking the peasant by the shoulder. The man looked round stupidly, but Rupert pointed to his wife, and again poured some spirits between her lips. This time she made a slight movement and opened her eyes. The peasant gave a wild scream of delight, and poured forth a volume of words, of which Rupert understood nothing; but the peasant kneeling beside him, bent his forehead till it touched the ground, and then kissed the lappet of his coat—an action expressive of the intensity of his gratitude.

Rupert continued his efforts until the woman was able to sit up, and look round with frightened and bewildered air. When her eye caught her husband, she burst into tears; and as Hugh raised the baby and placed it in her arms she clasped it tightly, and rocked to and fro, sobbing convulsively.

"Look, Hugh, see if you can find something like a spade in that little garden; let us bury this poor little child."

Hugh soon found a spade, and dug a little grave in the corner of a garden, under the shade of an old tree.

Then the lads returned to the spot where the husband

and wife, quiet now, were sitting hand in hand crying together. Rupert made a sign to him to lift the body of his little girl, and then led the way to the little grave. The father laid her in, and then fell on his knees by it with his wife, and prayed in a loud voice, broken with sobs. Rupert and Hugh stood by uncovered, until the peasant had finished. Then the little grave was filled in; and Rupert, pointing to the ruined house, placed five gold pieces in the woman's hand. Then they mounted their horses again and rode on, the man and his wife both kneeling by the roadside praying for blessings on their heads.

A week later, Rupert again had occasion to pass through the village, and dismounted and walked to the little grave. A rough cross had been placed at one end, and some flowers lay strewn upon it. Rupert picked a few of the roses which were blooming neglected near, and laid them on the grave, and then rode on, sighing at the horrors which war inflicts on an innocent population.

This time their route lay through a thickly wooded mountain, to a town beyond, where one of the cavalry regiments had its head-quarters. Rupert was the bearer of orders for it to return to head-quarters, as a general movement of the army was to take place. The road was a mere track, hilly and wild, and the lads rode with pistols cocked, in case of any sudden attack by deserters or stragglers from the Bavarian army. The journey was, however, performed without adventure; and having delivered their orders, they at once started on their homeward way.

CHAPTER XIII.

BLENHEIM.

ALTHOUGH the sun had not set when Rupert and Hugh rode into the forest on their return journey, they had not been long among the trees when the light began to fade. The foliage met overhead, and although above the sky seemed still bright, the change was distinctly felt in the gloom of the forest. The ride had been a long one, and Rupert feared to press his horse, consequently they wound but slowly up the hill, and by the time they reached its crest, it was night.

"This is unpleasant, Hugh, for I can scarcely see my horse's head; and as there are several tracks crossing this, we are likely enough to go wrong."

"I think, Master Rupert, we had better dismount and lead our horses; we shall break our necks if they tread on a stone on this rocky path."

For half-an-hour they walked on in silence, then Hugh said,—"I think we are going wrong, Master Rupert, for we are not descending now; and we ought to have been at the foot of the hill, if we had been right, by this time."

"I am afraid you are right, Hugh. In that case we had better make up our minds to halt where we are till morning; it is no use wandering on, and knocking up the horses. It seems rather lighter just ahead, as if the trees opened a little; we may find a better place to halt."

In another minute they stood in a small clearing. The stars were shining brightly; and after the dense darkness of the forest, they were able to see clearly in the open. It was a clearing of some sixty feet diameter, and in the middle stood, by the path, a hut.

"Stay where you are, Hugh, with the horses; I will go quietly forward. If the place is occupied, we will go back. We can't expect hospitality in Bavaria."

The hut proved to be empty. The door hung loosely on its hinges, and clearly the place was deserted.

Rupert called Hugh up, and fastening the horses outside, the lads entered.

"Shall we light a fire, Master Rupert?"

"No, Hugh; at any rate unless we see that the shutters and door will close tightly. There may be scores of deserters in the wood, and we had better run no risk. The night is not cold. We will just sit down against the wall till morning. Before we do, though, we will look round, outside the hut; if it has been lately inhabited, there may be a few vegetables or something the horses can munch."

Nothing, however, was found.

"We will take it by turns to watch, Hugh. I will take first watch; when I am sleepy I will wake you."

Without a word Hugh unstrapped his cloak, felt for a level piece of ground in the hut, and with his cloak for a pillow, was soon asleep.

Rupert sat down on the log of a tree, that lay outside the hut, and leaned against its wall. For two hours he sat, and thought over the adventures and the prospects of the war, and then gradually a drowsiness crept over him, and he fell fast asleep.

His waking was not pleasant; indeed, he was hardly aware that he was awake; for he first came to the consciousness that he was lying on the ground, with a number of wild-looking figures around him, some of whom bore torches, while Hugh, held by two of them, was close by.

It was Hugh's voice, indeed, that first recalled him to a consciousness of what had happened.

"Master Rupert, Master Rupert!" he exclaimed, "tell me that you are not killed!"

"No, I am not killed, Hugh," Rupert said, raising himself on his elbow. "But it would have served me right if I had been, for going to sleep on my watch."

One of their captors now stooped down, seized Rupert by the shoulder, and gave him a rough kick to intimate that he was to get up.

"I am sorry, Hugh, that I have sacrificed your life as well as my own by my folly, for I have no doubt these fellows mean to kill us; they are charcoal-burners, as rough a lot as there exists in Europe, and now naturally half mad at the flames they see all over the land."

In the meantime, a dialogue was going on between their captors as to the best and most suitable method of putting them to death.

"They are fond of burning houses," one said at last," "let them try how they like it; let us make a blaze here, and toss them in, and let them roast in their own shells."

The proposal was received with a shout of approval. Some of them scattered in the forest, and soon returned laden with dry branches and small logs, which were piled up in a great heap against the hut, which was itself constructed of rough-hewn logs. The heap of dry wood was then lighted, and ere long a great sheet of flame arose, the logs and the shingles of the roof caught, and ere many minutes the hut was a pile of fire.

"They're going to throw us in there, Hugh."

"God's will be done, Master Rupert; but I should like to have died sword in hand."

"And I too, Hugh. I wish I could snatch at a weapon and die fighting; but this man holds my hands like a vice, and those heavy axes of theirs would make short work of us. Well, the fire will not take an instant, Hugh; it will be a momentary death to be thrown into that mass of flame. Say a prayer to God, Hugh, for those at home, for it is all up with us now."

The blaze of fire had attracted other bodies of charcoal burners and others, and their captors only delayed to obtain as large a number of spectators as possible · for their act of vengeance.

The fire was now at its height, and even the savage charcoal burners felt a grudging admiration for the calm demeanour, and fearless, if pale, faces, with which these lads faced death. There was, however, no change of purpose. The horrors that had been perpetrated on the plains had extinguished the last spark of pity from their breasts, and the deed that they were about to do seemed to them one of just and praiseworthy retribution.

The man who acted as leader gave the word, and the powerful woodsmen lifted the two lads as if they had been bundles of straw, and advanced towards the hut.

"Good-bye, Master Rupert!"

"Good-bye, Hugh. May God receive"—when a terrible scream rent the air, and a wild shout.

Then from the back of the crowd, two figures who had just arrived at the spot burst their way. With piercing cries a woman with a baby in her arms flung herself down on the ground on her knees, between Rupert and the flames, and clasping the legs of the men who held him, arrested their movement; while the man, with a huge club swinging round his head, planted himself also in the way, shouting at the top of his voice.

A mighty uproar arose; and then the leader obtained silence enough to hear the cause of the interruption.

Then the man began, and told the tale of the restoration to life and consciousness of his wife, and of the burial of his child, with an eloquence and pathos that moved many of his rough audience to tears; and when he had finished, his wife, who had been sobbing on her knees while he spoke, rose to her feet, and told how that morning, as she went down from the wood towards her little one's grave, she saw Rupert ride up and dismount, and how when she reached the place she found fresh-gathered flowers laid on her darling's grave.

A dead hush fell upon the whole assembly. Without a word the leader of the charcoal burners strode away into the forest, and returned in another minute with the two horses. Rupert and Hugh wrung the hands of the peasants to whom they owed their lives, and leapt into the saddle.

The leader took a torch and strode on ahead along the path, to show them their way; and the crowd, who had hitherto stood still and silent, broke into a shout of farewell and blessing.

It was some time before either Rupert or Hugh spoke, the emotion had been too great for them. That terrible half hour facing death—the sudden revulsion at their wonderful deliverance—completely prostrated them, and they felt exhausted and weak, as if after some great exertion. On the previous occasions in which they had seen great danger together—at the mill of Dettingheim, the fight on the Dykes, the scuttling of the boat—they had been actively engaged. Their energies were fully employed, and they had had no time to think. Now they had faced death in all his terrors, but without the power of action; and both felt they would far rather go through the three first risks again, than endure five minutes of that terrible watching the fire burn up.

Hugh was the first to speak when, nearly an hour after starting, they emerged from the wood into the plain at the foot of the hill.

"My mother used to say, Master Rupert, that curses, like chickens, came home to roost, and surely we have proved it's the case with blessings. Who would have thought that that little act of kindness was to save our lives?"

"No, indeed, Hugh. Let it be a lesson to us to do good always when we can."

At this moment they reached the main road from which that over the hill branched off.

Their guide paused, pointed in the direction they were to go, and with a "God-speed you," in his own language, extinguished his torch on the road, turned, and strode back by the path that they had come by.

The lads patted their horses, and glad to be again on level ground, the animals went on at a sharp canter along the road. Two hours later they reached camp.

The Duke of Marlborough had already laid siege to the fortress of Ingoldstadt, the siege operations being conducted by Prince Louis of Baden with a portion of his troops, while the main army covered the siege. But early in August the Elector of Bavaria left Augsburg with his army, and, altogether abandoning his dominions, marched to join Marshal Tallard, who was now coming up.

Marlborough at once broke up his camp, leaving Prince Louis to continue the siege of Ingoldstadt, and collecting as many of his troops as he could, marched with all speed in the same direction; as Prince Eugene, who, with his army, had marched in a parallel line with the French, now ran the risk of being crushed by their united force.

By dint of great exertion, Marlborough joined the prince with his cavalry on the 10th of August, and the infantry came up next day.

The two great armies now faced each other, their numerical force being not unequal, the French being about 60,000 strong, and the allies 66,000. In other respects, however, the advantage lay wholly with the enemy. They had ninety guns, while the allies had but fifty-one, while out of the 60,000 troops under Marshal Tallard 45,000 were the best troops France could

produce.   The allied army was a motley assembly,
composed of nearly equal numbers of English, Prussians, Danes, Wurtemburghers, Dutch, Hanoverians,
and Hessians.   But although not more numerous than
the troops of other nationalities, it was felt by all that
the brunt of the battle would fall upon the British.

These had, throughout the three campaigns, shown
fighting qualities of so high a character, that the whole
army had come to look upon them as their mainstay in
battle.   The heavy loss which had taken place among
these, the flower of his troops, at the assault of Schless-
ingen greatly decreased the fighting power of Marlborough's army.

The weakness caused by the miscellaneous character
of the army was so much felt, that Marlborough was
urged to draw off, and not to tempt fortune under such
unfavourable circumstances.

Marshal Villeroi was, however, within a few days'
march with a large force, and Marlborough felt that if
he effected a junction with Tallard, Austria was lost.
It was therefore necessary, at all hazards, to fight at
once.

The French position was an exceedingly strong one.
Their right rested on the Danube; and the village of
Blenheim, close to its bank, was held by twenty-six
battalions and twelve squadrons, all native French
troops.

Their left was equally protected from attack by a
range of hills, impregnable for guns or cavalry.   In the
centre of their line, between their flanks, was the village
of Oberglau, in and around which lay thirty battalions
of infantry, among whom was the fine Irish regiments.

From Blenheim to Oberglau, and thence on to Lutzingen, at the foot of the hills, the French line occupied
somewhat rising ground, in front of them was the rivu-
let of the Nebel running through low swampy ground
very difficult for the passage of troops.

Prince Maximilian commanded the French left, where the Bavarians were posted, Marshal Marsin the line on to Oberglau and the village itself, Marshal Tallard the main body thence to the Danube.

The French marshals, strong in the belief of the prowess of their troops, equal in number, greatly superior in artillery, and possessing an extremely strong position, scarcely paid sufficient attention to what would happen in the event of a defeat. The infantry being posted very strongly in the three villages, which were very carefully intrenched and barricaded, insufficient attention was paid to the long line of communications between them, which was principally held by the numerous cavalry. This was their weak point, for it was clear that if the allies should get across the rivulets and swamps and break through the cavalry line, the infantry would be separated and unable to reunite, and the strong force in Blenheim would run a risk of being surrounded without a possibility of retreat, as the Danube was unfordable.

Upon the side of the allies the troops were divided into two distinct armies. That under Prince Eugene, consisting of eighteen battalions of infantry and seventy-four squadrons of horse, was to attack the French left. The main army under the duke, consisting of forty-eight battalions and eighty-six squadrons, was to attack the centre and right.

The British contingent of fourteen battalions and fourteen squadrons, formed part of Marlborough's command.

It was arranged that Prince Eugene should commence the attack, and that when he had crossed the rivulets in front of the French left, Marlborough should advance and attempt to carry out the plan he had laid out, namely, to cut the French line between Oberglau and Blenheim.

Prince Eugene's advance took the French by surprise. So confident were the marshals in the strength
of their position and the belief of the superiority of their
troops over the polyglot army of Marlborough, that
they had made up their minds that he was about to
retreat.

The morning was misty, and Eugene's advance
reached the French pickets before they were perceived.

Their difficulties now began. The rivulets were
deep, the ground treacherous; fascines had to be laid
down, and the rivulets filled up, before guns could get
over; and even when across they could but feebly answer the French artillery, which from the higher
ground commanded their whole line; thus the allies lost
2000 men before Eugene got the army he commanded
across the marshes. Then at half-past twelve he sent
word to Marlborough that he was ready.

While the cannon roar had been incessant on their
right, the main army remained motionless, and divine
service was performed at the head of every regiment
and squadron.

The moment the aide-de-camp arrived with the news
that Prince Eugene was in readiness, the artillery of
Marlborough's army opened fire, and the infantry, followed closely by their cavalry, advanced to the attack.

The British division, under Lord Cutts, as the most
trustworthy, had assigned to them a direct attack upon
the strong position of Blenheim, and they advanced
unwaveringly under a storm of fire, crossed the swamps
and the Nebel, and advanced towards Blenheim.

General Rowe led the front line, consisting of five
English battalions and four Hessians, and he was supported by Lord Cutts with eleven battalions and fifteen
squadrons.

Advancing through a heavy artillery fire, General
Rowe's troops had arrived within thirty yards of the

palisade before the French infantry opened fire. Then a tremendous volley was poured into the allies, and a great number of men and officers fell. Still they moved forward, and Rowe, marching in line with his men, struck the palisade with his sword before he gave the order to fire.

Then desperately the British strove to knock down the palisade and attack their enemy with the bayonet, but the structure was too strong, and the gallant force melted away under the withering fire kept up by the great force of French infantry which occupied the village.

Half Rowe's force fell, he himself was badly wounded, most of his officers down, when some squadrons of French horse fell upon their flank, threw them into confusion, and took the colours of the regiment.

The Hessians, who so far had been in reserve, fell upon the French, and re-took the colours.

Fresh squadrons of French cavalry came up, and General Lumley sent some squadrons of cavalry across to Rowe's assistance. Then, with a cheer, the dragoons rode at the French, who were twice their strength. In an instant every one was engaged in a fierce conflict, cutting, slashing, and using their points.

The French gave way under the onslaught, but fresh squadrons came up from their side, a heavy musketry fire broke out from the enclosure round Blenheim, and leaving many of their number behind them, the British horse and foot fell back to the stream.

Marlborough, seeing that Blenheim could not be taken, now resolved upon making his great effort to break the French line midway between Oberglau and Blenheim.

On the stream at this part stood the village of Unterglau, having a stone bridge across the Nebel. This was but weakly held by the French, who, upon seeing

the allies advancing at full speed, fired the village to
check the advance, and then fell back.

General Churchill's division rushed through the
burning village, crossed the bridge, and began to open
out on both sides.   Then the duke gave the order for
the whole cavalry to advance.   Headed by the English
dragoons, they came down in good order through the
concentrated fire of the enemy's batteries to the edge of
the stream; but the difficulties here were immense; the
stream was divided into several branches, with swampy
meadows between them, and only by throwing down
fascines could a footing be obtained for the horses.

"I don't call this fighting, Master Rupert," Hugh
said, as they floundered and struggled through the deep
marshes, while the enemy's shell burst in and around
the ranks; "it's more like swimming.   Here come the
French cavalry, and we've not even formed up."

Had the French charge been pressed home, the
dragoons must have been crushed; but Churchill's infantry on their right opened such a heavy fire that the
French cavalry at that end of the line paused.   On
their left, however, near Blenheim, the dragoons, suffering terribly from the artillery and musketry fire from
that village, were driven back by the French cavalry to
the very edge of the swamp.

Marlborough, however, anxiously watching the
struggle, continued to send fresh bodies of horse across
to their assistance, until the Dutch and Hanoverian
squadrons were all across, and the allied cavalry formed
in two long lines.

While this had been going on, a serious fight had
been raging in front of Oberglau; and here, as at Blenheim, the allies suffered disaster.   Here, the Hanoverians, led by the Prince of Holstein, had attacked.
The powerful body of French and Irish infantry did
not, however, wait for the assault, but, 9000 strong,

charged down the slope upon the 5000 Hanoverians before they had formed up after crossing the river, repulsed them with great loss, and took the prince himself prisoner.

This was a serious disaster, as, by the rout of the Hanoverians the connexion between Marlborough's army and that of Prince Eugene was broken.

Marlborough's eye, however, was everywhere; and galloping to the spot, he put himself at the head of some squadrons of British cavalry, and, closely followed by three battalions of fresh infantry, charged the Irish battalions, who, in the impetuosity of their pursuit, had fallen into disorder. The cavalry charge completed their confusion, and the infantry opening fire in flank on the lately victorious column, drove it back with immense slaughter. Thus the battle was restored at this point.

All this time the fight had raged between Eugene's army and the Bavarians and French opposed to them. At first the prince had been successful, and the Danes and Prussians under his orders captured a battery of six guns. His cavalry, however, while advancing in some disorder, were charged by the French, driven back across the Nebel, and the guns were re-taken. Twice the prince himself rallied his cavalry, and brought them back to the charge, but each time the Bavarian horse, led by the elector, drove them back, defeated and broken, across the river. The Prussian and Danish infantry stood their ground nobly, although the enemy charged them over and over again; but, cheered by the presence of Prince Eugene, who took his place amongst them, they beat off all attacks.

The Duke of Marlborough, after restoring the battle at Oberglau, rode back to his centre, and prepared for the grand attack by his cavalry. Marshal Tallard, in preparation for the attack he saw impending, brought

up six battalions of infantry, and placed them in the
centre of the ridge. Marlborough brought up three
battalions of Hessians to front them, placed the rest of
his infantry to cover the left of the cavalry from the
attack of the strong battalions in Blenheim, and then,
drawing his sword, placed himself in front of his troops,
and ordered the trumpets to sound the advance.

This grand and decisive charge is thus described by
Allison in his "Life of Marlborough:"—

"Indescribably grand was the spectacle that ensued.
In compact order, and in the finest array, the allied
cavalry, mustering 8000 sabres, moved up the gentle
slope in two lines—at first slowly, as on a field day, but
gradually more quickly as they drew near, and the fire
of the artillery became more violent. The French
horse, 10,000 strong, stood their ground at first firmly.
The choicest and bravest of their chivalry were there;
the banderolls of almost all the nobles of France floated
over the squadrons.

"So hot was the fire of musketry and cannon when
the assailants drew near, that their advance was
checked. They retired sixty paces, and the battle was
kept up for a few minutes only by a fire of artillery.
Gradually, however, the fire of the artillery slackened;
and Marlborough, taking advantage of the pause, led
his cavalry again to the charge. With irresistible vehemence the line dashed forward at full speed, and soon
the crest of the ridge was passed. The French horsemen discharged their carbines at a considerable distance with little effect, and immediately wheeled about
and fled.

"The battle was gained. The allied horse rapidly
inundated the open space between the two villages; the
six battalions in the middle were surrounded, cut to
pieces, or taken. They made a noble resistance; and
the men were found lying on their backs in their ranks
as they had stood in the field."

Thus at one blow the whole French line of defence was broken up. Blenheim was entirely cut off; and the rear of their left beyond Oberglau threatened.

General Marsin's cavalry, seeing the defeat of their main body, fell back to avoid being taken in rear; and Prince Eugene, seeing the Bavarian infantry left unsupported, called up all his reserves, and advanced at the head of the Danes and Prussians against them. The Bavarian infantry fought stubbornly, but the battle was lost, their line of retreat threatened by the allied horse, who were now masters of the field, and setting fire to the villages of Oberglau and Lutzingen, they fell back sullenly.

In the meantime, Marshal Tallard was striving bravely to avert the defeat. He brought up his last reserves, rallied his cavalry, and drew them up in line stretching towards Blenheim in hopes of drawing off his infantry from that village. Marlborough brought up his whole cavalry force, and again charging them, burst through their centre, and the French cavalry, divided into two parts, fled in wild disorder—the one portion towards the Danube, the other towards Hochstadt. Marlborough at the head of fifty squadrons pursued the first body; Hanpesch with thirty followed the second. Marlborough drove the broken mass before him to the Danube, where great numbers were drowned in attempting to cross; the rest were made prisoners. Marshal Tallard himself, with a small body of cavalry who still kept their ranks, threw himself into the village of Sonderheim, and was there captured by the victorious squadrons. Hanpesch pursued the flying army as far as Hochstadt, captured three battalions of infantry on the way, and halted not until the French were a mere herd of fugitives, without order, riding for their lives.

There now remained only the garrison of Blenheim

to dispose of, and the infantry were brought up to attack them. So strong were the defences, however, so desperate the resistance offered by the brave body of Frenchmen, who were now alone against an army, that the infantry attack was beaten back. The guns were then brought up, and opened fire, and the French, whose case was now hopeless, surrendered.

The battle of Blenheim was over. In this great battle Marlborough's army lost 5000 men, Eugene's 6000. In all 11,000 men. The French and Bavarians lost in killed and wounded 12,000, together with 1200 officers and 13,000 privates made prisoners, and 47 cannon. Their total loss, including desertions in their retreat through the Black Forest, was estimated by their own historians at 40,000 men—a defeat as complete and disastrous as that of Waterloo.

CHAPTER XIV.

THE RIOT AT DORT.

THE Duke of Marlborough lost no time in utilizing the advantages gained by the victory of Blenheim. He at once raised the siege of Ingoldstadt, which, when all the country was in his power, must sooner or later surrender, and detached a portion of the force which had been there engaged to besiege Ulm, an important fortress on the Danube. Then with the bulk of his army he marched to the Rhine, crossed at Philipsburg on the 6th of September, and advanced towards Landau.

Marshal Villeroi had constructed an entrenched camp to cover the town; but on the approach of the victor of Blenheim he fell back, leaving Landau to its fate. Marlborough followed him, and made every effort to bring the French to a battle; but Villeroi fell back behind the Lauter, and then behind the Motter, abandoning without a blow one of the strongest countries in Europe.

On the 11th of September Ulm surrendered, with 250 pieces of cannon; and upon the following day, Landau was invested. The Prince of Baden with 20,000 men conducted the siege, and Marlborough and Eugene with 30,000 covered the operations. Marlborough, however, determined on ending the campaign, if possible, by driving the French beyond the Moselle, and leaving Prince Eugene with 18,000 men, marched with 12,000 men on the 14th of October.

After a tremendous march through a wild and desolate country, he arrived with his exhausted troops at Treves on the 29th, one day before the arrival of 10,000 French, who were advancing to occupy it. The garrison of 600 men in the citadel evacuated it at his approach. He immediately collected and set to work 6000 peasants to restore the fortifications. Leaving a garrison, he marched against the strong place of Traes-bach. Here he was joined by twelve Dutch battalions from the Meuse; and having invested the place, he left the Prince of Hesse to conduct the siege—which speedily ended in the surrender of the place—and marched back with all haste to rejoin Prince Eugene.

Leaving Eugene to cover the siege of Landau, Marl-borough now hurried away to Hanover and Berlin, to stimulate the governments of Hanover and Prussia to renewed exertion; and by his address and conciliatory manner succeeded in making arrangements for 8000 fresh Prussian troops to be sent to the imperial armies in Italy, as the Duke of Savoy had been reduced to the last extremity there by the French.

The Electress of Bavaria, who had been regent of that country since her husband left to join the French, had now no resource but submission, and she accord-ingly agreed to disband her remaining troops, and to make peace.

The Hungarian insurrection was suppressed by Aus-tria, now able to devote all its attention to that point; and Landau surrendered towards the end of November, when its garrison was reduced from 7000 to 3500, who became prisoners of war.

All these decisive results arose from the victory of Blenheim. Had the British Government during the winter acceded to Marlborough's request, and voted men and money, he would have been able to march to Paris in the next campaign, and could have brought the war to an end; but the mistaken parsimony then, as often since, crippled the British general, allowed the French to recover from their disaster, prolonged the war for years, and cost the country very many times the money and the men that Marlborough had asked for to bring the war to a decisive termination.

But while the English and Dutch governments refused to vote more money or men, and the German government, freed from their pressing danger, became supine and lukewarm, the French upon the contrary, set to in an admirable manner to retrieve the disasters they had suffered, and employed the winter in well-conceived efforts to take the field with a new army, to the full as strong as that which they had lost; and the fruits of Blenheim were, with the exception of the acquisition of a few fortresses, entirely thrown away.

At the battle of Blenheim, Rupert Holliday escaped untouched, but Hugh was struck with a fragment of shell, and severely wounded. He was sent down the Rhine by water to the great military hospital which had been established at Bonn; and Rupert, who was greatly grieved at being separated from his faithful follower, had the satisfaction of hearing ere long that he was doing well.

Rupert had assigned him as orderly a strong, active young fellow, named Joe Sedley, who was delighted at his appointment, for the "little cornet" was, since his defeat of the German champion, the pride of the regiment. Joe was a Londoner, one of those fellows who can turn their hand to anything, always full of fun, getting sometimes into scrapes, but a general favourite with his comrades.

The campaign over, Rupert, who was now a lieutenant, asked and obtained leave to go home for the winter; he had long since been reconciled with his mother; and it was two years and a half since he had left home. Hugh and Joe Sedley had also obtained leave, upon Rupert's application on their behalf.

On his way down Rupert resolved to pay a visit for a few days to his kind friends at Dort. They had writ-

ten begging him to come and see them; and a postscript which Maria had put in her last letter to him, to
the effect that she had reason to believe that her old
persecutor was in the neighbourhood, and that her
father had taken renewed precautions for her safety,
added to his desire to visit Dort.

"That fellow's obstinacy is really admirable in its
way," Rupert said, on reading this news. "He has
made up his mind that there is a fortune to be obtained
by carrying off Maria Von Duyk, and he sticks to it
with the same pertinacity which other men display in
the pursuit of commerce or of lawful trade, or that a
wild beast shows in his tireless pursuit of his prey."

Had it not been for the postscript, Rupert would
have deferred his visit to Dort until after his return
from England, but the news caused him serious uneasiness. He knew but too well the unscrupulous nature
of this desperate man, whom he had heard of since his
last attempt upon his life as being a leader of one of
the bands of freebooters who, formed of deserters and
other desperate men, frequented the Black Forest, the
Vosges mountains, the Ardennes, and other forests and
hill districts. That he would dare lead his band down
into the plains of Holland, Rupert had no fear; still he
could have no difficulty in finding men of ruined fortunes even there to join in any wild attempt.

Leaving the army when it went into winter quarters,
Rupert travelled by land to Bonn, and there picked up
Hugh, who was now completely restored to health,
and then, taking boat, journeyed down the Rhine.
Then he took horse again, and rode to Dort.

Mynheer Von Duyk and Maria were delighted to see
him; and Hugh and Sedley were hospitably received
by the servants, with whom Hugh had, on the occasion
of his last visit, made himself a prime favourite.

From the first day of their arrival Rupert had all the

talking to do, and his adventures to relate from the time he set sail from Dort. He had of course written from time to time, but his letters, although fairly full, did not contain a tithe of the detail which his friends were anxious to learn. The next morning, after breakfast, he asked his host if he was unwell, for he looked worn and anxious.

"I am well in body, but disturbed in mind," he said. "Six months ago I stood well with my fellow-citizens, and few were more popular in Dort than myself. Now, save among the better class, men look askance at me. Subtle whispers have gone abroad that I am in correspondence with France; that I am a traitor to Holland; that I correspond with the Spanish at Antwerp. In vain have I tried to force an open accusation, in order that I might disperse it. The merchants, and others of my rank, scoff at these rumours, and have in full council denounced their authors as slanderers; but the lower class still hold to their belief. Men scowl as I walk along; the boys shout 'Traitor!' after me; and I have received threatening letters."

"But this is abominable," Rupert said, hotly. "Is there no way of dealing with these slanderers?"

"No," the merchant said; "I see none, beyond living it down. Some enemy is at work, steadily and powerfully."

"Have you an enemy you suspect?"

"None, save indeed that rascal countryman of yours. He is desperate, and, as you know, relentless. My house has always been guarded by six stout fellows since we returned from The Hague; and any open attempt to carry off my daughter would be useless. It is difficult to see what he proposes to himself by stirring up a party against me; but he might have some scheme which we cannot fathom. Our Dutchmen are slow but obstinate, and once they get an idea in their head it is difficult to discharge."

"You do not fear any public tumult, surely?" Rupert said.

"I do not anticipate it, and yet I regard it as possible," Von Duyk said; "the people in our town have been given to bursts of frenzy, in which some of our best men have been slain."

"Why don't you go down to The Hague again till this madness has passed by?"

"I cannot do that. My enemies would take advantage of it, and might sack my house and warehouses."

"But there is the burgher guard; and all the respectable citizens are with you."

"That is true enough," the merchant said; "but they are always slow to take action, and I might be killed, and my place burned before they came on to the ground. I will send Maria with you down to The Hague to her aunt's. If this be the work of the man we wot of, it may be that he will then cease his efforts, and the bad feeling he has raised will die away; but in truth, I shall never feel that Maria is safe until I hear that his evil course has come to an end."

"If I come across him, I will bring it to an end, and that quickly," Rupert said, wrathfully. "At any rate, I think that the burgomaster ought to take steps to protect the house."

"The council laught at the idea of danger," Von Duyk said. "To them the idea that I should be charged with dealing with the enemy is so supremely ridiculous that they make light of it, and are inclined to think that the state of things I describe is purely a matter of my own imagination. If I were attacked they would come as quickly as they could to my aid; but they may be all too late. There is one thing, Rupert. This enemy hates you, and desires your death as much as he wishes to carry off my daughter, and through her to become possessed of my money bags. If, then, this work is his doing, assuredly he will bring it to a head while you are here, so as to gratify both his hate and his greed at once."

"It is a pity that you cannot make some public statement, that unless your daughter marries a man of whom you approve you will give her no fortune whatever."

"I might do that," Von Duyk said; "but he knows that if he forced her to marry him, I should still give her my money; in the second place, she has a large fortune of her own, that came to her through her mother; and lastly, I believe that it is not marriage he wishes now, for he must be sure that Maria would die rather than accept him, but to carry her off, and then place some enormous sum as a ransom on condition of her being restored safe and unharmed to me. He knows that I would give all that I possess to save her from his hands."

"The only way out of it that I see," Rupert said, "is for me to find him, and put an end to him."

"You will oblige me, Rupert, if, during the time you remain here, you would wear this fine mail shirt under your waistcoat. You do not wear your cuirass here; and your enemy might get a dagger planted between your shoulders as you walk the streets. It is light, and very strong; it was worn by a Spanish general who fell, in the days of Alva, in an attack upon Dort. My great-grandfather shot him through the head, and kept his mail shirt as a trophy."

"It is a useful thing against such a foe as this," Rupert said, putting it on at once. "I could not wear it in battle, for it would be an unfair advantage; but against an assassin all arms are fair."

During the day Rupert went out with his host, and the scowling looks which were turned upon the latter convinced him that the merchant had not exaggerated the extent to which the feeling of the lower class had

12

been excited against him. So convinced was he of the danger of the position, that, to the immense surprise of Hugh and Joe Sedley, he ordered them to lie down at night in their clothes, with their swords and pistols ready by them. With eight armed men in the house— for four of the porters engaged in the merchant's warehouse slept on truckle beds placed in the hall—Rupert thought that they ought to be able to repel any assault which might be made.

It was on the fourth night after Rupert's coming to Dort, that he was aroused by a touch on his shoulder. He leapt to his feet, and his hand, as he did so, grasped his sword, which lay ready beside him."

"What is it?" he exclaimed.

"There is mischief afloat," Von Duyk said. "There is a sound as of a crowd in front of the house. I have heard the tramp of many footsteps."

Rupert went to the window and looked out. The night was dark, and the oil lamps had all been extinguished; but it seemed to him that a confused mass filled the space in which the house stood.

"Let me get the men under arms," he said, "and then we can open the window, and ask what they want."

In two minutes he returned.

"Now, sir, let us ask them at once. They are probably waiting for a leader or order."

The merchant went to the window, and threw it open.

"Who is there?" he asked. "And what means this gathering at the door of a peaceful citizen?"

As if his voice had been the signal for which they waited, a roar went up from the immense crowd. A thunder of axes at the door and shutters, and a great shout arose,—

"Death to the traitor! Death to the Frenchmen!"

Shots were fired at the windows, and at the same

moment the alarm-bell at the top of the house pealed
loudly out, one of the serving-men having previously
received order to sound the signal if needed. In answer to the alarm bell, the watchman on the tower,
whose duty it was to call the citizens from their beds in
case of fire, struck the great bell, and its deep sounds
rang out over the town; two minutes later the church
bells joined in the clamour; and the bell on the town
hall with quick, sharp strokes called the burgher guard
to arms.

Von Duyk, knowing now that all that could be done
had been effected, ran to his daughter's room, bade her
dress, and keep her door locked until she heard his
voice, come what may; then he ran downstairs to join
the defenders below.

"The shutters are giving everywhere," Rupert cried.
"We must hold this broad staircase. How long will it
be, think you, before the burgher guard are here?"

"A quarter of an hour, maybe."

"We should beat them back for that time," Rupert
said. "Light as many lights as you can, and place
them so as to throw the light in their faces, and keep
us in the shade."

In two or three minutes a smashing of timber and
loud shouts of triumph proclaimed that the mob were
effecting an entrance.

"For the present I will stand in front, with one of
these good fellows with their axes on each side of me.
The other two shall stand behind us, a step or two
higher. You, Hugh and Joe, take post with our host
in the gallery above with your pistols, and cover us by
shooting any man who presses us hard. Fire slowly,
pick off your men, and only leave your posts and join
me here on the last necessity."

They had just taken the posts assigned to them when
the door fell in with a crash, and the mob poured in,

just as a rush took place from the side passages by those who had made their way in through the lower windows.

"A grim set of men," Rupert said to himself.

They were indeed a grim set. Many bore torches, which, when once need for quiet and concealment was over, they had lighted.

Dort did a large export trade in hides, and in meats to the towns lying below them, and it was clear that it was from the butchers and skinners that the mob was chiefly drawn. Huge figures, with pole-axes and long knives, in leathern clothes spotted and stained with blood, showed wild and fierce in the red light of the torches, as they brandished their weapons, and prepared to assault the little band who held the broad stairs.

Rupert advanced a step below the rest, and shouted,—

"What means this? I am an officer of the Duke of Marlborough's army, and I warn you against lifting a hand against my host and good friend Mynheer Von Duyk."

"It's a lie!" shouted one of the crowd. "We know you; you are a Frenchman masquerading in English uniform. Down with him, my friends! Death to the traitors!"

There was a rush up the stairs, and in an instant the terrible fight began.

On open ground, Rupert, with his activity and his straight sword, would have made short work of one of the brawny giants who now attacked him, for he could have leapt out of reach of the tremendous blow, and have run his opponent through ere he could again lift his ponderous axe. But there was no guarding such swinging blows as these with a light sword; and even the advantage of the height of the stairs was here of little use.

At first he felt that the combat was desperate; soon, however, he regained confidence in his sword. With it held ever straight in front of him, the men mounting could not strike without laying open their breasts to the blade. There must, he felt, be no guarding on his part; he must be ever on the offensive.

All this was felt rather than thought in the whirl of action. One after another the leaders of the assailants fell, pierced through the throat while their ponderous axes were in the act of descending. By his side the Dutchman's retainers fought sturdily, while the crack of the pistols of Hugh, Joe Sedley, and the master of the house were generally followed by a cry and a fall from the assailants.

As the difficulty of their task became more apparent, the yells of fury of the crowd increased. Many of them were half drunk, and their wild gestures and shouts, the waving of their torches, and the brandishing of knives and axes, made the scene a sort of pandemonium.

Ten minutes had passed since the first attack, and still the stairs were held. One of the defenders lay dead, with his head cloven to his shoulders with a pole-axe, but another had taken his place.

Suddenly, from behind, the figure of a man bounded down the stairs from the gallery, and with a cry of "Die, villain!" struck Rupert with a dagger with all his strength, and then bounded back into the gallery. Rupert fell headlong amid his assailants below.

Hugh and Joe Sedley, with a shout of rage and horror, dashed from their places, sword in hand, and leaping headlong down the stairs, cutting and hewing with their heavy swords, swept all opposition back, and stood at the foot, over the body of Rupert.

The three Dutchmen and Von Duyk followed their example, and formed a group round the foot of the stairs. Then there was a wild storm of falling blows, the clash of sword and axe, furious shouts, loud death-cries, a very turmoil of strife, when there was a cry at the door of "The watch!" and then a loud command,—

"Cut the knaves down! slay every man! Dort! Dort!"

There was a rush now to escape; down the passages fled the late assailants, pursued by the burgher guard, who, jealous of the honour of their town, injured by this foul attack upon a leading citizen, cut down all they came upon; while many who made their escape through the windows by which they had entered, were cut down or captured by the guard outside. The defenders of the stairs made no attempt at pursuit.

The instant the burgher guard entered the hall, Hugh and Joe threw down their blood-stained swords, and knelt beside Rupert.

"Ough!" sighed the latter, in a long breath.

"Thank God! he is not dead."

"Dead!" Rupert gasped, "not a bit of it; only almost trodden to death. One of my stout friends has been standing on me all the time, though I roared for mercy so that you might have heard me a mile off, had it not been for the din."

"But are you not stabbed, Master Rupert?"

"Stabbed! no; who would have stabbed me? One of you somehow hit me on the back, and down I went; but there is no stab."

"He had a dagger; I saw it flash," Hugh said, lifting Rupert to his feet.

"Had he?" Rupert said; "and who was he? If it was an enemy, it is your coat of mail has saved me," he continued, turning to Von Duyk. "I have never taken it off since. But how did he get behind me, I wonder? Run," he continued energetically, "and see if the lady is safe. There must have been mischief behind."

Mynheer Von Duyk, closely followed by the others, ran upstairs to his daughter's room. The door was open. He rushed into the room. It was empty. The window was open; and looking out, two ladders were seen, side by side.

It was clear that while the fray had been raging, Maria Von Duyk had been carried off.

CHAPTER XV.

THE END OF A FEUD.

AFTER the first cry of rage and grief at the discovery of the abduction of Maria Von Duyk there was a moment's silence.   Rupert broke it, laying his hand on the shoulder of Von Duyk, who had dropped despairingly into a chair,—

"We will find her," he said, "wherever she be.   Let us lose no moments in sorrow.   Call up the burgomaster, or whoever leads the burghers, and let us consult."

In another minute or two four of the principal magistrates of Dort had joined the party, and Von Duyk told them what had happened.

"I told her to lock the door, and not to open until she heard my voice.   Doubtless she was standing there listening to the strife without, when the men burst in at the window, and seized her before, in her surprise and terror, she had time to unlock the door.   Now what is to be done to recover her?   They have, no doubt, carried her off by boat, for they could not pass through the landward gate of the town.   Will you order two fast boats, to be manned by strong parties of rowers, with well-armed men?   One had better go up the river, one down; for we know not in which direction they will take their flight.   What think you, Master Holliday?"

"I think that a boat had better go either way, without a moment's loss of time," Rupert said.   "But I doubt whether either will find them.   But send the boats without a moment's delay, with orders to overhaul and search every craft they overtake."

The magistrates at once called in an officer of the guard, and gave him the necessary instructions.

"And why do you not think that either up or down

the river they will overtake them?" Von Duyk asked Rupert, as the officer left the room.

"Because they will know that a fleet horseman will pass them; and that by morning the people at the towns on the banks will all be on the look-out for them. So, having sent off the boats, I should now send off horsemen up and down the river, with a letter from you, sirs, to the authorities at all the towns, begging them to stop and search every boat."

Again the necessary orders were given.

"It was right to take these steps," Rupert said, "for they may be greater fools than I take them to be; but I think that they have done one of two things. They have gone either up or down the river to some place, probably not far away, where horses are in readiness, or —or, they may be still in the town."

"Still in the town!"

"Yes," Rupert said; "they will know that we should pursue them up and down the river; that we should scour the country round; but they may think that we should not suspect that she is still here. There must be lots of secure hiding-places in an old town like this; and they may well think it safer to keep her hidden here until they force her into marriage, or wring a fabulous ransom from you."

"We will search every house," the burgomaster said, "from cellar to roof."

"It would be useless," Rupert said. "There must be secret hiding-places where she could be stowed away, bound and gagged perhaps, and which you could never detect. I would lose no moment of time in sending out horsemen to every village on either side of the river above and below us, for a circle of twenty miles. If horsemen have passed through, some villager or other is sure to have been awoke by the clatter of the horses. If we get news, we must follow up the traces wherever they go. If not, it will be strong proof that they are still here. In any case, our pursuit all over the country will lead them to think that we have no suspicion that she is here, and we shall have far more chance of lighting upon a clue than if they thought we suspected it. Get trusty men to work at once; question the prisoners your men have taken, with some sharp pain that will wring the truth from them; but let all be done quietly; while on the other hand, let the chase through the country be as active and public as possible."

Threats, and the application of a string twisted round the thumb, and tightened until the blood spurted from beneath the nails—rough modes of questioning which had not yet died out—soon elicited from the captives the place where the arch-conspirator had been staying while he laid the train for the explosion; but, as was expected, a search showed that the bird had flown, without leaving a trace behind him.

Then, as there was nothing more to do until morning, and two score of horsemen had been sent off in different directions, and the officers most acquainted with the haunts of the bad characters were set quietly to work to search for some clue that might help to find the hiding place of Maria, the magistrates took their leave with many expressions of regret and commiseration with the merchant, and with confession of a consciousness of deep fault that they had not taken to heart his warnings.

Long ere this the bodies of the score of rioters who had fallen on the stairs, hall, and passages had been removed; and leaving the afflicted merchant for awhile to his thoughts, Rupert retired to his room, telling Hugh and Joe to follow him. He explained to them exactly the steps which had been taken, and his opinion as to the true state of things; and bade them think the matter over in every light, and to come to him at daybreak, and let him know if any plan for the conduct of the search had occurred to them.

The result of the night's thoughts and of the morning's deliberations was conveyed to Mynheer Von Duyk by Rupert.

"The first thing to be done is to offer a large reward, sir, for any news which may lead to the discovery of your daughter. This may or may not bring us in some information. The next thing is to have an eye kept on every boat by the quay which may have a cabin or half-deck capable of concealing a person wrapped up and bound. Also, that a watch should be set upon any fishing boat anchored in the river, or moored against the banks, for miles round. It is very possible that she was carried on board, and that there she may be kept, close to us, for days, or even weeks, until the hotness of the search is over, and they can pass up or down the river without being stopped and overhauled."

"We will have every boat at the quay searched at once; and boat parties shall be sent off to examine every craft at anchor or moored in the river."

"I think, sir, that it behoves us to act with care," Rupert said; "for knowing the desperate nature of this villain, I think it probable that he would wreak his hate upon your daughter, and do some terrible crime when he found that he was discovered, for he knows that his life is already forfeit. When we find out where she is confined, to my mind the serious difficulty only commences, for it is absolutely necessary that the arrest be so prompt and sudden, that he shall not have time even to level a pistol at her."

Von Duyk acknowledged the justice of Rupert's reasoning.

"Hugh has suggested that it is likely that he has in his pay the same boatmen whom he employed last year to murder us. As a first step, let one of your clerks go down with an officer to the quay, and inquire what boats left here yesterday or in the night. Hugh will put on a rough fisherman's suit, and with his hat well down over his brows, will stroll along by the water, to see if he recognizes the face of any of the men."

At eight o'clock in the morning there was a meeting of the council of the town, to determine upon the measures to be taken to discover the authors of this disgraceful outbreak, and to take steps for the recovery of the daughter of the leading citizen of the town. Criers had already gone round to offer rewards for information; and a proclamation was now issued by the magistrates, calling upon every citizen to do his best to aid in the search. A committee was appointed to investigate all information which might be brought in.

All Dort was in a state of excitement; parties of the burgher guard still patrolled the town; numerous arrests were made in the skinners' and butchers' quarters; groups of people assembled and talked over the events of the night; and indignation at the riot and assault upon Mynheer Von Duyk, and pity for himself and his daughter, were loudly expressed on all sides. The authorities forbad any one from leaving the town by land or water without a special permit signed by the magistrates.

The investigation as to the sailing of boats upon the previous day produced a long list of craft of various sizes and kinds that had left Dort. Besides those that had actually sailed, one or two had left the quay, and had anchored out in the river, and made fast to buoys there.

Hugh returned with the intelligence that he had recognized in a boatman loitering on the quay one of the crew of the boat in which Rupert and he had had so narrow an escape from drowning. The captain of one of the merchant's own craft, of which there were several at Dort, was sent for, and having received instructions as to his course, accompanied Hugh to the quay, and having had the fisherman pointed out to him, sauntered along, and after speaking to several men, entered into conversation with him. A confidential agent of the merchant was also ordered to keep at a distance, but to watch every movement, however minute and insignificant, of the suspected man.

The captain's report was soon given in. He had asked the man if he wanted a berth in a ship just going to sail for England, one of the crew having fallen sick at the last moment. He had refused, as he belonged to a boat just about to sail for Bergen-op-Zoom, and he had nodded towards a large decked boat riding in the river. Fearing to excite suspicion, he had asked no further questions, but had turned to another man standing near, and asked him if he would make the voyage.

It was considered certain by Rupert and Von Duyk that Maria was either already confined in that boat, or that she would be taken there when it was considered safe to start. A close scrutiny of the boat with a telescope showed that two men were on board her. They appeared to be smoking, and idling about.

In the meantime, at the Town Hall the committee were busy in examining the reports brought in by the horsemen—whose tales agreed, inasmuch as in none of the villages visited by them had any stir or unusual movement been heard through the night—and in hearing the evidence of innumerable people, who were all anxious to give information which appeared to them to bear upon the outrage.

Von Duyk himself, like one distracted, wandered from place to place.

Presently the spy set to watch the fisherman came in with his report. He said that it was clear that the man was anxious and ill at ease; that after an hour's waiting, a man came up and spoke a word to him, and passed on; that the fisherman then got into a small boat and rowed out towards his vessel, but that he did not watch him further, thinking it better to follow the man up who had spoken to him.   After walking about aimlessly for a short time, as if to see whether he was watched, he had proceeded some distance along the quay, and had then gone into a large house used as a tavern and sailors' boarding-house, but which did but a small trade, the landlord having a bad name in the place.

A boat, with a strong armed party, was ordered to be in readiness to follow at once if the fishing boat sailed; to keep at a distance, but to follow her wherever she went, and at her next landing-place to pounce suddenly upon her and search her.   Then the whole attention of the searchers was directed to the tavern in question. It was agreed that Maria was not likely to be in confine- ment there, as, it having been the house at which it had been ascertained that Sir Richard Fulke had, previous to the last attempt on Rupert, stayed in hiding, it would be suspected, and might be searched.   The strictest watch was now set upon the house, and every one leav- ing it was followed.   Many came out and in, sailors from the quay or the ships lying there; but in none of their movements was anything suspicious found.

At five in the afternoon a boy of twelve years old, a son of the landlord, came out.   He looked suspiciously round, and then walked along the quay.   As he passed a house of considerable size, he again looked round, pulled the bell twice, hastily, and then walked on.   He made a long *détour*, and returned to the tavern.

Not a moment was lost in following up the clue.   The house in question had been unoccupied for some time; the owner was, however, known to Von Duyk, who at once called upon him.   He said that he had let it some weeks before, to a person who had stated that he was a merchant of Amsterdam, and intended to open a branch house at Dort. He had paid him six months' rent in advance, and had received the keys of the house. He believed that some of his party had arrived, as he had himself seen two men go in, but the house was certainly not yet open for business.

Rupert who had been all day at work following out other clues given by persons who had come forward, returned just as Mynheer Von Duyk came back with the news.

"Thank God!" he said, "there is an end to uncertainty. Your daughter is in that house, beyond all doubt. It is only a question of action now. Let us call in the burgomaster and the chief constable, and discuss how the rescue is to be effected. It is probable that he has with him a dozen desperate fellows of his Black Forest gang, and the task of so arranging it that we may interpose between her and the arch-villain is a difficult one indeed. While you send for these officials, I will go and reconnoitre the house; it is quite dark."

The house differed little from its fellows. It was old, with gables, and each floor projected beyond the one below it. A dim light was visible in one of the upper rooms, while a far brighter light shown through the folds of curtains which had been drawn across a window lower down.

Rupert drew his own conclusions.

Returning, he found the burgomaster and chief constable already with Mynheer Von Duyk. After much discussion it was agreed that thirty picked men should be at Rupert's orders at ten that night, an hour at which all Dort would already be sound asleep.

The chief constable then proceeded with Rupert to the houses situated behind that which was intended to be attacked. It was reconnoitred from that side, and found to be in darkness. The owners of these houses, strictly charged to secrecy, were informed of what was going on, and promised all aid in their power. A dozen ladders of various lengths were now got together.

Then they went to the house adjoining, and made their way out on to the roof. This, like many of the Dort houses, was furnished with a terrace, placed between the gabled roofs, which rose sharply on either side. Here the owner, if disposed, could sit and smoke, and look on the river. A table and benches were placed here, and a few tubs with shrubs and flowers. A short, light ladder was brought up, and Rupert climbed up the steep roof, drew up his ladder, and descended on the other side. The steep roof of the next house now faced him, and he was soon over this also, and stood on the little terrace of the house where he believed Maria was a prisoner. It in all respects resembled that he had left. The door leading to it appeared strong and firmly fastened. He now retraced his steps.

Then some light ladders were brought up and placed in position on the two roofs, and all was ready for a party to pass over on to the terrace.

At ten o'clock, then, accompanied by Mynheer Von Duyk and the two troopers, he went to the spot where the force was assembled, and told them off to the duties he had assigned to them.

Eight were to enter the next house with Hugh and Joe Sedley, were to pass, by means of the ladders, over the roof on to the terrace. They were to carry heavy axes and crowbars, and to beat down the door and rush downstairs the instant the signal was given.

Sixteen were to raise eight ladders at the back of the house, and place them close to the windows. Two were to take post at each, ready to burst in the window and rush in at the signal.

The remaining six were to bring a long ladder to the front of the house, and place it against the upper window, where the light was. Two were to follow Rupert up this ladder, the other four to place themselves at the front door, and cut down all who tried to escape.

Rupert's object at attacking at so many different points was so to confuse the occupants of the house by the suddenness and noise of the assault that they would be unable to rally and carry out any plan they might have formed, before the assailants could muster in sufficient force to overcome them.

Orders were also issued for a party of men to proceed to the quay, and to arrest and carry off any one they might find hanging about there.

All arranged, the party moved off, and the work was begun. Thick rolls of flannel had been fastened round the ends of the ladders, so as to prevent the slightest noise being made when they came in contact with the wall. Rupert saw the ladders planted at the back of the house, and the men ready to climb to their places. He then moved round to the front; here the ladder was also fixed. A light flashed down from the terrace above showed that here too the party were in position; and Rupert began to mount, followed by Von Duyk, who had insisted upon taking that post, so as to be ready to spring to the assistance of his child at the first attack. The ladder reached exactly to the window, and as his eyes reached the level Rupert peered anxiously in. At a table, on which burned a candle, sat a man with a huge bowl of liquor and a brace of pistols before him. On a pallet bed in a corner lay a figure, which Rupert felt sure was that of Maria. Rupert doubted not in the least that the order to the watcher was to kill her at the first alarm. Twice he raised his pistol, twice withdrew it. If he did not kill the man on the spot, Maria's life would be clearly forfeited. Under such circumstances he dared not fire. After a moment's thought he gave a sharp tap at the window, and then shrank below the level of the window, and with both his pistols pointed upwards, he waited. As he expected, in a moment the window darkened, and the figure of a man was seen trying to look out into the darkness. As he leaned against the glass, Rupert discharged both his pistols into his body, and then, leaping up, dashed in the window, and leapt over the man's body into the room.

Maria had sprung up with a scream.

"You are safe, Maria," Rupert exclaimed, as he ran to the door. "Here is your father."

The discharge of the pistol had been the signal, and with it came a sound of heavy blows, the crashing of timber, and the shivering of glass. Then rose shouts and furious exclamations, and then a great tramping sounded through the late silent house. Doors and windows had all given way at the onset; and as Sir Richard Fulke with eight comrades rushed upstairs, Hugh and his party ran down.

Torches had been provided and lanterns, and as three of Hugh's men carried them the broad landing was lighted up. Sir Richard Fulke first turned to the door of Maria's room, but there Rupert and two followers stood with drawn swords.

"Cut them down! cut them down!" he shouted; but the rush of Hugh, Joe Sedley, and the rest swept him back, and he fought now to defend his life.

Up the stairs from behind ran the officers who had gained entry by the windows; and the outlaws saw themselves surrounded and hedged in. They fought desperately but vainly, and one by one fell under the blows of their assailants.

Rupert stood immovable on guard; he knew the desperate nature of his enemy, and feared that if he himself were drawn for a moment from his post into the conflict he would rush past and endeavour to avenge himself upon them all by killing Maria.

At last, when most of his followers had fallen, Sir Richard Fulke made a sudden dash through his assailants, and fled up the stairs towards the door on the roof. Rupert, who had never for a moment taken his eye off him, followed at full speed, shouting to Hugh to bring torches and follow.

Short as was the start that was gained, it nearly sufficed for the desperate man's escape; as Rupert gained the terrace, he was already nearly at the top of the ladder against the roof. Rupert seized the ladder, and jerked it sideways. Sir Richard made a grasp at the crest of the roof, and then rolled down on to the terrace.

Rupert rushed forward, but the torches had not yet come, and his enemy was on his feet and upon him, with the advantage which the light coming up the stairs afforded him, and striking down his guard, rushed in and grappled with him. Rupert dropped his sword, which was useless now, and struggled for his life. He felt what his enemy's object was, to throw both over the end of the terrace. He was strong and athletic, but he was far from being a match for his older opponent, to whom rage, despair, and hatred lent a prodigious strength.

"Hugh," he shouted, "quick! quick!"

Joe Sedley was the first to leap to the terrace with a torch, and stood for a moment aghast as he saw the deadly struggle going on, close to the slight wooden railing which ran along the edge of the terrace; then he sprang forward, and just as the struggling foes crashed through the woodwork, and were in the very act of falling over the low stone parapet, he dashed the torch in Sir Richard's face, while at the same moment he grasped Rupert's shoulder with a grip of iron, and dragged him back as his foe loosed his grasp when the torch struck him in the face, and dropped in the darkness.

"A close squeak that, sir; the fellow died hard," Joe Sedley said, cheerily.

"It was indeed, Joe; I owe my life to you."

"Oh, it was all in the way of business, sir; you'll likely enough do as much for me in our next charge."

Hugh was up a moment after Joe Sedley, for the latter had been nearer to a man with a torch, but he just saw the narrow escape his master had, and was so shaken that his hand trembled as he wrung that of his comrade.

"I must stick to my sword another time," Rupert said; "I am David without his sling without it, and any Goliath who comes along can make short work of me. Now let us go below and see after Miss Von Duyk, and assure ourselves that our enemy is dead at last. As he said in the boat, I shall never feel quite safe till I know for certain that he is dead."

CHAPTER XVI.

RAMILIES.

NEITHER Rupert Holliday nor Maria Von Duyk
would be troubled more with Sir Richard Fulke. He
was absolutely and unquestionably dead; he had fallen
on his head, and death had been instantaneous. In the
man whom Rupert shot through the window, Hugh
and he recognized the fellow who had been his accom-
plice in the attempt to carry off Maria in London.

Maria was wholly uninjured, although she was days
before she was able to speak with comfort, so roughly
had the gag been thrust into her mouth. She had not
seen her chief abductor after she had been carried off,
as Sir Richard must have felt that it was in vain either
to threaten or to sue until he had got her in safety far
from Dort.

Leaving the rest of the gang to be dealt with by the
authorities, Rupert with his followers left Dort two
days later, happy in having finally freed his friends from
the danger which had so long menaced them. Mynheer Von Duyk said but little; but Rupert knew how
deep were his feelings of gratitude; and he again sighed
deeply over the fact that Rupert was still but little over
eighteen. Maria herself was equally grateful. Von
Duyk would have freighted a shipful of presents to Rupert's friends in England, but the latter would not hear
of it; he insisted, however, on sending a pipe of magnificent old Burgundy for the colonel's drinking; while
Maria sent a stomacher of antique workmanship, with
valuable gems, to Madame Holliday.

No adventure marked their homeward journey.
Their ship took them rapidly with a fair wind to London Bridge; and Rupert and Hugh started next day by

the coach for Derby, the former having made Joe Sedley a handsome present, to enable him to enjoy his hol-
iday, and an invitation to come down to Windthorpe
Chace when he was tired of London.

A letter had been written from Holland a few days
before starting, to announce their coming, but it was,
of course, impossible in the days of sailing ships to fix
a day for arrival.

Hiring a chaise, they drove to Windthorpe Chace,
where the delight both of Mistress Holliday and of the
colonel was unbounded.   Hugh, too, was greeted very
warmly by both, for Rupert had done full justice to the
services he had rendered him.   It was difficult to recognize in the dashing-looking young officer and the stal-
wart trooper the lads who but two years and a half
before had ridden away post-haste from the Chace.
Hugh was driven off to the farm; and Rupert remained
alone with his mother and the colonel, who overwhelmed him with questions.

The colonel had changed but little, and bid fair to
live to a great age.   His eye was bright, and his bearing
still erect.   He scarcely looked sixty-five, although he
was more than ten years older.   Mistress Dorothy was,
Rupert thought, softer and kinder than of old.   Her
pride, and to some extent her heart, had met with a rude
shock, but her eyes were now fully open to the worth-
lessness of her former suitor, who had lately been
obliged to fly the country, having been detected at
cheating at cards.

Colonel Holliday rejoiced when he heard of the pipe
of prime Burgundy, which started from London on the
day Rupert left; while Mistress Dorothy was enchanted
with the stomacher, which her son produced from his
trunk.

"Have you ever heard from M. Dessin, grandfather?
You told me that he said he would write and tell you his
real name."

"I doubt not that he did so, Rupert; but the carriage of letters between this and France is precarious. Only smugglers or such like bring them over, and these, except when specially paid, care but little for the trouble. That he wrote I am certain, but his letter has not reached me, which I regret much."

The six months at home passed rapidly. Rupert fell into his old ways; rode and hawked, and occasionally paid state visits to the gentry of the neighbourhood, by whom, as one of Marlborough's soldiers, he was made much of.

"I think this soldiering life makes one restless, Master Rupert," Hugh said, one day when the time was approaching for their start; "I feel a longing to be with the troop again, to be at work and doing."

"I feel the same, Hugh; but you would not find it so, I think, if you had come home for good. Then you would have your regular pursuits on the farm, while now you have simply got tired of having no work to do. When the war is over, and we have done soldiering, you will settle down on one of the farms of the Chace. Madame says you shall have the first that falls vacant when you come home. Then you will take a wife, and be well content that you have seen the world, and have something to look back upon beyond a six miles' circuit of Derby."

The next campaign may be passed over briefly. The parsimony of England and Holland, and the indifference of Germany, spoiled all the plans of Marlborough, and lost the allies all the benfits of the victory of Blenheim. The French, in spite of their heavy losses, took the field in far greater force than the allies; and instead of the brilliant offensive campaign he had planned, Marlborough had to stand on the defensive.

The gallantry of his English troops, and the effect which Blenheim had produced upon the *morale* of the

French, enabled him to hold the ground won, and to
obtain several minor successes, one notably at the Dyle,
where Villeroi's troops were driven out of lines considered impregnable, but where the pusillanimity and ill-
will of the Dutch generals prevented any substantial
results being obtained; but no important action took
place, and the end of 1705 found things in nearly the
same state that 1704 had left them.

The non-success of the campaign undid some of the
harm which the success of that of 1704 had effected.   In
Flanders the genius of the duke had enabled the allies
to maintain their ground; but on the Rhine they had
done badly, and in Italy the French had carried all
before them; therefore while after Blenheim an apathy
had fallen on the victors, so now the extent of the danger moved them to fresh exertions.

Marlborough, after seeing his army into winter quarters, visited the capitals of Vienna, Berlin, and The
Hague, and again by the charm of his manner succeeded in pacifying jealousies, in healing quarrels, and
in obtaining the promises of vigorous action and larger
armaments in the spring.

The bad conduct of the Dutch generals had created
such a general cry of indignation through Europe, that
the States-General were compelled by the pressure of
public opinion to dismiss several of the men who had
most distinguished themselves by thwarting the plans
of Marlborough, and interposing on every occasion
between him and victory.   Consequently the campaign
of 1706 seemed likely to open with far brighter prospects of success than its predecessors had done.

Suddenly, however, all the arrangements broke down.
The Imperialists had just suffered another reverse in
Italy; and matters looked so desperate there, that Marlborough proposed to pass the Alps with an army of
40,000 men to their assistance, and there, as he would

have the warm co-operation of Prince Eugene instead of the cowardice of the Dutch generals, and the incapacity and obstinacy of the Prince of Baden, he anticipated the complete discomfiture of the French.

In these hopes, however, he was thwarted. The Prince of Baden would do nothing beyond defending his own dominion; the cabinets of Berlin and Copenhagen fell to quarrelling, and both refused to supply their promised contingents; the Hanoverians and Hessians had also grievances, and refused to join in any general plan, or to send their troops to form part of the allied army. Thus all ideas of a campaign in the south were destroyed; but Marlborough persuaded the Dutch to send 10,000 of the troops in their pay across the Alps to assist Prince Eugene, under the promise that he with the English and Dutch troops would defend Flanders.

So the campaign commenced; and on the 19th of May Marlborough joined his army, which lay encamped on the Dyle, on the French frontier. On the 22d a Danish contingent, which had at the last moment been despatched in answer to an urgent appeal of the duke, arrived; and his army now consisted of 73 battalions and 123 squadrons, in all 60,000 men, with 120 guns. Marshal Villeroi's force, which lay on the other side of the Dyle, consisted of 74 battalions and 128 squadrons—62,000 men, with 130 guns. They had also, as at Blenheim, the advantage that the troops were all of one nationality, and accustomed to act together, while Marlborough's army consisted of troops of three nations, at least half of them new to war, and unused to act with each other.

Marlborough opened the campaign by moving towards Tirlemont, with a view of laying siege to Namur, where many of the citizens were anxious to throw off the French yoke. Villeroi, anxious to cover Namur, moved his troops out from their quarters on

the Dyle to stop the advance of the allies, and bring on
a battle in the open field.

The ground taken up by the French marshal was exceedingly strong. Marlborough was aware of the great
importance of the position, and had made every effort
to be the first to seize it; but the French had less distance to march, and when the allied troops arrived
within sight of the ground, the French were already in
camp upon Mons St. André.

Mons St. André is an extensive and elevated plateau,
being, indeed, the highest ground in Brabant. From it
four rivers take their rise—the Great Gheet, the Little
Gheet, the Dyle, and the Mehaigne. The French camp
was placed immediately above the sources of the two
Gheets.

The plan of the battle should be examined carefully,
and the events of the great battle will then be understood without difficulty.

The descents from the plateau to the Great Gheet are
steep and abrupt. The other rivers rise in wet marshes,
in some places impassable. The French left was on
the crest of the ridge, above the marshes of the Little
Gheet, and extended to the village of Autre Eglise,
while the extreme right stood on the high ground over-
looking the sources of the Mehaigne. The village of
Tavieres, in front of the right, was strongly held; while
in the villages of Offuz and Ramilies, opposite their
centre, were numerous infantry, no less than twenty
battalions occupying Ramilies.

The great bulk of the French cavalry were arranged
in two lines on their right, the extreme right of their
cavalry being in front of the tomb, or barrow, of the
.ancient German hero Ottomond, the highest part of the
ridge, and commanding the whole field of battle.

Marlborough, having with the Dutch General Overkirk, a loyal and gallant old man, reconnoitred the
ground, immediately formed his plan of attack.

The French position was somewhat in the form of a bow, the ends being advanced. They would therefore have more difficulty in sending troops from one end to the other of their line than would the allies, who could move in a direct line along, as it were, the string of the bow; and the ground was sufficiently undulating to enable the movements of troops to be concealed from the enemy on the plateau.

The commanding position of Ottomond's tomb appeared the key of the whole battle-ground; and Marlborough determined to make his main attack on this point, first deceiving the enemy by a feigned attack on their left. Accordingly, he formed in a conspicuous position, a heavy column of attack, opposite the French left, and menacing the village of Autre Eglise.

Villeroi, believing that the main attack would be made there, moved a considerable body of his infantry from his centre behind Offuz, to reinforce Autre Eglise.

As the column of attack advanced, a large portion was withdrawn by a dip behind the rising ground on which the others advanced, and moved rapidly towards the left centre, the Danish horse, twenty squadrons strong, being directed to the same spot. The smoke of the advance towards Autre Eglise, and the nature of the ground, concealed all these movements from the French, who directed a very heavy artillery fire on the column advancing against Autre Eglise.

Suddenly the real attack began. Five Dutch battalions advanced against Tavieres; twelve battalions under General Schultz, supported by a strong reserve, moved to attack Ramilies.

The vehemence of their attack showed Villeroi that he had been deceived; but he had now no infantry available to move to reinforce the troops in the threatened villages. He therefore ordered fourteen squadrons of dragoons to dismount, and with two Swiss battalions to advance to the support of Tavieres. They arrived, however, too late, for before they could reach the spot, the Dutch battalions had, with great gallantry, carried the village; and the Duke of Marlborough, launching the Danish horse on the supports as they came up, cut them up terribly, and threw back the remnant in confusion upon the French cavalry, advancing to charge.

Overkirk now charged the French cavalry with the first line of the allied horse, broke and drove them back; but at this moment, when the allied cavalry were in disorder after their success, the second line of French cavalry, among whom were the Royal life guards, burst upon them, drove them back in great confusion, and restored the battle in that quarter.

The danger was great, for the victorious cavalry might have swept round, and fallen upon the rear of the infantry engaged in the attack upon Ramilies. Marlborough saw the danger, and putting himself at the head of seventeen squadron of dragoons, and sending an aide-de-camp to order up twenty squadrons still in reserve, charged the French life guards. The French batteries on the heights behind Ramilies poured in so dreadful a fire that the cavalry hesitated, and some French troopers recognizing the duke, made a dash at him as he rode ahead of the troops.

In an instant he was surrounded; but before any of his troops could ride to his rescue, he cut his way through the French troopers, sword in hand. As his horse tried to leap a wall it fell, and the enemy were again upon him. At this moment Rupert Holliday, whose troop was in the front line, arrived on the spot, followed by Hugh and half a dozen other troopers, and some of the Duke's personal staff. A desperate fight raged round the general, until the cavalry charged heavily down to the rescue of their beloved leader. But they were still overmatched and pressed backwards by the French guards. At this critical time, however, the twenty squadrons of the reserve arrived on the ground, and charged the French cavalry in front, while the Danish cavalry, who had been detained by the morasses, fell at the same moment on their flank, and the French cavalry fell back in confusion. Forming the allied cavalry in two lines, Marlborough led them forward in person, and sweeping aside all resistance, they halted not until they reached the summit of Ottomond's tomb, where they were visible to the whole army, while a tremendous shout told friend and foe alike that the key of the whole position had been gained, and victory in that part of the field secured.

All this time the twenty French battalions in Ramilies under the Marquis Maffie had fought obstinately, although far removed from succour. Gradually, however, they were driven out of the village; the British had fresh battalions of infantry available, and these were sent against them, and the victorious horse charging them in flank, they were almost all made prisoners or destroyed.

The fight had lasted but three hours, and the victory was complete on the right and left. The confusion was, however, great, and Marlborough halted his troops and re-formed them, before advancing to the final attack; while Marshal Villeroi strove on his part also to re-form his troops, and to take up a new front. The roads were, however, choked with baggage-waggons and artillery, and before the troops could take up their fresh posts, the allies were ready. The charge was sounded, and horse and foot advanced to the attack on the centre, while the troops who had commenced the battle by their demonstration against Autre Eglise joined in the general attack. Confused and disheartened, the French did not await the onslaught, but broke and fled. The Spanish and Bavarian horse guards made a gallant at-

tempt to stem the tide of defeat, but were cut to pieces.
The battle was now over. It was a rout and a pursuit,
and the British horse, under Lord Orkney, pursued the
fugitives until they reached Louvain, at two o'clock in
the morning.

In the battle of Ramilies the French lost in killed and
wounded 7000 men, and 6000 were taken prisoners.
They lost 52 guns, their whole baggage and pontoon
train, and 80 standards. Among the prisoners were the
Princes de Soubise and Rohan, while among the killed
were many nobles of the best blood of France.

The Allies lost 1066 killed and 2567 wounded, in all
3633 men.

But great as was the victory itself, the consequences
were even more important. Brussels, Louvain, Mech-
lin, Alost, Luise, and all the chief towns of Brabant,
speedily opened their gates to the conqueror; Ghent and
Bruges, Darn and Oudenarde, followed the example.
Of all the cities of Flanders, Antwerp, Ostend, Nieuport, and Dunkirk, with some smaller fortresses, alone
held out for the French.

The Duke of Marlborough issued the most stringent
orders for the protection and fair treatment of the inhabitants, and so won such general good-will among
the population, that when he advanced on Antwerp the
local troops and citizens insisted on a surrender; and the
French troops capitulated, on condition of being allowed to march out with the honours of war, and to be
escorted safely to the French frontier. Ostend was
then besieged, and captured after a brave resistance;
and then, after a desperate resistance, the important
and very strong fortress of Menin, was carried by assault, 1400 of the storming party, principally British,
being slain at the breach. Dindermande and Ath were
next taken, and the allied army then went into winter
quarters, after a campaign as successful, and far more
important in its results, than that of Blenheim.

CHAPTER XVII.

A PRISONER OF WAR.

IN the brilliant results which arose from the victory at Ramilies, Rupert Holliday had no share. The 5th dragoons formed part of the cavalry force which, when the battle was over, pursued the broken French cavalry to the gates of Hochstad.

In the pursuit, along a road encumbered with deserted waggons, tumbrils, and guns, the pursuers after nightfall became almost as much broken up as the pursued.

Rupert's horse towards the end of the pursuit went dead lame, and he dismounted in order to see if he could do anything to its hoof. He found a sharp stone tightly jammed in the shoe, and was struggling to get this out when the troop again moved forward. Not doubting that he would overtake them in a minute or two, and fearing that unless his horse was relieved of the stone it would become so lame that it would not be able to carry him back, Rupert hammered away at it with a large boulder from the road. It was a longer job than he had anticipated, and five minutes elapsed before he succeeded in getting the stone out, and then, mounting his horse, he rode briskly forward. Presently he came to a point where the road forked. He drew rein and listened, and thought he heard the tramping of horse on the road that led to the left. As he rode on the noise became louder, and in another five minutes he came up to the troop.

It was quite dark, and riding past the men, he made his way to the head of the column.

"I have had an awful bother in getting rid of that stone," he said, as he rode up to the leader. "I began to think that I should lose you altogether. It is quite a chance I took this road."

"An unfortunate chance, sir, for you; a fortunate one for us," the officer he addressed said in English, but with a strong accent, "since you are our prisoner," and as he spoke he laid his hand on Rupert's bridle.

Rupert gave an exclamation of horror at finding the mistake that he had made, but he saw at once that resistance would be useless.

"Je me rends, monsieur. But what horrible luck."

The three French officers at the head of the troop burst into a laugh.

"Monsieur," the one who had first spoken said, now in his native tongue, "we are indebted to you, for you have made us laugh, and heaven knows we have had little enough to laugh at to-day. But how came you here? Your cavalry have taken the upper road. We were drawn up to make a last charge, when we heard them turn off that way; and were, I can tell you, glad enough to get off without more fighting; we have had enough of it for one day."

As the speaker proceeded, Rupert became more and more convinced that he knew the voice; and the fact that the speaker was acquainted with English, the more convinced him that he was right.

"I stopped to get rid of a stone in my horse's hoof," he said. "If I had only had a fight for it I should not have minded, but not even to have the pleasure of exchanging a pass or two with one of you gentlemen is hard indeed."

"It is just as well that you did not," one of the officers said, "for M. le Marquis de Pignerolles is probably the best swordsman in our army."

"The Marquis de Pignerolles," Rupert said, courteously; "it would have been a pleasure to have crossed swords with him, but scarcely fair, for he knows already that he is not a match for me."

"What!" exclaimed the marquis himself, and the two officers, in astonishment. "You are pleased to joke, sir," the marquis said haughtily.

"Not at all," Rupert said, gravely. "You have met two persons who were your match. You remember M. Dalboy?"

"Dalboy!" the marquis said. "Surely, surely, le Maitre Dalboy, yet—?"

"No, I am assuredly not M. Dalboy," Rupert said. "And the other?"

The marquis reined in his horse suddenly.

"What!" he said, "you are—?"

"Rupert Holliday, my dear M. Dessin."

"My dear, dear lad," the marquis exclaimed, "what pleasure! what delight!" and drawing his horse by the side of Rupert he embraced him with affection.

"My friends," he said to the other officers, who were naturally astonished at this sudden recognition between their prisoner and their colonel, "gentlemen, this English officer is my very dear friend. What kindness have I not received from his grandfather during my time of exile! while to himself I am deeply indebted. What a fortunate chance, that if you were to have the bad luck to be made prisoner, you should fall into my hands of all men. I wish that I could let you go, but you know—"

"Of course, of course," Rupert said. "Really I am hardly sorry, since it has brought us together again."

"Did you recognize my name?" the marquis said.

"No indeed," Rupert answered. "The letter which, we doubted not, that you wrote to my grandfather, never came to hand, and we never knew what M. Dessin's real name was, so that Colonel Holliday did not know to whom to write in France."

"I wrote twice," the marquis said, "but I guessed that

14

the letters had never arrived; and the good gentleman your grandfather, he is still alive and well?"

"As well as ever," Rupert said, "and will be delighted to hear of you. Mademoiselle is well, I trust?"

"Quite well, and quite a belle at the court, I can assure you," the marquis said. "But there are the gates of Louvain. You will, of course, give me your parole not to try to escape, and then you can come straight to my quarters with me, and I need not report you for a day or so. We shall be in fearful confusion to-night, for half our army is crowding in here, and every one must shift for himself. Peste! what a beating you have given us! That Marlborough of yours is terrible. I know some people here," he said, turning to the officers; "they will take us four in, and the men must picket their horses in the courtyard and street, and lie down in their cloaks. To-morrow we will see what is to be done, and how many have escaped from the terrible débacle."

The streets of Louvain were crowded with fugitives, some of them had thrown themselves down by the sidewalks, utterly exhausted; others mingled with the anxious townsmen, and related the incidents of the disastrous day; while the horses stood, with drooping heads, huddled together along the middle of the street. It was only by making long détours that the Marquis de Pignerolles reached the house of which he was in search. Late as was the hour, the inmates were up, for the excitement at Louvain was so great that no one had thought of going to bed; and M. Cardol, his wife and family, did all in their power for their guests. Supper was quickly laid for the four gentlemen; a barrel of wine was broached for the troops, and what provisions were in the house were handed over to them.

"Now let us look at you," the Marquis de Pignerolles said, as they entered the brightly lighted room. "Ah, you are a man now; but your face has little changed—scarcely at all."

"I am scarcely a man yet," Rupert said, laughing. "I am just twenty now; it is rather more than four years since we parted, without even saying good-bye."

"Yes, indeed, Rupert. I tried to do you a good turn in the matter of the Brownlows. I hope it succeeded."

"It did indeed," Rupert said. "We are indeed indebted to you for your intervention then. You saved my lady mother from a wretched marriage, and you saved for me the lands of Windthrope Chace.

"Ah, I am glad it came off well. But I am your debtor still, mind that; and always shall be. And now to supper. First, though, I must introduce you formally to my comrades, and to our host and hostess, and their pretty daughters.

Very much surprised were the latter when they heard that the handsome young officer was an Englishman and a prisoner.

"He does not look very terrible, does he, this curly-haired young fellow, maidemoiselles; but he is one of those terrible horse which have broken the cavalry of the Maison du Roi to-day, and scattered the chivalry of France. As to himself, he is a Rustium, a Boabdil, if he has, as I doubt not, kept up his practice—" and he looked at Rupert, who nodded smilingly; for he had indeed, during the four years he had been in Flanders, not only practised assiduously in the regimental fencing salles, but had attended all the schools kept by the best Spanish, Italian, and German teachers, keeping himself in practice, and acquiring a fresh pass here, an ingenious defence there, and ever improving—"the first swordsman in France would run a poor chance against this good-tempered-looking lad with his blue eyes."

The French girls opened their eyes in astonishment, but they were not quite sure whether the marquis was not making fun of them.

"Parbleu!" the two officers exclaimed. "You are not in earnest surely, marquis?"

"I am, indeed, gentlemen; and I can claim some share of the merit, for I taught him myself, and before he was sixteen he was a better swordsman than I was; and as he loved the art, he will have gone on improving, and must be miraculous. By the way," he said, suddenly, "there was a story went through Flanders near four years back of the best swordsmen in the German army being killed by a mere boy in an English regiment, and I said then, I think that this must be my pupil; was it so?"

"It was," Rupert said; "it was a painful affair; but I was forced into it."

"Make no excuse, I beg," the marquis said, laughing. "Now, young ladies, let us to supper; but beware of this prisoner of war, for if he is only half as formidable with his eyes as with his wrist, it is all up with your poor hearts."

Then, with much merriment, the four officers sat down to table, their host and hostess joining for company, and the young ladies acting as attendants.

No one would have guessed that three of the party had formed part of an army which that day had been utterly routed, or that the other was their prisoner; but the temperament of the French enables them to recover speedily from misfortune; and although they had been dull and gloomy enough until Rupert so suddenly fell into their hands, the happy accident of his being known to their colonel, and the pleasure and excitement caused by the meeting, sufficed to put them in high spirits again, especially as their own corps had suffered but slightly in the action, having been in reserve on the left, and never engaged except in a few charges to cover the retreat.

When the battle was alluded to, the brows of the French officers clouded, and they denounced in angry terms the fatal blunder of the marshal of weakening his centre to strengthen the left against a feigned attack; but the subject soon changed again, for, as the marquis said,—

"It would be quite time to talk it over to-morrow, when they would know who had fallen, and what were the losses;" for from their position on the left, they had little idea of the terrible havoc which had been made among the best blood in France.

Long after all the others had retired, the marquis and Rupert sat together talking over old times. Rupert learned that even before he had left the Chace the marquis had received news that the order of banishment, which the king had passed against him because he had ventured to speak in public in terms of indignation at the wholesale persecution of the Protestants, had been rescinded, and that the estates, which had also been confiscated, were restored. The Protestant persecutions had become things of the past, the greater portion of the French Protestants having fled the country; and the powerful friends of De Pignerolles had never ceased to interest themselves in his favour. The king, too, was in need of experienced soldiers for the war which was about to break out; and lastly, and by the tone in which his friend spoke Rupert saw that the subject was rather a sore one, his Majesty wished to have Adèle near the court.

"Mademoiselle Dessin!" Rupert said, in astonishment.

"Well, not exactly Mademoiselle Dessin," the marquis said, smiling, "but La Marquise Adèle de Pignerolles, who is by her mother's side—she was a Montmorency—one of the richest heiresses in France, and as inheriting those lands, a royal ward, although I, her father, am alive."

"But even so," Rupert said, "what can his Majesty wish to have her at court for?"

"Because, as a very rich heiress, and as a very pretty one, her hand is a valuable prize, and his Majesty may well intend it as a reward to some courtier of high merit."

"Oh, M. Dessin!" Rupert said, earnestly; "surely you do not mean that?"

"I am sorry to say that I do, Master Rupert. The Grand Monarque is not in the habit of considering such trifles as hearts or inclinations in the bestowal of his royal wards; and although it is a sort of treason to say so, I would rather be back in England, or have Adèle to myself, and be able to give her to some worthy man whom she might love, than to see her hand held out as a prize of the courtiers of Versailles. I have lived long enough in England to have got some of your English notions, that a woman ought at least to have the right of refusal."

Rupert said nothing, but he felt sorry and fully of pity at the thought of the young girl he remembered so well being bestowed as a sort of royal gift upon some courtier, quite irrespective of the dictates of her own heart. After sitting some time in silence, the marquis changed the subject suddenly.

"I am afraid you will not be exchanged before next winter, Rupert; there are, no doubt, plenty of prisoners in Marlborough's hands, but the campaign is sure to be a stirring and rapid one after this defeat; he will strike heavy blows, and we shall be doing our best to avoid them. It will not be until the fighting is over that the negotiations for the exchange of prisoners will begin."

The next morning the Marquis de Pignerolles went off early to the headquarters of the commandant; and Rupert remained chatting with the family of his host. Two hours later he returned.

"Things are worse than I even feared," he said; "the royal guards are almost destroyed, and the destruction wrought in all our noble families is terrible. It is impossible to estimate our total loss at present, but it is put down at 20,000, including prisoners. In fact, as an army it has almost ceased to exist; and your Marlborough will be able to besiege the fortresses of Flanders as he likes. There has been a council of all the general officers here this morning. I am to carry some despatches to Versailles—not altogether a pleasant business, but some one must do it, and of course he will have heard the main incidents direct from Villeroi. I leave at noon, Rupert, and you will accompany me, unless indeed you would prefer remaining here on the chance of getting an earlier exchange."

Rupert naturally declared at once for the journey to Paris. Officers on parole were in those days treated with great courtesy, especially if they happened to have a powerful friend. He therefore looked forward to a pleasant stay in Paris, and to a renewal of his acquaintance with Adèle, and to a sight of the glories of Versailles, which, under Louis XIV., was the gayest, the most intellectual, and the most distinguished court of Europe.

Louis XIV. could not be termed a good man, but he was unquestionably a great king. He did much for France, whose greatness and power he strove to increase; and yet it was in no slight degree owing to his policy that, seventy years later, a tempest was to burst out in France, which was to sweep away the nobility and the crown itself; which was to deluge the soil of France with its best blood, to carry war through Europe, and to end at last by the prostration of France beneath the feet of the nations to whom she had been a scourge.

The tremendous efforts made by Louis XIV. to maintain the Spanish succession, which he had secured for France; the draining of the land of men; and the im-

poverishing of the nobles, who hesitated at no sacrifices
and efforts to enable the country to make head against
its foes, exhausted the land; while the immense extrava-
gance of the splendid court in the midst of an impover-
ished land, ruined not only by war, but by the destruction of its trade, by the exile of the best and most
industrious of its people on acount of their religion,
caused a deep and widespread discontent throughout
the towns and country of France.

Three hours later, Rupert set out with the Marquis
of Pignerolles and two troopers.   After two days' ride
through Belgium they reached Valenciennes, where the
uniform of Rupert, in the scarlet and bright cuirass of
the British dragoons, excited much attention, for British prisoners were rare in France.

On the evening of the fifth day they reached Paris,
where they rode to the mansion of the marquis.   Rupert
was aware that he would not see Adèle, who was, her
father had told him, at Versailles, under the care of
Madame de Soissons, one of the ladies of the court.
Rupert was told to consider himself at home; and then
the marquis rode on to Versailles.

"I saw his Majesty last night," he told Rupert when
he returned next morning, "and he was very gracious.
I hear that even Brousac, who brought the news of our
defeat, was kindly received.   I am told that he feels the
cutting up of his guards very much.   A grand entertainment, which was to have taken place this week, has
been postponed, and there will be no regular fêtes this
autumn.   I told his Majesty that I had brought you
with me on parole, and the manner of your capture.
He charged me to make the time pass pleasantly for
you, and to bring you down to Versailles, and to present you at the evening reception.   We must get tailors
to work at once, Rupert, for although you must of
course appear in uniform, that somewhat war-stained

coat of yours is scarcely fit for the most punctilious court in Europe. However, as they will have this coat for a model, the tailors will soon fashion you a suit which would pass muster as your uniform before Marlborough himself. I saw Adèle, and told her I had brought an English officer, who had galloped in the darkness into our ranks, as a prisoner. I did not mention your name. It will be amusing to see if she recognizes you. She was quite indignant at my taking you prisoner, and said that she thought soldiers ought not to take advantage of an accident of that kind. In fact, although Adèle, as I tell her, is very French at heart, the five years she passed in Derby have left a deep impression upon her. She was very happy at school; every one, as she says, was kind to her; and the result is, that although she rejoices over our victories in Italy and Germany, she talks very little about the Flanders campaign, about which, by the way, were she even as French as possible, there would not be anything very pleasant to say."

Rupert was at once furnished from the wardrobe of the marquis with clothes of all kinds, and as they were about the same height—although Rupert was somewhat broader and heavier—the things fitted well, and Rupert was able to go about Paris, without being an object of observation and curiosity by the people.

Rupert was somewhat disappointed in Paris. Its streets were narrower than those of London, and although the public buildings were fine, the Louvre especially being infinitely grander than the Palace of St. James, there was not anything like the bustle and rush of business which had struck Rupert so much on his arrival in London.

Upon arriving at Versailles, however, Rupert was struck with wonder. Nothing that he had seen could compare with the stately glories of Versailles, which was then the real capital of France. A wing of the magnificent palace was set apart for the reception of the nobles and military men whose business brought them for short periods to the court, and here apartments had been assigned to the marquis. The clothes had already been sent down by mounted lackeys, and Rupert was soon in full uniform again, the cuirass alone being laid aside. The laced scarlet coat, and the other items of attire, were strictly in accordance with the somewhat lax regulations as to the dress of an officer of dragoons; but the lace cravat falling in front, and the dress lace ruffles of the wrists, were certainly more ample than the Duke of Marlborough might have considered fit for strict regimental attire. But indeed there was little rule as to dress in those early days of a regular British army.

Rupert's knee-breeches were of white satin, and his waistcoat of thick brocaded silk of a delicate drab ground. Standing as he did some six feet high, with broad shoulders, and a merry, good-tempered face, with brown curls falling on his lace collar, the young lieutenant was as fine a looking specimen of a well-grown Englishman as could be desired.

"Ma foi!" the marquis said, when he came in in full dress to see if Rupert was ready, "we shall have the ladies of the court setting their caps at you, and I must hasten to warn my countrymen of your skill with the rapier, or you well be engaged in a dozen affairs of honour before you have been here as many days. No," he said, laughing at Rupert's gestures of dislike to duelling, "his gracious Majesty has strictly forbidden all duelling, and—well, I will not say that there is none of it, but it goes on behind the scenes, for exile from court is the least punishment, and in some cases rigorous imprisonment when any special protégé of the king has been wounded. And now, Rupert, it is time to be off.

The time for gathering in the antechamber is at hand. By the way, I have said nothing to the king of our former knowledge of each other. There were reasons why it was better not to mention the fact."

Rupert nodded as he buckled on his sword and prepared to accompany his friend.

Along stately corridors and broad galleries, whose magnificence astonished and delighted Rupert, they made their way until they reached the king's ante-chamber.

Here were assembled a large number of gentlemen, dressed in the extreme of fashion, some of whom saluted the marquis, and begged particulars of him concerning the late battles; for in those days news travelled slowly, newspapers were scarcely in existence, special correspondents were a race of men undreamed of.

To each of those who accosted him the marquis presented Rupert, who was soon chatting as if at St. James's instead of Versailles. In Flanders he had found that all the better classes spoke French, which was also used as the principal medium of communication between the officers of that many-tongued body the allied army, consequently he spoke it as fluently and well as he had done as a lad.

Presently the great door at the end of the antechamber was thrown back, and the assembled courtiers fell back on either side. Then one of the officers of the court entered, crying:

"The king, gentlemen, the king!"

And then Louis himself, followed by some of the highest officers of state, entered.

CHAPTER XVIII.

THE COURT OF VERSAILLES.

As the King of France entered the ante-chamber a dead hush fell upon all there, and Rupert Holliday looked eagerly to see what sort of man was the greatest sovereign in Europe.,

Louis was under middle height, in spite of his high-heeled shoes, but he had an air of dignity which fully redeemed his want of stature. Although he was sixty-six years of age, he was still handsome, and his eyes were bright, and his movements quick and vivacious.

The courtiers all bent low as the king moved slowly down the line, addressing a word here and there. The king's eye quickly caught that of the young Englishman, who with his companion was taller than the majority of those present.

Louis moved forward until he stopped before him.

"So, Sir Englishman," he said, "you are one of those who have been maltreating our soldiers. Methinks I have more reason than you have to complain of the fortune of war, but I trust that in your case the misfortune will be a light one, and that your stay in our court and capital will not be an unpleasant one."

"I have no reason, sire, to complain of the fortune of war," Rupert said, "since to it I owe the honour of seeing your gracious Majesty, and the most brilliant court in the world!"

"Spoken like a courtier," the king said with a slight smile. Pray consider yourself invited to all the fêtes at court and to all our entrées and receptions, and I hope that all will do their best to make your stay here agreeable."

Then with a slight inclination of the head he passed

on, saying in an audible tone to the nobles who walked next, but a little behind him,—

"This is not such a bear as are his island countrymen in general!"

"In another hour, Rupert, is the evening reception, at which the ladies of the court will be present; and although all set fêtes have been arrested owing to the news of the defeat at Flanders, yet as the king chooses to put a good face upon it, every one else will do the same, therefore you may expect a brilliant assembly. Adèle will of course be there. Shall I introduce you, or leave it to chance?"

"I would rather you left it to chance," Rupert said, "except, that as you do not desire it to be known that we have met before, it would be better that you should present me personally; but I should like to see if she will recognize me before you do so."

"My daughter is a young lady of the court of his most puissant Majesty Louis XIV," the marquis said, somewhat bitterly, "and has learned not to carry her heart upon her sleeve. But before you show yourself near her, I will just warn her by a word that a surprise may take place in the course of the evening, and that it is not always expedient to recognize people unless introduced formally. That will not be sufficient to give her any clue to your being here, but when she sees you she will recall my warning, and act prudently."

Presently they entered the immense apartment, or rather series of apartments, in which the receptions took place.

Here were gathered all the ladies of the court, all the courtiers, wits, and nobles of France, except those who were in their places with the army. There was little air of ceremony. All present were more or less acquainted with each other.

In a room screened off by curtains, the king was play-

ing at cards with a few highly privileged members of the
court, and he would presently walk through the long
suite of rooms, but while at cards his presence in no
ways weighed upon the assembly. Groups of ladies
sat on fauteuils surrounded by their admirers, with
whom volleys of light badinage, fun, and compliments
were exchanged.

Leaving Rupert talking to some of those to whom he
had been introduced in the king's ante-chamber, and
who were anxious to obey the royal command to make
themselves agreeable to him, the Marquis de Pignerolles
sauntered across the room to a young lady who was
sitting with three others, surrounded by a group of gentlemen.

Rupert was watching him, and saw him stoop over
the girl, for she was little more, and say a few words in
her ear. A surprised and somewhat puzzled expression passed across her face, and then as her father left
her she continued chatting as merrily as before.

Rupert could scarcely recognize in the lovely girl of
seventeen the little Adèle with whom he had danced and
walked little more than four years before.

Adèle de Pignerolles was English rather than French
in her style of beauty, for her hair was browner, and her
complexion fresher and clearer, than those of the great
majority of her countrywomen. She was vivacious, but
her residence in England had taught her a certain re-
straint of gesture and motion, and her admirers, and she
had many, spoke of her as l'Anglaise.

Rupert gradually moved away from those with whom
he was talking, and, moving round the group, went
through an open window on to a balcony, whence he
could hear what was being said by the lively party,
without his presence being noticed.

"You are cruel, Mademoiselle d'Etamps," one of the
courtiers said. "I believe you have no heart; you love

to drive us to distraction, to make us your slaves, and then you laugh at us."

"It is all you deserve, M. de Duc. One would as soon think of taking the adoration of a butterfly seriously. One is a flower, butterflies come round, and when they find no honey, flit away elsewhere. You amuse yourself, so do I. Talk about hearts, I do not believe in such things."

"That is treason," the young lady who sat next to her said, laughing. "Now, I am just the other way; I am always in love, but then I never can tell whom I love best, that is my trouble; you are all so nice, messieurs, that it is impossible for me to say whom I love most."

The young men laughed.

"And you, Mademoiselle de Rohan, will you confess?"

"Oh, I am quite different," she said. "I quite know whom I love best, but just as I am quite sure about it, he does something disagreeable or stupid—all men are really disagreeable or stupid when you get to know them—and so then I try another, but it is always with the same result."

"You are all very cruel," the Duc de Carolan laughed. "And you, Mademoiselle de Pignerolles? But I know what you will say, you have never seen any one worth loving."

Adèle did not answer; but her laughing friends insisted that as they confessed their inmost thoughts, she ought to do the same.

For a moment she looked serious, then she laughed, and again put on a demure air.

"Yes," said she, "I have had a grande passion, but it came to nothing."

A murmur of "Impossible!" ran round the circle.

"It was nearly four years ago," she said.

"Oh, nonsense, Adèle, you were a child four years ago," one of her companions said.,

"Of course I was a child," Adèle said, "but I suppose children can love, and I loved an English boy."

"Oh, oh, mademoiselle, an English boy!" and other amused cries ran round the circle.

"And did he love you, mademoiselle?" the Duc de Carolan asked.

"Oh, dear no," the girl answered. "I don't suppose I should have loved him if he had. But he was strong, and gentle, and brave, and he was nearly four years older than I was, and he always treated me with respect. Oh, yes, I loved him."

"He must have been the most insensible of boys," the Duc de Carolan said; "but no doubt he was very good and gentle, this youthful islander; but how do you know that he was brave?"

The sneering tone with which the duke spoke was clearly resented by Adèle, for her cheek flushed, and she spoke with an earnestness quite different from the half-laughing tone she had hitherto spoken in.

"I know that he was brave, M. le Duc, because he fought with, and ran through the body, a man who insulted me."

The girl spoke so earnestly that for a moment a hush fell upon the little group; and the Duc de Carolan, who clearly resented the warm tone in which she spoke, said,—

"Quite a hero of romance, mademoiselle. This unfortunate who incurred your Paladin's indignation was clearly more insolent than skilful, or Sir Amadis of sixteen could hardly have prevailed against the dragon."

This time Adèle de Pignerolles was seriously angry:

"M. le Duc de Carolan," she said quietly, "you have honoured me by professing some admiration of my poor person, and methinks that good taste would have demanded that you would have feigned, at least, some interest in the boy who championed my cause. I was wrong, even in merry jest, to touch on such a subject, but I thought that as French gentlemen you would understand that I was half serious, half jesting at myself for this girlish love of mine. He is not here to defend himself against your uncourteous remarks; but, M. le Duc, allow me to inform you that the fact that the person who insulted me paid for it almost with his life was no proof of his great want of skill, for monsieur my father will inform you, if you care to ask him, that had you stood opposite to my boy hero, the result would probably have been exactly the same; for, as I have often heard him say that this boy was fully a match for himself, I imagine that the chance of a nobleman who, with all his merits, has not, so far as I have heard, any great pretensions to special skill with his sword, would be slight indeed."

The duke, with an air of bitter mortification on his face, bowed before the indignant tone in which Adèle spoke; and as the little circle broke up, the rumour ran round the room that L'Anglaise had snubbed the Duc de Carolan in a crushing manner.

Scarcely had the duke, with a few murmured excuses, withdrawn from the group, than the marquis advanced towards his daughter with a tall figure by his side.

"Adèle," he said, "allow me to introduce to you the English officer whose own unlucky fate threw him into my hands. He desires to have the honour of your acquaintance. You may remember his name, for his family lived in the country in which we passed some time. Lieutenant Rupert Holliday, of the English dragoons."

Adèle had not looked up as her father spoke. As he crossed the room towards her she had glanced towards his companion, whose dress showed him to be the English officer who was as she knew, with him; but something in her father's tone of voice, still more the sentences with which he introduced the name, warned her that this was the surprise of which he had spoken, and the name, when it came at last, was almost expected. Had it not been for the manner in which she had just been speaking, and the vague wonder that flashed through her mind whether he could have heard her, she could have met Rupert, with such warning as she had had, as a perfect stranger. What she had said was perfectly true, that as a child he had been her hero; but a young girl's heroes seldom withstand the ordeal of a four years' absence, and Adèle was no exception. Rupert had gone out of her existence, and she had not thought of him, beyond an occasional feeling of wonder whether he was alive, for years; and had it not been for that unlucky speech—which, indeed, she could not have made had any of her girlish feeling remained, she could have met him as frankly and cordially as in the days when they danced together. In spite, therefore, of her efforts, it was with a heightened colour that, as demanded by etiquette, Adèle rose, and making a deep reverence in return to the even deeper bow of Rupert, extended her hand, which, taking the tips of the fingers, Rupert bent over and kissed; then, looking up in her face, he said,—

"The marquis your father has encouraged me to hope that you will take pity upon a poor prisoner, and forget and forgive his having fought against your compatriots."

Adèle adroitly took up the line thus offered to her, and was soon deep in a laughing contest with him as to the merits of their respective countries, and above all as to his opinion of French beauty. Rupert answered in the exaggerated compliments characteristic of the time. After talking with her for some little time he withdrew, saying that he should have the honour of calling upon the following day with her father.

The next day when they arrived Rupert was greeted with a frank smile of welcome.

"I am indeed glad to see you again, M. Rupert; but tell me why was that little farce of pretending that we were strangers, played yesterday?"

"It was my doing, Adèle," her father said. "You know what the king is. If he were aware that Rupert were an old friend of ours he would imagine all sorts of things."

"What sort of things, papa?"

"To begin with, that M. Rupert had come to carry you off from the various noblemen for one or other of whom his Majesty destines your hand."

The girl coloured.

"What nonsense! However," she went on, "it would anyhow make no difference so far as the king is concerned, for I am quite determined that I will go into a convent and let all my lands go to whomsoever his Majesty may think fit to give them rather than marry any one I don't care for. I couldn't do it even to please you, papa, so you may be quite sure I couldn't do it to please the king. And now let me look at you M. Rupert. I talked to you last night, but I did not fairly look at you. Yes, you are really very little altered except that you have grown into a man; but I should have known you anywhere. Now, would you have known me?"

"Not if I had met you in the street," Rupert said. "When I talk to you, and look at you closely, Mademoiselle Adèle Dessin comes back again; but at a casual glance you are simply Mademoiselle Adèle de Pignerolles."

"I wish I were Adèle Dessin again," she said. "I should be a thousand times happier living with my father than in this artificial court, where no one is what they seem to be; where every one considers it his duty to say complimentary things; where every one seems to be gay and happy, but every one is as much slaves as if they wore chains. I break out sometimes, and astonish them."

A slight smile passed over Rupert's face; and Adèle knew that he had overheard her the evening before. The girl flushed hotly. Her father and Madame de Soissons were talking together in a deep bay window at the end of the room.

"So you heard me last night, M. Rupert. Well, there is nothing to be ashamed of. You were my hero when I was a child; I don't mind saying so now. If you had made me your heroine it would have been different, but you never did, one bit. Now don't try to tell stories. I should find you out in a moment; I am accustomed to hear falsehoods all day."

"There is nothing to be ashamed of, mademoiselle. Every one must have a hero, and I was the only boy you knew. No one could have misunderstood you; and even to those artificial fops who were standing round you, there seemed nothing strange or unmaidenly in your avowal that when you were a little girl you made a hero of a boy. You are quite right, I did not make a heroine of you; boys, I think, always make heroines of women much older than themselves. I looked upon you as a dear, bright little girl, whom I would have cared for and protected as I would my favourite dog. Some boys are given to heroine-worship. I don't think that is my line. I am only just getting out of my boyhood now, and I have never had a heroine at all."

So they sat and chatted, easily and pleasantly, as if four years had been rolled back, and they were boy and girl again in the garden of Windthorpe Chace.

"I suppose I shall see you every evening at the court?" Rupert said.

"I suppose so," the girl sighed. "But it will be much more pleasant here; you will come with papa, won't you?"

"Whenever he will be good enough to bring me," Rupert said.

"You remember what I told you about Adèle," the marquis said, as they walked back to their rooms in the palace.

"Surely, sir," Rupert replied.

"I think it would be as well, both for her sake and your own, that you should not frequent her society in public, Rupert. His Majesty intends to give her hand to one of the half-dozen of his courtiers who are at present intriguing for it. Happily, as she is little over sixteen, although marriages here are often made at that age, the question does not press; and I trust that he will not decide for a year, or even longer. But if you were to be seen much at her side, it might be considered that you were a possible rival, and you might, if the king thought that there was the slightest risk of your interfering with his plans, find yourself shut up in the Bastille or at Loches, or some other of the fortress dungeons, and Adèle might be ordered to give her hand at once to the man he selected for her. There is hope in time. Adèle may in time really come to love one of her suitors, and if he were one of those whom the king would like to favour, he would probably consent to the match. Then, the king may die. It is treason even to suppose such a thing possible; still he is but mortal; or something else may occur to change the course of the future. Of one thing I have decided: I will not see Adèle sacrificed. I have for the last four years managed to transmit a considerable portion of the revenues of my estates to the hands of a banker in Holland; and if needs be I will again become an exile with her, and wait patiently until some less absolute monarch mounts the throne."

It was not so easy, however, to silence the mouths of the gossips of Versailles as the Marquis de Pignerolles

had hoped. It was true that Rupert was seldom seen
by the side of Adèle in the drawing-room of the palace,
but it was soon noticed that he called regularly every
morning with the marquis at Madame de Soissons', and
that, however long the visits of the marquis might be,
the young English officer remained until he left.

Adèle's English bringing up, and her avowed liking
for things English, were remembered; and the Duc de
Carolan, and the other aspirants to Adèle's hand, began
to scowl angrily at the young Englishman whenever
they met him.

Upon the other hand, among the ladies Rupert was a
general favourite, but he puzzled them altogether. He
was ready to chat, to pay compliments, to act as chevalier to any lady, but his compliments never passed beyond the boundary of mere courtly expression; and in a
court where it appeared to be almost the duty of every
one to be in love, Rupert Holliday did not seem to
know what love meant.

The oddness of this dashing-looking young officer—
who was, the Marquis de Pignerolles assured every one,
a very gallant soldier, and who had killed in a duel the
finest swordsman in the German army—being perfectly
proof to all blandishments, and ready to treat every
woman with equal courtesy and attention, was a mystery to the ladies of the court of Versailles; and Rupert
was regarded as a most novel and amusing specimen of
English coldness and impenetrability.

Rupert himself was absolutely ignorant of the opinion
with which men and women alike regarded him. He
dreamt not that it was only the character which so high
an authority as the Marquis de Pignerolles had given
him as a swordsman of extraordinary skill, that prevented the Duc de Carolan and some of Adèle's other
admirers from forcing a quarrel upon him; still less did
he imagaine that the ladies of the court considered it in

the highest degree singular that he did not fall in love with any of them. He went his way, laughed, talked, was pleasant with every one, and enjoyed his life, especially his morning visits to Madame de Soissons.

The first intimation that was given of the jealousy with which the Duc de Carolan and others regarded Rupert, was a brief order that the Marquis de Pignerolles received from the king to retire with his prisoner to Paris, an intimation being given that although the marquis would as heretofore be received at court, yet that Rupert was not to leave the circuit of the walls of Paris. The marquis, who had foreseen the gathering storm in a hundred petty symptoms, was not surprised at the order. He knew the jealousy with which the king regarded any person who appeared even remotely likely to interfere with any plans that he had formed, and was sure that a mere hint from some favourite as to the possibility of Rupert's intimacy at Madame de Soissons proving an obstacle to the carrying out of his wishes with regard to the disposal of Adèle's hand, would be sufficient to ensure the issue of an order for his instant dismissal from Versailles. Rupert was astonished and indignant at the order.

"At any rate I may call and say 'Good-bye' to mademoiselle, may I not?"

"I think that you had better not, Rupert; but I have simply orders to leave Versailles at one o'clock to-day. I can therefore only ask you to be here at that hour. It is now eleven."

"Very well, sir," Rupert said, "I will be here in time; and as I am not a prisoner, and can go about where I like, I do not think that even the king could object to my paying a visit of adieu."

On presenting himself at Madame de Soissons', Rupert heard that, in accordance with the king's command that morning received, Madame de Soissons and Mademoiselle de Pignerolles had gone out to the hunt, one of the royal carriages having come for them."

Rupert, determined not to be baulked, hurried back to the stables where the horses of the marquis, one of which was always at his disposal, were kept. In a few minutes he was riding out towards the forest of St. Germains, where he learned that the royal chase had gone.

He rode for some time, until at last he came up with one of the royal carriages which had got separated from the others. He saw at once that it contained two of the ladies of the court with whom he was most intimate. They gave an exclamation of surprise as he reined up his horse at the window.

"You, Monsieur Holliday! How imprudent! Every one knows that you are in disgrace, and exiled to Paris; how foolish of you to come here!"

"I have done nothing to be ashamed of," Rupert said. "Besides, I was ordered to leave at one o'clock, and it is not one o'clock yet."

"Oh, we are all angry with you, M. l'Anglais, for you have been deceiving us all for the last three months; but, now mind, we bear no malice; but pray ride off."

As she spoke she made a sign to Rupert to alight and come to the window, so that the coachman might not overhear what was said.

"Do you know," she said, earnestly, "that you are trifling with your safety, and, if la belle Anglaise loves you, with her happiness? You have already done more than harm enough. The king has to-day, when he joined the hunt, presented to her formally before all the court the Duc de Carolan as her future husband. Remember, if you are found here you will not only be sent straight to some fortress, where you may remain till you are an old man, but you will do her harm by compromising her still further, in which case the king might be so enraged, that he might order her to marry the duke to-morrow."

"You are right. Thank you," Rupert said, quietly; "and I have indeed, although most unwittingly done harm. Why you should all make up your minds I love Mademoiselle de Pignerolles I know not. I have never thought of the matter myself. I am but just twenty, and at twenty in England we are still little more than boys. I only know that I liked her very much, just as I did when she was a little girl."

"Oh, monsieur, but you are sly, you and l'Anglaise. So it was you that she owned was her hero; and the monsieur the marquis introduced you as a stranger. Oh, what innocence! but there," she went on kindly, "you know your secret is safe with us. And, monsieur," and she leant forward, "although you would not make love to me, I bear no malice, and will act as your deputy. A very strict watch is certain to be kept over her; if you want to write to her, enclose a note to me; trust me, she shall have it. There, do not stop to thank me; I hear horses' hoofs; gallop away, please; it would ruin all were you caught here."

Rupert pressed the hands the two ladies held out to him to his lips, mounted his horse, and rode furiously back to Versailles, where he arrived just in time to leave again for Paris at the hour beyond which their stay was not to be delayed.

CHAPTER XIX.

THE EVASION.

Upon the ride from Versailles to Paris Rupert told the marquis what he had done and heard.

"It is bad news, Rupert. I will ride back this afternoon, when I have lodged you in Paris, and see Adèle. If she objects—as I know she will object to this marriage—I shall respectfully protest. That any good will come of the protest I have no thought, but my protest may strengthen Adèle's refusal, by showing that she has her father's approval. Adèle will of course be treated coldly at first, then she will have pressure put upon her, then be ordered to choose between a convent and marriage. She will choose a convent. Now in some convents she could live quietly and happily, in others she would be persecuted. If she is sent to a convent chosen for her, it will be worse than a prison. Her life will be made a burden to her until she consents to obey the king's command. Therefore, my object will be to secure her retreat to a convent where she will be well treated and happy. But we will talk of this again."

It was not until the following afternoon that the marquis returned from Versailles.

"I am off to the front again," he said. "I had an audience with his Majesty this morning, and respectfully informed him of my daughter's incurable repugnance to the Duc de Carolan, and of her desire to remain single until at least she reached the age of twenty. His Majesty was pleased to say that girls' whims were matters to which it behoved not to pay any attention. He said, however, that for the present he would allow it to remain in abeyance, and that he begged me to see Adèle, and to urge upon her the necessity for making up her mind to accept his Majesty's choice. He also said that the news from the army was bad, that good officers were urgently required there, and that it would be therefore advisable for me to repair at once to the front and again take the command of my regiment. He said that he wished me to take you with me as far as Lille, and that you should there take up your residence."

"Of course I will accompany you, sir," Rupert said; "but I will withdraw my parole as soon as you hand me over, and take my chance of escaping."

"Yes, I should do that, Rupert; indeed, as you gave your parole to me, you can give it back to me now, if you choose. I will run the risk of some little anger on the part of the king, if you quit me on your way to Lille and make the best of your way to the frontier."

"No, I thank you," Rupert said; "there can't be much difficulty in escaping from a town when one wants to do so; and it would do you an evil turn indeed to incense the king against you at the present time."

The next morning, just as they were setting out, a lackey placed a note in Rupert's hands.

"I hear you are sent off to Lille. I have a cousin there, and have written to recommend you to his care. I will keep my promise, and let you know, if needs be, of what is happening to the young person we spoke of.—DIANA."

Rupert wrote a few words of earnest thanks, and imitating the example set him, gave it unaddressed and unsigned to the lackey, with a handsome present to himself.

On the way to Lille, the marquis told Rupert his plans for the withdrawal of Adèle from court, and her concealment, should Louis insist on the marriage being pressed on.

Arriving at Lille, Rupert was handed over to the gov-

ernor, and having formally withdrawn his parole to
make no effort to escape, he was assigned quarters in
barracks, whence he was allowed to go into the town
during daylight, being obliged, however, to attend at
roll-call at midday.   The fortifications of the town were
so strong and well-guarded that it was supposed that
the chance of escape was small.

The following day the Marquis de Pignerolles took
an affectionate leave of Rupert and went on to join the
army; and an hour or two later Captain Louis
d'Etamps, the cousin of whom Diana had written, called
upon him, and placed himself at his service.   His cousin had told him of the supposed crime for which Rupert had been sent away from court, and felt much sym-
pathy with what she considered his hard treatment.   Not
only Louis d'Etamps, but the French officers of the
garrison showed great kindness and attention to the
English prisoner, for the Duke of Marlborough had
treated the French officers who fell into his hands at
Ramilies with such kindness and courtesy that the
French were glad to have an opportunity of reciprocat-
ing the treatment when the chance fell in their way.
Late in the autumn, the Marquis de Pignerolles was
brought back to Lille seriously wounded in one of the
last skirmishes of the campaign.   Rupert spent all the
time he was allowed to be out of barracks at his friend's
quarters.   The wound was not considered dangerous,
but it would keep the marquis a prisoner to his room for
weeks.

A few days after the marquis was brought in, Louis
d'Etamps came into Rupert's room early in the morning.

"I have a note for you from my fair cousin," he said.
"It must be something particular, for she has sent a
special messenger with a letter to me, and on opening it
I found only a line asking me to give you the enclosed

instantly. Rupert opened the letter from Diana d'Etamps; it was as follows:—

"Adèle has been ordered to marry the Duc de Carolan on the 15th; unless she consents, she is on the 14th to be sent to the nunnery of St. Marie, the strictest in France, where they will somehow or other wring consent from her before many weeks are over. They have done so in scores of cases like hers. I promised to tell you, and I have done so. But I don't see that anything can be done. I hear Monsieur le Marquis is badly wounded, but even were he here, he could do nothing. The king is resolute. The Duc de Carolan has just given 200,000 crowns towards the expenses of the war."

"May I see?" Louis d'Etamps said, for the young men were now fast friends.

Rupert handed him the note.

"What can you do, my poor boy?" he said.

"I will go and see the marquis, and let you know afterwards," Rupert said. "I shall do something, you may be sure."

"If you do, you will want to escape from Lille. I will see about the arrangements for that. There is no time to be lost. It is the 10th to-day."

Rupert's conversation with the Marquis de Pignerolles was long and interesting. The marquis chafed at being confined to a sick bed and permitting Rupert to run the risk, which was immense, of the attempt alone. However, as he could not move, and as Rupert was determined to do something, the marquis entered into all the plans he had drawn up, and intended to follow when such an emergency occurred. He gave him a letter for Adèle, and then they parted.

At his room Rupert found Louis.

"Quick," he said, "there is no time to lose; at ten o'clock a convoy of wounded leave for Paris. The doctor in charge is a friend of mine and a capital fellow. I have just seen him. All is arranged. Come along to my quarters, they are on the line that the convoy goes to the gate. Jump in bed, then I will bandage up your head with plaisters so that not more than space to see and breathe out of will be left. When the convoy arrives at the door, he will have an empty litter ready, will bring up four men who will lift you in, supposing you to be a wounded French officer, carry you down, and off you go with the convoy, not a soul save the doctor, you, and I, the wiser. He has got a pass to leave the city with forty-eight sick and ten soldiers, and he has only to tell one of those marked to go that he is not well enough to be moved, and will go with the next convoy. The messenger who brought the letter has started again, and has taken with him a led horse of mine. He will be at the hostelry of Henri IV, at the place where you will stop to-night. He will not know who you are, I have told him that a friend of mine will call for the horse, which I had promised to send him. When you halt for the night, the doctor will order you to be carried into his own room. You will find two or three suits of clothes in the litter, a lackey's suit of our livery which may be useful, a country gentleman's, and one of mine. When you are alone with the doctor and all is safe, get up, put on the country gentleman's suit, say good-bye to him and go straight to the stables at the Henri IV. You are the Sire de Nadar. I have written a note here, telling you the horse will be there and you are to fetch it—here it is. The messenger will know my seal."

"I am indeed obliged to you," Rupert said, "you have thought of everything; but how will the doctor explain my not being forthcoming in the morning?"

"Oh, he will arrange that easily enough. The soldiers will all sleep soundly enough after this march; besides, they will not, in all probability, be near his quar-

ters, so he will only have to say that he found you were
too ill to continue the journey, and had therefore had
you carried to a confrere of his. You must be under
no fear, Rupert, of any evil consequences to any one,
for no one will ever connect you with the convoy. You
will be missed at roll-call, but that will go for nothing.
When you are absent again at six o'clock, you will be
reported as missing. Then it will be supposed that you
are hid in the city, and a sharp watch will be set at the
gates; but after a few days it will be supposed that you
have either got over the walls, or that you have gone
out disguised as a peasant. A prisoner of war more or
less makes but little difference, and there will never be
any fuss about it."

Soon after dusk on the evening of the 13th of October, Adèle de Pigncrolles was sitting alone in a large
room in the house of Madame de Soissons. A wood
fire was blazing, and even in that doubtful light it might
have been seen that the girl's eyes were swollen with
crying. She was not crying now, but was looking into
the fire with a set, determined look in her face.

"I don't care," she said; "they may kill me at St.
Marie, but I will never say yes. Oh, if papa were but
here."

At that moment there was a knock at the door, and a
bright-looking waiting-maid entered.

"A note, mademoiselle, from Mademoiselle d'Etamps
—and mademoiselle," and she put her finger mysteri-
ously to her lips, "it is a new lackey has brought it. I
told him to come again in ten minutes for an answer;
for I thought it better he should not come in to be
looked at by Francois and Jules."

"Why not, Margot?" Adèle asked in great surprise.

"Because, mademoiselle, he seemed to me—I may be
wrong, you know—but he seemed to me very, very
like—"

"Like whom, Margot?   How mysterious you are."

"Like the English officer," Margot said, with an arch nod.

Adèle leapt to her feet.

"You must be mad, Margot.   There, light a candle." But without waiting, Adèle knelt down close to the fire, and broke open the letter.

A flush, even ruddier than that given by the fire, mounted over her face.

"It is him, Margot.   He has come from my father. Now we are to do what I told you about.   We are to go off to-night under his charge, to your mother's, my dear old nurse, and there I am to live with you, and be as your cousin, till papa can get me out of the country."

"And is the young officer to live there till the marquis comes?" Margot asked, slily; "he might pass as another cousin, mademoiselle."

"How foolish you are, Margot, and this is no time for folly.   But listen.   My father says, 'Rupert will be in the street round the corner, with three horses, at eleven o'clock.   You and Margot are to be dressed in the boys' clothes that I bade you prepare.   Take in bundles two of Margot's dresses.   Do not be afraid to trust yourself with Rupert Holliday; regard him as a brother; he has all my confidence and trust.' "

"We must remember that," Margot said.

"Remember what, Margot?"

"Only that you are to regard him as a brother, made-moiselle."

"Margot, Margot, I am surprised at you, joking like a child when we have a terrible business before us.   But indeed I feel so happy at the thought of escape from that terrible convent, that I could joke like a child also."

"You had better write a line for him, mademoiselle. It was from chance that I happened to be in the hall when he rang; and we don't want him to come in to be stared at by Francois while you write an answer."

Quickly Adèle sat down at a table, and wrote,—
"At the hour and place named, expect us.—Yours,
trustfully, ADELE."

As the clock struck eleven two slight figures stole
noiselessly out of the garden gate of Madame de Soissons' house at Versailles. The town was hushed in
sleep, and not a sound was moving in the street. They
carried bundles with them, and walked with rapid steps
to a small lane which led off the street by the side of the
garden wall. It was quite dark, and they could see
nothing, but a voice said,—"Adèle!"

"Rupert!" one of the figures answered, in shy, trem-
bling tones.

"Please stay where you are," Rupert said; "it is
lighter in the street."

The horses were led forth noiselessly, for Rupert had
fastened cloths round their feet, to prevent the iron
shoes sounding on the round pebbles which paved the
streets.

Not a word was said. There was a warm clasp of
the hand, and Rupert lifted Adèle into the saddle; Margot climbed into another, and the three rode rapidly
down the streets. Not a word was spoken until they
were in the open country.

"Thank God, you are safe thus far, Adèle. The last
time I helped you on to a horse was the day you went
out to see my hawk kill a heron."

"Oh, Rupert," the girl said, "it seems like a dream.
But please do not let us talk yet about ourselves. Tell
me about papa. How is he?"

Rupert told her; and gradually as they talked the excitement and agitation passed off.

"And where did you get the horses, Rupert?"

"The one I am riding is Louis d'Etamps'," he said,
"the others are your father's. I brought orders from
him to his steward in Paris, that two of his best horses

16

were to be sent this morning to a stable in Versailles, and left there, and that a person with an order from him would call for them."

"I cannot see you in the least; are you dressed as M. d'Etamps' lackey still?"

"No, I am now a quiet country gentleman, riding down from Paris with my two sons, who have been up with me to see their aunt who lives in the Rue du Temple."

"Talk French, please, Rupert; Margot will understand then; and she is so brave and good, and shares my danger, so she ought to be as one of us."

Adèle's spirits rose as they got farther from Versailles, and they talked and laughed cheerfully, but in low tones.

Three miles from Versailles, as they rode past a cross-road, two mounted men dashed out suddenly.

"Stand, in the king's name! Who are you?"

"We are travellers," Rupert said, quietly, "and go where we will. Who are you?"

"We are guards of the court, and we must know who you are before we suffer you to pass. None ride at night near Versailles but with a pass."

"I am an exception then," Rupert said, "and I advise you not to interfere with us," and he urged his horse a few feet in advance of his companions.

One of the horsemen seized his bridle, while another drew a pistol.

Rupert's sword leaped from its scabbard and cut down the man who held the rein. The other fired, but Rupert threw himself forward on the horse's neck and the bullet whizzed over his head; he rode at the garde, and with a heavy blow with the pommel of the sword struck him senseless from his horse.

"Now," he said to Adèle, "we can ride on again. You are not frightened, I hope?"

"Not so frightened as I was the first time you drew sword in my behalf," the girl said; "but it is very dreadful. Are they killed, Rupert?"

"Not a bit of it," Rupert said; "one has got a gash on the head which will cost him a crown in plaister, the other may have lost some teeth. It would have been wise to have killed them, for their tale in the morning is likely to be regarded as throwing some light upon your disappearance; but I could not kill men who were only doing their duty. At any rate we have twelve hours' start, even if they take up the clue and pursue us on this line to-morrow. It is about ten miles this side of Poitiers that your mother lives, is it not, Margot?"

"Yes, M. Rupert. How surprised she will be at my arrival with my cousins."

"Oh, we are both your cousins, are we, Margot?"

"Mademoiselle Adèle is to pass as my cousin, monsieur, and I suppose you must be either another cousin, or else her brother."

"Margot," Adèle said, "you chatter too much."

"Do I, mademoiselle? It is better than riding through the darkness without speaking. I was very glad when the cloths were off the horses' feet, for we seemed like a party of ghosts."

"How long shall we be getting there?" Adèle asked, presently.

"Six days, if we do it all with the same horses," Rupert said; "and I am afraid to hire horses and leave them on the way, as it would look as if we were pressed for time. No, for to-day we are safe—but for to-day only. Messengers will be sent in all directions with orders for our arrest. They will take fresh relays of horses; and really our only hope is in disguise. I propose that we go the first stage without halting as far as our horses will carry us. I think we can get to Orleans. There we will put them up and take rooms. Then Margot must slip out in her own dress and buy two peasant girls' attire, and I will pick up at some dealer in old clothes a suit which will enable me to pass as a wounded soldier making his way home. Then we will strike off from the main road and follow the lanes and get on some other road. They will inquire all along the road and will hear of a gentleman and two youths, and will for a while have that in their minds. No one will particularly notice us, and we shall get into Tours safely enough. We must never enter a house or town together, for they will be on the look out for three people, and neither a soldier with his head bound up, nor two peasant girls, will attract attention. At Tours I will get a farmer's dress, and will buy a horse and cart, and a load of hay, and will pick you up outside the town. You can get on the hay, and can cover yourselves over if you see any horsemen in pursuit; after that it will be all easy work."

"Why could you not get the cart at Orleans, Rupert?" Adèle asked.

"I might," he said; "but I think that the extra change would be best, as they would then have no clue whatever to follow. They will trace us to Orleans, and you may be sure that there will be a hot hue and cry, and it may be that the fact of a horse and cart having been sold would come out. They will not know whether we have made east, west, or south from there, so there will be a far less active search at Tours than there will at Orleans."

So the journey was carried out, and without any serious adventure, although with a great many slight alarms, and some narrow escapes of detection, which cannot be here detailed, the party arrived at the spot where the lane leading to the little farm occupied by Margot's mother left the main road. Here they parted, the girls taking their bundles, and starting to trudge the last few miles on foot. Margot discreetly went on a little ahead, to give her mistress the opportunity of speaking to Rupert alone, but she need not have done so, for all that Rupert said was,—

"I have been in the light of your brother this time, Adèle, as your father gave you into my charge. If I ever come again, dear, it will be different."

"You are very good, Rupert. Good-bye;" and with a wave of the hand she ran after Margot; while Rupert, mounting the cart, drove on into Poitiers.

Here he sold his load of hay to a stable-keeper, drove a mile or two out of the town, entered a wood, and then took the horse out of the cart, and leaving the latter in a spot where, according to all appearances, it was not likely to be seen for months, drove the horse still further into the wood, and, placing a pistol to its head, shot it dead. Then he renewed his disguise as a soldier, but this time dispensed with the greater part of his bandages, and set out on his return, in high spirits at having so successfully performed his journey.

He pursued his journey as far back as Blois without the slightest interruption, but here his tramp came to a sudden termination. Secure in the excellence of his French, Rupert had attempted no disguise as to his face beyond such as was given by a strip of plaister, running from the upper lip to the temple. He strode gaily along, sometimes walking alone, sometimes joining some other wayfarer, telling every one that he was from Bordeaux, where he had been to see his parents, and get cured of a sabre cut.

As he passed through the town of Blois, Rupert suddenly came upon a group of horsemen. Saluting as he passed—for in those days in France no one of inferior rank passed one of the upper classes without uncovering—he went steadily on.

"That is a proper looking fellow," one of the party said, looking after him.

"By our Lady," exclaimed another, "I believe I have seen that head and shoulders before. Yes, I feel sure. Gentlemen, we have made a prize: unless I am greatly mistaken, this is the villainous Englishman who it is believed aided that malapert young lady to escape."

In another moment Rupert was surrounded, his hat was knocked off, and the Duc de Carolan, for it was he, exclaimed in delight,—

"I thought that I could not be mistaken, it is himself."

Rupert attempted no resistance, for alone and on foot it would have been hopeless.

The governor of the royal castle of Blois was one of the party, and Rupert found himself in another ten minutes standing, with guards on each side of him, before a table in the governor's room, with the governor and the Duc de Carolan sitting as judges before him.

"I have nothing to say," Rupert said, quietly. "I escaped from Lille because I had been, as I deemed it, unworthily treated in Paris. I had withdrawn my parole, and was therefore free to escape if I could. I did escape, but finding the frontier swarmed with French troops, I thought it safer to make for central France, where a wayfarer would not be looked upon as suspiciously as in the north. Here I am. I decline to answer any further questions. As to the lady of whom you question me, I rejoice to find, by the drift of your questions, that she has withdrawn herself from the persecution which she suffered, and has escaped being forced into marriage with a man whom she once described in my hearing as an ape in the costume of the day."

"And that is all you will say, prisoner?" the governor asked, while the Duc de Carolan gave an exclamation of fury.

"That is all, sir; and I would urge, that as an English officer I am entitled to fair and honourable treatment, for although I might have been shot in the act of trying to escape from prison, it is the rule that an escaping prisoner caught afterwards, as I am, should have fair treatment, although his imprisonment should be stricter and more secure than before. As to the other matter, there cannot be, I am assured, even a tittle of evidence to connect me with the event you mention. As far as I hear from you, I escaped on the 10th from Lille, which date is indeed accurate. Three days later Mademoiselle de Pignerolles left Versailles. The connexion between the two events does not appear in any way clear to me."

"It may or it may not be," the governor said; "however, my duty is clear, to keep you here in safe ward until I receive his Majesty's orders."

Four days later the royal order came. Rupert was to be taken to the dreaded fortress prison of Loches, a place from which not one in a hundred of those who entered in ever came forth alive.

CHAPTER XX.

LOCHES.

"A BRITISH officer, broke out from Lille, Ah!" the
Governor of Loches said to himself, as he glanced over
the royal order. "Something else beyond that, I fancy.
Prisoners of war who try to break prison are not sent to
Loches. I suppose he has been in somebody's way
very seriously. A fine young fellow, too—a really
splendid fellow. A pity really; however, it is not my
business. Number four, in the south tower," he said,
and Rupert was led away.

Number four was a cell on the third story of the south
tower. More than that Rupert did not know. There
was no looking out from the loopholes that admitted
light, for they were boarded up on the outside. There
was a fireplace, a table, a chair, and a bedstead. Twice
a day a goaler entered with provisions; he made no reply to Rupert's questions, but shook his head when
spoken to.

For the first week Rupert bore his imprisonment
with cheerfulness, but the absolute silence, the absence
of anything to break the dreary monotony, the probability that he might remain a prisoner all his life, was
crushing even to the most active and energetic temperament.

At the end of a month the gaoler made a motion for
him to follow him. Ascending the stairs to a great
height, they reached the platform on the top of the
tower.

Rupert was delighted with the sight of the sky, and
of the wide-spreading fields—even though the latter was
covered with snow. For a half-an-hour he paced rap-

idly round and round the limited walk. Presently the
gaoler touched him, and pointing below, said,—

"Look!"

Rupert looked over the battlement, and saw a little
party issue from a small postern gate far below him,
cross the broad fosse, and pause in an open space
formed by an outlying work beyond. They bore with
them a box.

"A funeral?" Rupert asked.

The man nodded.

"They all go out at last," he said, "but unless they tell
what they are wanted to tell, they go no other way."

Five minutes later Rupert was again locked up in his
cell, when he was, in the afternoon of the same day, visited by the governor, who asked if he would say where
he had taken Mademoiselle Pignerolles. "You may as
well answer," he said; "you will never go out alive unless you do."

Rupert shook his head.

"I do not admit that I know aught concerning the
lady you name; but did I do so, I should prefer death
to betraying her."

"Ay," the governor said, "you might do that; but
death is very preferable to life at Loches."

In a day or two Rupert found himself again despond-
ing.

"This will not do," he said earnestly, "I must arouse
myself. Let me think, what have I heard that prisoners do? In the first place they try to escape; and some
have escaped from places as difficult as Loches. Well,
that is one thing to be thought very seriously about. In
the next place, I have heard of their making pets of spiders and all sorts of things. Well, I may come to that,
but at present I don't like spiders well enough to make
pets of them; besides I don't see any spiders to make
pets of. Then some prisoners have carved walls, but I

have no taste for carving. I might keep my muscles in
order and my health good by exercise with the chair and
table, get to hold them out at arm's length, lift the table with one hand, and so on. Yes, all sorts of exercise
might be continued in that way, and the more I take
exercise the better I shall sleep at night and enjoy my
meals. Yes, with nothing else to do I might become
almost a Samson here. There, now my whole time is
marked out—escape from prison, and exercise. I'll try
the last first, and then think over the other."

For a long time Rupert worked away with his furniture until he had quite exhausted himself; then feeling
happier and better than he had done since he was shut
up, he began to think of plans to escape. The easiest
way would of course be to knock down and gag the
gaoler, and to escape in the clothes; but this plan he put
aside at once, as it was morally certain that he should be
no nearer to his escape after reaching the courtyard of
the prison, than he was in his cell. There remained
then the chimney, the loophole, and the solid wall. The
chimney was the first to disappear from the calculation.
Looking up it Rupert saw that it was crossed by a dozen
iron bars, the height too was very great, and even when
at the top the height was immense to descend to the
fosse. The loophole was next examined. It was far
too narrow to squeeze through, and was crossed by
three sets of bars. The chance of widening the narrow
loophole and removing the bars without detection was
extreme; besides, Rupert had a strong idea that loophole looked into the courtyard. Finally he came to the
conclusion, that if an escape was to be made it must be
by raising a flag of the floor, tunnelling between his
room and that underneath it, and working out through
the solid wall. It would be a tremendous work, for the
loophole showed him that the wall must be ten feet
thick; still, as he said to himself, it will be at least some-

thing to do and to think about, and even if it takes five years and comes to nothing, it will have been useful.

Thus resolved, Rupert went to work, and laboured steadily. His exercise with the chair and table succeeded admirably, and after six months he was able to perform feats of strength with them that surprised himself. With his scheme for escape he was less fortunate. Either his tools were faulty, or the stones he had to work upon were too compact and well built, but beyond getting up the flag, making a hole below it in the hard cement which filled in the space between the floor, large enough to bury a good sized cat, Rupert achieved nothing.

He had gone into prison in November, it was now August, and he was fast coming to the idea that Loches was not to be broken out of by the way in which he was attempting to do it. One circumstance gave him intense delight, Adèle's hiding-place had not been discovered. This he was sure of, by the urgency with which the governor strove to extract from him the secret of her wherabouts. Their demands were at the last meeting mingled with threats, and Rupert felt that the governor had received stringent orders to wring the truth from him. So serious did these menaces become that Rupert ceased to labour at the floor of his cell, being assured that ere long some change or other would take place. He was not mistaken. One day the governor entered, attended, as usual, by the gaoler and another official.

"Sir," he said to Rupert, "we can no longer be trifled with. I have orders to obtain from you the name of the place to which you escorted the young lady you went off with. If you refuse to answer me, a different system to that which has hitherto been pursued will be adopted. You will be removed from this comfortable room and placed in the dungeons. Once there, you must either

speak or die, for few men are robust enough to exist
there for many weeks. I am sorry, sir, but I have my
duty to do. Will you speak, or will you change your
room?"

"I will change my room," Rupert said, quietly. "I
may die; but if by any chance I should ever see the light
again, be assured that all Europe shall know how officers taken in war are treated by the King of France."

The governor shrugged his shoulders, made a sign
to the gaoler, who opened the door, and as the governor
left four other warders entered the room. Rupert
smiled, he knew that this display of force was occasioned
by the fact that his gaoler, entering his room suddenly,
had several times caught him balancing the weighty table on his arm or performing other feats which had astounded the Frenchman. The work at the cell wall
had always been done at night.

"I am ready to accompany you," Rupert said, and
without another word followed his conductor down
stairs. Arrived at a level with the yard, another door
was unlocked, and the party descended down some
stairs, where the cold dampness of the air struck a chill
to Rupert's heart. Down some forty feet, and then a
door was unlocked, and Rupert saw his new abode. It
was of about the same size as the last, but was altogether
without furniture. In one corner, as he saw by the light
of a lantern which the gaoler carried, was a stone bench
on which was a bundle of straw. The walls streamed
with moisture, and in some places the water stood in
shallow pools on the floor; the dungeon was some
twelve feet high; eight feet from the ground was a narrow loophole, eighteen inches in height and about three
inches wide. The gaoler placed a pitcher of water and
a piece of bread on the bench, and then without a word
the party left.

Rupert sat quiet on the bench for an hour or two before his eyes became sufficiently accustomed to the darkness to see anything, for but the feeblest ray of light made its way through so small a loophole in a wall of such immense thickness.

"The governor was right," he muttered to himself. "A month or two of this place would kill a dog."

It was not until the next day that the gaoler made his appearance. He was not the same one who had hitherto attended him, but a powerful-looking ruffian who was evidently under no orders as to silence such as those which had governed the conduct of the other.

"Well," he began, "and how does your worship like your new palace?"

"It is hardly cheerful," Rupert said; "but I do not know that palaces are ever particularly cheerful."

"You are a fine fellow," the gaoler said, looking at Rupert by the light of his lantern. "I noted you yesterday as you came down, and I thought it a pity then that you would not say what they wanted you to. I don't know what it is, and don't want to; but when a prisoner comes down here, it is always because they want to get something out of him, or they want to finish with him for good and all. You see you are below the level of the moat here, the water comes at ordinary times to within six inches of that slit up there. And in wet weather it happens sometimes that the stream which feeds the moat swells, and if it has been forgotten to open the sluice gates of the moat, it will rise ten feet before morning. I once knew a prisoner drowned in the cell above this."

"Well," Rupert said, calmly. "After all one may as well be drowned as die by inches. I don't owe you any ill-will, but I should be almost glad if I did, for then I should dash your brains out against the wall, and fight till they had to bring soldiers down to kill me."

The man gave a surly growl,—

"I have my knife," he said.

"Just so," Rupert answered; "and it may be, although I do not think it likely, that you might kill me before I knocked your brains out; but that would be just what I should like. I repeat, it is only because I have no ill-will towards you that I don't at once begin a struggle which would end in my death one way or another."

The gaoler said no more; but it was clear that Rupert's words had in no slight degree impressed him, for he was on all his future visits as civil as it was within his nature to be.

"Whenever you wish to see the governor, he will come to you," he said to Rupert one day.

"If the governor does not come till I send for him," Rupert answered, "he will never come."

Even in this dungeon, where escape seemed hopeless, Rupert determined to do his best to keep life and strength together. Nothing but the death of the king seemed likely to bring relief, and that event might be many years distant. When it took place, his old friend would, he was sure, endeavor in every way to find out where he was confined, and to obtain his release. At any rate he determined to live as long as he could; and he kept up his spirits by singing scraps of old songs, and his strength by such gymnastic exercises as he could carry out without the aid of any movable article. At first he struck out his arms as if fighting, so many hundred of times; then he took to walking on his hands; and at last he loosened one of the stones which formed the top of the bed, and invented all sorts of exercises with it.

"What is the day of the month?" he said one day to his gaoler.

"It is the 15th of October."

"It is very dark," Rupert said, "darker than usual."

"It is raining," the gaoler said; "raining tremendously."

Late that night Rupert was awoke by the splashing of water. He leaped to his feet. The cell was already a foot deep in water.

"Ha!" he exclaimed, "it is one thing or the other now."

Rupert had been hoping for a flood; it might bring death, but he saw that it was possible that it might bring deliverance.

The top of the loophole was some two and a half feet from the vaulted roof; the top of the door was about on the same level, or some six inches lower. The roof arched some three feet above the point whence it sprang.

Rupert had thought it all over, and concluded that it was possible, nay almost certain, that even should the water outside rise ten feet above the level of his roof, sufficient air would be pent up there to prevent the water from rising inside, and to supply him with sufficient to breathe for many hours. He was more afraid of the effects of cold than of being drowned. He felt that in a flood in October the water was likely to be fairly warm, and he congratulated himself that it was now, instead of in December, that he should have to pass through the ordeal.

Before commencing the struggle, he kneeled for some time in prayer on his bed, and then, with a firm heart, rose to his feet and awaited the rising of the water. This was rapid indeed, it was already two feet over his bed, and minute by minute it rose higher.

When it reached his chin, which it did in less than a quarter of an hour from the time when he had first awoke, he swam across to the loophole, which was now but a few inches above the water, and through which a stream of water still poured. Impossible as it was for any human being to get through the narrow slit, an iron bar had been placed across it. Of this Rupert took hold, and remained quiescent as the water mounted higher and higher; presently it rose above the top of the loophole, and Rupert now watched anxiously how fast it ran. Floating on his back, and keeping a finger at the water level against the wall, he could feel that the water still rose.   It seemed to him that the rise was slower and slower, and at last his finger remained against a point in the stones for some minutes without moving.   The rise of the water inside the dungeon had ceased.

That is continued outside he guessed by a slight but distinct feeling of pressure in the air, showing that the column of water outside was compressing it. He had no fear of any bad consequences from this source, as even a height of twelve feet of water outside would not give any unbearable pressure.   He was more afraid that he himself would exhaust the air, but he believed that there would be sufficient; and as he knew that the less he exerted himself the less air he required, he floated quietly on his back, with his feet resting on the bar across the loophole, now two feet under water.   He scarcely felt the water cold.   The rain had come from a warm quarter; and the temperature of the water was actually higher than that of the cold and humid dungeon.   Hour after hour passed.   The night appeared interminable.   From time to time Rupert dived so as to look through the loophole, and at last was rewarded by seeing a faint dull light.   Day was beginning; and Rupert had no doubt that with early morning the sluices would be opened, and the moat entirely cleared of water.

He had, when talking with his gaoler one day, asked him how they got rid of the water in the dungeon after a flood, and the man said there were pipes from the floor of each dungeon into the moat.   At ordinary times these pipes were closed by wooden plugs, as the water outside was far above the floor; but that after a flood the water was entirely let out of the moat, and the plugs removed from the pipes, which thus emptied the dungeons.

From the way in which the fellow described the various arrangements, Rupert had little doubt that the sluice gates were at times purposely left closed, in order to clear off troublesome prisoners who might otherwise have remained a care and expense to the state for years to come.

Long as the night had seemed, it seemed even longer before Rupert felt that the water was sinking. He knew that after the upper sluice had opened the fosse might take some time to fall to the level of the water inside the dungeon, and that until it did the water inside would remain stationary.

He passed the hours by changing his position as much as possible; sometimes he swam round and round, at other times he trod water, then he would float quietly, then cling to the bar of the loophole.

The descent of the water came upon him at last as a surprise. He was swimming round and round, and had not for some time touched the wall, when suddenly a ray of light flashed in his face. He gave a cry of joy. The water had fallen below the top of the loophole, and swimming up to it, he could see across the fosse, and watch the sunlight sparkling on the water. It was two months since he had seen the light, and the feeling of joy overpowered him more than the danger he had faced. Rapidly the water fell, until it was level with the bottom of the loophole.

Then hours passed away; for the fosse would have to be emptied before the drain leading from the dungeon could be opened. However, Rupert hardly felt the time long. With his hands on the bar and in the loophole, he remained gazing out at the sunlight.

The water in the fosse sank and sank, until he could

17

no longer see it; but he could see the sun glistening on the wet grass of the bank, and he was satisfied. At last he was conscious of a strain on his arm, and withdrawing his gaze from without, he saw that the water had fallen six inches.

It now sank rapidly; and in an hour he could stand with his head above it. Then he was able to sit down on his bed; but when the water sank to a depth of two feet, he again lay on his back and floated. He knew that a thick deposit of mud would be left, and that it was essential for his plan that he should drift to the exit hole of the water, and there be found, with the mud and slime undisturbed by footsteps or movement. Another ten minutes, and he lay on his back on the ground in a corner of the dungeon to which the water had floated him, having taken care towards the end to sink his head so that his hair floated partly over it, and as the water drained off remained so.

He guessed it to be about midday, and he expected to be left undisturbed until night.

After a time he slept, and when he awoke it was dark, and soon after he heard steps coming down the stairs. Now was the moment of trial. Presently the door opened and four of the gaolers came in. They bore between them a stretcher.

"This is the fifth," one said, and he recognized the voice of his own attendant. "It is a pity! he was a fine fellow. Well, there's one more, and then the job's done."

He bent over Rupert, who ceased breathing.

"He's the only one with his eyes closed," he said. "I expect there's some one would break her heart if she knew he was lying here. Well, lift him up, mates."

The two months' imprisonment in the dungeon had done one good service for Rupert, the absence of light had blanched his face, and even had he been dead he could hardly have looked more white than he did. The long hours in the water had made his hands deadly cold, and the hair matted on his face added to the deathlike aspect.

"Put the stretcher on the ground, and roll him over on to it," one of the men said. "I don't mind a dead man, but these are so clammy and slimy that they are horrible to touch. There, stand between him and the wall, put a foot under him, roll him over. There, nothing could be better! Now then, off we go with him. The weight's more than twice as much as the others."

Rupert lay with his face down on the stretcher, and felt himself carried upstairs, then along several long passages, then through a door, and felt the fresh evening air. Now by the sound he knew that he was being carried over the bridge across the moat to the burying-ground. Then the stretcher was laid down.

"Now then, roll him over into the hole," one said, "and let us go back for the last. Peste! I am sick of this job, and shall need a bottle of eau de vie to put me straight again."

One side of the stretcher was lifted, and Rupert was rolled over. The fall was not deep, some three or four feet only, and he fell on a soft mass, whose nature he could well guess at. A minute later he heard the retreating footsteps of his gaolers, and leaping from the grave, stood a free man by its side.

He knew that he was not only free, but safe from any active pursuit, for he felt sure that the gaolers, when they returned with their last load, would throw it in and fill up the grave, and that no suspicion that it contained one short of the number would arise.

This in itself was an immense advantage to him, for on the escape of a prisoner from Loches—an event which had happened but once or twice in its records—a gun was fired and the whole country turned out in pursuit of the prisoner.

Rupert paused for two minutes before commencing his flight, and kneeling down, thanked God for his escape. Then he climbed the low ramparts, dropped beyond them, and struck across country.

The exercise soon sent the blood dancing through his hands again, and by the morning he was thirty-five miles from Loches.

He had stopped once, a mile or two after starting, when he came to a stream. Into this he had waded, and had washed the muck stains from his clothes, hair, and face.

With the morning dawn his clothes were dry, and he presented to the eye an aspect similar to that which he wore when captured at Blois nearly a year before, of a dilapidated and broken-down soldier, for he had retained in prison the clothes he wore when captured; but they had become infinitely more dingy from the wear and tear of prison, and the soaking had destroyed all vestige of colour.

Presently he came to a mill by a stream.

"Hallo!" the miller said cheerily, from his door. "You seem to have been in the wars, friend."

"I have in my way," Rupert said. "I was wounded in Flanders. I have been home to Bordeaux, and got cured again. I started for the army again, and some tramps who slept in the same room with me robbed me of my last shilling. To complete my disaster, last night, not having money to pay for a bed, I tramped on fell into a stream, and was nearly drowned."

"Come in," said the miller. "Wife, here is a poor fellow out of luck; give him a bowl of hot milk, and some bread."

CHAPTER XXI.

BACK IN HARNESS.

"You must have had a bad time of it," the miller said, as he watched Rupert eating his breakfast. "I don't know that I ever saw any one so white as you are, and yet you look strong too."

"I am strong," Rupert said, "but I had an attack, and all my colour went. It will come back again soon, but I am only just out. You don't want a man, do you? I am strong and willing. I don't want to beg my way to the army, and I am ashamed of my clothes. There will be no fighting till the spring. I don't want high pay, just my food and enough to get me a suit of rough clothes, and to keep me in bread and cheese as I go back."

"From what part of France do you come?" the miller asked. "You don't speak French as people do hereabouts."

"I come from Brittany," Rupert said; "but I learnt to speak the Paris dialect there, and have almost forgotten my own, I have been so long away."

"Well, I will speak to my wife," the miller said. "Our last hand went away three months since, and all the able-bodied men have been sent to the army. So I can do with you if my wife likes you."

The miller's wife again came and inspected the wanderer, and declared that if he were not so white he would be well enough, but that such a colour did not seem natural.

Rupert answered her that it would soon go, and offered that if, at the end of a week, he did not begin to show signs of colour coming, he would give up the job.

The bargain was sealed. The miller supplied him

with a pair of canvas trousers and a blouse, Rupert cut off his long hair, and set to work as the miller's man.

In a week the miller's wife, as well as the miller himself, was delighted with him. His great strength, his willingness and cheeriness kept, as they said, the place alive, and the pallor of his face had so far worn off by the end of the week that the miller's wife was satisfied that he would, as she said, soon look like a human being, and not like a walking corpse.

The winter passed off quietly, and Rupert stood higher and higher in the liking of the worthy couple with whom he lived, the climax being reached when, in mid-winter, a party of marauders—for at that time the wars of France and the distress of the people had filled the country with bands of men who set the laws at defiance—five in number, came to the mill and demanded money.

The miller, who was not of a warlike disposition, would have given up all the earnings which he had stored away, but Rupert took down an old sword which hung over the fire-place, and sallying out, ran through the chief of the party, desperately wounded two others, and by sheer strength tossed the others into the mill stream, standing over them when they scrambled out, and forcing them to dig a grave and bury their dead captain and to carry off their wounded comrades.

Thus when the spring came, and Rupert said that he must be going, the regrets of the miller and his wife were deep, and by offer of higher pay they tried to get him to stay. Rupert however was, of course, unable to accede to their request, and was glad when they received a letter from a son in the army, saying that he had been laid up with fever, and had got his discharge, and was just starting to settle with them at the mill.

Saying good-bye to his kind employers, Rupert started with a stout suit of clothes, fifty francs in his pocket, and a document signed by the Maire of the parish to the effect that Antoine Duprat, miller's man, had been working through the winter at Evres, and was now on his way to join his regiment with the army of Flanders.

Determined to run no more risks if he could avoid it, he took a line which would avoid Paris and all other towns at which he had ever shown himself. Sometimes he tramped alone, more often with other soldiers who had been during the winter on leave to recover from the effects of wounds or of fevers. From their talk Rupert learned with satisfaction that the campaign which he had missed had been very uneventful, and that no great battles had taken place. It was expected that the struggle that would begin in a few weeks would be a desperate one, both sides having made great efforts to place a predominating force in the field. As he had no idea of putting on the French uniform even for a day, Rupert resolved as he approached the army frontier to abandon his story that he was a soldier going to take his place in the ranks.

When he reached Amiens he found the streets encumbered with baggage waggons taking up provisions and stores to the army. The drivers had all been pressed into the service. Going into a cabaret, he heard some young fellow lamenting bitterly that he had been dragged away from home when he was in three weeks to have been married. Waiting until he left, Rupert followed him, and told him that he had heard what he had said and was ready to go as his substitute, if he liked. For a minute or two the poor fellow could hardly believe his good fortune; but when he found that he was in earnest he was delighted, and hurried off to the contractor in charge of the train—Rupert stopping with him by the way to buy a blouse, in which he looked more fitted for the post. The contractor seeing that

Rupert was a far more powerful and useful-looking man than the driver whose place he offered to take, made no difficulty whatever; and in five minutes Rupert, with a metal plate with his number hung round his neck, was walking by the side of a heavily loaded team, while their late driver, with his papers of discharge in his pocket, had started for home almost wild with delight. For a month Rupert worked backwards and forwards, between the posts and the depôts. As yet the allies had not taken the field, and he knew that he should have no chance of crossing a wide belt of country patrolled in every direction by the French cavalry. At the end of that time the infantry moved out from their quarters and took the field, and the allied army advanced towards them. The French army, under Vendôme, numbered 100,000 men, while Marlborough, owing to the intrigues of his enemies at home, and the dissensions of the allies, was able to bring only 70,000 into the field.

The French had correspondents in most of the towns in Flanders, where the rapacity of the Dutch had exasperated the people against their new masters, and made them long for the return of the French.

A plot was on foot to deliver Antwerp to the French, and Vendôme moved forward to take advantage of it; but Marlborough took post at Halle, and Vendôme halted his army at Soignies, three leagues distant. Considerable portions of each force moved much closer to each other, and lay watching each other across a valley but a mile wide.

Rupert happened to be with the waggons taking ammunition up to the artillery in an advanced position, and determined, if possible, to seize the opportunity of rejoining his countrymen. A lane running between two high hedges led from the foot of the hill where he was standing, directly across the valley, and Rupert slipping away unnoticed, made the best of his way down the lane. When nearly half across the valley, the hedges ceased, and Rupert issued out into open fields.

Hitherto, knowing that he had not been noticed, he had husbanded his breath, and had only walked quickly, but as he came into the open he started at a run.

He was already nearly half way between the armies, and reckoned that before any of the French cavalry could overtake him he would be within reach of succour by his friends.

A loud shout from behind him showed that he was seen, and looking round he saw that a French general officer, accompanied by another officer and a dragoon, were out in front of their lines reconnoitring the British position. They seeing the fugitive, set spurs to their horses to cut him off. Rupert ran at the top of his speed, and could hear a roar of encouragement from the troops in front. He was assured that there was no cavalry at this part of the lines, and that he must be overtaken long before he could get within the very short distance that then constituted musket range. Finding that escape was out of the question, he slackened his speed, so as to leave himself breath for the conflict. He was armed only with a heavy stick. The younger officer, better mounted, and anxious to distinguish himself on so conspicuous an occasion, was the first to arrive.

Rupert faced round, his cap had fallen off, and grasping the small end of the stick, he poised himself for the attack.

The French officer drew rein with a sudden cry,—

"You!" he exclaimed, "you! What, still alive?"

"Yes, no thanks to you, Monsieur le Duc," Rupert said, bitterly. "Even Loches could not hold me."

His companions were now close at hand, and with a

cry of fury the duke rode at Rupert; the latter gave the horse's nose a sharp blow as the duke's sweeping blow descended; the animal reared suddenly, disconcerting the aim, and before its feet touched the ground the heavy knob of Rupert's stick, driven with the whole strength of his arm, struck the duke on the forehead. At the same instant as the duke fell, a lifeless mass, over the crupper, Rupert leaped to the other side of the horse, placing the animal between him and the other assailants as they swept down upon him. Before they could check their horses he vaulted into the saddle, and with an adroit wheel avoided the rush of the dragoon.

The shouts of the armies, spectators of the singular combat, were now loud, and the two Frenchmen attacked Rupert furiously, one on each side. With no weapon but a stick, Rupert felt such a conflict to be hopeless, and with a spring as sudden as that with which he had mounted he leapt to the ground, as the general on one side and the dragoon on the other cut at him at the same moment. The spring took him close to the horse of the latter, and before the amazed soldier could again strike, Rupert had vaulted on to the horse, behind him. Then using his immense strength—a strength brought to perfection by his exercise at Loches, and his work in lifting sacks as a miller's man—he seized with both hands the French soldier by the belt, lifted him from the seat, and threw him backwards over his head, the man flying through the air some yards before he fell on the ground with a heavy crash. Driving his heels into the horse, he rode him straight at the French general, as the latter—who had dashed forward as Rupert unseated the trooper— came at him. Rupert received a severe cut on the left shoulder, but the impetus of the heavier horse and rider rolled the French officer and his horse on to the ground. Rupert shifted his seat into the saddle, leapt the fallen

"HE LIFTED HIM FROM HIS SEAT AND THREW HIM BACKWARDS OVER HIS HEAD."

horse, and stooping down seized the officer by his
waist-belt, lifted him from the ground as if he had been
a child, threw him across the horse in front of him, and
galloped forward towards the allied lines, amid a perfect roar of cheering, just as a British cavalry regiment
rode out from between the infantry to check a body of
French dragoons who were galloping up at full speed
from their side.

With a thundering cheer the British regiment reined
up as Rupert rode up to them, the French dragoons
having halted when they saw that the struggle was
over.

"Why, as I live," shouted Colonel Forbes, "it's the
little cornet!"

"The little cornet! the little cornet!" shouted the sol-
dies, and waved their swords and cheered again and
again, in wild enthusiasm, as Colonel Forbes, Lauriston, Dillon, and the other officers, pressed forward to
greet their long-lost comrade.

Before, however, a word of explanation could be uttered, an officer rode up.

"The Duke of Marlborough wishes to see you," he
said, in French.

"Will you take charge of this little officer, colonel?"
Rupert said, placing the French general, who was half
suffocated by pressure, rage, and humiliation, on his
feet again.

"Now, sir," he said to the officer, "I am with you."

The latter led the way to the spot where the duke
was sitting on horseback surrounded by his staff, on
rising ground a hundred yards behind the infantry regiment.

"My Lord Duke," Rupert said, as he rode up, "I beg
to report myself for duty."

"Rupert Holliday!" exclaimed the duke, astonished.
"My dear boy, where do you come from, and where

have you been? I thought I was looking at the deeds of some modern Paladin, but now it is all accounted for. I wrote myself to Marshal Villeroi to ask tidings of you, and to know why you were not among the officers exchanged; and I was told that you had escaped from Lille, and had never been heard of since.

"He never heard of me, sir, but his Majesty of France could have given you further news. But the story is too long for telling you now."

"You must be anxious about your friends, Rupert. I heard from Colonel Holliday just before I left England, begging me to cause further inquiries to be made for you. He mentioned that your lady mother was in good health, but greatly grieving at your disappearance. Neither of them believed you to be dead, and were confident you would reappear. And now, who is the French officer you brought in?"

"I don't know, sir," Rupert said, laughing, "there was no time for any formal introduction, and I made his acquaintance without asking his name."

An officer was at once sent off to Colonel Forbes to inquire the name of the prisoner.

"There is one of your assailants making off," the duke said; and Rupert saw that the trooper had regained his feet and was limping slowly away.

"He fell right," Rupert said; "he was no weight to speak of."

The other officer is killed, I think," the duke said, looking with a telescope.

"I fancy so," Rupert said, drily. "I hit him rather hard. He was the Duc de Carolan, and as he had given much annoyance to a friend of mine, not to mention a serious act of disservice to myself, I must own that if I had to kill a Frenchman in order to escape, I could not have picked out one with whom I had so long an account to settle."

The officer now rode back, and reported that the prisoner was General Mouffler.

"A good cavalry officer," the duke said; "it is a useful capture. And now, Rupert, you will want to be with your friends. If we encamp here to-night, come in to me after it is dark and tell me what you have been doing. If not, come to me the first evening we halt."

Rupert now rode back to his regiment, where he was again received with the greatest delight.

The men had now dismounted, and Rupert, after a few cordial words with his brother officers, went off to find Hugh.

He found the faithful fellow leaning against a tree, fairly crying with emotion and delight, and Rupert himself could not but shed tears of pleasure at his reunion with his attached friend. After a talk with Hugh, Rupert again returned to the officers, who were just sitting down to a dinner on the grass.

After the meal was over Rupert was called upon to relate his adventures. Some parts of his narrative were clear enough, but others were singularly confused and indistinct. The first parts were all satisfactory. Rupert's capture was accounted for. He said that in the person of the commanding officer he met an old friend of Colonel Holliday, who took him to Paris, and presented him at Versailles. Then the narrative became indistinct. He fell into disgrace; his friend was sent back to the army, and he was sent to Lille.

"But why was this, Rupert," Captain Dillon—for he was now a captain—asked. "Did you call his Majesty out? or did you kiss Madame de Maintenon? or run away with a maid of honour?"

A dozen laughing suggestions were made, and then Rupert said gravely,—

"There was an unfounded imputation that I was interfering with the plans which his Majesty had formed for the marriage of a lady and gentleman of the court."

Rupert spoke so gravely that his brother officers saw that any joking here would be ill-timed; but sly winks were exchanged as Rupert, changing the subject, went on to recount his captivity at Lille.

The story of his escape was listened to eagerly, and then Rupert made a long pause, and coloured lightly.

"Several things of no importance then happened," he said, "and as I was going through the streets of Blois,—"

"The streets of where?" Colonel Forbes asked, in astonishment. "You escape from Lille, just on the frontier, what on earth were you doing down at Blois, a hundred miles south of Paris?"

Rupert paused again.

"I really cannot explain it, colonel. I shall make a point of telling the duke, and if he considers that I acted wrongly, I must bear his displeasure; but the matter is of no real importance, and does not greatly concern my adventures. Forgive me, if I do not feel justified in telling it. All the rest is plain sailing."

Again the narrative went on, and the surprise at hearing that Rupert had been confined at Loches, well known as a prison for dangerous political offenders was only exceeded by that occasioned by the incidents of his escape therefrom. Rupert carried on his story to the point of the escape from the French, which they had just witnessed.

There was a chorus of congratulations at his having gone safely through such great dangers; and Dillon remarked,—

"It appears to me that you have been wasting your time and your gifts most amazingly. Here have you been absent just two years, and with the exception of a paltry marauder you do not seem to have slain a single Frenchman, till you broke that officer's skull to-day. I think, my friends, that the least we can do is to pass a formal vote of censure upon our comrade for such a grievous waste of his natural advantages. The only thing in his favour is, that he seems to have been giving up his whole attention to growing, and he has got so prodigiously broad and big that now he has again joined us he will be able to make up for the otherwise sinful loss of time."

A chorus of laughter greeted Dillon's proposal, and the merry group then broke up, and each went off to his duty.

Rupert's first effort was to obtain such clothes as would enable him to appear in his place in the ranks without exciting laughter. Hugh told him that all his clothes and effects were in store at Liege, but indeed it was questionable whether any would be of use to him. He was not taller indeed than he was two years before, but he was broader by some inches, than before. From the quartermaster he obtained a pair of jack-boots which had belonged to a trooper who had been killed in a skirmish two days before, and from the armourer he got a sword, cuirass, and pistols. As to riding-breeches there was no trouble, for several of the officers had garments which would fit him, but for a regimental coat he could obtain nothing which was in any way large enough. Hugh was therefore despatched to Halle to purchase a riding-coat of the best fashion and largest size that he could find, and a hat as much as possible in conformity with those generally worn.

An hour or two later Lord Fairholm and Sir John Loveday rode over, the news of the singular fight on the ground between the armies, and of the reappearance of the famous "little cornet" of the 5th dragoons having spread apace through the army.

Joyous and hearty were the greetings, and after a while, the party being joined by Dillon, Rupert gave his three friends a full account of his adventures omitting some of the particulars which he had not deemed it expedient to speak of in public.

"I understand now," Lord Fairholm said, "the change in your face which struck me."

"Is my face changed?" Rupert said. "It does not seem to me that I have changed in face a bit since I joined, six years ago."

"It is not in features, but in expression. You look good-tempered now, Rupert, even merry when you smile, but no man could make a mistake with you now. There is; when you are not speaking, a sort of intent look upon your face, intent and determined—the expression which seems to tell of great danger expected and faced. No man could have gone through that two months in the dungeon of Loches and come out unchanged. All the other dangers you have gone through —and you always seem to be getting into danger of some kind—were comparatively sharp and sudden, and a sudden peril, however great, may not leave a permanent mark; but the two months in that horrible den, from which no other man but yourself would deem escape possible, could not but change you. When you left us, although you were twenty, you were in most things still a boy; there is nothing boyish about you now. It is the same material, but it has gone through the fire; you were good iron, very tough and strong, but you could be bent; now, Rupert, you have been tried in the furnace and have come out steel."

"You are very good to say so," Rupert said, smiling, "but I don't feel all that change which you speak of. I hope that I am just as much up to a bit of fun as ever I was. At present I strike you perhaps as being more quiet; but you see I have hardly spoken to a soul for eighteen months, and have got out of the way rather. All that I do feel is, that I have gained greatly in strength, as that unfortunate French trooper found to his cost to-day. But there, the trumpets are sounding; it's too late for a battle to-day, so I suppose we have got a march before us."

CHAPTER XXII.

OUDENARDE.

THE trumpet call which summoned Rupert and his friends to horse was, as he suspected, an indication that there was a general movement of the troops in front.

Vendôme had declined to attack the allies in the position they had taken up, but had moved by his right to Braine-le-Leude, a village close to the ground on which more than a hundred years later, Waterloo was fought, and whence he threatened alike Louvain and Brussels. Marlborough moved his army on a parallel line to Anderleet. No sooner had he arrived there, than he found that Vendôme was still moving towards his right—a proof that Louvain was really the object of the attack. Again the allied troops were set in motion, and all night, through torrents of rain, they tramped wearily along, until at daybreak they were in position at Parc, covering the fortress of Louvain. Vendôme, finding himself anticipated, fell back to Braine-le-Leude without firing a shot.

But though Marlborough had so far foiled the enemy, it was clear that he was not in a condition to take the offensive before the arrival of Prince Eugene, who would, he trusted, be able to come to his assistance; and for weeks the armies watched each other without movement.

On the 4th of July, Vendôme suddenly marched from Braine-le-Leude, intending to capture the fortress of Oudenarde. Small bodies of troops were sent off at the same time to Ghent and Bruges, whose inhabitants rose and admitted the French. Marlborough, seeing the danger which threatened the very important fortress of Oudenarde, sent orders to Lord Chandos who commanded at Ath, to collect all the small garrisons in the neighbourhood, and to throw himself into Oudenarde. This was done before Vendôme could reach the place, which was thus secured against a coup-de-main. Vendôme invested the fortress, brought up his seige train from Tournay, and removed towards Lessines with his main army, to cover the seige.

The loss of Ghent and Bruges, the annoyances he suffered from party attacks at home, and the failure of the allies to furnish the promised contingents, so agitated Marlborough that he was seized with an attack of fever.

Fortunately, on the 7th of July Prince Eugene arrived. Finding that his army could not be up in time, he had left them, and, accompanied only by his personal staff, had ridden on to join Marlborough.

The arrival of this able general and congenial spirit did much to restore Marlborough; and after a council with the prince, he determined to throw his army upon Vendôme's line of communications, and thus force him to fight with his face to Paris.

At two in the morning of the 9th of July, the allies broke up their camp, and advanced in four great columns towards Lessines and the French frontier. By noon the heads of the columns had reached Herfelingen, fourteen miles from their starting point, and bridges were thrown across the Dender, and the next morning the army crossed, and then stood between the French and their own frontier.

Vendôme, greatly disconcerted at finding that his plans had all been destroyed, ordered his army to fall back to Gavre on the Scheldt, intending to cross below Oudenarde.

Marlborough at once determined to press forward, so as to force on a battle, having the advantage of coming upon the enemy when engaged in a movement of retreat. Accordingly, at daybreak on the 11th, Colonel Cadogan, with the advanced guard, consisting of the whole of the cavalry and twelve battalions of infantry, pushed forward, and marched with all speed to the Scheldt, which they reached by seven o'clock. Having thrown bridges across it, he marched to meet the enemy, his troops in battle array, the infantry opposite Eynes, the cavalry extending to the left towards Schaerken. Advancing strongly down the river in this order, Cadogan soon met the French advanced guard under Biron, which was moving up from Gavre. In the fighting the French had the advantage, retaining possession of Eynes, and there awaiting the advance of the English.

Meanwhile Marlborough and Eugene, with the main body of the army, had reached the river, and were engaged in getting the troops across the narrow bridges, but as yet but a small portion of the forces had crossed. Seeing this, Vendôme determined to crush the British advanced guard with the whole weight of his army, and so halted his troops and formed order of battle.

The country in which the battle of Oudenarde was about to be fought is undulating, and cut up by several streams, with hedgerows, fields, and enclosures, altogether admirably adapted for an army fighting a defensive battle.

The village of Eynes lies about a mile below Oudenarde and a quarter of a mile from the Scheldt. Through it flows a stream formed by the junction of the two rivulets. At a distance of about a mile from the Scheldt, and almost parallel with that river, runs the Norken, a considerable stream, which falls into the Scheldt below Gavre. Behind this river the ground rises into a high plateau, in which, at the commencement of the fight, the greater portion of the French army were posted. The appearance of Colonel Cadogan with his advanced guard completely astonished the

French generals. The allies were known to have been fifteen miles away on the preceding evening, and that a great army should march that distance, cross a great river, and be in readiness to fight a great battle, was contrary to all their calculations of probabilities. The Duke of Burgundy wished to continue the march to Ghent. Marshal Vendôme pointed out that it was too late, and that although a country so intersected with hedges was unfavorable ground for the army which possessed the larger masses of men, yet that a battle be fought. This irresolution and dissension on the part of the French generals wasted time, and allowed the allies to push large bodies of troops across the river unmolested. As fast as they got over Marlborough formed them up near Bevere, a village a few hundred yards north of Oudenarde. Marlborough then prepared to take the offensive, and ordered Colonel Cadogan to retake Eynes. Four English battalions, under Colonel Sabine, crossed the stream and attacked the French forces in the village, consisting of seven battalions under Pfiffer, while the cavalry crossed the rivulets higher up, and came down on the flank of the village. The result was three French battalions were surrounded and made prisoners, and the other four routed and dispersed.

The French generals now saw that there was no longer a possibility of avoiding a general action. Vendôme would have stood on the defensive, which, as he had the Norken with its steep and difficult ground in his front, was evidently the proper tactics to have pursued; he was, however, overruled by the Duke of Burgundy and the other generals, and the French accordingly descended from the plateau, crossed the Norken, and advanced to the attack. The armies were of nearly equal strength, the French having slightly the advantage. The allies had 112 battalions and 180 squadrons, in all 80,000 men; the French, 121 battalions and 198 squadrons, in all 85,000 men. The French again lost time, and fell into confusion as they advanced, owing to Marshal Vendôme's orders being countermanded by the Duke of Burgundy, who had nominally the chief command, and who was jealous of Vendôme's reputation. Marlborough divined the cause of the hesitation, and perceiving that the main attack would be made on his left, which was posted in front of the Castle of Bevere, half a mile from the village of the same name, ordered twelve battalions of infantry under Cadogan to move from his right at Eynes to reinforce his left.

He then lined all the hedges with infantry, and stationing twenty British battalions under Argyle with four guns in reserve awaited the attack. But few guns were employed on either side during the battle, for artillery in those days moved but slowly, and the rapid movements of both armies had left the guns far behind

The French in their advance at once drew in four battalions, posted at Groenvelde, in advance of Eynes and then bearing to their right, pressed forward with such vigour that they drove back the allied left. At this point were the Dutch and Hanoverian troops Marlborough now despatched Eugene to take command of the British on the right, directed Count Lottum to move from the center with twenty battalions to reinforce that side of the fight, and went himself to restore the battle on the left.

Eugene, with his British troops, were gradually but steadily, in spite of their obstinate resistance, being driven back, when Lottum's reinforcements arrived, and with these Eugene advanced at once, and drove back the enemy. As these were in disorder, General Natzmer, at the head of the Prussian cuirassiers, charged them and drove them back, until he himself was fallen upon by the French horse guards in reserve,

while the infantry's fire from the hedgerows mowed
down the cuirassiers.   So dreadful was the fire that half
the Prussian cavalry were slain, and the rest escaped
with difficulty, hotly pursued by the French household
troops.

An even more desperate conflict was all this time
raging on the left.

Here Marlborough placed himself at the head of the
Dutch and Hanoverian battalions, and led them back
against the French, who were advancing with shouts
of victory, and desperate struggles ensued.   Alison in
his history says:—"The ground on which the hostile
lines met was so broken, that the battle in that quarter
turned almost into a series of partial conflicts and even
personal encounters.   Every bridge, every ditch, every
wood, every hamlet, every enclosure, was obstinately
contested, and so incessant was the roll of musketry,
and so intermingled did the hostile lines become, that
the field, seen from a distance, appeared an unbroken
line of flame.   A warmer fire, a more desperate series
of combats, was never witnessed in modern warfare; it
was in great part conducted hand to hand, like the battles of antiquity, of which Livy and Homer have left
such graphic descriptions.   The cavalry could not act,
from the multitude of hedges and copses which intersected the theatre of conflict; breast to breast, knee to
knee, bayonet to bayonet, they maintained the fight on
both sides with the most desperate resolution.   If the
resistance, however, was obstinate, the attack was no
less vigorous, and at length the enthusiastic ardour of
the French yielded to the steady valour of the Germans.
Gradually they were driven back, literally, at the bayonet's point; and at length, resisting at every point, they
yielded all the ground they had won at the commencement of the action.   So, gradually they were pushed
back as far as the village of Diepenbech, where so stub-

born a stand was made that the allies could no longer advance."

Overkirk had now got the rear of the army across the river, and the duke, seeing that the Hill of Oycke, which flanked the enemy's position, was unoccupied by them, directed the veteran general with his twenty Dutch and Danish battalions to advance and occupy it. Arrived there, he swung round the left of his line, and so pressed the French right, which was advanced beyond their outer bounds into the little plain of Diepenbeck. The duke commanded Overkirk to press round still further to his left by the passes of Mullem and the mill of Royeghem by which the French sustained their communication with the force still on the plateau beyond the Norken, and Prince Eugene to further extend his right so as to encompass the mass of French crowded in the plain of Diepenbeck.

The night was falling now, and the progress of the allies on either flank could be seen by the flashes of fire.

Vendôme, seeing the immense danger in which his right and centre were placed, endeavoured to bring up his left, hitherto intact; but the increasing darkness, the thick inclosures, and the determined resistance of Eugene's troops, prevented him from carrying out his intention. So far were the British wings extended round the plain of Diepenbeck, that they completely enclosed it, and Eugene's and Overkirk's men meeting fought fiercely, each believing the other to be French. The mistake was discovered, and to prevent any further mishap of this kind in the darkness, the whole army was ordered to halt where it was and wait till morning. Had the daylight lasted two hours longer, the whole of the French army would have been slain or taken prisoners; as it was, the greater portion made their way through the intervals of the allied army around them, and fled

to Ghent. Nevertheless, they lost 6000, killed and
wounded, and 9000 prisoners, while many thousands of
the fugitives made for the French frontier. Thus the
total loss to Vendôme exceeded 20,000 men, while the
allies lost in all 5000.

When morning broke, Marlborough despatched forty
squadrons of horse in pursuit of the fugitives towards
Ghent, sent off Count Lottum with thirty battalions
and fifty squadrons to carry the strong lines which the
enemy had constructed between Ypres and Warneton,
and employed the rest of his force in collecting and
tending the wounded of both armies.

A few days later the two armies, that of Eugene and
that of the Duke of Berwick, which had been marching
with all speed parallel to each other, came up and
joined those of Marlborough and Vendôme respectively. The Duke of Berwick's corps was the more
powerful, numbering thirty-four battalions and fifty-
five squadrons, and this raised the Duke de Vendôme's army to over 110,000, and placed him again
fairly on an equality with the allies. Marlborough
having by his masterly movement forced Vendôme to
fight with his face to Paris, and in his retreat to retire
still farther from the frontier, now had France open to
him, and his counsel was that the whole army should at
once march for Paris, disregarding the fortresses just as
Wellington and Blucher did after Waterloo. He was,
however, overruled, even Eugene considering such an
attempt to be altogether too dangerous, with Vendôme's army, 110,000 strong, in the rear; and it must
be admitted it would certainly have been a march altogether without a parallel.

Finding that his colleagues would not consent to so
daring and adventurous a march, Marlborough determined to enter France, and lay siege to the immensely
strong fortress of Lille. This was in itself a tremend-

ous undertaking, for the fortifications of the town were considered the most formidable ever designed by Vauban, the citadel within the town was still stronger, and the garrison of 15,000 picked troops were commanded by Marshal Bouflers, one of the most skilful generals in the French army. To lay siege to such a fortress as this, while Vendôme, with this army of 110,-000 men, lay ready to advance to its assistance, was an undertaking of the greatest magnitude.

In most cases the proper course to have taken would have been to advance against and defeat Vendôme before undertaking the siege of Lille; but the French general had entrenched his position with such skill that he could not be attacked, while he had, moreover, the advantage, that if the allies stood between him and France, he stood between them and their base, commanded the Scheldt and the canals from Holland, and was therefore in position to interfere greatly with the onerous operation of bringing up stores for the British army, and with the passage of the front of the immense siege train requisite for an operation of such magnitude as was now about to be undertaken, and for whose transport alone 16,000 horses were required.

CHAPTER XXIII.

THE SIEGE OF LILLE.

THE British cavalry suffered less severely at Oudenarde than did those of the other allied nationalities, as they were during the greater portion of the day held in reserve; and neither Rupert nor any of his special friends in the regiment were wounded. He was, however, greatly grieved at the death of Sir John Loveday, who was killed by a cannon-ball at the commencement of the action. Two of the captains in the 5th were also killed, and this gave Rupert another step. He could have had his captain's rank long before, had he accepted the Duke's offer, several times repeated, of a post on his staff; he preferred, however, the life with his regiment, and in this his promotion was, of course, regular, instead of going up by favour, as was, and still is, the case on the staff.

The train for the siege of Lille was brought up by canal from Holland to Brussels; and although the French knew that a large accumulation of military stores was taking place there, they could not believe that Marlborough meditated so gigantic an undertaking as the siege of Lille, and believed that he was intending to lay siege to Mons.

Berwick, with his army, which had since his arrival on the scene of action been lying at Douai, now advanced to Montagne; and Vendôme detached 18,000 men from his army, lying between Ghent and Bruges, to Malle, to intercept any convoy that might move out from Brussels.

Marlborough's measures were, however, well taken. Eugene, with twenty-five battalions and thirty squadrons, moved parallel to the convoy, which was fifteen miles in length, while the Prince of Wurtemburg, General Wood, the Prince of Orange, each with a large force, were so placed as to check any movement of the enemy.

The gigantic convoy left Brussels on the 6th of August, and reached the camp near Lille on the 15th, without the loss of a single waggon. Prince Eugene, with 53 battalions and 90 squadrons, in all 40,000 men, undertook the siege; while Marlborough, with the main army of 60,000 men, took post at Heldün, where he alike prevented Berwick and Vendôme from effecting a junction, and covered the passage of convoys from Brussels, Ath, and Oudenarde. No less than eighty-one convoys, with food stores, etc., passed safely along; and the arrangements for their safety were so perfect that they excited the lively admiration both of friends and foes.

Feuguieres, the French annalist, asks, "How was it possible to believe that it was in the power of the enemy to convey to Lille all that was necessary for the siege and supplies of the army, to conduct there all the artillery and implements essential for such an undertaking; and that these immense burdens should be transported by land over a line of twenty-three leagues, under the eyes of an army of 80,000 men, lying on the flank of a prodigious convoy, which extended over five leagues of road? Nevertheless, all that was done without a shot being fired or a chariot unharnessed. Posterity will scarcely believe it. Nevertheless, it was the simple truth."

To facilitate his operations, Marlborough threw six bridges across the Scheldt, and 10,000 pioneers were collected to commence the lines which were to surround the city. The lines were projected not only to shut in the city, but to protect the besiegers from attacks by a relieving army. Never since Cæsar be-

sieged Alesia had works upon so gigantic a scale been
constructed. They were fifteen miles in circumfer-
ence, and the ditch was fifteen feet wide and nine deep.

On the 23rd of August, the lines of circumvallation
being now nearly finished, Eugene opened his trenches
and began operations against the city, the parts selected
for attack being the gates of St. Martin and of the Madelaine. These points were upon the same side of the
city, but were separated from each other by the river
Dyle, which flows through the town.

On the morning of the 24th the cannonade opened,
Prince Eugene himself firing the first gun on the right,
the Prince of Orange that on the left attack. The
troops worked with the greatest energy, and the next
day forty-four guns poured their fire into the advanced
works round the chapel of the Madelaine, which stood
outside the walls. The same night the chapel was carried by assault; but the next night, while a tremendous
cannonade was going on, 400 French issued quietly
from their works, fell upon the 200 Dutch who held the
chapel, killed or drove them out, blew up the chapel,
which served as an advanced post for the besiegers, and
retired before reinforcements could arrive.

Marshal Vendôme now determined to unite with the
Duke of Berwick, and to raise the siege, and by making
a long and circuitous march, to avoid Marlborough's
force. This was accomplished; the two armies united,
and advanced to relieve Lille.

Marlborough, who foresaw the line by which they
would approach, drew up his army in order of battle,
with his right resting on the Dyle at Noyelles, and his
left on the Margne at Peronne. Two hours after he
had taken up his position, the French army, 110,000
strong, the most imposing France had ever put in the
field, appeared before him.

The Duke of Marlborough had been strengthened by

10,000 men despatched to him by Prince Eugene from the besieging army, but he had only 70,000 men to oppose to the French. And yet, notwithstanding their great superiority of numbers, the enemy did not venture to attack, and for a fortnight the armies remained facing each other, without a blow being struck on either side. The French were, in fact, paralyzed by the jealousy of the two great generals commanding them, each of whom opposed the other's proposals; and nothing could be decided until the king sent M. Chamillard, the French minister of war, to examine the spot, and give instructions for an attack.

The six days, however, which elapsed between the appearance of the French army in front of Marlborough and the arrival of M. Chamillard in camp, had given Marlborough time so to entrench his position, that upon reconnoitring it Chamillard, Vendôme, Berwick, and the other generals, were unanimous in their opinion that it was too strong to be attacked. The great army therefore again retired, and taking up its post between Brussels and Lille, completely interrupted the arrival of further convoys or stores to the British camp.

The siege meantime had been pressed hotly. From the 27th of August to the 7th of September 120 cannon and eighty mortars thundered continuously; and on the evening of the 7th two breaches were effected in the side of the bastions of the outworks that were to be assaulted.

Fourteen thousand men prepared to storm the outworks. The French allowed them to get, with but slight resistance, into the covered way, where a terrific fire was poured upon them, 800 were shot down in a few minutes, and two mines were exploded under them. The fighting was desperate; but the assailants managed to retain possession of two points in the outwork, a success most dearly purchased with a loss of 2000 killed, and as many wounded.

It was not until the 20th that a fresh attempt to carry the place by storm was made. At this time Marlborough's position was becoming critical. The fortress held out bravely; the consumption of ammunition was so enormous, that his supplies were almost exhausted, and a great army lay directly upon his line of communication. It became a matter of necessity that the place should be taken. Immense efforts were made to secure the success of the assault; enormous quantities of fascines were made for filling up the ditch; and 5000 British troops were sent by Marlborough from his army to lead the assault.

Rupert Holliday, with many other officers, accompanied this body as a volunteer. The troops were drawn up as the afternoon grew late, and just as it became dark they advanced to the assault.

The besieged in the outworks assaulted were supported by the fire of the cannon and musketry of the ramparts behind, from which, so soon as the dense masses of the stormers advanced, a stream of flame issued. So tremendous was the carnage, that three times the troops recoiled before the storm of balls.

On the fourth occasion Eugene himself led them to the assault, on either side of him were the Princes of Orange and Hesse, and a number of officers.

"Remember Hochstadt, Ramilies, and Oudenarde!" the prince shouted; but scarcely had he spoken when he was struck to the ground by a bullet, which struck and glanced over the left eye.

Then the troops dashed forward, and forced their way into the outwork. The French fought with magnificent resolution; and were from time to time reinforced by parties from the city.

For two hours the fight raged. With bayonets and

clubbed muskets, hand to hand, the troops fought; no one flinched or gave way; indeed it was safer to be in the front line than behind, for in front friends and foes were so mixed together, that the French on the ramparts were unable to fire, but had to direct their aim at the masses behind.

At last the allies gained ground. Gradually, foot by foot, the French were thrust back, and Rupert, who had been fighting desperately in the front line of the stormers' party, directed his efforts to a part where a French officer still held his ground, nobly backed by his men. The piled up dead in front of them showed how strenuous had been the resistance to the advancing wave of the allies.

Rupert gradually reached the spot, and had no difficulty in placing himself *vis-à-vis* to the French officer; for so terrible was his skill, that others willingly turned aside to attack less dangerous opponents. In a moment the swords crossed!

The light was a strange one, flickering and yet constant, with the thousands of firearms, which kept up an unceasing roar. The swords clashed and ground together, and after a pass or two both men drew back.

A bright flash from a musket not a yard away threw a bright though momentary light on their faces.

"M. Dessin!" Rupert exclaimed, in delight.

"What! Is it possible?" the Frenchman exclaimed. "Rupert Holliday!"

At the moment there was a tremendous rush of the British. The French were borne back, and hurled over the edge of the outwork; and before Rupert could avert the blow, the butt end of a musket fell with great force upon his late opponent's head.

Rupert leapt forward, and lifting him in his arms, made his way with him to the rear; for with that last rush the fight was over, and the allies had established themselves in the left demibastion of the outwork—an important advantage, but one which had cost them 5000 killed and wounded, of whom 3000 belonged to the English force, whom Marlborough had sent. The fact that more than half of them were *hors de combat* showed how fiercely they had fought.

Owing to the wound of Prince Eugene, the Duke of Marlborough had to direct the operations of the siege as well as to command the army in the field.

On the 23rd he followed up the advantage gained on the 20th, by a fresh attack in two columns, each 5000 strong, and headed by 500 English troops. After being three times repulsed, these succeeded in maintaining a lodgment in another outwork, losing, however, 1000 men in the attack, the greater part being destroyed by the explosion of a mine.

Both besiegers and besieged were now becoming straitened for ammunition, for the consumption had been immense.

The French generals succeeded in passing a supply into the fortress in a very daring manner.

On the night of the 28th, 2500 horsemen set out from Douai, under the command of the Chevalier de Luxembourg, each having forty pounds of powder in his valise. They arrived at the gate of the walls of circumvallation, when the Dutch sentry cried out,—"Who comes there?"

"Open quickly!" the leader answered, in the same language; "I am closely pursued by the French!"

The sentry opened the gate, and the horsemen began to pass in. Eighteen hundred had passed without suspicion being excited, when one of the officers, seeing that his men were not keeping close up, gave the command in French,—"Close up! close up!"

The captain of the guard caught the words, and suspecting something, ordered the party to halt; and then, as they still rode in, ordered the guard to fire. The discharge set fire to three of the powder bags, and the explosion spreading from one to another, sixty men and horses were killed. The portion of the troops still outside the gate fled, but the 1800 who had passed in rode forward through the allied camp and entered the town in safety, with 70,000 pounds of powder!

Another deed of gallantry, equal to anything ever told in fiction, was performed by a Captain Dubois of the French army.

It was a matter of the highest importance for the French generals to learn the exact state of things at Lille.

Captain Dubois volunteered to enter the fortress by water. He accordingly left the French camp, and swimming through seven canals, entered the Dyle near the place where it entered the besiegers' lines. He then dived, and aided by the current, swam under water for an incredibly long distance, so as entirely to elude the observation of the sentinels. He arrived in safety in the town, exhausted with his great exertions.

After having had dry clothes put on him, and having taken some refreshment, he was conducted round the walls by Marshal Boufflers, who showed him all the defensive works, and explained to him the whole circumstances of the position. The next night he again set out by the Dyle, carrying despatches in an envelope of wax in his mouth, and after diving as before through the dangerous places, and running innumerable risks of detection, he arrived in safety in the French camp.

But it was not the French alone who had run short of ammunition. Marlborough had also been greatly straitened, and there being now no possibility of getting through convoys from Brussels, he persuaded the home government to direct a considerable expedition, which had been collected for the purpose of exciting an alarm on the coast of Normandy, and was now on board ship in the Downs, to be sent to Ostend. It arrived there, to the number of fourteen battalions and an abundant supply of ammunition, on the 23rd of September, and Marlborough detached 15,000 men from his army to protect the convoy on its way up.

On the 27th of September, the convoy started, crossed the canal of Nieuport at Leffinghen, and directed its course by Slype to defile through the woods of Wynendale. General Webb, who commanded the troops detached for its protection, took post with 8000 men to defend its passage through the wood, which was the most dangerous portion of the journey; while Cadogan with the rest of the force was stationed at Hoglede to cover the march farther on. Vendôme had received information of the march of the column, and detached M. de la Mathe with 20,000 men to intercept the convoy. At five in the evening the force approached the wood, through which the convoy was then filing. Webb posted his men in the bushes, and when the French—confident in the great superiority of numbers which they knew that they possessed—advanced boldly, they were received by such a terrible fire of musketry, poured in at a distance of a hundred yards, that they fell into confusion. They, however, rallied, and made desperate efforts to penetrate the wood, but they were over and over driven back, and after two hours' fighting they retired, leaving the convoy to pass on in safety to the camp.

In this glorious action 8000 English defeated 20,000 French, and inflicted on them a loss of 4000 killed and wounded. Several fresh assaults were now made, and gradually the allies won ground, until on the eve of the grand assault, Marshal Boufflers surrendered the town, and retired with the survivors of the defenders into the citadel, which held out for another month, and then also surrendered. In this memorable siege, the greatest—with the exception of that of Sebastopol—that has ever taken place in history, the allies lost 3632 men killed, 8322 wounded, in all 11,954, and over 7000 from sickness. Of the garrison, originally 15,000 strong, and reinforced by the 1800 horsemen who made their way through the allied camp, but 4500 remained alive at the time of the final capitulation.

Marshall Boufflers only surrendered the citadel on the express order of Louis XIV. not to throw away any more lives of the brave men under him. At the time of the surrender the last flask of powder was exhausted, and the garrison had long been living on horseflesh.

After Lille had fallen, Marlborough, by a feint of going into winter quarters, threw the French generals off their guard, and then by a rapid dash through their lines fell upon Ghent and Bruges, and recaptured those cities before Vendôme had time to collect and bring up his army to save them.

Then ended one of the most remarkable campaigns in the annals of our own or any other history.

CHAPTER XXIV.

ADELE.

"My dear, dear lad," the Marquis of Pigncrolles said, as he made his way with Rupert back out of the throng in the captured outwork, "what miracle is this? I heard that you had died at Loches."

"A mistake, as you see," Rupert laughed. "But I shall tell you all presently. First, how is Mademoiselle?"

"Well, I trust," the marquis said; "but I have not heard of her for eighteen months. I have been a prisoner in the Bastille, and was only let out two months since, together with some other officers, in order to take part in the defence of Lille. Even then I should not have been allowed to volunteer, had it not been that the Duc de Carolan, Adèle's persecutor, was killed; and his Majesty's plans having been thus necessarily upset, he was for the time being less anxious to know what had become of Adèle."

"In that case you have to thank me for your deliverance," Rupert said; "for it was I who killed monsieur le duc, and never in my life did I strike a blow with a heartier goodwill."

"You!" the marquis exclaimed, in astonishment; "but I might have guessed it. I inquired about his death when I reached Lille, and was told by an officer who was there that he was killed in an extraordinary combat, in which General Mouffler, a trooper, and himself were put *hors de combat* in sight of the whole army, by a deserter of demoniacal strength, skill, and activity. I ought to have recognized you at once; and no doubt should have done so, had I not heard that you were dead. I never was so shocked, dear boy, in all my life, and have done nothing but blame myself for allowing you to run so fearful a risk."

On arriving at the camp Rupert presented his prisoner to the Duke of Marlborough, who having, when Rupert rejoined, heard the story of his discovery in the Marquis de Pignerolles of his old friend M. Dessin, received him with great kindness, and told him that he was free to go where he liked until arrangements could be made for his exchange. Rupert then took him to his tent, where they sat for many hours talking.

Rupert learned that after his escape from Lille the marquis was for three weeks confined to his bed. Before the end of that time a messenger brought him a letter from Adèle, saying that she was well and comfortable. When he was able to travel he repaired at once to Versailles, having received a peremptory order from the king, a few days after Rupert left, to repair to the court the instant he could be moved. He found his Majesty in the worst of humors; the disappearance of Adèle had thwarted his plan, and Louis XIV. was not a man accustomed to be baulked in his intentions. The news of Rupert's escape from Lille had further enraged him, as he connected it with Adèle's disappearance; and the fact that the capture of Rupert had thrown no light upon Adèle's hiding-place had still further exasperated him. He now demanded that the marquis should inform him instantly of her place of concealment. This command the marquis had firmly declined to comply with. He admitted that he could guess where she would take refuge; but that as he sympathized with her in her objection to the match which his Majesty had been pleased to make for her, he must decline to say a word which could lead to her discovery. Upon leaving the king's presence he was at once arrested, and conveyed to the Bastille.

Imprisonment in the Bastile, although rigorous, was

not, except in exceptional cases, painful for men of rank. They were well fed and not uncomfortably lodged; and as the governor had been a personal friend of the marquis previous to his confinement. he had been treated with as much lenity as possible.

After he had been a year in prison, the governor came to his room and told him that Rupert had been drowned by the overflowing of the moat at Loches, and that if therefore his daughter was, as it was believed, actuated by an affection for the Englishman in refusing to accept the husband that the king had chosen for her, it was thought that she might now become obedient. He was therefore again ordered to name the place of her concealment. The marquis replied that he was not aware that his daughter had any affection for Rupert beyond the regard which an acquaintance of many years authorized; and that as he was sure the news would in no way overcome her aversion to the match with the Duc de Carolan, he must still decline to name the place where he might suspect that she had hidden herself.

He heard nothing more for some months; and then the governor told him privately that the duke was dead, and that as it was thought that Lille would be besieged, two or three other officers in the Bastile had petitioned for leave to go to aid in the defence. Had the duke still lived, the governor was sure that any such request on the part of the marquis would have been refused. As it was, however, his known military skill and bravery would be so useful in the defence, that it was possible that the king would now consent. The marquis had therefore applied for, and had received, permission to go to aid in the defence of Lille.

Rupert then told his story, which excited the wonder and admiration of the marquis to the highest point. When he concluded, he said,—

"And now, monsieur le marquis, I must say what I

have never said before, because until I travelled with her down to Poitiers I did not know what my own feelings really were. Then I learned to know that which I felt was not a mere brotherly affection, but a deep love. I know that neither in point of fortune nor in rank am I the equal of mademoiselle, but I love her truly, sir, and the Chace, which will some day be mine, will at least enable me to maintain her in comfort. Monsieur le marquis, may I ask of you the hand of your daughter?"

"You may indeed, my dear Rupert," the marquis said, warmly, taking his hand. "Even when in England the possibility that this might some day come about occurred to me; and although then I should have regretted Adèle's marrying an Englishman, yet I saw in your character the making of a man to whom I could safely entrust her happiness. When we met again, I found that you had answered my expectation of you, and I should not have allowed so great an intimacy to spring up between you had I not been willing that she should, if she so wished it, marry you. I no longer wish her to settle in France. After what I have seen of your free England, the despotism of our kings and the feudal power of our nobles disgust me, and I foresee that sooner or later a terrible upheaval will take place. What Adèle herself will say I do not know, but imagine that she will not be so obstinate in refusing to yield to the wishes of her father as she has been to the commands of her king. But she will not bring you a fortune, Rupert. If she marries you, her estates will assuredly be forfeited by the crown. They are so virtually now, royal receivers having been placed in possession; but they will be formally declared forfeited on her marriage with you. However, she will not come to you a dowerless bride. In seven years I have laid by sufficient to enable me to give her a dowry which will add a few farms to the Chace. And now, Rupert, let us to sleep; day is breaking, and although your twenty-three years may need no rest, I like a few hours' sleep when I can get them."

Upon the following day the conversation was renewed.

"I think, Rupert, that my captivity is really a fortunate one for our plans. So long as I remained in France my every movement would be watched. I dared not even write to Adèle, far less think of going to see her. Now I am out of sight of the creatures of Louis, and can do as I please. I have been thinking it over. I will cross to England. Thence I will make my way in a smuggler's craft to Nantes, where the governor is a friend of mine. From him I will get papers under an assumed name for myself and daughter, and with them journey to Poitiers, and so fetch her to England."

"You will let me go with you, will you not?" Rupert exclaimed. "No one can tell I am not a Frenchman by my speech, and I might be useful."

"I don't know, Rupert; you might be useful, doubtless, but your size and strength render you remarkable."

"Well, but there are big Frenchmen as well as big Englishmen," Rupert said. "If you travel as a merchant, I might very well go as your serving-man, and you and I together could, I think, carry mademoiselle in safety through any odds. It will not be long to wait. I cannot leave until Lille falls, but I am sure the duke will give me leave as soon as the marshal surrenders the city; which cannot be very many days now; for it is clear that Vendôme will not fight, and a desperate resistance at the end would be a mere waste of life."

So it was arranged, and shortly afterwards Rupert took his friend Major Dillon into his confidence. The

latter expressed the wildest joy, shook Rupert's hand,
patted him on the back, and absolutely shouted in his
enthusiasm. Rupert was astonished at the excess of
joy on his friend's part, and was mystified in the extreme when he wound up,—

"You have taken a great load off my mind, Rupert;
you have made Pat Dillon even more eternally indebted
to you than he was before."

"What on earth do you mean, Dillon?" Rupert
asked. "What is all this extraordinary delight about?
I know I am one of the luckiest fellows in the world,
but why are you so overjoyed because I am in love?"

"My dear Rupert, now I can tell you all about it. I
told you, you know, that in the two winters you were
away I went, at the invitation of Mynheer Von Duyk,
to Dort, in order that he might hear whether there was
any news of you, and what I thought of your chance of
being alive, and all that, didn't I?"

"Yes, you told me all that, Dillon; but what on earth
has that got to do with it?"

"Well, my boy, I stopped each time something like
a month at Dort, and, as a matter of course, I fell over
head and ears in love with Maria Von Duyk. I never
said a word, though I thought she liked me well
enough; but she was for ever talking about you and
praising you, and her father spoke of you as his son,
and I made sure it was all a settled thing between you,
and thought what a sly dog you were never to have
breathed a word to me of your good fortune. If you
had never come back I should have tried my luck with
her; but when you turned up again, glad as I was to see
you, Rupert, I made sure that there was an end of any
little corner of hope I had had. When you told me
about your gallivanting about France with a young
lady, I thought for a moment that you might have been
in love with her; but then I told myself that you were

as good as married to Maria Von Duyk, and that the other was merely the daughter of your old friend, to whom you were bound to be civil. Now I know you are really in love with her, and not with Maria, I will try my luck there; that is, if she doesn't break her heart and die when she hears of the French girl."

"Break her heart! nonsense, man!" Rupert laughed. "She was two years older than I was, and looked upon me as a younger brother. Her father lamented that I was not older, but admitted that any idea of a marriage between us was out of the question. But I don't know what he will say to your proposal to take her over to Ireland."

"My proposal to take her over to Ireland!" repeated Dillon, in astonishment; "I should as soon think of proposing to take her to the moon! Why, man, I have not an acre of ground in Ireland, nor a shilling in the world, except my pay. No; if she will have me, I'll settle down in Dort and turn Dutchman, and wear big breeches, and take to being a merchant."

Rupert burst into a roar of laughter.

"You a merchant, Pat! Mynheer Von Duyk and Dillon! Why, man, you'd bring the house to ruin in a year. No, no; if Maria will have you, I shall be delighted; but her fortune will be ample without your efforts—you who, to my positive knowledge, could never keep your company's accounts without the aid of your sergeant."

Dillon burst out laughing too.

"True for you, Rupert; figures were never in my line, except it is such a neat figure as Maria has. Ah, Rupert! I always thought you a nice lad; but how you managed not to fall in love with her, though she was a year or so older than yourself, beats Pat Dillon entirely Now the sooner the campaign is over, and the army goes into winter quarters, the better I shall be pleased."

It was a dark and squally evening in November, when "La Belle Jeanne," one of the fastest luggers which carried on a contraband trade between England and France, ran up the river to Nantes.

She had been chased for twelve hours by a British war ship, but had at last fairly outsailed her pursuers, and had run in without mishap.

On her deck were two passengers, Maître Antoine Perrot, a merchant, who had been over to England to open relations with a large house who dealt in silks and cloths, and his servant, Jacques Bontemps, whose sturdy frame and powerful limbs had created the admiration of the crew of the "Belle Jeanne."

An hour later the lugger was moored against the quay, her crew had scattered to their homes, and the two travellers were housed in a quiet cabaret near, where they had called for a private room.

Half an hour later Maître Perrot left the house, inquired the way to the governor's residence, left a letter at the door, and then returned to the cabaret. At nine o'clock a cloaked stranger was shown into the room. When the door was closed he threw off his hat and cloak.

"My dear marquis, I am delighted to see you; but what means this wild freak of yours?"

"I will tell you frankly, De Brissac." And the Marquis de Pignerolles confided to the Count de Brissac his plan for getting his daughter away to England.

"It is a matter for the Bastille of his most Christian Majesty should he learn that I have aided you in carrying your daughter away, but I will risk it, marquis, for our old friendship's sake. You want a passport saying that Maître Antoine Perrot, merchant of Nantes, with his servant, Jacques Bontemps, is on his way to Poitiers, to fetch his daughter, residing near that town, and that that damsel will return with him to Nantes?"

"That is it, De Brissac. What a pity that it is not with us as in England, where every man may travel where he lists without a soul asking him where he goes, or why."

"Ah! well, I don't know," said the count, who had the usual aristocratic prejudice of a French noble of his time. "It may suit the islanders of whom you are so fond, marquis, but I doubt whether it would do here. We should have plotters and conspirators going all over the country, and stirring up the people."

"Ah! yes, count; but if the people had nothing to complain of, they would not listen to the conspirators. But there, I know we shall never agree about this. When the war is over you must cross the channel, and see me there."

"No, no," De Brissac said, laughing. "I love you, De Pignerolles, but none of the fogs and mists of that chilly country for me. His Majesty will forgive you one of these days, and then we will meet at Versailles."

"So be it," the marquis said. "When Adèle's estates have been bestowed upon one of his favourites, he will have no reason for keeping me in exile; but we shall see."

"You shall have your papers without fail to-morrow early, so you can safely make your preparations. And now good-bye, and may fortune attend you."

It was not until noon next day that Maître Perrot and his servant rode out from Nantes, for they had had some trouble in obtaining two horses such as they required, but had at last succeeded in obtaining two animals of great strength and excellent breeding. The saddle of Maître Perrot had a pillion attached behind for a lady, but this was at present untenanted. Both travellers carried weapons, for in those days a journey across France was not without its perils. Discharged soldiers, escaped serfs, and others, banded together in

the woods and wild parts of France; and although the
governors of provinces did their best to preserve order,
the force at their command was but small, as every man
who could be raised was sent to the frontier, which the
fall of Lille had opened to an invading army.

Until they were well beyond Nantes, Rupert rode
behind the marquis, but when they reached the open
country he moved up alongside.

"I do not know when I have enjoyed a week so much
as the time we spent at the Chace, Rupert. Your grandfather is a wonderful old man, as hard as iron; and
your lady mother was most kind and cordial. She
clearly bore no malice for my interference in her love
affair some years ago."

"Upon the contrary," Rupert said, "I am sure that
she feels grateful to you for saving her from the consequences of her infatuation."

Six days later, the travellers rode into Poitiers. They
had met with no misadventure on the way. Once or
twice they had met parties of rough fellows, but the
determined bearing and evident strength of master and
man had prevented any attempt at violence.

The next morning they started early, and after two
hours' riding approached the cottage where Adèle had
for two years lived with her old nurse.

They dismounted at the door.

"Go you in, sir," said Rupert, "I will hold the horses.
Your daughter will naturally like best to meet you
alone."

The marquis nodded, lifted the latch of the door, and
went in. There was a pause, and then he heard a cry
of "Father!" just as the door closed. In another instant it opened again, and Margot stole out, escaping
to leave her mistress alone with her father.

She ran down to the gate, looked at Rupert, and gave
a little scream of pleasure, leaping and clapping her
hands.

"I said so, monsieur; I always said so. 'When monsieur le marquis comes, mademoiselle, you be sure monsieur l'Anglais will come with him.'"

"And what did mademoiselle used to say?"

"Oh, she used to pretend she did not believe you would. But I knew better; I knew that when she said, over and over again, 'Is my father never coming for me?' she was thinking of somebody else. And are you come to take her away?"

Rupert nodded.

The girl's face clouded.

"Oh, how I shall miss her! But there, monsieur, the fact is—the fact is—"

"You need not pretend to be shy." Rupert said, laughing. "I can guess what 'the fact is.' I suppose that there is somebody in your case too, and that you are just waiting to be married till mademoiselle goes." Margot laughed and coloured, and was going to speak, when the door opened, and the marquis beckoned him in.

"Mr. Holliday," he said, as Rupert on entering found Adèle leaning on her father's shoulder, with a rosy colour, and a look of happiness upon her face, "I have laid my commands upon my daughter, Mademoiselle Adèle de Pignerolles, to receive you as her future husband, and I find no disposition whatever on her part to defy my authority, as she has that of his Majesty. There, my children, may you be happy together!"

So saying, he left the room, and went to look after the horses, leaving Adèle and Rupert to their new-found happiness.

CHAPTER XXV.

FLIGHT AND PURSUIT.

It was early in the afternoon when M. Perrot, with his daughter behind him on a pillion, and his servant riding a short distance in the rear, rode under the gateway of Parthenay. A party of soldiers were at the gateway, and a gendarmerie officer stood near. The latter glanced carelessly at the passport which the merchant showed him, and the travellers rode on.

"*Peste!*" one of the soldiers said; "what is monsieur the Marquis de Pignerolles doing here, riding about dressed as a bourgeois, with a young woman at his back?"

"Which is the Marquis de Pignerolles?" one of the others said.

"He who has just ridden by. He was colonel of my regiment, and I know him as well as I do you."

"It can't be him, Pierre. I saw Louis Godier yesterday, he has come home on leave—he belongs to this town, you know—wounded at Lille. He was telling me about the siege, and he said that the marquis was taken prisoner by the English."

"Prisoner or not prisoner," the other said, obstinately, "that is the marquis. Why, man, do you think one could be mistaken in his own colonel—a good officer too, rather strict perhaps, but a good soldier, and a lion to fight?"

The gendarme moved quietly away, and repeated what he had heard to his captain.

"The Marquis de Pignerolles travelling under the name of M. Perrot, silk merchant of Nantes, with a young lady behind him," the officer exclaimed, "while he is supposed to be a prisoner in England? This must be his daughter, for whom we made such a search two years ago, and who has been on our lists ever since. This is important, André. I will go at once to the prefecture, and obtain an order for their arrest. They will be sure to have put up at the 'Fleur de Lis,' it is the only hostelry where they could find decent accommodation. Go at once, and keep an eye on them. There is no great hurry, for they will not think of going further to-day, and the prefect will be at dinner just at present, and hates being disturbed."

The marquis and Adèle were standing over a blazing fire of logs in the best room of the 'Fleur de Lis,' when Rupert, who was looking out of the casemented window, said,—

"Monsieur le marquis, I do not want to alarm you unnecessarily, but there is a gendarme on the other side of the street watching this house. He was standing by a group of soldiers at the gate when we rode through; I happened to notice him particularly. He is walking slowly backwards and forwards. I saw him when I was at the door a quarter of an hour ago, and he is there still, and just now I saw him glance up at these windows. He is watching us. That is why I made an excuse to come up here to ask you about the horses."

"Are you sure, Rupert?"

"Quite sure," Rupert said, gravely.

"Then there is no doubt about it," the marquis said, "for I know you would not alarm us unnecessarily. What do you advise?"

"I will go down," Rupert said, "and put the saddles on quietly. The stable opens into the street behind. There is a flight of stairs at the end of the long passage here, which leads down into a passage below, at the end of which is a door into the stable-yard. I have just been examining it. I should recommend Adèle to put on her things, and to be in readiness, and then to remain in her room. If you keep a watch here you will see every one coming down the street, and the moment you see an officer approaching, if you will lock the door outside and take the key with you, then call Adèle, and come down the back stairs with her into the yard, I will have the horses in readiness. There is only one man in the stable, a crown piece will make him shut his eyes as we ride out, and they will be five minutes at the door before they find that we have gone."

The marquis at once agreed to the plan, and Rupert went down into the stable-yard, and began to re-saddle the horses.

"What, off again?" the ostler said.

"Yes," Rupert answered. "Between you and I, my master has just seen a creditor to whom he owes a heavy bill, and he wants to slip away quietly. Here is a crown for yourself, to keep your tongue between your teeth. Now lend me a hand with these saddles, and help bring them out quickly when I give the word."

The horses re-saddled and turned in their stables ready to be brought out without a moment's delay, Rupert took his place at the entrance, and watched the door leading from the hotel. In ten minutes it opened, and the marquis, followed by Adèle, came out.

"Quick with that horse," Rupert said to the ostler; and seeing to the other, they were in the yard as soon as the marquis came up.

"An officer and eight men," he whispered to Rupert, as he leapt into the saddle, while Rupert lifted Adèle on to the pillion.

"Mounted?"

"No."

"Then we have a good half-hour's start. Which is the way to the west gate?"

"Straight on, till you reach the wall; follow that to the right, it will bring you to the gate."

Rupert vaulted into his saddle, and the party rode out into the street and then briskly, but without any appearance of extraordinary haste, until they reached the gate.

The guardian of the gate was sitting on a low block of wood at the door of the guard-room.

There was, Rupert saw, no soldier about; indeed, the place was quiet, for the evening was falling, and but few people cared to be about in those times after night-fall.

An idea flashed across Rupert's mind, and he rode up to the marquis,—

"Please lead my horse," he said. "Wait for me a hundred yards on; I will be with you in three minutes."

Without waiting for an answer, he leapt from his horse, threw the reins to the marquis, and ran back to the gate, which was but thirty yards back.

"A word with you, good man," he said, going straight into the guard-room.

"Hullo!" the man said, getting up and following him in. "And who may you be, I should like to know, who makes so free?"

Rupert, without a word, sprang upon the man and bore him to the ground. Then, seeing that there was an inner room, he lifted him, and ran him in there, the man being too astonished to offer the slightest resistance. Then Rupert locked him in, and taking down the great key of the gate, which hung over the fire-place, went out, closed the great gate of the town, locked it on the outside, and threw the key into the moat. Then he went off at a run and joined the marquis, who with Adèle was waiting anxiously at the distance he had asked him.

"What have you been doing, Rupert?"

"I have just locked the great gate and thrown the key into the moat," Rupert said. "The gate is a solid one, and they will not get it open to-night. If they are to pursue us, they must go round to one of the other gates, and then make a circuit to get into this road again. I have locked the porter up, and I don't suppose they will find it out till they ride up, half-an-hour hence. They will try for another quarter of an hour to open the gate, and it will be another good half-hour's ride to get round by the road, so we have over one hour's start."

"Capital, indeed," the marquis said, as they galloped forward. "The dangers you have gone through have made you quick-witted indeed, Rupert. I see you have changed saddles."

"Yes, your horse had been carrying double all day, so I thought it better to give a turn to the other. It is fortunate that we have been making short journeys each day, and that our horses are comparatively fresh."

"Why did you come out by the west gate, Rupert? The north was our way."

"Yes, our direct way," Rupert said; "but I was thinking it over while waiting for you. You see with the start we have got and good horses, we might have kept ahead of them for a day; but with one horse carrying double, there is no chance for us doing so for eighty miles. We must hide up somewhere to let the horses rest. They would make sure that we were going to take ship, and would be certain to send on straight to Nantes, so that we should be arrested when we arrive there. As it is we can follow this road for thirty miles, as if going to La Rochelle, and then strike up for a forty miles ride across to Nantes!"

"Well thought of, indeed," M. de Pignerolles said. "Adèle, this future lord and master of yours is as long-headed as he is long-limbed."

Adèle laughed happily. The excitement, and the

fresh air and the brisk pace, had raised her spirits; and with her father and lover to protect her, she had no fear of the danger that threatened them.

"With ten miles start they ought not to overtake us till morning, Rupert."

"No," Rupert said, "supposing that we could keep on, but we cannot. The horses have done twenty-five miles to-day. They have had an hour and a half's rest, but we must not do more than as much farther, or we shall run the risk of knocking them up."

So they rode on at a fast trot for three hours.

"Here is a little road to the right," Rupert said; "let us ride up there, and stop at the first house we come to."

It was a mere by-road, and as once out of the main road they were for the present safe from pursuit, they now suffered the horses to break into a walk. It was not until two miles had been passed that they came to a small farm-house. Rupert dismounted and knocked at the door.

"Who is there?" a voice shouted within.

"Travellers, who want shelter and are ready to pay well for it."

"No, no," the voice said. "No travellers come along here, much less at this time of night. Keep away; we are armed, I and my son, and it will be worse for you if you do not leave us alone."

"Look here, good man, we are what I say," Rupert said. "Open an upstairs casement and show a light, and you will see that we have a lady with us. We are but two men. Look out, I say. We will pay you well. We need shelter for the lady."

There was more talking within, and then a heavy step was heard ascending the stairs. Then a light appeared in an upper room. The casement opened and a long gun was first thrust out, then a face appeared.

The night was not a very dark one, and he was able to see the form of the horse, and of a rider with a female figure behind him.

So far assured, he brought a light and again looked out. The inspection was satisfactory, for he said,—

"I will open the door directly."

Soon Adèle was sitting before a fire bright with logs freshly thrown on.

The horses, still saddled, were placed in a shed with an ample allowance of food. One of the sons, upon the promise of a handsome reward, started to go a mile down the road, with instructions to discharge his gun if he heard horsemen coming up it.

In a quarter of an hour Adèle, thoroughly fatigued with her day's exertion, went to lie down on the bed ordinarily used by the farmer's daughter, the marquis wrapped himself in his cloak and lay down in front of the fire, while Rupert took the first watch outside.

The night passed quietly, and at daybreak the next morning the party were again in their saddles. Their intention was to ride by cross lanes parallel to the main road, and to come into that road again when they felt sure they were ahead of their pursuers, who, with riding nearly all night, would be certain to come to the conclusion that they were ahead of the fugitives, and would begin to search for some signs of where they had left the road.

They instructed their hosts to make no secret of their having been there, but to tell the exact truth as to their time of arrival and departure, and to say that from their conversation they were going south to La Rochelle.

The windings of the country roads that they traversed added greatly to the length of the journey, and the marquis proposed that they should strike at once across it for Nantes.

Rupert, however, begged him to continue the line

that they had chosen and to show at least once on the La Rochelle road, so as to lead their pursuers to the conclusion that it was to that town that they were bound. In the middle of the day they halted for two hours at a farm-house, and allowed their horses to rest and feed, and then shifted the saddles again, for Rupert had, since starting in the morning, run the greater part of the way with his hand on the horse's saddle, so that the animal was quite fresh when they reached their first halting-place. They then rode on and came down into the La Rochelle road, at a spot near which they had heard that a way-side inn stood at which they could obtain refreshments. The instant they drew rein at the door, they saw from the face of the landlord that inquiries had been made for them.

"You had better not dismount, sir; these fellows may play you some trick or other. I will bring some refreshments out, and learn the news.'

So saying, Rupert leapt from his horse, took his pistols from their holsters, placed one in his belt, and having cocked the other, went up to the landlord.

"Bring out five *manchettes* of bread," he said, "and a few bottles of your best wine; and tell me how long is it since men came here asking if you had seen us?"

"This morning, about noon," the man said, "two gendarmes came along, and a troop of soldiers passed an hour since; they same from Parthenay."

"Did they say anything besides asking for us? Come, here is a louis to quicken your recollection."

"They said to each other, as they drank their wine, that you could not have passed here yet, since you could not get fresh horses, as they had done. Moreover, they said that troops from every place on the road were out in search of you."

"Call your man, and bid him bring out quickly the things I have named," Rupert said.

The man did so; and a lad, looking scared at the sight of Rupert's drawn pistol, brought out the wine and bread, and three drinking-horns.

"How far is it to La Rochelle?" Rupert asked.

"Thirty-five miles."

"Are there any by-roads, by which we can make a *détour*, so as to avoid this main road, and so come down either from the north or south into the town?"

The landlord gave some elaborate directions.

"Good!" Rupert said. "I think we shall get through yet."

Then he broke up two of the portions of bread, and gave them to the horses, removed the bits from their mouths, and poured a bottle of wine down each of their throats; then bridled up and mounted, throwing two louis to the host, and saying,—

"We can trust you to be secret as to our having been here, can we not?"

The landlord swore a great oath that he would say nothing of their having passed, and they then rode on.

"That landlord had 'rogue' written on his face," Adèle said.

"Yes, indeed," Rupert said. "I warrant me by this he has sent off to the nearest post. Now we will take the first road to the north, and make for Nantes. It is getting dark now, and we must not make more than another ten miles; these poor brutes have gone thirty already."

Two hours' further riding at an easy pace brought them to a village, where they were hospitably received at the house of the *maire* of the place.

The start was again made early.

"We must do our best to-day," the marquis said. "We have a fifty-five-mile ride before us; and if the horses take us there, their work is done, so we can press them to the utmost. The troops will have been march-

ing all night along the road on which the innkeeper set
them; but by this morning they will begin to suspect
that they have been put on a false scent, and as likely
as not will send to Nantes. We must be first there, if
possible."

The horses, however, tired by their long journeys on
the two preceding days, flagged greatly during the last
half of the journey, and it was late in the afternoon before they came in sight of Nantes. At a slight rise half
a mile from the town Rupert looked back along the
straight, level road on which they had ridden the last
few miles of the journey.

"There is a body of men in the distance, marquis. A
troop of cavalry, I should say. They are a long way
behind—three miles or so; and if they are in chase of
us, their horses must be fagged; but in five-and-twenty
minutes they will be here."

They urged their weary steeds into a gallop as far
as the town, and then rode quietly along the streets
into an inn-yard. Here they dismounted in a leisurely
way.

"Take the horses round to the stable, rub them down
and give them food," the marquis said to the ostler who
came out. Then turning to the host, he said, "A sit-
ting-room, with a good fire. Two bedrooms for myself and my daughter, a bedroom for my servant. Prepare a meal at once. We have a friend to see before we
enter."

So saying, he turned with his daughter, as if to re-
trace his steps up the street; but on reaching the first
side street, turned, and then, by another street, made his
way down to the river, Rupert following closely behind.

"There is 'La Belle Jeanne,'" the marquis exclaimed.
"That is fortunate. The captain said he should be returning in a week or ten days, so I hope he has his
cargo on board, and will be open to make a start at
once."

CHAPTER XXVI.

THE SIEGE OF TOURNAI.

In a few minutes they were alongside the lugger.

"Maître Nicolay! Maître Nicolay!" the marquis shouted.

"Holloa!" and a head showed up the companion.

On seeing who it was, the speaker emerged.

"It is you, Maître Perrot."

"Have you your cargo on board?"

"Every barrel," said the skipper; "we sail to-morrow morning."

"I will give you two hundred and fifty louis if you will sail in ten minutes, and as much more if you land us safely in England."

"Really?"

"Really."

"It is a bargain. Holloa! Pierre! Etienne!"

Two lads ran up from below.

"Run to the wine-shops on the quay, fetch the crew, just whisper in their ears, say I am casting off, that no man must wait to say good-bye to his wife, and that each down in five minutes will have as many louis, and that in ten I sail, if with only half the crew. Run! Run!

The two boys set off at full speed.

"I fear ten minutes will be impossible, Maître Perrot; but all that can be done, shall. Is ten absolutely necessary?"

"Twenty may do, Maître Nicolay; but if we are not off by that time, we shall not be able to go at all.'

"You are pursued?"

"Yes; in half an hour at latest a troop of soldiers will be here after us."

Maître Nicolay looked at the sky.

"There is wind enough when we once get well beyond the town; but unless we get a good start they will
overtake us in boats. Is it a state affair, Maître Perrot?
for I own to you I don't like running my head against
the state."

"I will tell you frankly, captain. I am the Marquis
de Pignerolles. This is my daughter; the king wants
her to marry a man she does not like, and I am running
away with her, to save her from being shut up in a convent till she agrees."

"And this one?" Maître Nicolay said, pointing to
Rupert.

"That is the gentleman whom both I and my daughter like better than the king's choice."

"That is all right," Maître Nicolay said; "there is no
hanging matter in that. But look, sir; if you should be
late, and they come up with us in boats, or warn the
forts at the entrance, mind, we cannot fight; you must
send us all below, with your swords and pistols, you
see, and batten us down, so that we shan't be responsible, else I could never show my face in a French port
again. Ah! here come four of the men; yes, and two
more after them. That is good. Now," he said, when
the men came up, "not a question, not a word. There
is money, but it has to be earned; now set to work.
Loosen the sails, and get all ready for casting off."

In a quarter of an hour from the moment the party
had reached the "Belle Jeanne" eight men had arrived,
and although these were but half her crew, the captain, who had been throwing himself heart and soul in
the work, declared that he would wait for no more; the
last rope was thrown off, and the lugger dropped out
into the stream.

It was running rapidly out; and as the wind caught
the sails, the "Belle Jeanne" began to move, standing
down towards the sea.

During the time the lugger had been prepared for sea the passengers had remained below, so as not to attract the attention of the little crowd of sailors whom the sudden departure had assembled on the quay. But they now came up on deck. Scarcely were they in the middle of the stream, and the sails had fairly gathered way on her, when Rupert exclaimed, "There they are!" as a party of horseman rode down on to the quay, now nearly a quarter of a mile away.

Then a faint shout came across the water, followed by a musket-shot, the ball splashing in the water a little way astern.

The men looked at each other and at their captain.

"Look here, lads, I will tell you the truth about this matter; and I know that, as men of La Vendee, you will agree with me. This gentleman who crossed with us before is a noble, and the king wants this lady, his daughter, to marry a man she does not like. The father agrees with her; and he and her *fiancé*, this gentleman here, have run away with her, to prevent her being locked up. Now we are bound, as true Vendeans, to assist them; and besides, they are going to pay handsomely. Each of you will get ten louis if we land them safe in England. But you know we cannot resist the law; so we must let these gentlemen, with their swords and pistols, drive us below, do you see? and then we shan't be responsible if the 'Jeanne' does not heave-to when ordered. Now let us make a bit of a scuffle; and will you fire a shot or two, gentlemen? they will be watching us with glasses from the shore, and will see that we make a fight for it."

The sailors entered into the spirit of the thing, and a mock fight took place. The marquis and Rupert flashed their swords and fired their pistols, the crew being driven below, and the hatch put on above them.

The fugitives had time to look around. Two boats

laden with soldiers had put out, and were rowing after them.

The marquis took the helm. "The wind is freshening, and I think it will be a gale before morning, Rupert; but they are gaining upon us. I fear they will overtake us."

"I don't think they will get on board if they do, sir," Rupert said. "Had not Adèle better sit down on deck under shelter of the bulwarks; for they keep on firing, and a chance shot might hit her?"

"It is no more likely to hit me than papa or you, Rupert."

"No more likely, my dear," her father said; "but we must run the risk, and you need not. Besides, if we are anxious about you, we shall not be so well able to attend to what we have to do."

Adèle sat down by the bulwark, but presently said,—

"If they come up close, papa, I might take the helm, if you show me which way to hold it. I could do it sitting down on deck, and you could help Rupert keep them off."

"Your proposal is a very good one, Adèle, and it pleases me much to see you so cool and steady."

The bullets were now whistling past the lugger, sometimes striking her sails, sometimes with a sharp tap hitting her hull or mast.

"We may as well sit down out of sight till the time comes for fighting, Rupert," the marquis said. "Our standing up does no good, and only frightens this little girl."

The firing ceased when they sat down, as it was clearly a waste of powder and ball continuing.

Rupert from time to time looked over the stern.

"The first boat is not more than fifty yards behind, the other thirty or forty behind it. They gain on us very slowly, but I think they will catch us."

"AS RUPERT, WITH THE BARREL POISED ABOVE HIS HEAD, REARED
HIMSELF ABOVE THE BULWARKS."

"Then we must do our best, Rupert; we have each our pistols, and I think we might begin to fire at the rowers."

"The pistols are not much good at that distance, sir. My idea is to let them come alongside; then I will heave that cask of water down into the boat, and there will be an end of it."

"That water cask!" the marquis said; "that is an eighteen-gallon cask; it is as much as we can lift it, much less heave it through the air."

"I can do it, never fear," Rupert said. "You forget my exercises at Loches, and as a miller's man. My only fear," he said in a low voice, "is that they may shoot me as I come to the side with it. For that reason we had better begin to fire. I don't want to kill any of them, but just to draw their fire. Then, just as they come alongside put a cap and a cloak on that stick, and raise them suddenly. Any who are still loaded are sure to fire the instant it appears."

The marquis nodded, and they began to fire over the stern, just raising their heads, and instantly lowering them. The boats again began to fire heavily. Not a man in the boats was hit, for neither of those in the lugger took aim. The men cheered, and rowed lustily, and soon the boat was within ten yards of the lugger, coming up to board at the side. Rupert went to the water barrel, and rolled it to the bulwarks at the point towards which the boat was making. The marquis stooped behind the bulwarks, a few paces distant, with the dummy.

"Now!" Rupert said, stooping over the barrel, as the boat made a dash at the side.

The marquis lifted the dummy, and five or six muskets were simultaneously discharged. Then a cry of amazement and horror arose, as Rupert, with the barrel poised above his head, reared himself above the bulwarks. He bent back to gain impetus, and then hurled the barrel into the boat as she came within a yard of the side of the lugger. There was a wild shout, a crash of timber, and in an instant the shattered boat was level with the water, and the men were holding on, or swimming for their lives. A minute later the other boat was on the spot, and the men were at work picking up their comrades. By the time all were in, she was only an inch or two out of the water, and there was only room for two men to pull; and the last thing those on board the lugger saw of her in the gathering darkness, she was slowly making her way towards shore.

Now that all immediate danger was at an end, the marquis took the tiller, and Rupert lifted the hatchway.

"The captain and two of the crew may come on deck if they promise to behave well," he said.

There was a shout of laughter, and all the sailors pressed up, eager to know how the pursuit had been shaken off.

When Rupert told them simply that he had tossed one of the water barrels into one of the boats and staved it, the men refused to believe him; and it was not until he took one of the carronades, weighing some five hundred weight, from its carriage, and lifted it above his head as if to hurl it overboard, that their doubts were changed into astonishment.

"I suppose our danger is not over, captain?" the marquis asked.

"No, we have the forts at the mouth of the river to pass, but we shall be there before it is light. They will send off a horseman when they get back to the town, but they will not be there for some time, and the wind is rising fast. I hope we shall be through before they get news of what has taken place. In any case, at the speed we shall be going through the water in another hour or two no row boat could stop us."

"I think, Captain Nicolay, it would be as well for you to keep only as many men as you absolutely want on deck, so that you can say we only allowed two or three up, and kept watch over you with loaded pistols."

"It would be better, perhaps," Maître Nicolay said. "There is safe to be a nice row about it, and it is always as well to have as few lies as possible to tell. Perhaps mademoiselle will like to go below. My cabin is ready for her, and I have told the boy to get supper for us all."

The captain's prediction about the rising wind was correct, and in another hour the "Belle Jeanne" was tearing down the river at a rate of speed which, had the road from Nantes to the forts been no longer than that by water, would have rendered the chance of any horseman arriving before it slight indeed; but the river was winding, and although they calculated that they had gained an hour and a half start, Captain Nicolay acknowledged that it would be a close thing. Long ere the forts were reached Adèle was fast asleep below, while her father and Rupert paced the deck anxiously.

The night was not a dark one. The moon shone out at times bright and clear between the hurrying clouds.

"There are the forts," Maître Nicolay said. "The prospect is hopeful, for I do not see a light."

The hands were all ordered below as they neared the forts, Maître Nicolay himself taking the helm.

All was dark and silent as they approached, and as "La Belle Jeanne" swept past them like a shadow, and all was still, a sigh of relief burst from the marquis and Rupert. Five minutes later the wind brought down the sound of a drum, a rocket soared into the air, and a minute or two later lights appeared in every embrasure of the forts on both sides.

"It has been a near thing," the marquis said; "we have only won by five minutes."

Three minutes later came a flash, followed by the

roar of a gun, and almost at the same moment a shot struck the water, fifty yards ahead of them on their beam.

"We are nearly a mile away already," the captain said; it is fifty to one against their crippling us by this light, though they may knock some holes in our sails, and perhaps splinter our timbers a little. Ah! just what I thought, here come the chasse marées, and he pointed to two vessels which had lain close under the shadow of the forts, and which were now hoisting sail. "It is lucky that they are in there, instead of cruising out-side, as usual. I suppose they saw the gale coming, and ran in for a quiet night."

The forts were now hard at work, and the balls fell thickly around; one or two went through the sails, but none touched her hull or spars, and in another ten min-utes she was so far away that the forts ceased firing.

By this time, however, the *chasse-marées* were under full sail, and were rapidly following in pursuit. "La Belle Jeanne" had, however, a start of fully a mile and a half.

"How do those craft sail with yours?" Rupert asked.

"In ordinary weather the 'Jeanne' could beat them, though they are fast boats; but they are heavier than we are, and can carry their sail longer; besides, our being underhanded is against us. It will be a close race, mon-sieur. It will be too rough when we are fairly out of them to use their guns. But the best thing that can happen for us is that there may be an English cruiser not far off. I must have the hands up, and take in some sail; she will go just as fast, for she has too much on to be doing her best now we are in the open sea. Now, gentlemen, I advise you to lie down for an hour or two. I will call you if they gain much upon us."

It was morning before the voyagers awoke, and made their way on deck. They looked round, but no sail was in sight, only an expanse of foaming sea and driving cloud.

The captain was on deck.

"I suspect they have given it up and run back," he said; "and no fools either. It is not weather for any one to be out who has a choice in the matter. But the 'Jeanne' is a good sea boat, and has been out in worse weather than this. Not but that it is a big gale, but it is from the north, and the land shelters us a bit. If it keeps on like this, I shall lie-to a few hours. The sea will be tremendous when we get beyond Ushant."

For three days the gale blew furiously, and the "Jeanne" lay-to. Then the storm broke, and the wind veered round to the south, and "La Belle Jeanne" flew along on her way towards England.

It was at a point on the Hampshire coast, near Lymington, that she was to run her cargo, and on the fifth day after leaving the river she was within sight of land. They lowered their sails, and lay a few miles off land until nightfall, and then ran in again. Two lights on the shore, one above the other, told that the coast was clear, and the boats were quickly lowered. The marquis, who had come well provided with gold to meet all emergencies, handed over to Maitre Nicolay fifty pounds over the sum agreed on, and in a few minutes the travellers set foot on shore. Six days later, a post-chaise brought them to the door of Windthorpe Chace, where Madame Holliday and the colonel stood on the steps to welcome Rupert's future wife. The very day after their return, Rupert mooted to the marquis the subject of an early marriage, but the latter said at once,—

"I must first take a place for Adèle to be married from. Mademoiselle Adèle de Pignerolles must not be married like the daughter of a little bourgeois. Moreover, Rupert, it is already near the end of the year. In three months you will be setting out to join your regi-

ment again. It would be cruel to Adèle for you to
marry her before the war is over, or until you at any rate
have done with soldiering. You tell me that you have
gone through enough, and that the next campaign shall
be your last. At any rate you can obtain a year's leave
after nine years of campaigning. So be it, when you
return at the end of next year's campaign you shall find
all ready, and I will answer for it that Adèle will not
keep you waiting. It is but a fortnight since you were
affianced to each other, you can well wait the year."

And so it was arranged, for Rupert himself saw that
it would be cruel to expose Adèle to the risk of being
made a widow after a few weeks only of married life.

The winter passed very quietly and happily.

The marquis was always talking of taking a house,
but Adèle joined her voice with those of the others in
saying that it would be cruel indeed for him to take her
away from the Chace until it was time for Rupert to
start for the war again.

In the middle of March he received orders to join his
regiment, as large numbers of recruits had been sent
out, and every officer was required at his post.

During the winter of 1708, Marlborough had laboured strenuously to obtain a peace which would sat-
isfy all parties. Louis offered great concessions, which
the duke urged strongly should be accepted; but the
English and Dutch wanted terms so severe and hu-
miliating that Louis would not accept them, and both
sides prepared for a great final struggle.

The King of France addressed an appeal to his people, telling them that he had offered to make the greatest possible sacrifices to obtain peace for them, but that
the enemy demanded terms which would place France
at their mercy, he therefore appealed to their patriotism
to come forward to save the country.

The people responded readily to the summons, and

Marshal Villars took the field in the spring with 110,000 men, a force just equal to that of the allies.

The French had taken up a position of such extraordinary strength, that it was hopeless for the allies to attempt to attack. His left wing was covered by the stream of Roubaix; his center by the marsh of Cambriu; his right by the canal between Douai and Lille; and this naturally strong position had been so strengthened by artificial inundations, ditches, abattis, and earthworks, as to be practically impregnable.

Marlborough and Eugene made, however, as if they would attack, and Villars called to him as many men as could be spared from the garrisons round. The allies then by a sudden night march arrived before Tournai, and at once commenced its investment. Tournai was an immensely strong town, but its garrison was weak. The heavy artillery was brought up from Ghent, and on the 6th of July the approaches were commenced, and on the 29th of that month, the governor, finding that the allies were gradually winning fort after fort, and that Villars made no movement to relieve him, surrendered the town, and retired into the citadel, which was then besieged.

This was one of the most terrible sieges ever undertaken, for not only were the fortifications enormously strong, but beneath each bastion and outwork, and far extending beyond them, an immense number of galleries had been driven for mines. At all times soldiers, even the bravest, have found it difficult to withstand the panic brought about by the explosion of mines, and by that underground warfare in which bravery and strength were alike unavailing, and where the bravest as well as the most cowardly were liable at any moment to be blown into the air, or smothered underground. The dangers of this service, at all times great, were immensely aggravated by the extraordinary pains taken

by those who had constructed the fortifications to prepare for subterranean warfare by the construction of
galleries.   The miners frequently met underground,
breaking into each other's galleries; sometimes the
troops, mistaking friend for foe, fought with each other;
sometimes whole companies entered mines by mistake
at the very moment that they were primed for explosion.   They were often drowned, suffocated with smoke,
or buried alive.   Sometimes scores were blown into the
air.

It was not surprising that even the hearts of the allied
troops were appalled at the new and extraordinary dangers which they had to face at the siege of Tournai; and
the bravest were indeed exposed to the greatest danger.
The first to mount a breach, to effect a lodgment in an
outwork, to enter a newly discovered mine, was sure to
perish.   First there was a low rumbling noise, then the
earth heaved, and whole companies were scattered with
a frightful explosion.

On the 15th of August, a sally made by the besieged
was bravely repulsed, and the besiegers pressing closely
upon them, effected a lodgment, but immediately a
mine was sprung, and 150 men blown into the air.

On the 20th, the besieged blew down a wall which
overhung a sap, and two officers and thirty-four soldiers
were killed.

On the 23rd a mine sixty feet long and twenty feet
broad was discovered, just as a whole battalion of Hanoverian troops had taken up their place above it.   All
were congratulating themselves on the narrow escape,
when a mine placed below that they had discovered exploded, burying all in the upper mine in the ruins.

On the 25th, 300 men posted in a large mine which
had been discovered, were similarly destroyed by the
explosion of another mine below it; and the same night
100 men posted in the ditch were killed by a wall being

blown out upon them. In resisting the attack upon one side of the fortress only, thirty-eight mines were sprung in twenty-six days, almost every one with fatal effect.

It is no detriment to the courage of the troops to say, that they shrank appalled before such sudden and terrible a mode of warfare, and Marlborough and Eugene in person visited the trenches and braved the dangers in order to encourage the men.

At last, on the 3rd of September, the garrison, reduced to 3000 men, surrendered, and were permitted to march out with the honours of war, and to return to France on the promise not to serve again.

This siege cost the allies 5000 men.

CHAPTER XXVII.

MALPLAQUET, AND THE END OF THE WAR.

DURING all the time the allies had been employed upon the siege of Tournai, Marshal Villars had laboured to form an impregnable line of entrenchments, barring all farther advance. Marlborough, however, a day or two previously to the fall of Tournai, sent off the Prince of Hesse Cassel, who by a rapid and most masterly march fell upon the French lines, at a part where the French had no expectation of there being an enemy within thirty miles of them. No opposition was made, and the prince marching rapidly to the plateau of Jemappes, invested Mons on the French side. The rest of the army followed. The effect caused throughout France, and indeed through Europe, by the success of this masterly movement, was immense, and it was evident that a great battle was at hand. Villars moved his army rapidly up. A detachment of Eugene's troops were left to watch Mons, and the allied army, 93,000 strong, advanced to meet them, and on the night of the 7th bivouacked in a line three miles long, and five from that occupied by the French. Marshal Villars had with him 95,000 men. The forces therefore were as nearly as possible equal; but the allies had 105 guns, against eighty of the French. The position taken up by Villars was of great natural strength, being a plateau, interspersed with woods and intersected with streams, and elevated from a hundred and fifty to two hundred feet above the meadow-land of the Trouville, across which their assailants must pass. Malplaquet stood on this plateau. On the slopes from the plateau to the plain, the woods were extremely thick, and the only access to the plateau, for troops, were two clearings cut through the woods, known as the Trouées de la Louvière, and d'Aulnoit.

On the morning of the 8th, when the French definitely took up their position, Marlborough and Eugene were in favour of making an instant attack, before the French could add to the great natural strength of their position by entrenchments. The Dutch deputies, however, were altogether opposed to an assault on so formidable a front. Finally a compromise was adopted—a compromise which, as is often the case, was the very worst course which could have been adopted. The army should neither fall back, as the Dutch wished; nor attack at once, as Marlborough desired. It was resolved not to abandon the siege of Mons, and to attack the enemy if they would not take the offensive, but to wait until St. Ghislain, which commanded a passage on the Haine, was taken, and until twenty-six battalions on the march from Tournai arrived. It was two days before these conditions were fulfilled; and Villars had used these two precious days in throwing up a series of immensely strong works. The heights he occupied formed a concave semicircle, enfilading on all sides the little plain of Malplaquet, and this semicircle now bristled with redoubts, palisades, abattis, and stockades; while the two trouées, or openings, by which it was presumed that the allies would endeavour to force an entrance, were so enfiladed by cross batteries as to be well-nigh unassailable. Half the French army by turns had laboured ceaselessly at the works, during the two days which the cowardly folly of the Dutch deputies had given them; and the result was the works resembled rather the fortifications of a fortress, than ordinary field works. Marlborough and Eugene had seen from hour to hour the progress of these formidable works, and resolved to mask their front attack by a strong demonstration on the enemy's rear. The troops coming up from Tournai, under General Withers, were ordered not to join the main army, but to cross the Haine at St. Ghislain, and to attack the extreme left of the enemy at the farm of La Folie. Baron Schulemberg was to attack the left flank of the entrenchments in the wood of Taisnière, with forty of Eugene's battalions, supported by as many cannon; while Count Lottum was to attack the right flank of the wood with twenty-two battalions. The rest of the army was to attack in front; but it was from Eugene's attack in the wood of Taisnière that success was chiefly hoped.

At three o'clock on the morning of the 11th the men were got under arms, divine service was performed at the head of each regiment, and then the troops marched to the posts assigned to them in the attack. Both armies were confident, the French enthusiastic. The allies relied on their unbroken series of victories. Never once since the war begun had they suffered defeat; and with Eugene as well as Marlborough with them, they felt confident of their power to carry a position which, even to the eye of the least instructed soldier, was yet formidable in the extreme.

The French were confident, in being commanded by their best and most popular generals, Villars and Boufflers, they were strong in the enthusiasm which the king's appeal had communicated to the whole nation, and they considered it absolutely impossible for any enemy to carry the wonderful series of works that they had erected.

At half-past seven all was ready, and the fog which had hitherto hung over the low ground cleared up, and the two armies came into view of each other, and the artillery on both sides opened a heavy fire. The whole line advanced; but the left was halted for awhile, while Count Lottum, with his twenty-two battalions formed in three lines, attacked the right of the wood of Taisnière, and Schulemberg, with whom was Eugene himself attacked their left.

Without firing a single shot, Schulemberg's men marched through the storm of grape which swept them until within twenty paces of the entrenchments, when the musketry fire of the French troops was so terrible that the attacking columns recoiled two hundred yards, where they were steadied, and brought back to the charge by the heroic efforts of Eugene, who exposed himself in front of the line.

While this conflict was raging, some Austrian battalions which had formed the extreme right of Schulemberg's corps, but had been unable to advance, owing to a deep marsh, stole round unperceived into the northeastern angle of the wood of Taisnière, and were soon in conflict with the French. Lottum's division had, with immense bravery, crossed a deep morass under a tremendous fire, and stormed a portion of the entrenchments; but Villars, who was directly in rear, led on a fresh brigade, who drove back the assailants.

Marlborough then charged at the head of D'Auvergne's cavalry, and some of Lottum's battalion again forced their way in.

Meanwhile Withers was quietly making his way through the wood from La Folie, and had made considerable progress before the French could muster in force at this point. As this threatened the rear of his front position, Villars fell back from the entrenchments in front of the wood, and took up the second and far stronger position he had prepared on the high ground.

On the left an even more desperate fight had been raging. The Prince of Orange commanded here. The prince was full of courage and impetuosity. The troops under him were Dutch, or auxiliaries in the Dutch pay, among them a Scotch brigade under the Marquis of Tullibardin. The corps advanced in the most gallant manner, the Scotch and Dutch rivalling each other in bravery. Two lines of the enemy's entrenchments were carried at the bayonet; and had there been a reserve at hand, the battle would have been won at this point. But the prince had thrown his whole force into the attack, and his forty battalions were opposed by seventy French battalions, while the assailants were swept by the fire from the high ground. Tullibardin and General Spau were killed, and the assailants, fighting with extraordinary obstinacy, were yet driven back, with a loss of 3000 killed and twice as many wounded. The French sallied out to attack them, but the Prince of Hesse Cassel charged them with his cavalry, and drove them back into their works.

The news of the terrible slaughter and repulse on the right brought Eugene and Marlborough from the center and left, where all was going well. Reserves were brought up, and the battle restored.

News now came that Villars, alarmed at the progress made on his left by Withers, had withdrawn the Irish brigade and some other of his best troops from his center, to drive back the allies' right.

Eugene galloped off with all haste to lead the right and carry them forward, while Marlborough directed Lord Orkney to attack the weakened French center with all his strength, and ordered the cavalry to follow on the heels of the infantry. The fight on the right was fierce indeed, for here Villars and Eugene alike led their men. Both were wounded; Villars in the knee. He refused to leave the field, but insisted on being placed in a chair where he could see the battle and cheer on his men. The agony he suffered, however, and the great loss of blood, weakened him so that at last he fainted, and was carried off the field, the command devolving on Marshal Boufflers.

Eugene was wounded in the head. In vain his staff

pressed him to retire in order that the wound might be dressed.

"If I am to die here," he said, "of what use to dress the wounds? if I survive, it will be time enough in the evening."

So with the blood streaming over his shoulders, he kept his place at the head of his troops, who, animated by his example and heroism, rushed forward with such impetuosity that the works were carried.

In the centre an even more decisive advantage had been gained.

Lord Orkney made the attack with such vigour, that the entrenchments, weakened by the forces which had been withdrawn, were carried, and the horse, following close behind, broke through the openings of the works, and spread themselves over the plateau, cutting down the fugitives.

The guns in the works were wheeled round, and opened a tremendous fire on the dense masses of the French drawn up behind other parts of the entrenchments.

Thrown into confusion by the fire, the French began to waver, and Marlborough gave the order for the great battery of forty guns in the allied centre to advance. These advanced up the hill, passed through the entrenchments and opened a fire right and left upon the French.

Although the French still strove gallantly, the battle was now virtually over. The centre was pierced, the right turned, and Boufflers prepared to cover the necessary retreat with his cavalry. With 2000 picked horsemen of the royal horse guards, he charged the allied cavalry when scattered and blown by their pursuit, and drove them back, but was himself repulsed by the fire of Orkney's infantry, and fell back, leaving half his force dead on the plain.

Again and again Boufflers brought up fresh cavalry, and executed the most desperate charges to cover the retreat of his infantry, who were now falling back along the whole line, as the Prince of Orange, benefiting by the confusion, had now carried the entrenchments on the French left.

Boufflers formed his infantry into three great masses, and fell back in good order in the direction of Bavai.

Such was the victory of Malplaquet. A victory indeed, but won at such a cost that a few more such successes would have been ruin.

The allies had gained the French position, had driven the enemy from the field, and had prevented the raising of the siege of Mons, the great object of the French, but beyond that their advantage was slight, for the enemy retired in good order, and was ready to have fought again, if attacked, on the following day.

The allies captured fourteen guns and twenty-five standards, the French carried off thirty-two standards, principally Dutch. The French lost 14,000 men in killed and wounded, the allies fully 20,000.

The French historians have done full justice to the extraordinary bravery of the allied troops. One of their officers wrote after the battle,—

"Eugene and Marlborough ought to be well satisfied with us on that day, since up to that time they had not met with a resistance worthy of them. They may now say with justice that nothing can stand before them; and indeed what should be able to stay the rapid progress of those heroes, if an army of 100,000 men of the best troops, strongly posted between two woods, trebly entrenched, and performing their duty as well as any brave men could do, were not able to stop them one day? Will you not then own with me that they surpass all the heroes of former ages?"

The siege of Mons was now undertaken, and after a

month's gallant defence, fell, and the two armies then went into winter quarters, there remaining now only the fortress of Valenciennes between the allies and Paris.

Rupert Holliday was not present with the army at the siege of Mons. He had distinguished himself greatly in the desperate cavalry fight which took place upon the plateau after the British infantry had forced their way in. More than once, fighting in front of his regiment, he had been cut off and surrounded when the allied cavalry gave way before the valiant charge of the French cavalry, but each time his strength, his weight, and the skill with which he wielded the long, heavy sword he carried, enabled him to cut his way through the enemy's ranks, and to rejoin his regiment. He had not, however, come off scatheless, having received several severe sabre cuts. Hugh had also been wounded, and Rupert readily obtained leave to retire to England to be cured of his wounds, the Duke of Marlborough raising him to the rank of colonel on the field of battle.

He had, during the campaign, received many letters from Adèle, who told him that the marquis had taken a house, but to each inquiry that Rupert made as to its locality, she either did not answer the question at all, or returned evasive answers. All he knew was that she was staying at the Chace, and that the marquis was away, seeing to the renovation of his house.

It was not until Rupert returned that he obtained the clue to this little mystery.

The Marquis de Pignerolles had bought the Haugh, formerly the property of Sir William Brownlow, and intended the estate as a dowry for Adèle. The Pignerolles estate was indeed very large, and two or three years of his savings were sufficient, not only to purchase the estate, but to add to and redecorate and refurnish the house.

Madame Holliday handed over to Rupert the title-deeds of the whole of the Windthorpe estate owned by her, as the income from her savings was more than enough to maintain her at Windthorpe Chace. One only condition the marquis exacted with the dowry, which was that the combined estates should, after Rupert finally came into possession of the Chace, be known not as the Haugh, but as Windthorpe Chace.

"It was at Windthorpe Chace, my dear Rupert, that you first knew and drew sword for Adèle, and the name is dear to her as to you. It is only right that I should unite the two estates, since I prevented their union some ten years ago. I am in treaty now for a small estate two miles on the other side of Derby, so that, until the king either forgives me or dies, I shall be near you.

The wedding did not take place quite so soon as Rupert had hoped, for his wounds were more severe than he had at first been willing to allow, and it was not until the last week of the year that the wedding took place.

For many years after the event the marriage of Rupert Holliday with Mademoiselle de Pignerolles was talked of as the most brilliant event which had taken place in the county of Derby during the memory of man. The great Duke of Marlborough himself and his duchess came down to be present at the ceremony; from Holland came over Major Dillon, and four or five others of the officers of the 5th dragoons; Lord Fairholm was also there, and Hugh was not the least welcome to Rupert of those assembled at the wedding.

Hugh was still a private, for although he could long ere this have been a sergeant had he chosen, he had always refused promotion, as it would have removed him from service as Rupert's orderly.

There was also present at the wedding a young Dutch lady engaged to be married to Major Dillon, and her father. Rupert had written over to say how glad he should be to see them at his marriage, but that he could not think of asking them to come so far. Mynheer Von Duyk had, however, written to say that he and his daughter would certainly come, for that regarding Rupert as a son it would be extraordinary indeed for him to be absent. And so they arrived at the Chace two days before the wedding; and on the morning before going to church he presented Rupert with a cheque which simply astounded the young soldier. At first, indeed, he absolutely refused to accept it. The merchant, however, insisted so strongly upon it—urging that his own wealth was so large, that, as he had only Maria to inherit it, it was really beyond his wants, or even his power to spend, and that he had, ever since Rupert saved Maria from the attempts of Sir Richard Fulke, which but for him must have succeeded, regarded him as his adopted son—Rupert saw that his refusal would really give pain, and therefore with warm gratitude he accepted the cheque, whose value exceeded that of the united estates of the Haugh and the Chace. Maria brought a magnificent set of jewels for Adèle— not indeed that that young lady in any way required them, for the marquis had had all her mother's jewels, which were superb, reset for the occasion. They were married first at the Roman Catholic chapel at Derby, for Adèle was of course a Catholic, and then at the church in the village of Windthorpe. After which there was a great dinner, and much rejoicing and festivity at it.

Rupert Holliday went no more to the wars.

He obtained leave to reside on his estate for a year. That year, 1710, little was done in Flanders. The duke's enemies at home had now gained the upper hand, and he was hampered in every way. The allies seeing that a change of government was imminent in England, and that the new party would in all probability make peace at any cost and leave them to themselves, carried on quiet negotiations with France, and so throughout the summer no great battle took place, although the allies gained several material advantages. In the following year, envy, intrigue, and a woman's spite, conquered. Godolphin fell, and the new ministry hastened to make the most disgraceful peace recorded in the annals of the history of this country. By it the allies of England were virtually deserted, and the fruits of ten years of struggle and of victory for the most part abandoned. Marlborough refused to sign the disgraceful peace of Utrecht, and, exiled and disgraced, lived quietly on the continent until the death of Anne, a living monument of national injustice. When George the First ascended the throne, the hero was recalled, and remained the war minister of the country until within a year or two of his death, honoured and loved by the people for whom he had done so much.

There is little more to tell about Rupert Holliday.

His grandfather lived until past ninety years of age, and Madame Holliday died suddenly a few weeks after her father-in-law. Rupert was now one of the largest landowners in the country, and was one of the most popular men. The home farm round the Chace was held for generations by the Parsons, for Hugh married not many months after his master. At the death of Louis, the Marquis de Pignerolles passed over again to France, and there, at least when England and France were at peace, Colonel Rupert Holliday and his wife paid him long visits. As his daughter had married a foreigner she could not inherit the estates, which went to a distant relation; but at the death of the marquis, at a good old age, he left a fortune to his daughter, which enabled her husband still further to extend his estates. Had Rupert desired it, he could have been raised to the peerage, but he preferred remaining one of the wealthiest private gentlemen in England. From time to time they received visits from Major Dillon and his wife, both of whom were great favourites with the young Hollidays.   Between Rupert and Hugh a real affection prevailed all through their lives, and the latter was never so happy as when the children first, and, years after, the grandchildren, of Rupert and Adèle came down to the farm to eat cake, drink syllabub, and listen to wonderful tales about the doings of the "Cornet of Horse."

THE END.